Learning to Read, Step by Step!

Ready to Read Preschool–Kindergarten
• big type and easy words • rhyme and rhythm • picture clues
For children who know the alphabet and are eager to begin reading.

Reading with Help Preschool–Grade 1
• basic vocabulary • short sentences • simple stories
For children who recognize familiar words and sound out new words with help.

Reading on Your Own Grades 1–3
• engaging characters • easy-to-follow plots • popular topics
For children who are ready to read on their own.

Reading Paragraphs Grades 2–3
• challenging vocabulary • short paragraphs • exciting stories
For newly independent readers who read simple sentences with confidence.

Ready for Chapters Grades 2–4
• chapters • longer paragraphs • full-color art
For children who want to take the plunge into chapter books but still like colorful pictures.

STEP INTO READING® is designed to give every child a successful reading experience. The grade levels are only guides; children will progress through the steps at their own speed, developing confidence in their reading.

Remember, a lifetime love of reading starts with a single step!

The authors would like to thank Kaitlin Dupuis and Deanna Ellis for their help in creating this book.

Text copyright © 2019 by Kratt Brothers Company Ltd.

All rights reserved. Published in the United States by Random House Children's Books, a division of Penguin Random House LLC, 1745 Broadway, New York, NY 10019, and in Canada by Penguin Random House Canada Limited, Toronto.

Wild Kratts® © 2019 Kratt Brothers Company Ltd. / 9 Story Media Group Inc. Wild Kratts®, Creature Power® and associated characters, trademarks, and design elements are owned by Kratt Brothers Company Ltd. Licensed by Kratt Brothers Company Ltd.

Step into Reading, Random House, and the Random House colophon are registered trademarks of Penguin Random House LLC.

Visit us on the Web!
StepIntoReading.com
rhcbooks.com

Educators and librarians, for a variety of teaching tools, visit us at
RHTeachersLibrarians.com

ISBN 978-1-101-93914-7 (trade) — ISBN 978-1-101-93915-4 (lib. bdg.) —
ISBN 978-1-101-93916-1 (ebook)

Printed in the United States of America
10 9 8 7 6 5 4 3 2 1

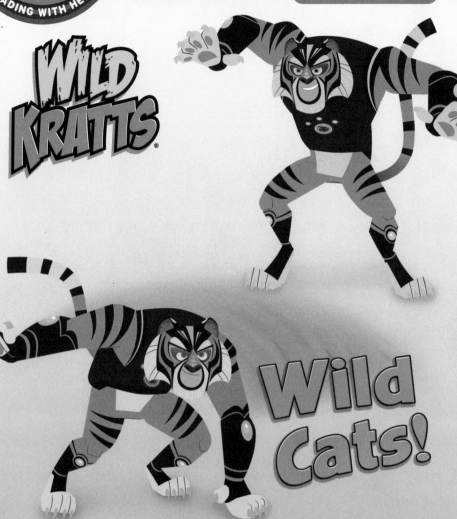

WILD KRATTS

Wild Cats!

by Martin Kratt and Chris Kratt

Random House 🏠 New York

Wild Cats

Big or small, wild or tame,
cats are one of the Wild Kratts'
favorite predators.

Members of the cat family are smart, fast, and strong. And those are just a few of their Creature Powers!

Cats Around the World

There are 38 species
of wild cats in the world.

lion   tiger

There are big wild cats,

such as **lions** and **tigers**.

There are medium-sized wild cats,
such as **lynxes** and **caracals**.

lynx

caracal

There are even small ones,
such as **margays**
and **African wildcats**.

margay

African wildcat

Cubs and Kittens

The young of big cats
are called **cubs**.

The young of medium
and small cats
are called **kittens**.

Mother cats care for their young
and teach them how to hunt.

How Cats Hunt

Cats are very good hunters.
Some cats rely on speed
to hunt. Others use
their size and strength.

Cats have sharp claws, sharp teeth, and powerful jaws that help them catch their prey.

Big Wild Cats

Lions live in savannas

and dry forests.

They are one of the biggest cats.

They mostly hunt big mammals, such as zebras and wildebeests. Lions often hunt in groups to take down animals that a single lion could not.

That's teamwork!

Medium Wild Cats

Caracals are great jumpers!

Their main prey is birds.

Their cousin, the **serval**,
hunts rodents
and other small prey.
Both of these cats live in
the same areas as lions.

Orange and Black Stripes!

Many types of cats have stripes, but the **tiger** is the most famous. Their stripes hide them in the forest shadows while they hunt.

Spot the Cat

Like stripes, spots help cats such as **ocelots** blend in with their surroundings.

Ocelots are very good tree climbers.
They hunt lizards, monkeys, and other small prey.

Spotted Speedsters

Cheetahs are the fastest
of all cats.

Their bodies have evolved
to run at great speeds.

Unlike most cats, their claws
always stick out a little
to grip the ground
when they run.

Versatile Hunters

Jaguars are stocky and muscular. They mostly live in the jungles of Central and South America. They hunt on land and in the water.

Leopards are lean and muscular.

They live in Asia and Africa.

They climb high into trees

to keep their food

away from lions.

Big Foot

Furry **lynxes** often live
in very cold areas.

Their big feet enable them
to run on top of the snow.

Their prey include hares, rabbits,
and other small creatures.

We have
big feet
too!

Name Game

Mountain lions live in the Americas. They have many habitats, ranging from the desert to snowy mountains. They also have different names in different places . . .

The **Florida panther** is a type of mountain lion. It has been known to clash with another fierce predator—the alligator!

There are less than
250 Florida panthers
left in the wild.
They may soon
disappear forever.

Some wild cats, such as the Caspian tiger, have died out. Bengal tigers are endangered, and cheetah numbers are declining.

Wild cats are amazing creatures.
Humans should try to help
wild cats survive so we can
always find them out there . . .

. . . on the prowl

and in the wild!

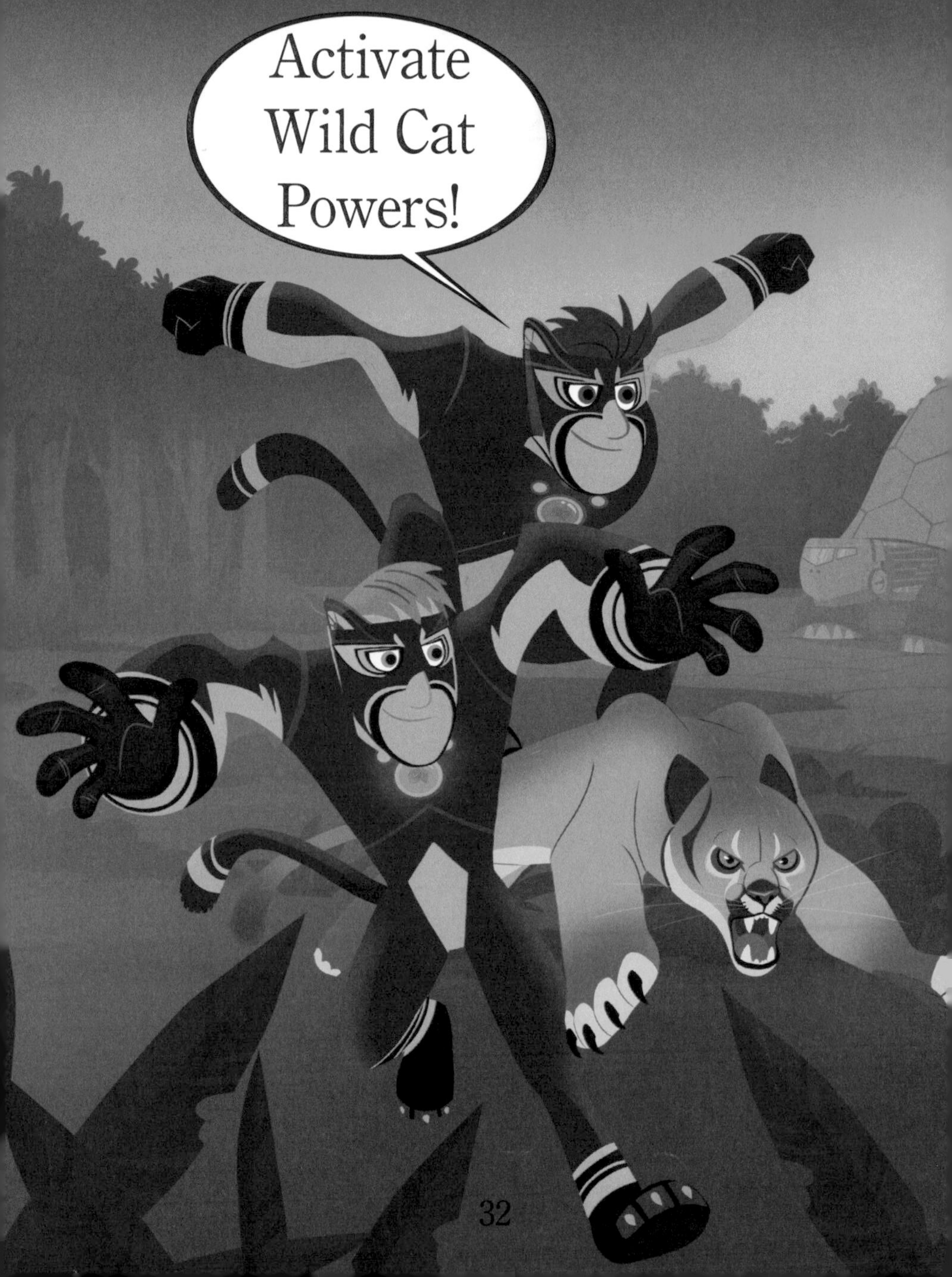

FOUNDATIONS OF PROBABILITY THEORY,

STATISTICAL INFERENCE,

AND STATISTICAL THEORIES OF SCIENCE

VOLUME III

THE UNIVERSITY OF WESTERN ONTARIO
SERIES IN PHILOSOPHY OF SCIENCE

A SERIES OF BOOKS

ON PHILOSOPHY OF SCIENCE, METHODOLOGY,

AND EPISTEMOLOGY

PUBLISHED IN CONNECTION WITH

THE UNIVERSITY OF WESTERN ONTARIO

PHILOSOPHY OF SCIENCE PROGRAMME

VOLUME 6

FOUNDATIONS OF PROBABILITY THEORY, STATISTICAL INFERENCE, AND STATISTICAL THEORIES OF SCIENCE

Proceedings of an International Research Colloquium held at the University of Western Ontario, London, Canada, 10–13 May 1973

VOLUME III

FOUNDATIONS AND PHILOSOPHY OF STATISTICAL THEORIES IN THE PHYSICAL SCIENCES

Edited by

W. L. HARPER and C. A. HOOKER

University of Western Ontario, Ontario, Canada

D. REIDEL PUBLISHING COMPANY

DORDRECHT-HOLLAND / BOSTON-U.S.A.

QA
276
A1
F68

Library of Congress Cataloging in Publication Data
Main entry under title:

Foundations and philosophy of statistical theories in the physical
      sciences.

      (Foundations of probability theory, statistical inference
and statistical theories of science ; v. 3) (The University of Western
Ontario series in philosophy of science ; v. 6)
      Papers and discussions from a colloquium held at the
University of Western Ontario, May 10–13, 1973.
      Includes bibliographies.
      1.   Mathematical statistics—Congresses.   2.   Probabil-
ities—Congresses.   3.   Quantum theory—Congresses.   I.
Harper, William.   II.   Hooker, Clifford Alan.   III.   Series.
IV.   Series: London, Ont. University of Western Ontario.
Series in philosophy of science ; v. 6.
QA276.A1F68   519.5′02′45   75–33879
ISBN 90–277–0620–4
ISBN 90–277–0621–2 pbk.

The set of three volumes (cloth) ISBN 90–277–0614–X
The set of three volumes (paper) ISBN 90–277–0615–8

Published by D. Reidel Publishing Company,
P.O. Box 17, Dordrecht, Holland

Sold and distributed in the U.S.A., Canada, and Mexico
by D. Reidel Publishing Company, Inc.
Lincoln Building, 160 Old Derby Street, Hingham,
Mass. 02043, U.S.A.

Printed in The Netherlands by D. Reidel, Dordrecht

CONTENTS

CONTENTS OF VOLUMES I AND II

VOLUME II

Foundations and Philosophy of Statistical Inference

GENERAL INTRODUCTION

In May of 1973 we organized an international research colloquium on foundations of probability, statistics, and statistical theories of science at the University of Western Ontario.

During the past four decades there have been striking formal advances in our understanding of logic, semantics and algebraic structure in probabilistic and statistical theories. These advances, which include the development of the relations between semantics and metamathematics, between logics and algebras and the algebraic-geometrical foundations of statistical theories (especially in the sciences), have led to striking new insights into the formal and conceptual structure of probability and statistical theory and their scientific applications in the form of scientific theory.

The foundations of statistics are in a state of profound conflict. Fisher's objections to some aspects of Neyman-Pearson statistics have long been well known. More recently the emergence of Bayesian statistics as a radical alternative to standard views has made the conflict especially acute. In recent years the response of many practising statisticians to the conflict has been an eclectic approach to statistical inference. Many good statisticians have developed a kind of wisdom which enables them to know which problems are most appropriately handled by each of the methods available. The search for principles which would explain why each of the methods works where it does and fails where it does offers a fruitful approach to the controversy over foundations. The colloquium first aimed both at a conceptually exciting clarification and enrichment of our notion of a probability theory and at removing the cloud hanging over many of the central methods of statistical testing now in constant use within the social and natural sciences.

The second aim of the colloquium was that of exploiting the same formal developments in the structure of probability and statistical theories for an understanding of what it is to have a statistical theory of nature, or of a sentient population. A previous colloquium in this series has already examined thoroughly the recent development of the analysis of quantum mechanics in terms of its logico-algebraic structure and brought out many of the sharp and powerful insights into the basic physical significance of this theory which that formal approach provides. It was our aim in this colloquium to extend the scope of that inquiry yet further afield in an effort to understand, not just one particular idiosyncratic theory, but what it is in general we are doing when we lay down a formal statistical theory of a system (be it physical or social).

Our aim was to provide a workshop context in which the papers presented could benefit from the informed criticism of conference participants. Most of the papers that appear here have been considerably rewritten since their original presentation. We have also included comments by other participants and replies wherever possible. One of the main reasons we have taken so long to get these proceedings to press has been the time required to obtain final versions of comments and replies. We feel that the result has been worth the wait.

When the revised papers came in there was too much material to include in a single volume or even in two volumes. We have, therefore, broken the proceedings down into three volumes. Three basic problem areas emerged in the course of the conference and our three volumes correspond. Volume I deals with problems in the foundations of probability theory; Volume II is devoted to foundations of statistical inference, and Volume III is devoted to statistical theories in the physical sciences. There is considerable overlap in these areas so that in some cases a paper in one volume might just as well have gone into another.

INTRODUCTION TO VOLUME III

One of the major influences on recent developments in foundations research in probability theory has been the striking role of probability theory in twentieth century scientific theories. Relativity theory aside, twentieth century theoretical physics research has been dominated by the exploration of statistical mechanics and quantum theory, and by the search for an understanding of the relation between them. Quantum theoretic use of probability theory has raised increasingly profound questions about the mathematical and physical conception of probability. The papers in this volume are almost entirely devoted to the exploration of these issues – but with a significant twist: most of them belong to an emerging tradition of foundations research in physics, of great power and potential, which takes a highly abstract approach to physical theory. Concerning this tradition one of us (CAH) wrote, in the introduction of a related work [2], as follows:

The twentieth century has witnessed a striking transformation in the understanding of the theories of mathematical physics. There has emerged clearly the idea that physical theories are significantly characterized by their abstract mathematical structure. This is in opposition to the traditional opinion that one should look to the specific applications of a theory in order to understand it. One might with reason now espouse the view that to understand the deeper character of a theory one must know its abstract structure and understand the significance of that structure, while to understand how a theory might be modified in light of its experimental inadequacies one must be intimately acquainted with how it is applied.

Quantum theory itself has gone through a development this century which illustrates strikingly the shifting perspective. From a collection of intuitive physical maneuvers under Bohr, through a formative stage in which the mathematical framework was bifurcated (between Schrödinger and Heisenberg) to an elegant culmination in von Neumann's Hilbert space formulation the elementary theory moved, flanked even at the later stage by the ill-understood formalisms for the relativistic version and for the field-theoretic alternative; after that we have a gradual, but constant, elaboration of all these quantal theories as abstract mathematical structures (their point of departure being von Neumann's formalism) until at the present time theoretical work is heavily preoccupied with the manipulation of purely abstract structures.

The papers by Bub, Demopoulos, Finch, Finkelstein, Gudder, Mittelstaedt and Randall and Foulis all belong, in their several distinct ways, to this tradition. (If the reader will consult their other publications, in the light of [1] and [2], he will discern an interlocking pattern of development in this abstract approach to physical theory.) There is emerging from this work a new and deeper understanding of the role of probability structures in theoretical physics.

The papers by Chernoff and Marsden and by Tisza, too, belong to an abstract structural approach, though not of a purely or strongly logico-algebraic sort. Bunge offers a clarification of the logico-semantic framework for probability in physics (cf. Tisza). Lubkin remarks on interesting applications of a generalized quantum approach to other subject matters.

W. L. HARPER and C. A. HOOKER

BIBLIOGRAPHY

[1] *Contemporary Research in the Foundations and Philosophy of Quantum Theory* (ed. by C. A. Hooker), Reidel, Dordrecht, 1974.
[2] *The Logico-Algebraic Approach to Quantum Theory* (ed. by C. A. Hooker), Vol. I, 1975, Vol. II, 1976.

JEFFREY BUB

THE STATISTICS OF
NON-BOOLEAN EVENT STRUCTURES

Quantum mechanics incorporates an algorithm for assigning probabilities to ranges of values of the physical magnitudes of a mechanical system:

$$p_W(a \in S) = \mathrm{Tr}(W P_A(S))$$

where W represents a statistical state, and $P_A(S)$ is the projection operator onto the subspace in the Hilbert space of the system associated with the range S of the magnitude A. (I denote values of A by a.) The statistical states (represented by the statistical operators in Hilbert space) generate all possible (generalized) probability measures on the partial Boolean algebra of subspaces of the Hilbert space.[1] Joint probabilities

$$P_W(a_1 \in S_1 \,\&\, a_2 \in S_2 \,\&\, \ldots \,\&\, a_n \in S_n) = $$
$$= \mathrm{Tr}(W P_{A_1}(S_1) P_{A_2}(S_2) \ldots P_{A_n}(S_n))$$

are defined only for compatible[2] magnitudes $A_1, A_2, \ldots A_n$, and there are no dispersion-free statistical states.

The problem of hidden variables concerns the possibility of representing the statistical states of a quantum mechanical system by measures on a classical probability space, in such a way that the algebraic structure of the magnitudes is preserved.[3] This is the problem of imbedding the partial algebra of magnitudes in a commutative algebra or, equivalently, the problem of imbedding the partial Boolean algebra of idempotent magnitudes (properties, propositions) in a Boolean algebra. The imbedding turns out to be impossible; there are no 2-valued homomorphisms on the partial Boolean algebra of idempotents of a quantum mechanical system, except in the case of a system associated with a 2-dimensional Hilbert space.[4]

Thus, the transition from classical to quantum mechanics involves the generalization of the Boolean propositional or event structures of classical mechanics[5] to a particular class of non-Boolean structures. This may be understood as a generalization of the classical notion of validity: the class of models over which validity is defined is extended to include partial Boolean algebras which are not imbeddable in Boolean algebras.[6]

Harper and Hooker (eds.), Foundations of Probability Theory, Statistical Inference, and Statistical Theories of Science, Vol. III, 1–16. All Rights Reserved.
Copyright © 1976 by D. Reidel Publishing Company Dordrecht-Holland.

In a Boolean algebra $\mathscr{B}$, there is a 1-1 correspondence between atoms, ultrafilters, and 2-valued homomorphisms, essentially because an ultrafilter Φ in $\mathscr{B}$ contains a or a', but not both, for every $a \in \mathscr{B}$.[7] In a partial Boolean algebra $\mathscr{A}$ that is not imbeddable in a Boolean algebra, this correspondence no longer holds. The partial Boolean algebra may be regarded as a partially ordered system, so the notion of a filter (and hence an ultrafilter as a maximal filter) is still well-defined. But it is no longer the case that if Φ is an ultrafilter, then for each $a \in \mathscr{A}$ either $a \in \Phi$ or $a' \in \Phi$, and hence ultrafilters do not define 2-valued homomorphisms on $\mathscr{A}$.[8] An atom in $\mathscr{A}$ will correspond to an ultrafilter but not to a prime filter, and hence will not define a 2-valued homomorphism on $\mathscr{A}$.

A measure on a classical probability space $(X, \mathscr{F}, \mu)$ may be interpreted as a measure over ultrafilters or atoms in a Boolean algebra $\mathscr{B}$, the points $x \in X$ corresponding to ultrafilters in $\mathscr{B}$ and the singleton subsets $\{x\}$ in $\mathscr{F}$ corresponding to atoms in $\mathscr{B}$. (Under the Stone isomorphism,[9] every element in a Boolean algebra is mapped onto the set of ultrafilters containing the element.) Thus, the probability of an event a[10] may be understood as the measure of the set of ultrafilters containing a, or the measure of the set of atomic events that can occur together with the event a:

$$p(a) = \mu(\Phi_a)$$

The conditional probability of a given b, $p(a \mid b)$, is the measure of the set of ultrafilters containing a in the set of ultrafilters containing b, with respect to a renormalized measure assigning probability 1 to the set Φ_b:

$$p(a \mid b) = \frac{\mu(\phi_a \cap \phi_b)}{\mu(\phi_b)} = \frac{p(a \wedge b)}{p(b)}$$

Loosely: We 'count' the number of atomic events that can occur together with the event b, in the set of atomic events that can occur together with the event a. (Notice that if b is an atom, the conditional probability is a 2-valued measure.)

The statistical states of quantum mechanics define probability measures in the classical sense on each maximal Boolean subalgebra of the partial Boolean algebra of propositions of a quantum mechanical system. Consider a system associated with a 3-dimensional Hilbert space $\mathscr{H}_3$. Let A and B be two incompatible (non-degenerate)[11] magnitudes with eigenvalues a_1, a_2, a_3 and b_1, b_2, b_3, respectively. The corresponding eigenvectors are α_1, α_2, α_3 and β_1, β_2, β_3. I shall also denote the atoms (atomic propositions or events) in the maximal Boolean subalgebras $\mathscr{B}_A$ and $\mathscr{B}_B$ of $\mathscr{A}_3$ by a_i and b_j, i.e. I shall use the same symbols to denote properties of the systems represented by these values of the magnitudes.

The statistical state with the vector α_1 assigns probabilities

$$p_{\alpha_1}(a_1) = 1, \quad p_{\alpha_1}(a_2) = 0, \quad p_{\alpha_1}(a_3) = 0$$

to the atomic propositions in $\mathscr{B}_A$, and probabilities

$$p_{\alpha_1}(b_1) = |(\beta_1, \alpha_1)|^2, \quad p_{\alpha_1}(b_2) = |(\beta_2, \alpha_1)|^2,$$
$$p_{\alpha_1}(b_3) = |(\beta_3, \alpha_1)|^2$$

to the atomic propositions in $\mathscr{B}_B$. How are these probabilities to be understood? The problem at issue is this: Suppose a system S has the property a_1. The statistical algorithm of quantum mechanics assigns non-zero probabilities to properties incompatible with a_1, for example $p_{\alpha_1}(b_1) = $ $= |(\beta_1, \alpha_1)|^2$. Now, the probability assigned to b_1 by the statistical state p_{α_1} (the projection operator onto the 1-dimensional subspace spanned by the vector α_1) cannot be interpreted as the relative measure of the set of ultrafilters containing b_1 in the set of ultrafilters containing a_1 because, firstly, a_1 and b_1 are atoms in $\mathscr{A}_3$ and, secondly, a_1 and b_1 cannot be represented as non-atomic properties in a Boolean algebra because no Boolean imbedding of $\mathscr{A}_3$ is possible. Thus, since there are no 2-valued homomorphisms on $\mathscr{A}_3$, the probability $p_{\alpha_1}(b_1)$ cannot be interpreted as the conditional probability, $p(b_1 \mid a_1)$, that the proposition b_1 is true (or the corresponding event obtains) given that the proposition a_1 is true, i.e. the probability that the value of the magnitude B is b_1 given that the value of the magnitude A is a_1. What do these probabilities mean?

Usually, the problem of interpreting the quantum statistics is posed rather differently. It is pointed out that the statistics defined by p_{α_1}, for the magnitude B cannot be understood in terms of a statistical ensemble constituted of systems in quantum states[12] β_1, β_2, β_3 with weights $|(\beta_1, \alpha_1)|^2$, $|(\beta_2, \alpha_1)|^2$, $|(\beta_3, \alpha_1)|^2$. Such an ensemble is represented by the statistical operator

$$W = \sum_{i=1}^{3} |(\beta_i, \alpha_1)|^2 \, P_{\beta_i}$$

which yields the same statistics as P_{α_1} only for magnitudes compatible

with B. Thus, the problem of interpreting the quantum statistical relations between incompatible magnitudes is presented as the problem of
making sense of the statistics of *pure ensembles*, insofar as these ensembles
are not reducible to *mixtures*: probability distributions of systems in quantum states represented by Hilbert space vectors.

Those interpretations which follow the Copenhagen interpretation of
Bohr and Heisenberg propose that a (micro-) system, at any one time, is
characterized by a set of properties which form a Boolean algebra – a
maximal Boolean subalgebra in the partial Boolean algebra of quantum
mechanical properties.[13] The appropriate Boolean subalgebra is related
to the experimental conditions defined by macroscopic measuring instruments. In effect, this amounts to saying that a system is always represented
by some mixture of quantum states (in the limiting case, by a mixture with
0, 1 weights), the constituents of the mixture being determined by the experimental conditions. If the experimental conditions are such as to
determine the maximal Boolean subalgebra $\mathscr{B}_A$ associated with the (non-
degenerate) magnitude A, then the system is actually in one of the states
α_1, α_2, α_3, and hence represented by a statistical operator of the form

$$\sum_{i=1}^{3} w_i P_{\alpha_i}.$$

If the state is known, $w_i = 1$ or 0. The probabilities assigned to the 'complementary' propositions in $\mathscr{B}_B$ by a pure statistical operator P_{α_i}, representing a statistical ensemble of systems all in the state α_i, are to be
understood as the probabilities of finding particular B-values, if the
experimental conditions are altered so as to determine the maximal Boo-
lean subalgebra $\mathscr{B}_B$, given that the system is in the state α_i. The quantum
mechanical description of a physical system, in terms of a partial Boolean
algebra of properties, allows the consideration of all possible experimental
conditions, but the application of this description to a particular system
is always with respect to the experimental conditions obtaining for the
system, which specify a particular maximal Boolean subalgebra of properties.

The Copenhagen interpretation leads to an insoluble measurement
problem, if the experimental conditions for a system $S^{(1)}$ are assumed to
be determined (in principle, at least) by a physical interaction between
$S^{(1)}$ and a second system $S^{(2)}$ (which, even if macroscopic, ought to be

reducible to a complex of interacting microsystems).[14] Suppose that a particular maximal Boolean subalgebra $\mathscr{B}_{A^{(1)}}$[15] is selected for $S^{(1)}$ by an interaction with $S^{(2)}$ governed by the quantum mechanical equation of motion. Suppose, further, that $S^{(2)}$ is a measuring instrument suitable for measuring the $S^{(1)}$-magnitude $A^{(1)}$, so that correlations are established during the interaction between the possible values of $A^{(1)}$ and the possible values of an $S^{(2)}$-magnitude $A^{(2)}$ (in the sense that the probability assigned by the statistical operator of the composite system $S^{(1)} + S^{(2)}$ to the pair of values $a_i^{(1)}$, $a_j^{(2)}$ ($i \neq j$) is zero). If the initial quantum state of $S^{(1)}$ is represented by the vector

$$\psi = \sum_i (\alpha_i^{(1)}, \psi)\, \alpha_i^{(1)},$$

what is apparently required is an interaction which results in the representation

$$W = \sum_i w_i P_{\alpha_i^{(1)} \otimes \alpha_i^{(2)}},$$

with $w_i = |(\alpha_i^{(1)}, \psi)|^2$, for the statistical state of the composite system $S^{(1)} + S^{(2)}$.[16] Since the statistics defined by W for $S^{(1)}$ is given by the operator[17]

$$W^{(1)} = \sum_i w_i P_{\alpha_i^{(1)}},$$

the quantum state of the system $S^{(1)}$ may be regarded as belonging to the set $\alpha_1^{(1)}$, $\alpha_2^{(1)}$, $\alpha_3^{(1)}$, and the probabilities w_i as a measure of our ignorance of the actual state.

Now, of course, there can be no quantum mechanical interaction which results in the transition

$$P_{\Psi_0} \to W$$

where P_{Ψ_0} is the statistical operator of the initial pure ensemble of composite systems all in the quantum state Ψ_0.[18] For the evolution of a quantum mechanical system is governed by Schrödinger's equation of motion, represented by a *unitary* transformation of the Hilbert space vector defining the quantum state of the system, and the transition $P_{\Psi_0} \to W$, from the pure ensemble represented by P_{Ψ_0} to the mixture represented by W, is *non-unitary*.

Attempted solutions to this problem exploit the similarity between W

and the statistical operator P_Ψ, with

$$\psi = \sum_i (\alpha_i^{(1)}, \psi) \, \alpha_i^{(1)} \otimes \alpha_i^{(2)}.$$

The transition $P_{\Psi_0} \to P_\Psi$ is unitary, and the statistics defined by P_Ψ for $S^{(1)}$ is also given by the operator

$$W^{(1)} = \sum_i w_i P_{\alpha_i^{(1)}}.$$

But W may be taken as representing a statistical ensemble of systems in quantum states $\alpha_i^{(1)} \otimes \alpha_i^{(2)}$ with weights w_i, which is manifestly different from the pure ensemble represented by P_Ψ and constituted of systems each in the state Ψ. In fact, P_Ψ and W define the same statistics for $S^{(1)}$-magnitudes, $S^{(2)}$-magnitudes, and for $S^{(1)} + S^{(2)}$-magnitudes compatible with the magnitude $A^{(1)} + A^{(2)}$ (whose eigenvectors are $\alpha_i^{(1)} \otimes \alpha_j^{(2)}$), but differ for general $S^{(1)} + S^{(2)}$-magnitudes.[19]

Actually, these considerations, which are usually laboured in discussions on the measurement problem, are largely irrelevant. The objections to the transition $P_{\Psi_0} \to P_\Psi$ as a process which selects a maximal Boolean subalgebra of propositions for the measured system $S^{(1)}$ apply with equal force to the transition $P_{\Psi_0} \to W$. Clearly, P_Ψ does not yield a representation for $W^{(1)}$ as a unique mixture of orthogonal pure states, represented by the eigenvectors of the magnitude measured. For we may have

$$\Psi = \sum_i (\alpha_1^{(1)}, \psi) \, \alpha_i^{(1)} \otimes \alpha_i^{(2)}$$
$$= \sum_j (\beta_j^{(1)} \otimes \beta_j^{(2)}, \Psi) \, \beta_j^{(1)} \otimes \beta_j^{(2)}$$

where $\beta_j^{(1)}$, $\beta_j^{(2)}$ ($j = 1, 2, 3$) are the eigenvectors of magnitudes $B^{(1)}$, $B^{(2)}$ incompatible with $A^{(1)}$, $A^{(2)}$, respectively, so that the statistics defined by P_Ψ for $S^{(1)}$ is given by the operator

$$W^{(1)} = \sum_i w_i P_{\alpha_i^{(1)}} = \sum_j w_j' P_{\beta_j^{(1)}}$$

with $w_i = |(\alpha_i^{(1)}, \psi)|^2$, $w_j' = |(\beta_j^{(1)} \otimes \beta_j^{(2)}, \Psi)|^2$.[20] But since the representation of a statistical operator as a weighted sum of pure statistical operators is in general not unique,[21] even assuming some physical grounds for restricting the representation to statistical operators associated with orthogonal vectors in Hilbert space, the mixture defined by $W =$

$=\sum_i w_i P_{\alpha_i^{(1)} \otimes \alpha_i^{(2)}}$, $w_i = |(\alpha_i, \psi)|^2$, does not always determine the representation for the system $S^{(1)}$ given by $W^{(1)} = \sum_i w_i P_{\alpha_i^{(1)}}$. For a suitable ψ we may have

$$W^{(1)} = \sum_i w_i P_{\alpha_i^{(1)}} = \sum_i w_i P_{\gamma_i^{(1)}}$$

where $\gamma_i^{(1)}$ ($i = 1, 2, 3$) are the eigenvectors of a magnitude $C^{(1)}$ incompatible with $A^{(1)}$.[22]

Thus, the Copenhagen interpretation, with its measurement problem, is unacceptable as a solution to the problem of the quantum statistics.

I shall show that the pure statistical states of quantum mechanics (representing statistical ensembles homogeneous with respect to some atomic property) generate generalized measures which satisfy a law of large numbers in an analogous sense to the measures on a classical probability space or Boolean event structure.

Suppose $A^{(1)}$, $A^{(2)}, \ldots, A^{(n)}$ are independent random variables on a classical probability space X that are *statistically equivalent*, i.e.

$$p(a^{(i)} \in S) = \mu(A^{(i)-1}(S)) = f(S)$$

for all $A^{(i)}$, and all Borel sets S, so that

$$\mathrm{Exp}_\mu(A^{(i)}) = k$$

for all $A^{(i)}$.[23] Define the random variable

$$\bar{A} = 1/n(A^{(1)} + A^{(2)} + \cdots + A^{(n)})$$

Let Δk be a neighbourhood of k, i.e. an interval $(k - \delta, k + \delta)$ where $\delta > 0$. Then, it can be shown that for any Δk (i.e. for any $\delta > 0$)

$$p_\mu(\bar{a} \in \Delta k) \to 1$$

as $n \to \infty$. This is the classical law of large numbers.[24]

To put this another way: Consider the n-fold Cartesian product of the space X

$$\bar{X} = X^{(1)} \times X^{(2)} \times \cdots \times X^{(n)}$$

with probability measure

$$\bar{\mu} = \mu^{(1)} \times \mu^{(2)} \times \cdots \times \mu^{(n)},$$

where $\mu^{(i)}$ is the same probability on $X^{(i)}$ as $\mu^{(j)}$ is on $X^{(j)}$, the measure

μ. Define the random variable

$$\bar{A} = 1/n \, (A^{(1)} + A^{(2)} + \cdots + A^{(n)}),$$

where $A^{(i)}$ is the same random variable on $X^{(i)}$ as $A^{(j)}$ is on $X^{(j)}$, say A.[25] Let $\text{Exp}_\mu(A) = k$. Then for any Δk:

$$\bar{\mu}\,[\bar{A}^{-1}\,(\Delta k)] \to 1$$

as $n \to \infty$, i.e. the measure in $\bar{X}$ of the set of points assigning a value to the random variable $\bar{A}$ in an infinitesimally small range about $\text{Exp}_\mu(A)$ tends to 1 as the number of factor spaces in $\bar{X}$ tends to infinity.

Loosely: If we understand the probability space X as exhibiting the possible events open to a certain physical system (i.e. the propositional structure of a system), and these events are weighted by a measure function determining the average or expectation value of a random variable A as $\text{Exp}_\mu(A) = k$, then if we consider a very large number n of non-interacting copies of the system as a new composite system, in the limit as $n \to \infty$ the probability is 1 that the value of the magnitude $\bar{A}$ of the composite system is equal to k.

Now, the expectation value of an idempotent magnitude is the probability of the corresponding proposition or event. Thus, to say of a system that the probability of the proposition a corresponding to the idempotent magnitude P_a is $p_\mu(a)$, is to say that if we take n non-interacting copies of the system, then in the limit as $n \to \infty$ the probability is 1 that the value of the magnitude $\bar{P}_a$ of the composite system is equal to $p_\mu(a)$. In other words, *the probability tends to 1 that the composite system (i.e. the statistical ensemble) has the property $p_\mu(a)$, i.e. the property corresponding to this value of the magnitude $\bar{P}_a$.* And this property of the composite system is, loosely, the property that a fraction, $\text{Exp}_\mu(P_a) = p_\mu(a)$ of the component systems has the property a.

Notice that if the measure μ is a 2-valued measure assigning the probability 1 to the *atomic* proposition a, i.e. if the statistical ensemble is constituted of systems with the property a, then the probability in the ensemble tends to 1 that the value of the magnitude $\bar{P}_b$ for any idempotent $P_b \neq P_a$ is equal to 0. (For $\bar{P}_a$, of course, the value is 1.) In particular, the fraction of systems in the ensemble with an atomic property $b \neq a$ is zero.

In the case of a partial Boolean algebra like $\mathscr{A}_3$ the following theorem can be proved:[26] Let $\psi^{(i)}$ be a unit vector in $\mathscr{H}_3^{(i)}$, generating the statistics of a pure statistical state, so that $\text{Exp}_{\psi^{(i)}}(A^{(i)}) = k$ for the magnitude $A^{(i)}$. Consider the vector

$$\bar{\psi} = \psi^{(1)} \otimes \psi^{(2)} \otimes \cdots \otimes \psi^{(n)}$$

in the tensor product Hilbert space

$$\bar{\mathcal{H}}_3 = \mathcal{H}_3^{(1)} \otimes \mathcal{H}_3^{(2)} > \cdots \otimes \mathcal{H}_3^{(n)},$$

where $\psi^{(i)}$ is the same vector in $\mathcal{H}_3^{(i)}$, as $\psi^{(j)}$ is in $\mathcal{H}_3^{(j)}$, say ψ, and the magnitude

$$\bar{A} = 1/n \,(A^{(1)} + A^{(2)} + \cdots + A^{(n)}),$$

where $A^{(i)}$ is the same operator in $\mathcal{H}_3^{(i)}$ as $A^{(j)}$ is in $\mathcal{H}_3^{(j)}$, say A.[27] Then $\bar{\psi}$ is practically an eigenvector of the operator $\bar{A}$ in $\bar{\mathcal{H}}_3$, with the eigenvalue k, even though ψ is not an eigenvector of A in $\mathcal{H}_3$, i.e.

$$\lim_{n \to \infty} \|\bar{A}\bar{\psi} - k\bar{\psi}\| = 0.$$

This holds for any operator. What this theorem says is that if we take n non-interacting copies of a system whose statistics is generated by a vector ψ as a new composite system, then the statistics of *this* system is generated by a vector which is practically an eigenvector of the operator representing the magnitude $\bar{A}$, with eigenvalue $\text{Exp}_{\psi}(A)$, if n is large, for any magnitude A and any vector ψ. Thus, if we take n non-interacting copies of a system for which the proposition a_1 is true, so that the statistics of the ensemble is generated by the vector α_1, then the above theorem applied to the idempotent magnitude P_{b_1} yields:

$$\lim_{n \to \infty} \|P_{b_1}\bar{\alpha}_1 - k\bar{\alpha}_1\| = 0.$$

Loosely: in the limit as $n \to \infty$, $\bar{\alpha}_1$ is practically an eigenvector of the operator representing the magnitude $\bar{P}_{b_1}$ with eigenvalue k, where k is the expectation value of P_{b_1} specified by the vector α_1.

The expectation value of an idempotent magnitude is the probability of the corresponding proposition: $\text{Exp}_{\alpha_1}(P_{b_1}) = p_{\alpha_1}(b_1)$. And to say that $\bar{\alpha}_1$ is practically an eignevector of the operator representing the magnitude $\bar{P}_{b_1}$ with eigenvalue k, is to say, in effect, that the probability is very close to 1 that the magnitude $\bar{P}_{b_1}$ takes the value k, i.e. in the limit as $n \to \infty$, the probability is 1 that the magnitude $\bar{P}_{b_1}$ takes the value $P_{\alpha_1}(b_1)$. In other words, *the probability tends to 1 that the composite system (i.e. the ensemble) has the property* p_{α_1} *(b_1) i.e. the property corresponding to this value of the magnitude* $\bar{P}_{b_1}$. And this property of the composite system is, losely, the property that a fraction, $\text{Exp}_{\alpha_1}(P_{b_1}) = p_{\alpha_1}(b_1)$, of the component systems have the property b_1.

Thus, a system S with the atomic property a_1 is associated with the statistical state α_1, in the sense that with respect to the property b_1, say, S is to be regarded as a member of a statistical ensemble considered as a composite system with the property $p_{\alpha_1}(b_1)$ corresponding, loosely, to a fraction $p_{\alpha_1}(b_1)$ of the component systems having the property b_1. But this is not to say that some component systems in the ensemble have the property $a_1 \wedge b_1$, for there is no property $a_1 \wedge b_1$ in the sense of a property which is related to a_1 and b_1 as $a \wedge b$, a, b are related in the Boolean case.[28] The probabilities assigned to atoms in $\mathscr{B}_B$, $\mathscr{B}_C$, etc., are determined by the law of large numbers as properties of an ensemble homogeneous with respect to the atomic property a_1, but such an ensemble is not defined by a 2-valued measure on $\mathscr{A}_3$. In a Boolean propositional structure, the probabilities generated in this way are all 0. The assignment of non-zero probabilities in $\mathscr{A}_3$ to atoms incompatible with the designated atom is directly related to the non-trivial compatibility relation.

These considerations clarify the way in which the properties of a quantum mechanical system hang together, and the difference between this propositional structure and the Boolean structure of the properties of a classical mechanical system. Since the propositional structure of a quantum mechanical system is not imbeddable in a Boolean algebra, there is no sense in which this structure is 'incomplete' relative to the propositional structures of classical systems. A quantum mechanical system has all its properties in the same sense in which a classical mechanical system has all its properties: the difference lies in the way in which these properties are structured. In the Boolean case there is a 1-1 correspondence between atoms and 2-valued homomorphisms, hence 2-valued measures, and so an ensemble homogenous in some atomic property is characterized by a 2-valued measure which selects an ultrafilter of propositions, i.e. assigns probabilities 0 or 1 to every range of every magnitude. In a partial Boolean algebra like $\mathscr{A}_3$, the algebraic relations between the incompatible atoms in $\mathscr{B}_A$ and $\mathscr{B}_B$ determine multi-valued measures $p_{\alpha_i}(b_j) = p_{\beta_j}(a_i)$. Since these measures satisfy a law of large numbers, they may be regarded as probabilities in the same sense as the 2-valued measures of classical mechanics. There should be no special problem concerning the meaning of the multi-valued probabilities assigned to the properties of a quantum mechanical system by the specification of an atomic property of the system. They mean whatever the 0, 1 probabilities assigned to the properties of a classical system by the specification of an atomic property of the system are understood to mean.

University of Western Ontario and
Tel Aviv University

NOTES

[1] The term 'partial Boolean algebra' is due to S. Kochen and E. P. Specker, who have investigated these structures in the context of quantum mechanics (*J. Math. Mech.* **17** (1967), 59–87). They define a 'partial algebra' over a field $\mathscr{F}$ as a set $\mathscr{A}$ with a reflexive and symmetric binary relation $\leftrightarrow$ (termed 'comeasurability'), closed under the operations of addition and multiplication, which are defined only from $\leftrightarrow$ to $\mathscr{A}$, and the operation of scalar multiplication from $\mathscr{F} \times \mathscr{A}$ to $\mathscr{A}$. In addition, there is a unit element 1 which is 'comeasurable' with every element of $\mathscr{A}$, and if a, b, c are mutually 'comeasurable', then the values of the polynomials in a, b, c form a commutative algebra over the field $\mathscr{F}$. A partial Boolean algebra is a partial algebra over the field $\mathscr{Z}_2$ of two elements $\{0, 1\}$. If a, b, c are mutually 'comeasurable' elements in a partial Boolean algebra, then the values of the polynomials in a, b, c form a Boolean algebra.

I prefer the term 'compatible' for the relation $\leftrightarrow$ instead of 'comeasurable', which is suggestive in the wrong way. (The relation is not transitive, for example.) I shall use the term 'compatible' in the sense of the relation $\leftrightarrow$ throughout this article.

The set of self-adjoint operators on a Hilbert space forms a partial algebra over the field of real numbers, if the relation $\leftrightarrow$ is taken as commutativity. The idempotents of this set – the projection operators – form a partial Boolean algebra, and hence the subspaces of a Hilbert space (which are in 1-1 correspondence with the projection operators) form a partial Boolean algebra. Here, the Boolean operations $\wedge, \vee,$ and $'$ (which may be defined in terms of the ring operations $+, \cdot$ in the usual way: $a \wedge b = a \cdot b, a \vee b = a + b - a \cdot b, a' = 1 - a$) denote the supremum, infimum, and orthocomplement of subspaces. The partial Boolean algebra of subspaces of a Hilbert space may be pictured as 'pasted together' from its maximal Boolean subalgebras, corresponding to maximal commuting sets of projection operators.

By a *generalized* probability measure on a partial Boolean algebra, I mean a measure function satisfying the usual conditions for a probability measure on each maximal compatible subset of the partial Boolean algebra. A. M. Gleason (*J. Math. Mech.* **6** (1957) 885–893) proved that the algorithm of quantum mechanics generates all possible generalized probability measures on the partial Boolean algebra of subspaces of a Hilbert space.

For a further exposition of these notions see Sections 1 and 2 of the paper by

William Demopoulos in this volume ('The Possibility Structure of Physical Systems.')
[2] The magnitudes of a quantum mechanical system are represented by the self-adjoint operators on the Hilbert space of the system, idempotent magnitudes by projection operators. Compatible magnitudes are represented by commuting operators. If two magnitudes A_1, A_2 are represented by commuting operators, the projection operators $P_{A_1}(S_1), P_{A_2}(S_2)$ (for all Borel sets S_1, S_2) defined by the spectral theorem and associated with the ranges S_1, S_2 of the magnitudes A_1, A_2, respectively, commute, i.e. the corresponding idempotent magnitudes (and subspaces) are compatible. If A_1, A_2 are incompatible, the projection operators $P_{A_1}(S_1), P_{A_2}(S_2)$ will not in general commute (although they might commute for some Borel sets).

[3] As Kochen and Specker have pointed out (*op. cit.*), it is quite trivial that the statistical states of a quantum mechanical system can be represented by measures on a classical probability space if the algebraic structure of the magnitudes is *not* preserved. But such a representation has no theoretical interest *in itself*. Thus, 'hidden variable theories', which all involve some such representation, are interesting only insofar as the new structure is theoretically motivated. Invariably, the reasons proposed for considering a new algebraic structure of a specific kind are 'plausibility arguments' derived from some metaphysical view of the universe (allegedly 'quantum mechanical', but otherwise quite arbitrary), or arguments which confuse the construction of a hidden variable theory of this sort with a solution to the hidden variable problem.

[4] This result may be regarded as a corollary to Gleason's theorem (*op. cit.*). Kochen and Specker (*op. cit.*) prove directly that there is no 2-valued homomorphism on a *finite* partial Boolean subalgebra of the partial Boolean algebra of subspaces of a Hilbert space of 3 or more dimensions. This is a very powerful result, which excludes the possibility of a classical representation of the quantum statistics that preserves the algebraic structure of the magnitudes *even if it is assumed that not all self-adjoint operators represent physical magnitudes* (or not all projection operators represent idempotent physical magnitudes).

[5] The idempotent magnitudes (which have possible values 0 or 1) of a classical mechanical system form a Boolean algebra, a subalgebra of the commutative algebra of real-valued functions on the phase space of the system (representing all possible magnitudes). This is the algebra of characteristic functions on phase space, isomorphic to the field of Borel subsets of the space. The algebra of idempotent magnitudes of a mechanical system may be understood as representing the totality of possible properties of the system, the values 0 and 1 for the magnitude denoting the absence or presence of the property. Equivalently, the algebra of idempotents represents the propositional structure of the system, or the possible events open to the system (since all changes in events are correlated with changes in properties, and conversely).

[6] See Kochen and Specker, *op. cit.*, or J. Bub and W. Demopoulos 'The Interpretation of Quantum Mechanics', in *Boston Studies in the Philosophy of Science*, vol. XIII (ed. by R. S. Cohen and M. W. Wartofsky), D. Reidel Publ Co., Dordrecht, Holland, 1974.

[7] If b is an atom, either a or a' is above b, i.e. either $b \leqslant a$ or $b \leqslant a'$ for every $a \in \mathscr{B}$ (but not both, or else $b=0$). Hence, there can be at most one ultrafilter containing an atom. A 2-valued homomorphism is definable on $\mathscr{B}$ by mapping each element $a \in \mathscr{B}$ onto 1 or 0 according to whether a is or is not a member of the ultrafilter Φ.

[8] This is because ultrafilters (maximal filters) are no longer *prime* filters. A filter Φ is prime if it is proper (i.e. a proper subset of $\mathscr{A}$) and if $a \vee b \in \Phi$ only if either $a \in \Phi$ or $b \in \Phi$. Every ultrafilter in a partial Boolean algebra contains the unit, and hence con-

tains $a \vee a'$ for every $a \in \mathscr{A}$. But if Φ is an ultrafilter in the maximal Boolean subalgebra $\mathscr{B} \subset \mathscr{A}$, then neither a nor a' will belong to Φ if a and a' are outside $\mathscr{B}$, i.e. incompatible with the elements contained in Φ.

[9] I refer to M. H. Stone's representation theorem for Boolean algebras: every Boolean algebra is isomorphic to a field of subsets of its ultrafilters, members of the field being those subsets of ultrafilters containing an element of the algebra. For an account and references see R. Sikorski, *Boolean Algebras,* Springer-Verlag, Inc., New York, 1969.

[10] An event a is represented by a subset of X belonging to the field $\mathscr{F}$.

[11] A non-degenerate magnitude has (three) distinct eigenvalues. If two eigenvalues are equal, say $a_1 = a_2 = a$, then a 2-dimensional subspace $\mathscr{K}_a$ in $\mathscr{H}_3$ is associated with the value a, but since any vector in $\mathscr{K}_a$ is an eigenvector of A with the eigenvalue a, *any* orthogonal pair of vectors in $\mathscr{K}_a$ together with α_3 will form a complete orthonormal set (basis) in $\mathscr{H}_3$. Thus, a degenerate magnitude is not associated with a *unique* set of orthogonal 1-dimensional subspaces in the partial Boolean algebra of subspaces $\mathscr{A}_3$ of $\mathscr{H}_3$, and hence a degenerate magnitude is not associated with a *maximal* Boolean subalgebra in $\mathscr{A}_3$ (each maximal Boolean subalgebra being defined by 3 orthogonal atoms in $\mathscr{A}_3$, i.e. 3 orthogonal 1-dimensional subspaces in $\mathscr{H}_3$).

[12] The term 'state' in quantum mechanics has been much abused. I have used the term *statistical state* in the sense of the generator of an assignment of probabilities to ranges of values of the magnitudes of a quantum mechanical system, with reference to the statistical algorithm of the theory. The statistical states of quantum mechanics are represented by the statistical operators in Hilbert space. When the term 'quantum state' is used in the literature, it usually carries the connotation of a maximal specification of a system in terms of the theory, analogous to the specification of the state of a classical mechanical system by a point in phase space. The difficulty with this notion is that the sense of the analogy is quite unclear without a clear understanding of the significance of the state in classical mechanics, and what the difference between classical mechanics and quantum mechanics amounts to. On this issue, see Section 4 of the paper by William Demopoulos in this volume ('The Possibility Structure of Physical Systems'). If a classical state is understood as a Boolean ultrafilter, and the transition from classical to quantum mechanics is regarded as involving the transition from a Boolean to a non-Boolean propositional structure of a specific kind, then a 'quantum state' is presumably an ultrafilter in a quantum mechanical propositional structure, represented by a 1-dimensional subspace or vector in Hilbert space. But this conception is never proposed explicitly. Generally, the notion of state is understood operationally, so that the state of a system in classical and quantum mechanics is regarded as the result of physical operations which 'prepare' the state. Then 'pure states' (represented by vectors in Hilbert space) are distinguished from 'mixed states' (represented by probability measure over pure states).

I shall use the term 'quantum state' throughout the following to denote a concept used uncritically in the literature, sometimes carrying the connotation of an ultrafilter or an atom in a propositional structure, and sometimes carrying the connotation of a 'pure state' associated with a maximal non-interfering set of measurements or physical operations. (I regard the operational notion as quite confused.) Thus, my use of the term 'statistical state' is in the precise sense outlined above, while my use of the term 'quantum state' is purely expository.

[13] It seems to me that this view is common to all versions of the Copenhagen interpretation, but a detailed textual examination in support of this claim would be out of place here. The following remarks are intended as clarifying comments.

Bohr describes quantum mechanics as a formalism in which "the quantities by which the state of a physical system is ordinarily defined are replaced by symbolic operators subjected to a non-commutative algorism involving Planck's constant. This procedure prevents a fixation of such quantities to the extent which would be required for the deterministic description of classical physics, but allows us to determine their spectral distribution as revealed by evidence about atomic processes. In conformity with the non-pictorial character of the formalism, its physical interpretation finds expression in laws, of an essentially statistical type, pertaining to observations obtained under given experimental conditions". (Niels Bohr, *Essays 1958–1962 on Atomic Physics and Human Knowledge,* Vintage Books, New York, 1966, pp. 2, 3.)

Again: "In the treatment of atomic problems, actual calculations are most conveniently carried out with the help of a Schrödinger state function, from which the statistical laws governing observations obtainable under specified conditions can be deduced by definite mathematical operations. It must be recognized, however, that we are dealing with a purely symbolic procedure, the unambiguous physical interpretation of which in the last resort requires a reference to a complete experimental arrangement". (*Ibid.,* p. 5.)

By a 'complete experimental arrangement', I understand Bohr to mean an arrangement which selects a maximal Boolean subalgebra in the partial Boolean algebra of quantum mechanical properties (associated with a quantity represented by a non-degenerate operator in the 'non-commutative algorism'), as opposed to a non-maximal Boolean subalgebra (associated with a degenerate quantity).

[14] Bohr, certainly, would reject this assumption. But this amounts to the abandonment of any attempt at a straightforward realist interpretation of the quantum statistics in favor of what is, in the last analysis, crank metaphysics.

[15] Maximal in the partial Boolean algebra of properties of $S^{(1)}$ (i.e. the partial Booean algebra of subspaces of $\mathcal{H}^{(1)}$).

[16] The composite system $S^{(1)}+S^{(2)}$ is associated with the Hilbert space $\mathcal{H}^{(1)}\otimes\mathcal{H}^{(2)}$, the tensor product of the Hilbert spaces $\mathcal{H}^{(1)}$, $\mathcal{H}^{(2)}$ of $S^{(1)}$, $S^{(2)}$, respectively. If $\alpha_i^{(1)}$ $(i=1, 2, 3)$ and $\alpha_j^{(2)}$ $(j=1, 2, 3)$ are bases (complete orthonormal sets of vectors) in $\mathcal{H}^{(1)}$, $\mathcal{H}^{(2)}$, the vectors $\alpha_i^{(1)}\otimes\alpha_j^{(2)}$ $(i, j=1, 2, 3)$ form a basis in $\mathcal{H}^{(1)}\otimes\mathcal{H}^{(2)}$, i.e. any vector in $\mathcal{H}^{(1)}\otimes\mathcal{H}^{(2)}$ may be represented as a linear combination of these basis vectors. Obviously, not every vector in $\mathcal{H}^{(1)}\otimes\mathcal{H}^{(2)}$ is of the form $\psi^{(1)}\otimes\phi^{(2)}$.

[17] This follows from the theory of statistical operators for composite systems. See J. von Neumann, *Mathematical Foundations of Quantum Mechanics,* Princeton University Press, Princeton, 1955, Chapter VI.

[18] Say, $\Psi_0=\psi\otimes\phi$, where ϕ is the initial quantum state of the measuring instrument $S^{(2)}$, represented by a vector in the Hilbert space $\mathcal{H}^{(2)}$.

[19] For a detailed discussion of the measurement problem, see C. A. Hooker, 'The Nature of Quantum Mechanical Reality', in *Paradigms and Paradoxes: The Philosophical Challenge of the Quantum Domain* (ed by R. G. Colodny), University of Pittsburgh Press, Pittsburgh, 1972.

Furry developed this elementary point into a critique of the Einstein-Podolsky-Rosen paradox, which involves difficulties in the interpretation of the statistical correlations between coupled systems (W. H. Furry, *Phys. Rev.* **49** (1936), 393–399). Einstein, Podolsky, and Rosen (*Phys. Rev.* **47** (1935), 777–780) considered a composite quantum mechanical system represented by a quantum state of the form:

$$\Psi = \Sigma_i \, (\alpha_i^{(1)} \otimes \alpha_i^{(2)}, \quad \Psi) \, \alpha_i^{(1)} \otimes \alpha_i^{(2)}$$
$$= \Sigma_j \, (\beta_j^{(1)} \otimes \beta_j^{(2)}, \quad \Psi) \, \beta_j^{(1)} \otimes \beta_j^{(2)},$$

i.e the values of an $S^{(1)}$-magnitude $A^{(1)}$ are correlated with the values of an $S^{(2)}$-magnitude $A^{(2)}$, and the values of an $S^{(1)}$-magnitude $B^{(1)}$ are correlated with the values of an $S^{(2)}$-magnitude $B^{(2)}$, where $B^{(1)}$, $B^{(2)}$ are incompatible with $A^{(1)}$, $A^{(2)}$, respectively.

The aspect of the paradox usually stressed is the possible separation in space of the coupled systems, but this is irrelevant. While the spatial separation of the systems might create difficulties for certain interpretations of the quantum statistics – a disturbance theory of measurement, for example – the peculiar features of the quantum mechanical description of the coupled systems in no way depends on this separation. In fact, the Einstein-Podolsky-Rosen example is a paradigm of the measurement process: an interaction between two systems, $S^{(1)}$ and $S^{(2)}$ resulting in correlations between (some of) the magnitudes of $S^{(1)}$ and $S^{(2)}$, so that the value of an $S^{(1)}$-magnitude, say, can be inferred from the value of an appropriate $S^{(2)}$-magnitude, on the basis of the theory of the interaction.

[20] This is, in effect, the possibility envisaged by Einstein, Podolsky, and Rosen: that the interaction might establish similar correlations between magnitudes $B^{(1)}$, $B^{(2)}$ incompatible with $A^{(1)}$, $A^{(2)}$, respectively.

[21] See von Neumann, *op. cit.*, Chapter IV, §3, for a discussion of this non-uniqueness. The representation of a degenerate operator as a weighted sum of pure statistical operators corresponding to a complete orthonormal set of vectors in Hilbert space is not unique. In general, a degenerate self-adjoint operator does not determine a unique complete set of eigenvectors in Hilbert space via the spectral representation, which defines a set of projection operators onto subspaces of dimension greater than 1 for degenerate eigenvalues.

[22] This is the case if, for example, all the eigenvalues of $W^{(1)}$ are the same, i.e. $w_1 = w_2 = w_3 = w$. (The eigenvalue w is said to be degenerate and of multiplicity 3.) Then any set of 3 orthogonal vectors in $\mathscr{H}^{(1)}$ are eigenvectors of $W^{(1)}$ with eigenvalue w, i.e. $W^{(1)}$ may be regarded as a mixture of any 3 orthogonal quantum states in $\mathscr{H}^{(1)}$ with weights w. If $w_1 = w_2 = w \neq w_3$, any pair of orthogonal vectors in the subspace orthogonal to $\alpha_3^{(1)}$ are eigenvectors of $W^{(1)}$ with eigenvalue w, i.e. $W^{(1)}$ may be regarded as a mixture of $\alpha_3^{(1)}$ and any two orthogonal quantum states in the subspace orthogonal to $\alpha_3^{(1)}$, with weights w_3, w, w, respectively.

[23] Here f is the 'distribution function' of the random variable. To say that the random variables are statistically equivalent, is to say that they all have the same distribution function. The symbol $a^{(i)}$ is a variable denoting a general value of the magnitude $A^{(i)}$, so $a^{(i)} \in S$ is to be read: the value of the magnitude $A^{(i)}$ lies in the range S. By $A^{(i)-1}$ I mean the inverse image of S under the map $A^{(i)}$, i.e. the set of points in X mapped onto S by $A^{(i)}$.

[24] The symbol $\bar{a}$ is a variable denoting a general value of the magnitude $\bar{A}$. Thus $\bar{a} \in \Delta k$ is to be read: the value of the magnitude $\bar{A}$ lies in the range Δk.

For a concise and readable account of the classical law of large numbers relevant to this discussion (a variety of related results are referred to as 'laws of large numbers'), see 'The Theory of Probability', A. N. Kolmogorov, in *Mathematics: Its Content, Methods, and Meaning,* vol. 2, Ch. XI (ed by A. D. Aleksandrov *et al.*), M.I.T. Press, Cambridge, 1963.

[25] Actually, $\bar{A}$ should be defined as

$$\bar{A} = (1/n)(A^{(1)} \times I^{(2)} \times \cdots \times I^{(n)} + I^{(1)} \times A^{(2)} \times I^{(3)} \times \cdots \times I^{(n)} + \cdots + I^{(1)} \times \cdots \times I^{(n-1)} \times A^{(n)})$$

where $I^{(i)}$ is the unit random variable – real-valued function – on the space $X^{(i)}$.

[26] For a proof see D. Finkelstein, 'The Logic of Quantum Physics', *Transactions of the New York Academy of Science* **25** (1962–63), 621–637.

[27] Again, $\bar{A}$ should be defined as

$$\bar{A} = (1/n)(A^{(1)} \otimes I^{(2)} \otimes \cdots \otimes I^{(n)} + I^{(1)} \otimes A^{(2)} \otimes I^{(3)} \otimes \cdots \otimes I^{(n)} + \cdots + I^{(1)} \otimes \cdots \otimes I^{(n-1)} \otimes A^{(n)})$$

where $I^{(i)}$ is the unit operator on $\mathscr{H}_3{}^{(i)}$.

[28] In a partial Boolean algebra, $a \wedge b$ is defined as an element in the algebra if and only if a and b are compatible. In the partial Boolean algebra of subspaces of a Hilbert space, $K_a \wedge K_b$ denotes the infimum of the subspaces K_a and K_b. Now the infimum of two subspaces is *always* defined, even if the subspaces are incompatible. It might therefore appear gratuitous to restrict conjunction in the algebra of propositions of a quantum mechanical system to propositions corresponding to compatible subspaces, since conjunction in the sense of infimum is always defined: the subspaces of a Hilbert space actually form a lattice. The objection is misleading. There are no subspaces in the lattice which are left out of the partial Boolean algebra. The infimum and supremum of two incompatible subspaces K_a, K_b are elements in the partial Boolean algebra as well, only these elements are not related to K_a and K_b by the binary operations of the algebra.

Thus, in the example considered, the non-existence of systems in the ensemble having the property $a_1 \wedge b_1$ does not depend on an arbitrary restriction of the conjunction operation to compatible elements, which does not arise if the propositional structure is treated as a lattice.

MARIO BUNGE

POSSIBILITY AND PROBABILITY

1. Introduction

We shall be concerned with real possibility, such as the possibility of a physical event to happen. This kind of possibility is predicated of factual items – things, properties of things, or changes in properties of things. Real possibility is then radically different from conceptual possibility, such as the satisfiability of a formula in a model or the confirmability of a hypothesis by empirical evidence. Conceptual possibility concerns constructs, not things, and it is elucidated without the help of the probability concept – nor, for that matter, is it clarified with the help of modal logics. Not so real possibility: it concerns concrete objects and it is sometimes elucidated in probabilistic terms.

Probability exactifies real possibility of a certain kind – not of every kind. For example refrangibility (refractive power) is a disposition, or potential property, that is not construed probabilistically in classical dispersion theory. It is, as we shall say, a *causal disposition* to be contrasted to a *chance propensity* such as the probability an electron has to acquire a definite position. This difference, though radical, is not made by other advocates of real or physical possibility.

A scientific theory concerned with chance propensities is a probabilistic or stochastic theory. Prime examples of stochastic theories are of course classical statistical mechanics, quantum mechanics, quantum electrodynamics, genetics, the theory of birth and death processes, and most mathematical learning theories. In these theories certain properties are represented by random variables subject to definite conditions (law statements). In these theories chance propensities are exactified (moreover quantified) as probabilities, and the latter are interpreted as chance propensities. The exactification is performed without the help of the model theoretic notion of possibility as satisfiability in some model, or the concepts of possibility elucidated by modal logics. Nor are the exact concepts of real possibility built by the statistical theories of science reducible to

Harper and Hooker (eds.), Foundations of Probability Theory, Statistical Inference, and Statistical Theories of Science, Vol. III, 17–33. All Rights Reserved. Copyright © 1976 by D. Reidel Publishing Company, Dordrecht-Holland.

either the concept of relative frequency or the notion of degree of rational belief, let alone to that of uncertainty. In science, a statement such as "The probability of event e is p" should be interpreted as "e is a really possible event & The propensity (or tendency) for e to occur is p". Such a probability statement gives precision to the propositions "Event e may happen" and "Event e has a certain tendency to occur". It quantifies a real possibility of a certain kind, namely a chance propensity.

So much for an overview. The body of the paper will discuss the following subjects: real possibility, causal disposition, chance propensity, and modality and probability.

2. REAL POSSIBILITY

Unlike the notion of conceptual possibility, that of real (or ontic) possibility refers to factual items. That is, "p is really possible" assigns the factual referent(s) of the proposition p, not p itself, a real possibility. Our referents are then factual items not constructs. And a factual item is anything involving things: a thing is such and so are its properties and changes. Factual items are represented or described by propositions such as the following:

a is a thing.	Thing a has property P.
K is a kind of thing.	a is a thing of kind K.
s is a state.	Thing a is in state s.
e is a change.	Thing a undergoes change e.

A possible fact is of course a fact that may or may not occur or become actualized. The difference between possibles and actuals may be characterized in the following way. Possibles can conjoin and disjoin: if a and b are possible factual items represented by a set each, so are $a \cup b$, i.e. the complex possibility that a or b may be the case, and $a \cap b$, i.e. the possible joint occurrence of a and b. On the other hand there is no such thing as the actual fact that fact a or fact b will happen. Disjunction concerns possibles, not actuals. Likewise $\bar{a}$ is whatever is possible when a is not. But there is no such thing as the unique complement (or inverse or opposite) of an actual fact. Complementation (or negation) is, just as disjunction, a mark of possibility not of actuality. (Not the exclusive mark though, as constructs too may disjoin and invert.)

The possibility/actuality contrast can be summarized as follows. Call *P* the set of really possible factual items and $A \subset P$ the subset of *P* consisting of actuals. Then whereas *P* has the structure of an algebra of sets (and moreover is a sigma algebra), *A* has the structure of a semigroup. The actualization process is representable as the collapse of the richer structure into the poorer one: in this process union (or disjunction) and complementation (or negation) are forgotten. This characterization, though suggestive, is insufficient because it does not characterize unambiguously the set *P* of really possible factual items. So much so that any algebra of sets, whether concrete or abstract, fits the description. And this is not surprising: if an a priori theory of real possibility were true then we would have hardly any use for science, which is the study of real possibility.

Only science can tell us with precision which facts are really possible, which compossible, and so on. In science a fact is judged to be really possible just in case it is lawful, i.e. compatible with the stable objective patterns represented by law statements. The possible and the lawful coincide and so do the impossible and the lawless. For example, every solution of an equation of motion of a thing represents a possible trajectory. Consequently the set of all such solutions (the state space of the thing) represents the totality of possible motions of the thing. In other words, the lawful motions of the thing constitute its possible motions. (Equivalently: every possible state of the thing is represented by a point in the state space of the thing, and every possible motion of the thing is represented by a trajectory in that space.)

We are thus led to adopt a modified version of Bolzano's definition of physical possibility:

DEFINITION 1   A fact is possible iff it is lawful: If *x* is a fact then *x* is *possible* $=_{df}$ There is at least one law satisfied by *x*.

This definition of real (or ontic) possibility does not allow us to derive the concept of real necessity without further ado, namely by applying Aristotle's definition "$\Box p =_{df} \neg \Diamond \neg p$". For one thing $\neg$ applies to propositions not to facts: the expression '$\neg x$' makes no sense when *x* denotes a fact. But even if we were to reinterpret "$\neg x$" as "It is not the case that *x*", Aristotle's definition would not help us, because real or factual necessity has a component that is not included in lawfulness, namely *circumstance*. Indeed, for anything to actually happen and thus be necessary it must not only "obey" laws but must also "count on favorable circumstances". Not even a deterministic (nonstochastic) law statement describes what is actually the case: it only describes possibles. A fortiori stochastic laws describe even weaker possibilities, namely chance facts – i.e. facts occurring only with a certain frequency. In sum we can keep Aristotle's definition in terms of possibility and negation for the conceptual realm but it is inapplicable in science and in metaphysics. Consequently modal logics, all of which admit Aristotle's law, are irrelevant to both science and metaphysics.

To put things in a slightly different way: An actual state of affairs is best described as a conjunction of law statements with propositions representing circumstances (idiosyncrasies, initial conditions, boundary conditions, etc.). If the laws are deterministic, the corresponding facts may (but need not) be called *necessary*, while they may be called *contingent* if the laws are stochastic. Thus an unsupported coin will necessarily fall, it being contingent that it falls head up. Calling 'C' the set of circumstances that are jointly necessary and sufficient for a fact to occur either always or with a fixed frequency, we summarize:

Deterministic law, $C \vdash$ Necessary fact (occurs whenever C is the case)

Stochastic law, $C \vdash$ Contingent fact (occurs with a fixed frequency when C is the case).

Accordingly we have the following partitions of reality:

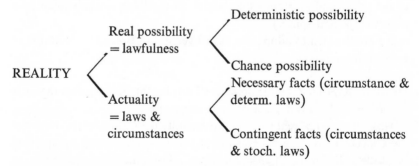

To conclude this section. Real possibility is identical with lawfulness. But real necessity is not definable in terms of possibility and negation. Never mind, for 'necessity' plays no role in factual science except as a synonym for 'actuality': whatever is the case must be and conversely. Nothing is gained by replacing "It is snowing" by "Necessarily it is snowing", or "The snowfall probability is $\frac{3}{4}$" by "Necessarily the snowfall probability is $\frac{3}{4}$", let alone by "The probability that it snows necessarily is $\frac{3}{4}$". The prefix 'necessarily' is unnecessary. And the very distinction between necessary facts and contingent facts, drawn a while ago, is unintelligible with reference to individual facts: it makes sense only for collections of facts. In fact an actual individual fact is a fact is a fact. Calling it 'necessary' is just a way of saying that, far from being merely possible, it is the case.

3. CAUSAL DISPOSITION

Thus far we have been concerned with the general concept of real possibility. Henceforth we shall study two special concepts of real possibility: causal disposition, as exemplified by fragility and inherited susceptibility to TB, and chance propensity, as exemplified by a photon that may go through either slit of a two slit screen. Let us start with the former, which is the simpler of the two though probably not the more basic.

A chunk of ice may melt in air, a lump of sugar may dissolve in water, a muscle cell may divide, a child may learn to read, a society may survive. These potentialities will be realized provided the proper environment or means is supplied: otherwise they will not. All such abilities are properties on a par with those actually "exercised" by the thing concerned. But they are derivative properties not basic ones: they are rooted or reducible to the very structure of the thing. Hence they are not to be counted separately when listing the properties of their carriers. We shall call them *causal dispositions*, *potentialities*, or *abilities*.

The peculiar trait of a disposition is that, when conjoined with suitable circumstances, it never fails to actualize: solubility becomes actual dissolution, divisibility division, viability continued existence, and so on. In clumsy but few words: *Disposition & Circumstances = Actuality*. Or, equivalently: disposition equals actuality minus certain circumstances. More precisely: a disposition is a condition that is necessary but not sufficient. Accordingly real possibility of this kind may be characterized as follows:

> If x is a fact, then x is really possible $=_{df}$ There is a fact y such that if y happens then x happens.

Real possibility of this kind is then insufficient condition: actuality ensues as soon as this shortcoming is remedied, i.e. when the missing conditions appear.

The circumstances favorable or unfavorable to the actualization of a causal disposition of a thing x involve some thing y other than x and forming part of the environment of x. (The additional thing y may but need not be a piece of experimental equipment.) The things x and y join to form a new thing $x \& y$. This composite thing possesses the property P into which the potentiality D has been actualized. I.e. the process is this:

Thing x with disposition D }
$x \& y$: thing with manifest property P.
Environment y of thing x

For example, if a piece of a magnetizable material is placed in a magnetic field, it becomes magnetic. The inherited susceptibilities to TB, schizophrenia and other illnesses are parallel: the environment will bring forth, or else inhibit, such an inborn disposition.

The preceding considerations can be summed up in the following convention:

DEFINITION 2   A property D of a thing x is called a *causal disposition* of x iff

(i) D is a derivative property of x [i.e. if x has another property B that precedes D, in the sense that D adds nothing to B, i.e. $B \& D = B$];

(ii) there is another thing y (the environment of x) that joins x to form the compound thing $x \& y$ such that

(iii) $x \& y$ has at least one property P, not possessed by either x or y, preceded by D.

A property that is not dispositional is called *manifest*. The totality of causal dispositions of a thing is called the *causal potentiality* of the thing. And one thing has a *greater causal potentiality* than another iff the causal potentiality of the former includes (set theoretically) that of the latter.

For example, the potentiality of an individual organism consists of its genetic make-up or program. A poor genetic endowment yields few possibilities of a rich experience, just as a poor environment cuts out many possibilites of using the genetic make-up. Second example: shortly before the birth of molecular biology it was considered preposterous to regard the human zygote as a potential man, or the acorn as a potential oak tree.

Both assertions would have been laughed away as so many remnants of preformationism. But contemporary biology is preformationist insofar as it holds the whole mature organisms to be programmed in the zygote. Third example: the psychological faculties or abilities, rejected by behaviorism, have been revived by N. Chomsky, G. A. Miller, and other psycholinguists. These scientists stress the difference between ability and performance – an instance of the potentiality-actuality difference. Performance, or the use of an ability, is an objectifier or index or the latter. Thus verbal behavior does not coincide with linguistic ability although it is an overt or observable manifestation of it. The ability is in this case the capacity to utter and understand sentences new to the speaker.

To conclude. Causal dispositions are as important as manifest properties but they can be reduced to the latter, though not as easily as the actualist would like to. The possibility of dissolving is not the same as actual dissolution: while the latter is a property of a complex system (solute *cum* solvent) the former is a property of one of its components. For example, the solubility of salt in water consists in a certain feature of the crystal structure of dry salt which, when joined with water, gives rise to actual dissolution. In general, a disposition of a thing x can be identified with a manifest property of the same thing x related to a joint manifest property of some complex thing $x \& y$. This is precisely what we had set out to do, i.e. to try and explain dispositions in terms of manifest properties without however dismissing them.

So much for causal disposition. Let us now look into a kind of propensity that is not reducible the way causal disposition is, namely chance propensity.

4. CHANCE PROPENSITY

An effective way of realizing the radical difference between chance propensity and causal disposition is to peep at quantum physics. Whereas classical physics assigns every point particle a definite position at each instant, the quantum mechanical "particle" possesses at each instant a definite position distribution, i.e. a whole range of possible positions, each with a given weight or probability. That is, in quantum mechanics position is a random variable. Likewise with other quantal properties such as linear momentum, angular momentum, and energy: save in exceptional cases each "particle" has a whole bunch (interval) of values of each of these properties. (The exceptions are constituted by the states of the "particle" that happen to be eigenstates of the corresponding property. For example, a system in a state that coincides with an energy eigenstate has a sharp energy value not a whole distribution of energy values. But such states, i.e. the stationary states, are privileged.)

Another way of describing this contrast between classical and quantal properties is as follows. Where classical physics offers a nonstochastic dynamical variable Q_c, quantum physics introduces a random variable $\psi^* Q \psi$ (a "local observable"), where Q is an operator acting on ψ, a place and time dependent function that determines the position probability density $\rho = |\psi(x)|^2$. (It may be assumed that these bilinear forms or densities constitute the basic dynamical variables of the system, whereas the operators Q are syncategorematic objects entering the construction of the random variables $\psi^* Q \psi$.) Every one of these random variables ("local observables") is a property of an individual thing not just a collective property of a whole aggregate of similar things. From a classical viewpoint this situation is unacceptable. Hence the classicist will interpret ψ as representing the state of a statistical ensemble of similar systems rather than as a property of an individual thing. This (Einstein's) interpretation is not possible, because (a) an expression such as '$\psi^* x \psi$', by containing a single position variable x, cannot be forced into representing a host of "particles", and (b) there is not enough momentum and energy to keep a whole assembly of "particles" in motion. As long as we accept quantum mechanics we must be reconciled with its nonclassical features, such as that position is a random variable with a number of alternative values (each with its own probability) for each microsystem. Only the average of such a distribution is a point and it happens to coincide with the classical value (in the nonrelativistic limit). In other words, classical physics gives only a global or superficial account of microentities by ignoring that the dynamical properties of the latter are random variables smeared over the whole space accessible to those entities.

It must be stressed that the $\psi^* Q \psi$ are not dispositions but are possessed all the time by a microsystem: that is, they are manifest (though not directly observable) properties. On the other hand a sharp value of Q, such as $Q_c = \langle Q \rangle_{AV}$, is a dispositional property of the thing concerned. In other words, a thing with a Q-distribution $\psi^* Q \psi$ has the *propensity* to acquire this or that sharp Q value, such as an eigenvalue or an average value of Q. For example, a photon travelling in free space is not concentrated at a point (is not sharply localized) but, when bumping into an atomic electron, it may suddenly contract – only to cease being a photon the next moment. And an electron may, under the influence of an external field, acquire a definite momentum value, though at the expense of its localization. In quantum physics distributions are basic and sharp values rather exceptional or just averages. On the other hand in classical physics sharp values are basic and distributions derivative: they result from the interplay of numerous entities. Only a classical reformulation of quantum physics could reinstate the primacy of the sharp actual value. But such a foundation, sweet dream of the nostalgic, is more than dubious: the deepest physical laws known heretofore are quantal not classical.

The upshot of the preceding discussion is this. We must admit that some stochastic properties (represented by random variables) are basic, and we may regard such properties as *propensities to acquire sharp values*. They are not causal dispositions such as fragility, because there is nothing necessary about them. In fact a distribution may collapse into any of a number of new states, each possible transition having only a definite probability. (For example, the initial superposition of states $\psi = c_1\psi_1 + c_2\psi_2$ collapses into state ψ_1 with probability $|c_1|^2$, or into state ψ_2 with probabil ty $|c_2|^2$.) For this reason we call this kind of real possibility *chance disposition* (in contrast to causal disposition) or *chance propensity*. Let us now try and sketch an analysis of this kind of property.

Call D a disposition of a thing and P a chance propensity of the same thing. Further, call A_i (with i a natural number) an actual or manifest property of the thing and C an external circumstance such as an environmental agent acting on the thing. There are two possible outcomes of the joint occurrence of possibility and circumstance, according to the kind of possibility:

$$D \ \& \ C \ \text{---} \rightarrow A \qquad \underline{\text{Causal disposition}}$$

$$P \ \& \ C \underset{\substack{P_1 \nearrow A_1 \\ \\ P_2 \rightarrow A_2 \\ \vdots \\ P_n \rightarrow A_n}}{} \qquad \underline{\text{Chance propensity}}$$

In the case of causal dispositions the environment offers opportunities or curtails them. In the case of chance propensities the possibilities inhere in the thing itself and the environment takes it pick. Whereas in the first case things are what they are, in the second things are whatever they may become.

To put it into a somewhat more exact way, we propose

DEFINITION 3   A property P of a thing x is called a *chance propensity* of x iff

(i) P is representable by a random variable or a probability distribution;

(ii) P is a primary, irreducible, or basic property [i.e. there is no other property Q of x such that $P \& Q = Q$].

The set of all chance propensities of a thing may be called the *chance potentiality* of the thing. A thing has a *greater chance potentiality* than another just in case the chance potentiality of the former includes (set theoretically) that of the latter. (For example, any atom has a greater chance potentiality than any of its components.) Finally, the *potentiality* of a thing is the (set theoretical) union of its causal potentiality and its chance potentiality.

Chance propensity is not reducible to causal disposition, let alone to nonstochastic manifest property. This is true not only of microphysics but also of biology and psychology. Thus Johnny's mathematical ability is a causal disposition resulting from a chance pairing of parental genes. His parents, as a couple, had a definite chance propensity of conceiving a child with mathematical ability.

5. PROPENSITY INTERPRETATION OF PROBABILITY AND PROBABILISTIC EXACTIFICATION OF REAL POSSIBILITY

Probability theory and any application of it (i.e. any stochastic theory) contain two basic or primitive concepts: the probability (or event) space F and the probability measure Pr defined on F. *A factual* or *objective interpretation* of probability theory, or of a stochastic theory, consists in assigning every point x of the probability space, and every value $\Pr(x)$ of the probability function, a factual meaning. One such possible interpretation consists in regarding the basic set S, out of which the probability space F is manufactured, as the state space of a thing. Since F is a certain collection of subsets of S (e.g. F = the power set of S), every element of F will be interpretable in this case as a bunch of states (or possible conditions) of the thing concerned. And $Pr(x)$ may then be interpreted as the strength of the probability to dwell in the state(s) x. Similarly, if x and y are states (or sets of states) of the thing, the conditional probability of y given x, i.e. $Pr(y \mid x)$, is a measure of the strength of the propensity or tendency the thing has to go from the state(s) x to the state(s) y.

Note the difference between the *propensity interpretation of probability* and the *probability exactification* (or elucidation) of the presystematic notion of propensity, tendency, or ability of the chance type. In the former case one attaches or assigns factual items to a concept, whereas in the latter one endows a factual concept (i.e. a concept with factual referent(s)) with a precise mathematical structure. In science and in scientific metaphysics we need both factual interpretation and mathematical elucidation (exactification). Note also that an interpretation of probability is incomplete unless it bears on the two primitives of the theory, F (or S) and Pr. Hence the objectivist interpretations of Poincaré, Smoluchowski, Fréchet and others are incomplete because they are restricted to assuming that a probability value is a "physical constant attached to an event E and to a category C of trials", as Fréchet put it. It is like saying that e is a physical constant without adding that it happens to be the electron charge.

It is instructive to contrast the propensity to the actualist (or frequency) interpretations of probability values, assuming that both interpretations agree on the nature of the support set F. (This assumption is a pretence: not only frequentists like von Mises but also Popper emphasized that facts have no probabilities unless they occur in experimentally controlled situations.) This contrast is sketched in Table I.

Note the following points. Firstly, a probability value makes sense only

TABLE I
Potentialist vs. actualist interpretation of probability

$p = Pr(x)$	Propensity	Frequency
0	x has almost nil propensity	x is almost never the case
$0 < p \ll 1$	x has a weak propensity	x is rare
$0 \ll p < 1$	x has a fair propensity	x is fairly common
$p \doteq 1$	x has a strong propensity	x is common
$p = 1$	x has an overpowering propensity	x is almost always the case

in relation to a definite probability (or sample or event) space. Likewise a frequency value makes sense only relative to a definite sample-population pair: for example the formula "x is rare" presupposes a certain set of occurrences, among which x is unfrequent. Secondly, zero probability is consistent with very rare happening: i.e. even if $\Pr(x)=0$, x may happen, albeit rarely as compared with all the other events represented in the probability space. Consequently a fact with probability one can fail to happen – which ruins the frequency interpretation. (Recall that the rationals have zero measure. Entire sets of states and events are assigned zero probability in statistical mechanics for that very reason, although the physical system of interest is bound to pass through them. This is what 'almost never' means in that context, namely that the states or the events in question are attained only denumerably many times – i.e. they are rather isolated.) Thirdly, the frequency column may, nay should be kept – though in a capacity other than interpretation or definition. Indeed although it fails to tell us what "$\Pr(x)=p$" *means* it does tell us the conditions under which such a formula is true. Long run frequency is, indeed, a *truth condition* for probability statements. (Frege and the Vienna Circle notwithstanding, truth conditions do not specify meanings.) Fourthly, note that our propensity interpretation differs from Popper's in that the latter requires that the system of interest be coupled to an experimental arrangement: his propensity is thus closer to our causal disposition than to our chance propensity. No such hang-up from the frequency or empiricist interpretation remains in our own version of the propensity interpretation. Nor do we require that only events (i.e. changes of states) be assigned probabilities, as an empiricist must (since states may be unobservable): states too may be assigned probabilities and in fact they are assigned in many a stochastic theory, such as statistical mechanics and quantum mechanics. In other words not only transition probabilities but also absolute probabilities can be factually meaningful. The requirement, set by some philosophers, that only transition probabilities be considered in science, is untenable for the following reasons. First, since a transition probability is a conditional probability and the latter is defined in terms of absolute probabilities (not the other way around), the former cannot have a factual meaning unless these latter have one. Second, an electron cloud (or position distribution for an electron) has a definite physical status, so much so that it can often be objectified by means of X-rays.

6. Probability and Modality

Probability exactifies possibility but not everything possible can be assigned a probability. There are possibilities in relation to which probability makes no sense for the simple reason that they are not the object of a stochastic theory. For example solubility and magnetic permeability are causal dispositions that are assigned no probabilities in classical physics. Even in atomic physics we have similar cases. For example a hydrogen atom in a given energy level occupies a $(2l+1)$-fold degenerate state, in the sense that the given energy level is consistent with $2l+1$ different possibilities of spatial orientation. An external field acting on the atom may throw it into any one of $2l+1$ nondegenerate states. This number measures the potential variety of the original (degenerate) state, or its potentiality. But as long as no probabilities are assigned to each of these possible nondegenerate states (or to the corresponding transitions to them) such possibilities remain nonquantified. In short, possibility does not warrant probability, be it in classical or in quantal science.

The converse holds: *wherever there is probability there is possibility.* In such cases, and in these only, "Probability is the *quantitative measure* of possibility" (Terletskii, 1971, p. 15). In other words, probability provides a numerical exactification of possibility just in case a stochastic theory of the facts of interest is available. Needless to say, a stochastic or probabilistic theory is one containing at least one random variable. In such a theory a particular probability value will occur only by postulation or by recourse to experience. For example, given a law of evolution of probabilities in the course of time, such as "$dp/dt = kp$", we may compute the value $p(t)$ of p at an arbitrary time t provided we give (by assumption or by observation) the initial value $p(0)$. If this additional piece of information is forthcoming then we are allowed to make the inference to any (past or future) value of p, namely thus: $p(t) = p(0) \exp(kt)$.

In other words, we adopt the principle that anything probable according to a scientific theory T is deemed to be possible on T and moreover that the strength or weight of a possibility is equal to the corresponding probability. This idea is perfectly consistent with our nomological concept of real possibility (Definition 1) because, by definition, a scientific theory contains law statements. When a stochastic theory about a collection F of facts is available then we can use the following possibility

CRITERION Let T be a stochastic theory concerning (referring to) a set F of facts. Call E a body of empirical evidence couched in the language of T and moreover relevant to T. Then if x is in F, x is *really possible according to T and E* iff $T \cup E$ contains the formula "$\Pr(x) \geqslant 0$".

Note that we are not equating zero probability with impossibility. Impossibility is construed instead as the absence of a probability value. That is, anything that fails to be assigned a probability with the help of a stochastic theory T and a body of relevant evidence E will be deemed to be *impossible on T and E* – not necessarily so according to alternative premises. And anything assigned the probability value one with the help of T and E may be called *necessary according to T and E*. Finally two facts will be held to be *compossible according to T and E* if the probability of their joint occurrence is defined in $T \cup E$.

We can also introduce the notion of a possibility field, namely thus. Let F be a set of facts and let T be a stochastic theory referring to F. Then F is a *possibility field* according to T iff T defines a probability measure on F, i.e. if, for every $x \in F$, $\Pr(x) \geqslant 0$. Consider now some subset F_0 of F. If the possible facts in F_0 are mutually exclusive, they can be said to constitute a *possibility bundle*. In general the threads in such a bundle are not equally strong.

In sum, whenever a set of facts constitutes a possibility field that is the concern of a stochastic theory, such a theory exactifies the modal notions. Table II exhibits the one-many correspondence between the handful of modal expressions and the infinitely many probability statements. The notions of almost impossibility and near necessity, which are not handled by modal logic, have been included out of generosity.

Whereas in modal logic there is a gap between possibility and necessity,

TABLE II

Exactification of modal notions by a stochastic theory

Modal language	Exact (probabilistic) language
x is possible.	There is a scientific theory in which $\Pr(x) \geqslant 0$.
x is contingent.	There is a scientific theory in which $0 < \Pr(x) < 1$.
x is necessary.	There is a scientific theory in which $\Pr(x) = 1$.
x is impossible.	There is no scientific theory in which $\Pr(x) \geqslant 0$.
x is almost impossible.	There is a scientific theory in which $\Pr(x) \doteq 0$.
x is almost necessary.	There is a scientific theory in which $\Pr(x) \doteq 1$.

in a probabilistic context there is a continuum between them. Moreover what is merely possible in the short run (for a small sample or a short run of trials) may become necessary or nearly so in the long run. Thus the probability that a single hydrogen atom will emit a certain 21 cm line is one in ten million per second – yet we can detect as many such waves as we wish. The most basic physical events are extremely unlikely (improbable) but they have an impact because of their sheer number. Give a chance to chance and it will turn into necessity. For this reason particle physicists and geneticists reject Borel's injunction to discard improbable events for being "meaningless'. Quite on the contrary, particle physicists accept the so-called "principle of compulsory strong interaction", originally formulated (with tongue in cheek) as follows: "Anything that is not forbidden is compulsory" (Gell-Mann, 1956). A more careful wording of the above principle is this: All possible repetitive chance events (in particular all those consistent with the conservation laws) are likely to occur in the long run.

To sum up, the classical modal concepts are much too poor to account for the continuum that lies between impossibility and necessity. Not even the ordinary concept of probability suffices, if only because of the ambiguity of the ordinary language phrase 'x is not probable', which may stand either for "$\Pr(x)$ is small" or for "$\Pr$ is not defined at x". Chance propensity can only be caught with the fine mesh of stochastic theories, which contain the mathematical theory of probability or rather parts of it.

7. CONCLUSION

Our discussion may be summarized as follows.

(i) There are two radically different kinds of possibility: conceptual and real. They are so utterly different that no single theory could cover both of them. Real possibility is a property of factual items – things, states of things, and changes in such states, i.e. events. It coincides with lawfulness. Reality is the union of real possibility and actuality.

(ii) Real possibility comes in several kinds, among them causal disposition and chance propensity. Causal disposition is the real possibility for something to acquire a definite property when supplied with the suitable environmental conditions. Paradigm: solubility. Chance propensity is the real possibility for something to acquire either of a number of definite properties (each with a definite probability). Paradigm: localizability.

(iii) A causal disposition of a thing is reducible to a manifest property of the thing-environment complex, as well as traceable to a deeper property of the thing. On the other hand a chance propensity is an irreducible property of the individual thing the latter possesses all the time.

(iv) Probability is essential to the elucidation of chance propensity – not however to clarifying causal dispositions. A probabilistic (stochastic) theory of certain factual items exactifies the chance propensities of the latter. Modal logic cannot perform this task, not only because it handles a qualitative notion of possibility but also because it is incompetent to treat real modalities. (Real necessity is not definable in terms of possibility and negation: it is definable in terms of laws and circumstances.)

(v) Our view is incompatible with narrow determinism (i.e. causal determinism), since it conceives of real possibility as inherent in things of certain kinds not as a disguise of human ignorance: in fact even an omniscient being would have to reckon with the primary probabilities of quantum theories and genetics.

(vi) Real possibility cannot be given an "operational definition", say in terms of frequency. For one thing whatever is actually observed, measured, or experimented on is an actual not a possible. Surely we should check possibility (e.g. probability) statements by contrasting them with bits of relevant empirical evidence, such as observed relative frequencies and measured variances. But such tests (or estimates) of probability values do not tell us what "real possibility" and "probability" mean. In general: interpretation is a conceptual matter and it precedes observation: it is part of scientific theory.

(vii) Our view on chance propensity is at variance with actualism, in particular with the kind of actualism that motivates partly the frequency misinterpretation of probability, according to which possible is whatever is sometimes the case. This may function as an empirical criterion of possibility but does not work for theoretical purposes. (Recall that the quantum mechanical properties, many of which are represented by random variables, are possessed by their carriers all the time.) Frequency is not a surrogate of probability but a manifestation of it – and not the only one. Moreover, a relative frequency is a frequency of occurrence, hence cannot be identical with a possibility although it serves as an index or estimate of the strength or weight of the latter.

(viii) Science is a study of real possibility. While in some cases this investigation involves the probability theory, in others it does not. Every theory of chance propensities is essentially probabilistic or stochastic – if the theory is any good, that is. (The converse is false: there may be stochastic theories which fail to be theories of chance propensities. This is the case with quality control theories, where probability serves mainly as a time saving device, since in principle random sampling could be replaced with individual inspection.) Probability exactifies chance propensity and some other concepts of real possibility – not that of causal disposition, though.

ACKNOWLEDGEMENT

The author wrote the present paper while holding a visiting professorship at the ETH Zürich on a John Simon Guggenheim Memorial Foundation fellowship.

McGill University, Montreal, and
ETH, Zürich

BIBLIOGRAPHY

Bunge, Mario, *Philosophy of Physics*, Reidel, Dordrecht, 1973.
Gell-Mann, Murray, *Nuovo Cimento Suppl.* 4 (1956), 848.
Popper, Karl, *Brit. J. Phil. Sci.* 10 (1959), 25.
Terletskii, Ya. P., *Statistical Physics* (transl. by N. Fröman), North-Holland, Amsterdam, Elsevier, New York 1971.

PAUL R. CHERNOFF AND JERROLD E. MARSDEN

SOME REMARKS ON HAMILTONIAN SYSTEMS AND QUANTUM MECHANICS*

1. INTRODUCTION

These notes contain some remarks on the general structure of a class of physical systems called Hamiltonian, and on quantum mechanical systems in particular. A complete treatment with emphasis on technical details is found in [6]; our goal here is to point out some unifying structures and special properties of physical systems that may be of interest to this conference. Thus many of our remarks are deliberately brief and sometimes vague. Most of the results are known in the literature (cf. [18, 23]) although perhaps from a different point of view.

We shall begin in Section 2 with the general features that a physical system admitting a probabilistic interpretation should have. The distinguishing features of classical and quantum mechanical systems are pointed out. In Section 3 the C*-algebra approach to quantum mechanics, as delineated by Segal, is reviewed. Then in Section 4 we study the dynamics of classical and quantum mechanics – we endeavor to show that both systems are Hamiltonian, when the latter condition is interpreted from the modern point of view of symplectic manifolds (see [2]). In Section 5 we briefly describe some other classes of Hamiltonian systems: specifically hydrodynamics and general relativity. Finally in Sections 6 and 7 we mention a few problems connected with hidden variables and the theory of measurement.

2. BASIC PROPERTIES OF PHYSICAL SYSTEMS

A physical system consts of two collections of objects, denoted $\mathscr{S}$ and $\mathscr{O}$ – called *states* and *observables* respectively, together with a mapping

$$\mathscr{S} \times \mathscr{O} \to (\text{Borel probability measures on the real line } \mathbb{R})$$
$$(\psi, A) \mapsto \mu_{A,\psi}$$

Additionally, there is usually a Hamiltonian structure described below in Section 4.

Harper and Hooker (eds.), Foundations of Probability Theory, Statistical Inference, and Statistical Theories of Science, Vol. III, 35–53. All Rights Reserved. Copyright © 1976 by D. Reidel Publishing Company, Dordrecht-Holland.

Elements $\psi \in \mathscr{S}$ describe the state of the system at some instant and elements $A \in \mathscr{O}$ is represent "observable quantities"; when A measured and the system is in state ψ, $\mu_{A,\psi}$ represents the probability distribution for the observed values of A. Thus if $E \subset \mathbb{R}$, $\mu_{A,\psi}(E) \in \mathbb{R}$ is the probability that we will measure the value of A to lie in the set E if the system is known to be in state ψ.

From the general point of view, the above seem to be minimal features that any physical system should possess. They have been axiomatized and studied by several authors; cf. Mackey [16]. The set $\mathscr{S}$ describes the basic mathematical structure we are dealing with, while $\mu_{A,\psi}$ provides the physical interpretation.

Normally there is some additional structure as well, namely the dynamics. The dynamics tells us how the system changes from time s to a (later) time t. Thus we are provided with a family of mappings

$$U_{t,s}: \mathscr{S} \to \mathscr{S},$$

called evolution operators.[1]

Causality, in the sense that a state at a given time uniquely determines the state at any other time[2] forces us to postulate the *flow property*:

$$\begin{cases} U_{t_2,t_1} = U_{t_2,s} \circ U_{s,t_1}\,; \\ U_{t,t} = \text{identity}. \end{cases}$$

If the dynamics or the 'law of motion' is idependent of time, then $U_{t,s}$ depends only on $t-s$; i.e. we can write $U_{t,s} = U_{t-s}$. Then U_t satisfies:

$$U_{t+s} = U_t \circ U_s.$$

One also calls U_t a semigroup or flow (nonlinear in general).

The flow $U_t: \mathscr{S} \to \mathscr{S}$ is determined by a law of motion: let $x \in \mathscr{S}$, write $x(t) = U_t(x)$ and set $A(x) = dx/dt \mid_{t=0}$. The flow property gives us the required law: $(d/dt)\, x(t) = A(x(t))$. We need enough structure on $\mathscr{S}$ for this to make sense; i.e. that $\mathscr{S}$ be a differentiable manifold.

The dynamics U_t determines and is usually determined by the operator A, called the *generator* of U_t. The differential equation $dx/dt = A(x)$ becomes the Schrödinger equation in quantum mechanics or Hamilton's canonical equations (or Newton's second law, if you wish) for classical mechanics.

Already at this stage the technical problems are enormous. For example, one wishes to know just what operators A generate flows. This is an active area of research, especially in the nonlinear case; cf. [5].

It is in connection with the dynamics that the Hamiltonian structure enters. However, let us first consider some other general features of classical and quantum mechanics. We begin with classical mechanics from the modern point of view [2].

2.1. *Classical Mechanics*

A *classical mechanical system* consists of a finite dimensional manifold P called the *phase space*; a *symplectic structure* ω on P, that is, a closed ($d\omega = 0$) differential 2-form of maximal rank; and a *Hamiltonian* or energy function $H:P \to \mathbb{R}$. From ω we can construct a measure, called Liouville measure: $\mu = \omega \wedge \ldots \wedge \omega$; from ω and H we can construct Hamilton's equations X_H, a vector field on P. X_H is determined by the relation $\iota_{X_H}\omega = dH$ where ι_X denotes the interior product and d the differential. Integrating the vector field X_H (i.e. solving a system of ordinary differential equations) yields the dynamics, $U_t:P \to P$.

Considerations from statistical mechanics lead to the following interpretation:

(a)   States: $\mathscr{S}$ consists of probability measures ν on P

(b)   Observables: $\mathcal{O}$ consists of measureable realvalued functions $A:P \to \mathbb{R}$

(c)   The map $\mathscr{S} \times \mathcal{O} \to$ (Borel measures on $\mathbb{R}$) is given by $\mu_{\nu,A}(E) = \nu(A^{-1}(E))$, where $E \subset \mathbb{R}$.

The states are measures rather than points of P to allow for the possibility that we may only have a statistical knowledge of the 'exact' state. Note that $\mathscr{S}$ is a convex set. Its extreme points are called *pure states* (see [7] for a detailed discussion of convex sets and extreme points; see [22] for details on the connections with statistical mechanics).

It is easy to see that the pure states are point measures, so are in one-to-one correspondence with points of P itself. Note that every observable A is *sharp* in a pure state; i.e. the corresponding measure $\mu_{\nu,A}$ on $\mathbb{R}$ is a point measure. In other words there is no dispersion when measuring any observable in a pure state.

Around 1930, B. O. Koopman noted that the above picture can be expressed in Hilbert space language. Let $\mathscr{H}$ denote the Hilbert space of all functions $\psi : P \to C$, square integrable with respect to Liouville measure. Each $\psi \in \mathcal{H}$ determines a probability measure $v_\psi = |\psi|^2 \mu$ if $\|\psi\| = 1$. If A is an observable, its expected value is

$$\mathcal{E}(A) = \int_P A |\psi|^2 \, \mathrm{d}\mu = \langle A\psi, \psi \rangle$$

where A is regarded as a (self adjoint) multiplication operator on $\mathcal{H}$.

The dynamics $U_t : P \to P$ on phase space P induces in a natural way, and (under certain conditions) is induced by, a dynamics on $\mathcal{S}$ and on $\mathcal{H}$.

Consider the map $\psi \mapsto v_\psi$ of $\mathcal{S}$ to $\mathcal{H}$. It is many-to-one. In fact $v_\psi = v_{\psi'}$ if $\psi' = e^{i\alpha} \psi$ where $\alpha : P \to \mathbb{R}$. These phase transformations $\psi \mapsto e^{i\alpha} \psi$ form the *phase group of classical mechanics*.

Remark. It is not hard to see that an operator A on $\mathcal{H}$ is a multiplication operator if and only if it commutes with all phase transformations. Classical observables are those A's which are self-adjoint, i.e. real valued.

Because the phase group is so large, neither the inner products $\langle \psi, \varphi \rangle$ nor their squares $|\langle \psi, \varphi \rangle|^2$ can have any physical meaning. This is related to the *absence* of *coherence phenomena* in classical mechanics.

The dynamics U_t on P is Hamiltonian; that is, U_t preserves the 2-form ω. In other words U_t consists of canonical transformations. In particular U_t preserves Liouville measure. Thus the induced dynamics on $\mathcal{H}$ is unitary. Hence the dynamics is consistent with the statistical interpretation: probability is conserved.

2.2. *Quantum Mechanics*

Quantum mechanics differs from classical mechanics in that the phase group is much smaller; interference and coherence – typical wave phenomena – now play a fundamental role. Furthermore, all predictions are necessarily statistical in that there are no dispersion-free states ($\psi \in \mathcal{S}$ is *dispersion-free* when $\mu_{A,\psi}$ is a point measure for each $A \in \mathcal{O}$).

In classical mechanics, each state $v \in \mathcal{S}$ was a 'mixture' of pure states, reflecting our ignorance of the true state. Increasing our knowledge will 'reduce' v to a measure with smaller variance.

In quantum mechanics there are 'irreducible' statistical phenomena even when the system is in a pure state. This is clearly illustrated by experiments with beams of plane-polarized coherent light, or even with single photons. In such experiments, states can be described by unit vectors $\psi \in \mathbb{R}^2$ giving the direction of polarization. The probability that a φ wave will pass through a ψ filter is observed to be $|\langle \varphi, \psi \rangle|^2$. Furthermore, the emerging wave is ψ-polarized. But a little thought shows that the φ-polarized state is not a statistical mixture of other polarized states.

This sort of experimental fact leads one to consider the states as being the unit rays in a Hilbert space $\mathscr{H}^3$. (These are the pure states; mixed states corresponding to v's above are introduced later.) Thus, letting $\mathscr{S}_0$ denote the rays in $\mathscr{H}$ ($\mathscr{S}_0$ is called projective Hilbert space), we have a map $\mathscr{H} \to \mathscr{S}_0$, again many-to-one. This time the *phase group* is the circle group $\{e^{i\alpha}, \alpha \in \mathbb{R}\}$. The reason $\mathscr{S}_0$ is chosen this way is that one imagines general *elementary selective measurements* wherein $|\langle \psi, \varphi \rangle|^2$, for each $\psi, \varphi \in \mathscr{H}$, $\|\psi\| = \|\varphi\| = 1$, is the object with physical meaning – it represents the probability that we will find φ in state ψ or, if you like, the 'transition probability' for going from φ to ψ.

More generally, we can imagine a general selection measurement. Let $F \subset \mathscr{H}$ be a (closed) subspace and $\varphi \in \mathscr{H}$. The probability of transition from φ to F is $\langle P_F \varphi, \varphi \rangle$ where P_F is the orthogonal projection onto F.

Once the above view is accepted, then as Mackey has shown, the rest of the picture of what $\mathscr{S}$, $\mathscr{O}$ and $\mu_{A, \phi}$ have to be is pretty much forced upon us. This can be seen as follows.

Consider an observable A. For each $E \subset \mathbb{R}$ we have $\mu_{A, \psi}(E)$, the probability of observing A to lie in E if the state is ψ. The previous discussion suggests there should be a projection operator P_E^A on $\mathscr{H}$ such that

$$\mu_{A, \psi}(E) = \langle P_E^A \psi, \psi \rangle$$

Since μ is a probability measure we must have:

(1) $\qquad P_\phi^A = 0, \qquad P_{\mathbb{R}}^A = I$

(2) $\qquad P_{\underset{i=1}{\overset{\infty}{\cup}} E_i}^A = \sum_{i=1}^{\infty} P_{E_i}^A$

if E_i are disjoint. It follows that the $P_{E_i}^A$ are mutually orthogonal. We also must have, by (2),

$$P_{E \cup F}^A = P_{E \setminus F}^A + P_{F \setminus E}^A + P_{E \cap F}^A$$

$$P_E^A = P_{E \setminus F}^A + P_{E \cap F}^A$$

and

$$P_F^A = P_{F\backslash E}^A + P_{E\cap F}^A$$

Hence

$$P_E^A P_F^A = P_{E\cap F}^A = P_F^A P_E^A; \quad \text{i.e. the } P_E^A\text{'s commute.}$$

The spectral theorem [4] now tells us that there is a unique self-adjoint operator, also denoted A, such that $A = \int_{-\infty}^{\infty} \lambda \, dP_\lambda^A$; $\{P_\lambda^A\}$ is the spectral measure of A. Conversely any self-adjoint operator A yields a spectral measure and hence defines $\mu_{A,\psi}$.

Thus, to every observable there is a self-adjoint operator A, but it is not clear that every self-adjoint operator is physically realizable. [5]

Notice that the expected value of A in a state ψ is

$$\mathscr{E}(A) = \int_{-\infty}^{\infty} \lambda \, d\mu_{A,\psi}(\lambda) = \int_{-\infty}^{\infty} \lambda \, d\langle P_\lambda^A \psi, \psi \rangle = \langle A\psi, \psi \rangle.$$

Thus a state φ yields a mapping $F \mapsto \langle P_F \varphi, \varphi \rangle$ of subspaces in $\mathscr{H}$ to $[0, 1]$ describing a transition probability. It is a 'probability measure' based on the closed subspaces.

We can generalize the notion of state so as to allow for the possibility of mixed states (with the same statistical interpretation as in the classical case) by just considering a general 'measure' defined on the closed subspaces of $\mathscr{H}$. It is a famous theorem of Gleason [6] that such a measure is given by $F \mapsto \text{trace}\,(P_F D)$ where D is a positive operator of trace one on $\mathscr{H}$, called a *density matrix*. (Here we must add the condition that $\mathscr{H}$ have dimension at least three.)

Thus quantum mechanics is specified as follows: we are given a complex Hilbert space $\mathscr{H}$ and set

$$\begin{cases} \mathscr{S} & = \text{ all density matrices, a convex set} \\ \mathcal{O} & = \text{ self adjoint operators on } \mathscr{H}. \\ \mu_{A,D}(E) & = \text{ trace } (P_E^A D), \, P_E^A \text{ the spectral projections of } A. \end{cases}$$

It is not hard to see that the pure states (extreme points of $\mathscr{S}$) are identifiable with unit vectors in $\mathscr{H}$, modulo the phase group – what we previously called $\mathscr{S}_0$.

We also postulate dynamics $U_t: \mathscr{S} \to \mathscr{S}$ on $\mathscr{S}$, and assume that U_t consists of convex automorphisms. It is a theorem (going back to Bargmann and Wigner) that U_t is naturally induced by a one-parameter unitary group V_t on $\mathscr{H}$. The generator of V_t is H, the Hamiltonian. Conversely if H is self adjoint, it determines V_t by Stone's theorem: $V_t = e^{iHt}$ (see [28]).

Actually this dynamics is Hamiltonian in the same sense that classical dynamics is, as discussed in 2.1 above. We shall see this in Section 4 below.

3. THE C^*-ALGEBRA APPROACH TO QUANTUM MECHANICS

There are many ways of generalizing the examples of physical systems given in Sections 2.1, 2.2 above. One of these, taken by von Neumann and Segal, is to regard the set of observables as an algebra. This is mathematically convenient although it may not correspond exactly with physical reality; for, as mentioned above, the sum of two observables need not be observable. Another type of generalization is the 'quantum logic' point of view described in other lectures and in [26].

In the classical case the algebra is the algebra of functions on phase space – a commutative algebra. The quantum case is distinguished by having a non-commutative algebra. Indeed any C^*-algebra which is commutative must be isomorphic to a space of continuous functions and so is, in this sense, classical.

Segal's version of this formulation proceeds as follows. Let $\mathfrak{A}$ be a C^*-algebra [7], (for example all bounded operators on Hilbert space). The observables [8] are the self-adjoint elements of $\mathfrak{A}$.

The *states* are the normalized positive linear functionals on $\mathfrak{A}$. They are automatically continuous. [9] We are to think of states in the same way as before. If $\mathscr{E}$ is a state, $\mathscr{E}(A)$ is the expectation of A in the state $\mathscr{E}$.

Of central importance is the Gelfand-Naimark-Segal construction: Let $\mathfrak{A}$ be a C^*-algebra and $\mathscr{E}$ a state of $\mathfrak{A}$. Then there is a Hilbert space $\mathscr{H}$, a unit (cyclic) vector $\psi \in \mathscr{H}$, and a *-representation $\pi : \mathfrak{A} \to \mathscr{L}(\mathscr{H})$ (the bounded operators on $\mathscr{H}$) such that

$$\mathscr{E}(A) = \langle \pi_\mathscr{E}(A)\psi, \psi \rangle \quad \text{for all} \quad A \in \mathfrak{A}$$

In face $\mathscr{H}, \psi, \pi$ are unique up to unitary equivalence. See Lanford [15] for details.

In this way, we can construct our probability measure $\mu_{A,\mathscr{E}}$. Thus we have a general example of a physical system – consisting of $\mathscr{S}$, $\mathcal{O}$ and the map $\mu_{A,\mathscr{E}}$ just constructed – which includes both classical and quantum systems as special cases.

The above construction is similar to Gleason's theorem in that it characterizes states. The Gelfand-Naimark-Segal construction essentially enables one to recover the Hilbert space formalism from the abstract C^*-algebra formalism. Often it is convenient to stick with the general formalism (e.g. see Section 6 below). For example, one can characterize pure states $\mathscr{E}$ as those for which $\pi_{\mathscr{E}}$ is irreducible.

Several other ideas carry over also. For example, a general form of the uncertainty principle is valid: for observables A, $B \in \mathfrak{A}$, and a state $\mathscr{E}$,

$$\sigma(A, \mathscr{E})\, \sigma(B, \mathscr{E}) \geqslant \tfrac{1}{2}\mathscr{E}(C); \qquad C = i(AB - BA)$$

where $\sigma(A, \mathscr{E})$ is the variance of the probability distribution $\mu_{A,\mathscr{E}}$:
$\sigma(A, \mathscr{E})^2 = \mathscr{E}(A^2) - (\mathscr{E}(A))^2 = \mathscr{E}((A - \mathscr{E}(A)I)^2)$.
Proof. Let $[X, Y] = \mathscr{E}(XY^*)$. This is an inner product on $\mathfrak{A}$, so obeys the Schwarz inequality. Note that it is enough to prove the inequality in case $\mathscr{E}(A) = 0$, $\mathscr{E}(B) = 0$ for we can replace A, B by $A - \mathscr{E}(A)\,I$, and $B - \mathscr{E}(B)\,I$. Then

$$\begin{aligned}
\mathscr{E}(C) &= i[\mathscr{E}(AB) - \mathscr{E}(BA)] \\
&= 2\,\mathrm{Im}\,[A, B] \\
&\leqslant 2\,[A, A]^{1/2}\,[B, B]^{1/2}
\end{aligned}$$

so $\tfrac{1}{2}\mathscr{E}(C) \leqslant \sigma(A, \mathscr{E})\,\sigma(B, \mathscr{E})$.   Q.E.D.

4. THE HAMILTONIAN STRUCTURE

A general Hamiltonian system consists of a manifold P, possibly infinite dimensional, together with (a) a (weakly) nondegenerate, closed two form ω on P (i.e. ω is an alternating bilinear form on each tangent space $T_x P$ of P, $d\omega = 0$, and for $x \in P$, $\omega_x(v, w) = 0$ for all $v \in T_x P$ implies $w = 0$) and (b) a Hamiltonian function $H : P \to \mathbb{R}$.

Then P, H, ω determine, in nice cases, a vector field X_H by the relation $i_{X_H}\omega = dH$; i.e.,

$$\omega(X_H(x), v) = dH_x \cdot v \quad \text{for all} \quad x \in P \quad \text{and} \quad v \in T_x P.$$

As in Section 2 we can require that X_H be the generator of a flow U_t on P.

Let us enrich our definition of a *physical system* as follows. It consists of

(a)   a convex set of states $\mathscr{S}$

(b)   a set $\mathcal{O}$ of observables

(c)   a map $(\psi, A) \mapsto \mu_{A,\psi}$ from $\mathscr{S} \times \mathcal{O}$ to (Borel probability measures on $\mathbb{R}$)

(d)   a flow of convex automorphism of $\mathscr{S}$, $U_t : \mathscr{S} \to \mathscr{S}$; this induces a flow $U_t : P \to P$, where P = extreme points of $\mathscr{S}$ = pure states.

We also assume:

(e)   The flow on P arises from a Hamiltonian system.

The fact that we deal with $\mathscr{S}$ rather than P is due to our ignorance about the precise initial state. This stochastic aspect of physical models is fundamental. Moreover, there are other related questions. Usually we don't know the dynamics exactly either, so only *stable* states are of physical interest. Here stability means that the time evolution should not be affected much by a perturbation of either the initial condition or the vector field itself. (The latter property is called structural stability.) Such questions are not simple and much remains to be discovered; cf. [1].

We have already explained the Hamiltonian structure for classical mechanics. It remains to discuss it for quantum mechanics. (cf. [17]).

Thus let $\mathscr{H}$ be complex Hilbert space and let P be the corresponding projective Hilbert space. Let A be a self-adjoint operator on $\mathscr{H}$. We claim that for a suitable symplectic form ω on $\mathscr{H}$, iA is Hamiltonian. By 'quotienting' by the phase group, it can be shown that this symplectic structure is inherited by P.

The symplectic form will be given by an antisymmetric bilinear form $\omega : \mathscr{H} \times \mathscr{H} \to \mathbb{R}$, namely

$$\omega(\psi, \varphi) = \operatorname{Im} \langle \psi, \varphi \rangle.$$

The energy is

$$H(\psi) = \tfrac{1}{2} \langle A\psi, \psi \rangle.$$

The Hamiltonian condition, namely

$$\omega(iA\psi, \varphi) = dH_\psi \cdot \varphi$$

is verified as follows:

$$
\begin{aligned}
\operatorname{Im}\langle iA\psi, \varphi\rangle \\
&= \operatorname{Re}\langle A\psi, \varphi\rangle \\
&= \tfrac{1}{2}[\langle A\psi, \varphi\rangle + \overline{\langle A\psi, \varphi\rangle}] \\
&= \tfrac{1}{2}[\langle A\psi, \varphi\rangle + \langle \varphi, A\psi\rangle] \\
&= \tfrac{1}{2}[\langle A\psi, \varphi\rangle + \langle A\varphi, \psi\rangle] \\
&= dH_\psi \cdot \varphi.
\end{aligned}
$$

Thus we conclude that the usual Hilbert space formalism of quantum mechanics satisfies all the requirements (a)–(e) listed above.

The structure of some of the basic observables in quantum mechanics can be derived by the elegant Mackey-Wightman analysis and other group-theoretic arguments. In particular, that the position and momentum operators have to be x^j and $i\,(\partial/\partial x^j)$ follows from very fundamental and non-controversial hypotheses. See [26], [6], and [13]. Note that the usual Heisenberg uncertainty principle follows, as was explained in Section 3.

5. SOME OTHER EXAMPLES OF HAMILTONIAN SYSTEMS

Several interesting physical systems can be put into the above Hamiltonian framework. They are all classical in the sense that $\mathscr{S}$ consists of the probability measures and $\mathcal{O}$ the real-valued functions on a given phase space P.
Examples are:

(a)   wave equations such as

$$
\frac{\partial^2\varphi}{\partial t^2} = \Delta\varphi - m^2\varphi - \alpha\varphi^p, \quad p \text{ an integer} \geqslant 2
$$
$$
\alpha\in\mathbb{R}, \quad m \geqslant 0.
$$

(b)   Maxwell's equations
(c)   hydrodynamics
(d)   conservative continuum mechanics
(e)   elasticity
(f)   Einstein's equations of general relativity.

Of course many of these examples are interrelated. For details, see [6] and [18]. We shall make a few brief remarks concerning (c) and (f).

5.1. *The Motion of a Perfect Fluid*

Let v be the velocity field of a perfect (incompressible, homogeneous, non-viscous) fluid in a region D of $\mathbb{R}^3$. Euler's equations assert:

$$\text{(E)} \quad \begin{cases} \dfrac{\partial v}{\partial t} + (v \cdot \nabla) v = - \operatorname{grad} p \\ \operatorname{div} v = 0 \\ v \text{ parallel to } \partial D \end{cases}$$

These equations are not in Hamiltonian form. But they can be so put as follows. Let $\eta(t, x) \in D$, $x \in D$, $t \in \mathbb{R}$ be defined by

$$\frac{d}{dt} \eta(t, x) = v(t, \eta(t, x))$$
$$\eta(0, x) = x.$$

Then $t \to \eta(t, x)$ is the trajectory followed by the particle which was initially at x. Let $\eta_t(x) = \eta(t, x)$. Then $\eta_t : D \to D$ is invertible (a diffeomorphism) and is volume-preserving. Let $\mathscr{D}_\mu$ denote all volume-preserving diffeomorphisms on D.

In 1967, V. Arnold showed that v satisfies (E) if and only if η_t is a geodesic on the infinite dimensional manifold $\mathscr{D}_\mu$. (The metric on $\mathscr{D}_\mu$ is canonically associated with the kinetic energy of the fluid.) Thus we immediately have the required Hamiltonian structure, since geodesics on a manifold M are well-known to arise from a Hamiltonian system on TM. See for example [2]. Thus $P = T\mathscr{D}_\mu$.

This point of view has turned out to be very useful technically for proving existence and representation theorems for the solutions of the equations of ydrodynamics. It may be of importance in problems of quantization as well.

5.2. *The Equations of General Relativity*

Consider a Lorentz manifold V and associated metric $^{(4)}g$. Outside regions of matter, Einstein's equations assert that V is Ricci-flat: $R_{\alpha\beta} = 0$. Pick a space-like hypersurface M in V and some orthogonal coordinate t; then, near M, V looks like $M \times$ (an interval in $\mathbb{R}$). Hence $^{(4)}g$ yields a curve $t \mapsto g_t$ of positive-definite Riemannian metrics on M. Let $\mathfrak{M}$ denote the set of all such metrics on M. Then one can show that $R_{\alpha\beta} = 0$ if and only if $t \mapsto g_t$ is a geodesic (with a potential term) in the space $\mathfrak{M}$.

Of course we can choose different M's and t-coordinates. In this way we get different Hamiltonian representations in $\mathfrak{M}$, but they are all equivalent.[11]

The phase space is thus $P = T\mathfrak{M}$. The symplectic structure is that associated with an indefinite, but non-degenerate metric on $\mathfrak{M}$ called the deWitt metric:

$$\mathscr{I}_g(h, k) = \int_M \{(\text{tr } h)(\text{tr } k) - \langle h, k \rangle\} \, d\mu_g$$

where tr is the trace, $\langle h, k \rangle = h^{ij} k_{ij}$ and $\mu_g = \sqrt{\det g_{ij}} \, dx^1 \wedge dx^2 \wedge dx^3$.

6. A HIDDEN VARIABLES THEOREM

The orthodox physical interpretation of quantum mechanics has discomforted many physicists, notably including Planck, Einstein, de Broglie, and Schrödinger; cf. [11]. It is hard to escape the feeling that a statistical theory must be, in some sense, an incomplete description of reality. One might hope that the probabilistic aspects of the theory are really due, as in the case of classical statistical mechanics, to some sort of averaging over an enormous number of 'hidden variables'; in a perfect description of a state, in which these hidden parameters would have well-determined values, all the observables would be sharp. However, von Neumann [27] has given a proof that the results of quantum mechanics are not compatible with a reasonably formulated hidden variable hypothesis. We shall outline an argument along von Neumann's lines, but in the more general setting of Segal's C^*-algebra formulation of quantum theory.

Let the observables of a given physical system be represented by the self-adjoint elements of a C^*-algebra $\mathfrak{A}$. If $A \in \mathfrak{A}$ is an observable and ρ is a state, the dispersion of A in the state ρ is given by $\sigma^2(A, \rho) = \rho(A^2) - \rho(A)^2 = \rho((A - \rho(A) I)^2)$. We shall say that ρ is a *dispersion-free state* provided that $\sigma^2(A, \rho) = 0$ for every observable $A \in \mathfrak{A}$. The results of experiment show that the states of quantum systems prepared in the laboratory are not dispersion-free. The hidden-variable hypothesis is that the physical state ρ owes its dispersion to the fact that it is a statistical ensemble of ideal dispersion-free states. (The latter need not be physically realizable – just as one cannot really prepare a classical gas with precisely determined positions and velocities for each of its molecules.) Mathematically, the hypothesis states that every state ρ is of the form

$$\rho(A) = \int_\Omega \rho_\omega(A)\,d\mu(\omega) \tag{1}$$

where each ρ_ω is a dispersion-free state and μ is a probability measure on some space Ω. The coordinate $\omega \in \Omega$ represents, of course, the indeterminate 'hidden variables'.

THEOREM. (Segal [24]). *A C^*-algebra $\mathfrak{A}$ admits hidden variables in the above sense only if $\mathfrak{A}$ is abelian. (The corresponding physical system is then 'classical'.)*

Proof. The first step is to show that a dispersion-free state ρ_ω is multiplicative. Note that the bilinear form $\langle\!\langle A, B \rangle\!\rangle = \rho_\omega(AB^*)$ is a Hermitian inner product on $\mathfrak{A}$. ($\langle\!\langle A, A \rangle\!\rangle = \rho_\omega(AA^*)$ is $\geqslant 0$ by hypothesis. From this it follows easily that $\rho_\omega(C^*) = \overline{\rho_\omega(C)}$ for any $C \in \mathfrak{A}$. In particular we have $\langle\!\langle B, A \rangle\!\rangle = \rho_\omega(BA^*) = \rho_\omega((AB^*)^*) = \overline{\rho_\omega(AB^*)} = \overline{\langle\!\langle A, B \rangle\!\rangle}$.) Hence, by the Schwarz inequality,

$$|\rho_\omega(AB)| \leqslant \rho_\omega(AA^*)^{1/2}\,\rho_\omega(B^*B)^{1/2}$$

for all $A, B \in \mathfrak{A}$. From this we see that if $\rho_\omega(AA^*) = 0$ then $\rho_\omega(AB) = 0$ for all B. Suppose that A is self-adjoint. Then, since $\mathfrak{A}$ is dispersion-free, $\rho_\omega((A - \rho_\omega(A) I)^2) = 0$. Therefore, for every B, $\rho_\omega((A - \rho_\omega(A)) B) = 0$. That is, $\rho_\omega(AB) = \rho_\omega(A)\,\rho_\omega(B)$. This holds as well for non-self-adjoint A by linearity. In particular, if $\mathfrak{A}$ is dispersion-free it follows that $\rho_\omega(AB) = \rho_\omega(BA)$.

But if A admits hidden variables, it follows immediately from (1) that every state ρ satisfies $\rho(AB) = \rho(BA)$. Since there are enough states to distinguish the members of $\mathfrak{A}$ (e.g. states of the form $A \mapsto \langle A\psi, \psi \rangle$), it follows that $AB = BA$. Thus $\mathfrak{A}$ is abelian. ∎

Remark. Conversely, a well-known theorem of Gelfand and Naimark states that every abelian C^*-algebra is isomorphic to $C(X)$, the set of continuous functions on some compact set X. (Many accounts of this result are available; a very readable one is in Simmons [25].) The states of $\mathfrak{A}$ are simply the probability measures on X, which are convex superpositions of the δ-measures at the points of X; the latter are, of course, precisely the dispersion-free states.

We can also dispose of a less stringent notion of hidden variables. According to Jauch [13], Mackey has proposed the consideration of 'ε-dispersion-free' states. A state ρ is called ε-dispersion-free if for every *projection* $E \in \mathfrak{A}$ we have $\sigma^2(E, P) < \varepsilon$. A system is said to admit 'quasi-hidden variables' if for all $\varepsilon > 0$, every state can be represented as $\int \rho_\omega \, d\mu(\omega)$ where all the states ρ_ω are ε-dispersion-free. If $\mathfrak{A}$ admits quasi-hidden variables and ρ is a *pure state* of $\mathfrak{A}$, then it is easy to see that ρ is ε-dispersion free for every ε. Then by the argument above ρ must be multiplicative on the algebra generated by the projections in $\mathfrak{A}$. This will be all of $\mathfrak{A}$ in many interesting cases – in particular, if $\mathfrak{A}$ is a von Neumann algebra (i.e. closed in the strong operation topology). But then, because the pure states separate elements of $\mathfrak{A}$, it follows as before that $\mathfrak{A}$ is abelian. (We must hasten to add that Jauch and Mackey were considering these questions in the context of lattices of 'questions' which are more general than the projection lattices which we have discussed; so from the foundational point of view the notion of quasi-hidden variables has raised problems which our simple argument cannot handle. But see [29].)

The essential point of the argument given above was the non-existence in general of a large supply of linear functionals on $\mathfrak{A}$ which carry squares to squares. A much deeper analysis has been carried out by Kochen and Specker [14]; cf. also Bell [3]. They have faced squarely the fact, which we have mentioned, that it is really not physically reasonable for the sum of non-commuting observables always to be an observable. Drastically reducing the algebraic operations which they allow, they nevertheless reach the same results; their functionals are required to be linear only on *commuting* observables. We shall not go into the details of their arguments, for which we refer the reader to their paper, which also includes an interesting discussion of the entire problem of hidden variables and various attempts to introduce them. Finally, we mention some recent experimental work in this area, centering around 'Bell's inequality'; the outcome argues against the hidden variable hypothesis. See [8, 12].

7. THE MEASUREMENT PROCESS

Let us now discuss the process of measurement in some detail, following von Neumann [27]. (A clear summary of von Neumann's ideas may be found in the book of Nelson [20]; see also Jauch [13] and de Broglie [9].)

Various solutions of the problems of measurement have been proposed; cf. [4] and J. Bub's lecture in this conference. However, it is not yet clear that the problems have been solved.

The measurement of an observable involves the interaction of a 'physical system' with an 'observing apparatus', so we should first describe the mathematical treatment of such composite systems.

If the pure states of a system S correspond to the unit rays of $\mathscr{H}$, and those of a second system S' correspond to the rays of $\mathscr{H}'$, then the pure states of the compound system consisting of S and S' correspond to the unit rays of the tensor product[12] $\mathscr{H} \otimes \mathscr{H}'$. (The tensor product of Hilbert spaces $\mathscr{H}$ and $\mathscr{H}'$ is by definition the completion of their algebraic tensor product with respect to the following inner product:

$$\left\langle \sum_i \varphi_i \otimes \varphi_i', \ \sum_j \psi_j \otimes \psi_j' \right\rangle = \sum_{i,j} \langle \varphi_i, \psi_j \rangle \langle \varphi_i', \psi_j' \rangle.$$

For example, $L^2(\mathbb{R}^3) \otimes L^2(\mathbb{R}^3) = L^2(\mathbb{R}^6)$. If $\{e_i\}$ and $\{f_j\}$ are orthonormal bases of $\mathscr{H}$ and $\mathscr{H}'$ respectively, then $\{e_i \otimes f_j\}_{i, \ j=1}$ is an orthonormal basis of $\mathscr{H} \otimes \mathscr{H}'$.) An observable A of S corresponds to the operator $A \otimes I$ on $\mathscr{H} \otimes \mathscr{H}'$; similarly the observable B of S' corresponds to $I \otimes B$. It can be shown that every observable of the composite system is a function of observables of the above sort, in the sense that every bounded operator on $\mathscr{H} \otimes \mathscr{H}'$ is a limit of operators of the form $\sum (A_i \otimes I) \cdot (I \otimes B_i)$. A state ρ of the compound system determines a state of S by the relation

$$\rho_S(A) = \rho(A \otimes I).$$

It is important to note that ρ_S will in general be a mixture even if ρ is pure. Thus, if ρ is given by the vector $\sum \varphi_i \otimes \varphi_i'$, with $\{\varphi_i\}$, $\{\varphi_i'\}$ orthogonal systems in $\mathscr{H}$ and $\mathscr{H}'$, we have

$$\rho_s(A) = \sum \|\varphi_i'\|^2 \langle A\varphi_i, \varphi_i \rangle,$$

so that ρ_s is given by the density matrix $\sum \|\varphi_i'\|^2 P_{\varphi_i}$.

Now let S be a physical system which we wish to study. Suppose that we wish to measure an observable A of S. For simplicity let us assume that A has a pure point spectrum, with eigenvectors $\varphi_1, \varphi_2, \ldots$. To measure A it is necessary to allow the system S to interact with an apparatus S'. A suitable apparatus for measuring A will have the property that, if the system S is initially in the state φ_i, after the interaction the composite system of S and S' will be in the state $\varphi_i \otimes \theta_i$, where $\{\theta_i\}$ is a sequence of orthonormal vectors in $\mathcal{H}'$. The interaction, of course, is governed by the Schrödinger equation for the composite system. Hence, if the initial state of S is given by $\psi = \sum_i^\infty c_i \varphi_i$, the final state of $S + S'$ will be $\theta = \sum_1^\infty c_i \varphi_i \otimes \theta_i$ by linearity. Now if B is an observable of S', then after the interaction the expected value of B will be

$$\langle (I \otimes B)\,\theta, \theta \rangle = \sum_{i=1}^\infty |c_i|^2 \, \langle B\theta_i, \theta_i \rangle,$$

so that, although $S + S'$ is in the pure state θ, S' is in the mixed state $\sum_{i=1}^\infty |c_i|^2 \, P_{\theta_i}$. Similarly, S is in the mixed state $\sum_{i=1}^\infty |c_i|^2 \, P_{\varphi_i}$.

Now the apparatus is supposed to be of a macroscopic nature; its orthogonal states θ_i represent, say, different counter readings. After the interaction the observer 'looks' at the apparatus. Through his faculty of introspection he realizes that the apparatus is in a definite state, say θ_j. (This occurs with probability $|c_j|^2$.) Once this act of consciousness has taken place it is no longer true that the state of $S + S'$ is $\sum_{i=1}^\infty c_i \varphi_i \times \theta_i$; it must be $\varphi_j \times \theta_j$. One then says that the system has been found to be in the state φ_j. This is the famous (or notorious) 'reduction of the wave packet'.[13]

We now venture to make some philosophical remarks. It is important to realize that analogous 'reduction' takes place in a *classical* statistical mechanical system when new information is gained. This is never regarded as a difficulty, because the classical probability packet is always viewed as a mere reflection of the observer's ignorance of the objective underlying state of the system. This is a perfectly consistent interpretation. Why can't the same interpretation serve in the quantum mechanical case?

As long as we are concerned only with a *single observable* (or with a commuting family of observables) it is perfectly possible to view the quantum system classically. That is, one can interpret the reduction from the mixture to the state φ_j as a reduction of classical type. But the existence of incompatible observables in quantum mechanics forces this interpretation to break down. Indeed, the entire point of the negative results concerning 'hidden variables' is that there is *no* 'objective underlying state' of the system!

Perhaps the quantum probability distributions can be interpreted as reflecting our partial knowledge, as long as we do not insist that there be an objective entity of which we have partial knowledge. This seems reminiscent of the problem of the golden mountain in the sentence 'The golden mountain does not exist'. If one asks 'what does not exist?' and answers 'the golden mountain', one is implying that the golden mountain is in fact an entity with some sort of 'existence'. Some philosophers tried to rescue the situation by stating that the golden mountain 'subsists' – that is, has enough of a shadowy sort of existence to serve as the subject of a sentence. Now Bertrand Russell has observed that the real solution of the problem is to recognize that the original sentence is implicitly quantified, and actually should be regarded as saying 'for every x it is false that x is both golden and mountainous'. In the absence of new physical discoveries, it seems not impossible that the same sort of purely grammatical trick may be the ultimate solution of the quantum measurement problem.

Department of Mathematics,
University of California at Berkeley, San Francisko

NOTES

* Presented by J. Marsden to this conference. Partially supported by NSF Grant GP-15735.
[1] This appears to require a universal Newtonian time, thereby excluding relativistic effects. In fact, as we shall see, general relativity can be included in this formalism.
[2] In other words, the state contains complete information of the system, and the dynamical laws are followed exactly. There is a serious philosophical point here which is further discussed in Section 4 below.
[3] We take $\mathscr{H}$ to be complex but it is not *a priori* clear why it shouldn't be real. There are good reasons for the complex structure related to the Hamiltonian structure; cf. [6] and [16] and related references.
[4] See for example [28]. Of course a self-adjoint operator (like the position operator) need not have any square integrable eigenfunctions. What is asserted to be of physical relevance is the probability measure $\mu_{A,\psi}$, which is always well defined. Of course, one must avoid trivial 'paradoxes' in quantum mechanics which arise from an inadequate understanding of the spectral theorem, or by ascribing more physical meaning (e.g. individual trajectories) to the theory than that given by the $\mu_{A,\psi}$; cf. [21].
[5] For example it is not clear how to measure (position)+(momentum)=$q+p$ in the laboratory.
[6] See Mackey [16] for further discussion. Gleason's theorem is proved in [26].
[7] See Dixmier [10] for their theory. Simmons [25] contains a very readable account of elementary facts.
[8] Unbounded operators like x, p are included via their spectral projections.
[9] See for example Lanford [15], p. 160. Real linearity is the main content of 'linear', for complex linearity is a convention by which the state extends from the self-adjoint operators to all of $\mathfrak{A}$. Countably additive states are called 'normal'.

[10] Whenever one has a symplectic manifold P and a symmetry group G acting on P once can construct another symplectic manifold, called the reduced phase space. Namely, let $P_\mu = \psi^{-1}(\mu)/G_\mu$ where $\psi: P \to \mathfrak{G}^*$ is a 'moment' or energy function for the action, $\mathfrak{G}^*$ is the dual of the Lie algebra and G_μ is the isotropy group of the action of G on $\mathfrak{G}^*$. In the quantum mechanical case $G = S^1$ is the quantum mechanical phase group and $\psi: \mathcal{H} \to \mathbb{R}$, $\varphi \to \frac{1}{2}\langle \varphi, \varphi \rangle$. See Marsden-Weinstein [19] for details.

[11] One can pass to a suitable reduced phase as one can do in quantum mechanics by dividing out the phase group. See [19].

[12] The tensor product $\mathcal{H} \otimes \mathcal{H}'$ is the direct product in the category of Hilbert spaces, just as the Cartesian product is in the category of manifolds (if P and P' are phase spaces for isolated systems $P \times P'$ is the phase space for the interacting system). A pure state in a composite quantum system is much more complicated than an ordered pair of pure states of the subsystems. This fact seems related to many, if not all, of the so-called 'paradoxes' of quantum theory.

[13] Of course, 'looking at the apparatus' involves interaction with some further apparatus – ultimately with the consciousness of the observer. But one can lump all that into S and the observer's mind into S'. Nevertheless, apparently one cannot find a mathematical device (within the framework of orthodox quantum mechanics) to yield the reduction of pure states. This is the fundamental problem in interpreting the foundations of quantum mechanics.

BIBLIOGRAPHY

[1] Abraham, R., *Introduction to Morphology*. Quatrième Rencontre entre mathématiciens et physiciens, Vol. 4, Fasc. 1 Publ. du Département de Mathématiques, Université de Lyon, France, 1972.

[2] Abraham, R. and Marsden, J., *Foundations of Mechanics* W. A. Benjamin, 1967.

[3] Bell, J. S., 'On the Problem of Hidden Variables in Quantum Mechanics', *Rev. Mod. Phys.* **38** (1966), 447–452.

[4] Bohm, D. and Bub, J., 'A Proposed Solution of the Measurement Problem in Quantum Mechanics by a Hidden Variable Theory', *Rev. Mod. Phys.* **38** (1966), 453–469, 470–475.

[5] Carroll, R., *Abstract Methods in Partial Differential Equations*, Harper and Row, 1969.

[6] Chernoff, P. and Marsden, J., 'Hamiltonian Systems and Quantum Mechanics', in preparation.

[7] Choquet, G., *Lectures on Analysis*, W. A. Benjamin, 1969.

[8] Clauser, J. F., Horne, M. A., Shimony, A., and Holt, R. A., 'Proposed Experiment to Test Local Hidden Variable Theories', *Phys. Rev. Letters* **23** (1969), 880–884.

[9] DeBroglie, L., *The Current Interpretation of Wave Mechanics*, Elsevier, 1964.

[10] Dixmier, J., *Les C* algèbres et leurs représentations*, Gauthier-Villars, 1964.

[11] Einstein, A., Podolsky, B., and Rosen, N., 'Can Quantum-Mechanical Description of Physical Reality be Considered Complete?', *Phys. Rev.* **47** (1935), 777–780.

[12] Freedman, S. J. and Clauser, J. F., 'Experimental Test of Local Hidden-Variable Theories', *Phys. Rev. Letters* **28** (1972), 938–941.

[13] Jauch, J. M., *Foundations of Quantum Mechanics*, Addison-Wesley, 1968.

[14] Kochen, S. and Specker, E. P., 'The Problem of Hidden Variables in Quantum Mechanics', *Jour. Math. and Mech.* **17** (1967), 59–88.

[15] Lanford, O. E., 'Selected Topics in Functional Analysis', in *Statistical Mechanics and Quantum Field Theory*, (ed. by C. DeWitt and R. Stora), Gordon and Breach, 1972.

[16] Mackey, G., *Mathematical Foundations of Quantum Mechanics*, W. A. Benjamin, 1963.

[17] Marsden, J., 'Hamiltonian One Parameter Groups', *Arch. Rat. Mech. and An.* **28** (1968), 362–396.

[18] Marsden, J., Ebin, D., and Fischer, A., 'Diffeomorphism Groups, Hydrodynamics and Relativity', *Proc. of 13th Biennial Seminar of Canadian Math. Congress*, (ed. by J. R. Vanstone), Montreal 1972.

[19] Marsden, J. and Weinstein, A., 'Reduction of Symplectic Manifolds with Symmetry', *Reports on Math. Phys.*, to appear.

[20] Nelson, E., *Dynamical Theories of Brownian Motion*, Princeton University Press, 1967.

[21] Robinson, M. C., 'A Thought Experiment Violating Heisenberg's Uncertainty Principle', *Can. Jour. Phys.* **47** (1969), 963–967.

[22] Ruelle, D., *Statistical Mechanics – Rigorous Results*, W. A. Benjamin, 1969.

[23] Segal, I., *Mathematical Problems of Relativistic Physics*, Amer. Math. Soc., 1963.

[24] Segal, I., 'A Mathematical Approach to Elementary Particles and Their Fields', University of Chicago Lecture Notes, 1955.

[25] Simmons, G. F., *Introduction to Topology and Modern Analysis*, McGraw-Hill, 1963.

[26] Varadarajan, V. S., *Geometry of Quantum Theory*, vols. I, II, Van Nostrand, 1968.

[27] Von Neumann, J., *Mathematical Foundations of Quantum Mechanics*, Princeton Univ. Press, 1955.

[28] Yosida, K., *Functional Analysis*, Springer-Verlag, 1965.

[29] Deliyannis, P. C., 'Generalized Hidden Variables Theorem', *Jour. of Math. Physics* **12** (1971), 1013–1017.

WILLIAM DEMOPOULOS

THE POSSIBILITY STRUCTURE OF PHYSICAL SYSTEMS

1. INTRODUCTION

This paper develops the logical interpretation of non-relativistic quantum mechanics initially proposed by Hilary Putnam [11]. (See also [1] and [2].) The main features of this interpretation are briefly summarized in this introduction.

Certain physical theories postulate abstract structural constraints which events are held to satisfy. Such theories are termed 'principle theories'. Interpretations of principle theories aim to explain their relation to the theories they replace. Interpretations are therefore concerned with the nature of the transitions between theories.

Theories of space-time structure provide the most accessible illustration of principle theories. For example, Newtonian mechanics in the absence of gravitation represents the 4-dimensional geometry of space-time by the inhomogeneous Galilean group, which acts transitively in the class of free motions, i.e. the inhomogeneous Galilean group is the symmetry group of the free motions: it is a subgroup of the symmetry group of every mechanical system, and the largest such subgroup. Einstein's special principle of relativity is the hypothesis that the symmetry group of the free motions is the Poincaré group. The transition from the Galilean group to the Poincaré group is associated with a corresponding modification in space-time structure. The absolute time and Euclidean metric of Newtonian mechanics are dropped altogether, and the metrical relations of space-time are determined by the Minkowski tensor.

The special theory of relativity represents the transition from Newtonian Mechanics to Maxwell's electro-dynamics as involving a modification of the structure of space-time. In this sense, the special theory may be regarded as an *interpretation* of classical electrodynamics.

Theoretical transitions in the class of space-time theories suggest an analogous approach to the interpretation of quantum mechanics. In this view, classical and quantum mechanics are represented as a particular type of principle theory. I call theories of this type 'theories of logical

Harper and Hooker (eds.), Foundations of Probability Theory, Statistical Inference, and Statistical Theories of Science, Vol. III, 55–80. All Rights Reserved. Copyright © 1976 by D. Reidel Publishing Company, Dordrecht-Holland.

structure' (or sometimes 'phase space theories'), since the type of structural constraint they introduce concerns the logical structure of events and this is given by the algebra of idempotent magnitudes of the theory. The logical structure of a physical system imposes the most general kind of constraint on the occurrence and non-occurrence of events. The event structures of classical mechanics are essentially Boolean algebras. The logical structure of a quantum mechanical system is represented by the partial Boolean algebra of subspaces of a Hilbert space. In general, this is not imbeddable into a Boolean algebra.

The mathematical investigations of Kochen and Specker [9] lead to a general concept of completeness applicable to phase space theories. The explication depends on the notion of a proper extension of a phase space theory. Extensions are defined relative to a category of algebraic structures (representing the phase spaces of the theory) and a suitable concept of statistical state: Let A denote the partial Boolean algebra of idempotents, S the set of statistical states ψ on A. Suppose there is an imbedding ϕ carrying A into A' such that for every $\psi \in S$, $\psi = \psi' \circ \phi$, where ψ' is a statistical state on A'. Then the theory (A', S') is an extension of the theory (A, S). The extension is proper if $\psi \neq \psi' \mid \phi[A]$, for some $\psi' \in S'$. Complete phase space theories have no proper extensions.

A proper extension of a phase space theory must not be confused with the more usual notion of a proper extension of a formal theory. Besides trivializing the notion, this would imply that completeness is a property of the theory's formalization. This, however, is not the case. The relevant notion of completeness is a mathematical property of a certain class of algebraic structures rather than a metamathematical one. There exists an important connection between completeness and the formal theory of this class of structures, but the concept of completeness does not depend on this connection.

A great deal of unclarity has surrounded the problem of completeness in quantum mechanics. An important consequence of this analysis is that classical mechanics and quantum mechanics are complete in exactly the same sense. In neither theory do there exist extensions in the category of algebraic structures associated with their respective phase spaces. As principle theories, classical mechanics and quantum mechanics specify different kinds of constraints on the possible events open to a physical system, i.e. they determine different possibility structures of events, and each theory is complete relative to the category of algebraic structures defined.

Finally, the approach to phase space theories outlined here has interesting consequences for the nature of logical truth. The logical structures of quantum mechanics include the Boolean algebras of classical mechanics. Such structures represent the possibility structure of events, that is, roughly speaking, they represent the way in which the properties of a physical system hang together. The quantum theory has shown that significantly different assumptions may be made concerning this structure. Now classical propositional validity is essentially validity in the category $\mathscr{B}$ of general Boolean algebras. The choice of Boolean algebras has an empirical justification in classical mechanics, for the magnitudes of this theory form a commutative algebra and therefore the subalgebra of idempotent magnitudes form a Boolean algebra. When viewed in this way, the justification of classical validity is intimately bound up with the logical structures postulated by classical mechanics. The quantum theory extends this class of structures to include all partial Boolean algebras of a certain type. The Boolean imbeddability properties of these structures have a model-theoretic characterization in terms of the validity of classical tautologies. Now a consequence of the work of Kochen and Specker is that there exists a classical tautology which is quantum mechanically refutable (i.e. refutable in a partial Boolean algebra of the quantum theory). In this sense, classical logic is false, and the truth of logic, an empirical question.

[One remark on the mathematical exposition: All qualifications regarding measurability, viz., the restriction to Borel functions, Borel subsets, and Boolean σ-algebras, have been omitted. This merely means that the exposition is not as general as it might be.]

2. PRELIMINARY NOTIONS

A partial algebra over a field K is a set A with a reflexive and symmetric binary relation $\leftrightarrow$ (termed 'compatibility') such that A is closed under the operation of scalar multiplication from $K \times A$ to A, and the operations of addition and multiplication defined from $\leftrightarrow$ to A. That is:

(i) $\leftrightarrow \subseteq A \times A$

(ii)   every element of A is compatible with itself
(iii)   if a is compatible with b, then b is compatible with a, for all a, $b \in A$
(iv)   if any a, b, $c \in A$ are mutually compatible, then $(a + b) \leftrightarrow c$, $ab \leftrightarrow c$, and $\lambda a \leftrightarrow b$ for all $\lambda \in K$.

In addition, there is a unit element 1 which is compatible with every element of A, and if a, b, c are mutually compatible, then the values of the polynomials in a, b, c form a commutative algebra over the field K.

A partial algebra over the field Z_2 of two elements is termed a *partial Boolean algebra*. The Boolean operations $\wedge$, $\vee$, and $'$ may be defined in terms of the ring operations in the usual way:

$$a \wedge b = ab$$
$$a \vee b = a + b - ab$$
$$a' = 1 - a.$$

If a, b, c are mutually compatible, then the values of the polynomials in a, b, c, form a Boolean algebra.

Clearly, if B is a set of mutually compatible elements in a partial algebra A, then B generates a commutative sub-algebra in A; and in the case of a partial Boolean algebra A, B generates a Boolean sub-algebra in A. Just as the set of idempotent elements of a commutative algebra forms a Boolean algebra, so the set of idempotents of a partial algebra forms a partial Boolean algebra.

We shall be mainly concerned with partial *Boolean* algebras. A *homomorphism*, h, between two partial Boolean algebras, A and A', is a map $h: A \to A'$ which preserves the algebraic operations, i.e. for all compatible $a, b \in A$:

$$h(a) \leftrightarrow h(b)$$
$$h(a + b) = h(a) + h(b)$$
$$h(ab) = h(a) h(b)$$
$$h(1) = 1$$

A homomorphism is an *imbedding* if it is one-to-one.
A *weak imbedding* is a homomorphism which is an imbedding on

Boolean sub-algebras of A. More precisely, a homomorphism, h, of A into A' is a weak imbedding if $h(a) \neq h(b)$ whenever $a \leftrightarrow b$ and $a \neq b$ in A. So that in the case of a weak imbedding, incompatible elements may be mapped onto the same element.

An algebra is *simple* if its only proper filter is the unit filter $\{1\}$. Z_2 is the only simple Boolean algebra. A necessary and sufficient condition for the imbeddability of a partial Boolean algebra A into a *Boolean algebra B*, is that for every pair of distinct elements a, $b \in A$ there exists a homomorphism $h: A \to Z_2$ which separates them in Z_2, i.e. such that $h(a) \neq h(b)$ in Z_2. This is Kochen and Specker's Theorem 0. The result depends on the semi-simplicity property of Boolean algebras, i.e. the fact that every Boolean algebra is imbeddable into a direct union of the simple Boolean algebra Z_2.

The direct union of a family $\{B_i\}_{i \in I}$ of Boolean algebras is defined on the set of all sequences $\{a_i\}_{i \in I}$ of elements of the B_i. The operations are defined point-wise, i.e.

$$\{a_i\}'_{i \in I} = \{a'_i\}_{i \in I}$$
$$\{a_i\}_{i \in I} \vee \{b_i\}_{i \in I} = \{a_i \vee b_i\}_{i \in I}$$
$$\{a_i\}_{i \in I} \wedge \{b_i\}_{i \in I} = \{a_i \wedge b_i\}_{i \in I}.$$

Semi-simplicity is equivalent to the homomorphism theorem: Every Boolean algebra admits a two-valued homomorphism, i.e. a homomorphism onto Z_2.

The semi-simplicity property and the homomorphism theorem are alternative formulations of Stone's representation theorem and the ultrafilter theorem (respectively). This is a consequence of the fact that in every Boolean algebra there is a natural one-to-one correspondence between ultrafilters and two-valued homomorphisms. Let S be the Stone space of a Boolean algebra B. (S is the set of all ultrafilters in B). Let $\mathscr{P}(S)$ denote the Boolean algebra of all subsets of S. Replacing ultrafilters by two-valued homomorphisms and subsets of S by the sequence of values of their characteristic functions yields Z_2^S – the direct union of Z_2 to the power of S – from $\mathscr{P}(S)$. In this context the Stone isomorphism becomes the imbedding $k: B \to Z_2^S$ given by

$$k(a) = \{h_t(a)\}_{t \in S}.$$

The mathematical connection of these ideas to logic arises in the following way. Propositional formulae are regarded as Boolean polynomials in a suitable first order language $\mathscr{L}$. Realizations of $\mathscr{L}$ are objects in the category $\mathscr{B}$ of general Boolean algebras. A formula $\phi(x_1, \ldots, x_n)$ is classically valid (C-valid) if, for any B in $\mathscr{B}$ every substitution of elements for the variables $x_1, \ldots, x_n$ yields the unit of B. If ϕ is a propositional formula not valid in B, i.e. if $\phi(a) \neq 1$ for some $a = (a_1, \ldots, a_n)$ in B^n, then $\phi(k(a)) \neq 1$ in Z_2^S, where $k(a) = (k(a_1), \ldots, k(a_n))$, so that ϕ is refutable in Z_2. Hence, by semi-simplicity, classical validity is equivalent to tautologousness, i.e. validity in Z_2.

Now extend the class of realizations of $\mathscr{L}$ to the category of partial Boolean algebras. Validity in a partial Boolean algebra N depends on the domain of a propositional formula. $\phi(x_1, \ldots, x_n)$ is valid in N if every substitution of elements from the domain of ϕ yields the unit of N. The concept of the domain of a propositional formula may be simply explained by an example.

Let $\phi = \psi \equiv \chi$ be the propositional formula

$$x_1 \wedge (x_2 \vee x_3) \equiv (x_1 \wedge x_2) \vee (x_1 \wedge x_3).$$

The domain of ϕ is the set of all elements $a = (a_1, a_2, a_3)$ of N such that:

$$a_1 \leftrightarrow a_2$$
$$a_1 \leftrightarrow a_3$$
$$a_2 \leftrightarrow a_3$$
$$a_1 \leftrightarrow (a_2 \vee a_3)$$
$$(a_1 \wedge a_2) \leftrightarrow (a_1 \wedge a_3)$$
$$a_1 \wedge (a_2 \vee a_3) \leftrightarrow (a_1 \wedge a_2) \vee (a_2 \wedge a_3),$$

for only then will the operations appearing in ϕ be defined in N.

It follows from the first three compatibilities that any three elements in the domain of ϕ generate a Boolean algebra, and hence, satisfy the distributive law. Hence ϕ is valid in all partial Boolean algebras. [Notice also that the last three compatibilities are therefore redundant.]

The generalized definition of propositional validity is: A propositional formula is Q-valid if it is valid in all partial Boolean algebras. The notion of Q-validity is formalized in [8].

The fundamental model-theoretic result in this field is:

(i) A partial Boolean algebra N is imbeddable into a Boolean algebra iff for every classical tautology of the form $\phi \equiv \psi$ the corresponding identity $\phi = \psi$ is valid in N, i.e. $\phi(a) = \psi(a)$ holds for all a in the intersection of the domains of ϕ and ψ.

(ii) N is weakly imbeddable into a Boolean algebra iff every classical tautology is not refutable in N.

(iii) There is a homomorphism from N into a Boolean algebra iff every classical tautology is not refutable in N. This is Theorem 4 of [9]. (See [2] for an exposition of the proof of this theorem.)

Notice that both C-validity and Q-validity have been defined algebraically, as the validity of propositional formulae in certain algebraic categories. In the case of classical validity, this definition differs sharply from more usual characterizations. Because of the equivalence of validity in $\mathscr{B}$ and validity in Z_2, classical propositional validity is defined as validity in the two-element *matrix* or *truth-table* $\langle \{0, 1\}, \{1\}, \vee, \neg \rangle$, where $\{1\}$ is the set of designated elements and $\vee$ and $\neg$ have their well-known matrix definitions. $\phi(x_1, \ldots, x_n)$ is a classical tautology if it yields the designated value 1 for all substitutions of the elements 0 and 1 for the variables $x_1, \ldots, x_n$.

The transition to Q-validity is greatly simplified when classical validity is understood algebraically. But there is another reason for replacing the matrix definition. First, it should be clear that a definition of classical validity is not merely a stipulation. Rather, one concept (or group of concepts) proved very fruitful in initiating the modern mathematical development of logic, and a definition of validity should provide some explication of this concept. The matrix definition is misleading since it ignores the connection of classical propositional logic with the theory of Boolean algebras. This connection is important for the whole development of the subject. For example, on the matrix definition it is trivial that classical propositional validity is effective. But when classical validity is defined algebraically, effectiveness depends on semi-simplicity, which is decidedly non-trivial. Hence the algebraic definition suggests that effectiveness did not play a major role in initial formulations of mathematical logic, and in fact, considerations of this type actually occur much later: viz., when the scope of logic came to be drawn in terms of the distinction between syntax and semantics.

3. PARTIAL BOOLEAN ALGEBRAS AND ORTHOMODULAR POSETS

Every partial Boolean algebra is isomorphic to a collection $L = \{L_i : i \in I\}$ of Boolean algebras satisfying the following conditions:

    (i)   The L_i have a common 1.

    (ii)   If $a \in L_i \cap L_j$, then $a^{\perp i} = a^{\perp j}$ ($\perp_i$ = orthocomplemention relative to L_i etc.)

    (iii)   If $a, b \in L_i \cap L_j$, then $a \wedge_i b = a \wedge_j b$.

    (iv)   Let $L = \bigcup \{L_i : i \in I\}$. Given any a, b, c in L such that any two of them lie in a common L_i, there exists an L_j such that $a, b, c \in L_j$.

Families of Boolean algebras satisfying (i)–(iv) are called *logical structures*. (Notice, the first three conditions simply insure that in any logical structure the operation of taking the intersection of two algebras makes sense.) The partial Boolean algebra associated with a logical structure is defined on $L = \bigcup L : a \leftrightarrow b$ iff there is an L_i containing a, b. The 1 of L is the common 1 of all the L_i. $a^{\perp} = a^{\perp i}$ for some L_i. If $a \leftrightarrow b$, then $a \wedge b = a \wedge_i b$ for some $i \in I$. (The zero and meet of L are thought of as being defined in the usual way.)

A partial Boolean algebra is said to be *transitive* if $a \leqslant b$, i.e. $a \wedge b = a$, and $b \leqslant c$ implies $a \leftrightarrow c$, in which case $a \leqslant c$. Logical structures associated with transitive partial Boolean algebras satisfy the further condition:

    (v)   If $a \leqslant_i b$ and $b \leqslant_j c$, there is an L_k such that $a, b, c \in L_k$.

Orthomodular posets are perhaps more familiar in the present context. They are structures $P = \langle P, \leqslant, \vee, \wedge, \perp, 0, 1 \rangle$ where $\leqslant$ is a partial order on P and $\perp$ is an orthocomplementation; 1 and 0 are greatest and least elements, and $\vee$, $\wedge$ are the l.u.b. and g.l.b. with respect to $\leqslant$. P is weakly modular: $a \vee b$ exists whenever a is orthogonal to b (i.e. $a \leqslant b^{\perp}$), and if $a \leqslant b$, then $a \vee (b \wedge a^{\perp}) = b$. In any orthomodular poset it is possible to define a relation C of compatibility: aCb if there exist mutually orthogonal elements a_1, b_1, c such that $a = a_1 \vee c$ and $b = b_1 \vee c$. (I.e., a and b are compatible if they are orthogonal except for an overlap.)

The representation theory for orthomodular posets has been established by Finch [3] (Theorems 1.1 and 3.1). The logical structures considered by Finch differ from those associated with transitive partial Boolean algebras with respect to condition (iv). In [3] this is replaced by the weaker (iv′) Suppose $a \leqslant_i b^{\perp i}$ for some a, $b \in L_i$. If $a \leqslant_j c^{\perp j}$ and $b \leqslant_k c^{\perp k}$ then there is an $m \in I$ such that $a, b, c \in L_m$.

That is, in an orthomodular poset we may have that $a, b \in L_i$, $a, c \in L_j$, and $b, c \in L_k$, but there is no L_m containing a, b, c.

A *compatible* orthomodular poset is one which satisfies the condition: $(a \vee b)Cc$ whenever a, b, c are pairwise compatible. This is a necessary and sufficient condition for every set of mutually compatible elements to be contained in a Boolean subalgebra of P.

There is a very simple connection between orthomodular posets and partial Boolean algebras: Every compatible orthomodular poset is a transitive partial Boolean algebra and conversely.

I have presented the connection between orthomodular posets and partial Boolean algebras in terms of their representation theory. A direct proof of these remarks has been given by Gudder in [6]. His formulation is based on the notion of an *associative* partial Boolean algebra: Suppose $a \leftrightarrow b$ and $b \leftrightarrow c$, $a, b, c \in L$. Then L is associative, if $(a \wedge b) \leftrightarrow c$ iff $a \leftrightarrow (b \wedge c)$, and hence $(a \wedge b) \wedge c = a \wedge (b \wedge c)$. (By a lemma of Gudder and Schelp ([7] Lemma 3.3) a partial Boolean algebra is associative if and only if it is transitive.) Gudder shows that every associative partial Boolean algebra is a compatible orthomodular poset, and conversely. (Theorems 2.3 and 2.4).

The partial Boolean algebra $B(H)$ of closed linear subspaces of a separable Hilbert space is a transitive partial Boolean algebra. The partial ordering is given by the subspace relation, and the operations of meet, join and orthocomplement are represented by the intersection, span and orthogonal complement of subspaces. The zero of $B(H)$ is the 0-dimensional subspace, and the unit is the whole space H. The definition of $\leftrightarrow$ is $a \leftrightarrow b$, if aCb, i.e. if there are mutually orthogonal subspaces a_1, b_1, c such that $b = b_1 \vee c$, and $a = a_1 \vee c$. Equivalently, the subspaces of H form a compatible orthomodular poset.

To sum up: The representation of H as an orthomodular poset is based on its order structure since it is the fact that H is partially ordered which is retained in the general concept of an orthomodular poset. The concept of a partial Boolean algebra is based on the compatibility structure of H, since it preserves the fact that every triple of pairwise compatible subspaces is contained in a Boolean subalgebra of H.

4. APPLICATIONS TO THE PROBLEM OF HIDDEN VARIABLES

Partial Boolean algebras were introduced by Kochen and Specker in connection with the problem of hidden variables. This is characterized as the problem of imbedding the non-commutative partial algebra of self-adjoint operators on H into the commutative algebra of real valued functions on a classical probability space. Their first theorem shows that there are no two-valued homomorphisms on a finite subalgebra of the partial Boolean algebra $B(E^3)$ of lines through a point in ordinary three dimensional Euclidian space. It follows from this that there are no two-valued homomorphisms on $B(H)$. (It is necessary to assume that the dimension of H be at least three.) Hence, by Theorem 0 there is no imbedding of $B(H)$ into a Boolean algebra. But the partial Boolean algebra of subspaces of H is isomorphic to the subalgebra of idempotent operators on H. Hence the partial algebra of physical magnitudes is not imbeddable into a commutative algebra.

By the equivalence of two-valued homomorphisms and two-valued probability measures (or dispersion-free states), the absence of two-valued homomorphisms is an immediate corollary to Gleason's theorem. An independent proof of this corrollary was first given by Bell. (See [1] for an exposition of the proof.) Kochen and Specker's proof differs from Bell's since it does not depend on the denseness of the unit sphere in H.

There is an interesting reformulation of the imbedding problem in terms of the concept of a logical structure (suggested by a paper of Macyznski [10]). This actually characterizes the problem of finding a *weak* imbedding of a partial Boolean algebra into a Boolean algebra. The problem may be further generalized by the concept of a homomorphic relation, but we shall not consider this here (see [9] Section 5). The interest of the reformulation from our point of view is that it clarifies an important distinction, viz. the distinction between a Boolean theory based on the idempotent magnitudes of quantum mechanics and a Boolean representation of the algebra of idempotent magnitudes.

Let $N = \{B_i : i \in I\}$ denote the logical structure associated with $B(H)$ for a three dimensional Hilbert space. $\{f_i^j : B_i \to B_j, i, j \in I\}$ is the set of inclusion homomorphisms from B_i into B_j. $f_i^i =$ the identity map. Notice that $f_j^k \circ f_i^j = f_i^k$, since N is a logical structure. Write $B_i \subseteq B_j$ if there is an f_i^j. A *Boolean representation* of N is a pair $(C, \{h_i\}_{i \in I})$ where C is a non-degenerate Boolean algebra and each $h_i : B_i \to C$ is an imbedding carrying B_i into C such that the following conditions are satisfied:

(i) $\bigcup_{i \in I} h_i[B_i]$ generates C.

(ii)   If $B_i \subseteq B_j$, then $h_i = h_j \mid f_i^j[B_i]$.

(iii)   Given any $(C', \{h_i'\}_{i \in I})$ satisfying (i) and (ii) there is a unique homomorphism $h : C \to C'$ such that $h \circ h_i = h_i'$.

The presence of condition (ii) implies that a Boolean representation of N is a weak imbedding of $B(H)$ into C.

Suppose that $(F, \{k_i\}_{i \in I})$ is the direct product of the B_i, e.g. F may be the field product of the Stone spaces X_i of the B_i. That is to say, take the Cartesian product $X = \prod_{i \in I} X_i$ of the spaces X_i. Associate each $Y_i \in F(X_i)$ with a subset of X by the mapping

$$Y_i \mapsto \{x \in X \mid x_i \in Y_i\}.$$

The field product $F(X)$ of the $F(X_i)$ is the field generated by the union of the images of the $F(X_i)$ under this correspondence. $F(X)$ contains an isomorphic copy of each $F(X_i)$, and hence, an isomorphic image of each B_i.

Condition (ii) distinguishes a Boolean representation of the B_i from their direct product. To see this consider an element a in $B_i \subseteq B_j$. a is mapped by k_i onto the set of points in X whose ith coordinate is an ultrafilter in B_i containing a. The image of $a = f_i^j(a)$ under k_j is the set of points whose jth coordinate is an ultrafilter in B_j containing a. It is clear that in general $k_i(a) \neq k_j(a)$.

Given the direct product, we may always obtain a structure satisfying condition (ii), but this is not necessarily a Boolean representation. To do this we proceed as follows. Let I be the ideal in F generated by all elements of the form: $k_i(a) - k_j(f_i^j(a)) \cup k_j(f_i^j(a)) - k_i(a)$. For Y, Z in F define $Y \sim Z$ if $Y - Z \cup Z - Y \in I$. F/I is the set of equivalence classes of elements of F under the relation $\sim$. Let $\phi : F \to F/I$ be the canonical homomorphism from F onto the quotient algebra F/I. Write $k_i' = \phi \circ k_i$. Then $(F/I, \{k'\}_{i \in I})$ is the *direct limit* of N. The direct limit is a Boolean representation if, and only if, it is non-degenerate.

It is always possible to construct a Boolean theory based on the idempotent magnitudes in the B_i simply by taking the direct product of the logical structure. This corresponds to Kochen and Specker's trivial hidden variable construction. Such a theory is excluded by condition (ii), for this condition makes the problem an imbedding problem. Rejecting this characterization of the problem is therefore equivalent to weakening the notion of a Boolean representation of a logical structure. But this overlooks the fact that *exactly the same* condition occurs in classical mechanics since, of the two representations, $(F, \{k_i\}_{i \in I})$ and $(F/I, \{k'_i\}_{i \in I})$, classical mechanics uses the direct limit, not the direct product. Hence, condition (ii), or equivalently, the condition of weak imbeddability, can hardly be regarded as an *ad hoc* restriction, arbitrarily introduced to exclude classical extensions of the quantum theory.

Orthomodular posets are mainly associated with the 'quantum logic' formulation of quantum mechanics. This represents a new axiomatic approach to the theory which aims at generalizing von Neumann's presentation in terms of Hilbert space. The principal question here is: "To what extent can von Neumann's formulation be recovered without explicitly using the concept of Hilbert Space". This is a mathematical investigation, motivated by mainly mathematical considerations. In this latter repect, it differs, not only from Kochen and Specker's investigations, but from von Neumann's as well.

Before von Neumann's treatise, the relationship between wave mechanics and matrix mechanics was obscure. For example, Dirac and Jordan viewed the similarity between the two theories in terms of a 'correspondence' between the 'points' over which matrices in matrix mechanics and differential operators in wave mechanics are defined – an idea which could not be consistently maintained as von Neumann showed. Von Neumann's presentation of these two theories in terms of Hilbert space was based on the observation that the algebraic structure of physical magnitudes is the same in both matrix and wave mechanics. This structure is represented by the noncommutative algebra of self-adjoint operators on a separable Hilbert space. The Hilbert space formalization is thus motivated by a question concerning the relationship between these two theories, and von Neumann presented the definitive clarification of the precise respect in which wave mechanics and matrix mechanics are equivalent.

In the quantum logic approach, the problem of hidden variables consists in showing that in any acceptable generalization of the theory there are no dispersion-free states. Now the difficulties with the notion of an *acceptable* generalization are obvious enough. However equally serious problems arise in connection with the notion of a *generalization* of quantum mechanics. For example, why should a generalization in any way preserve the algebraic structure of the theory? For this may be an inessential feature of the theory's formulation, and therefore, not properly part of any generalization of the theory. This is the criticism usually urged against hidden variable theorems.

These and similar difficulties are undercut by Kochen and Specker's formulation of the problem as an imbedding problem. First, this restricts the issue to the relationship between two *given* theories, viz., quantum mechanics and classical mechanics. The question is basically this: Is quantum mechanics a complete statistical theory? Or is it statistical in the sense of classical statistical mechanics? In this case the absence of dispersion-free states is the result of incomplete knowledge. Secondly, it completes the program initiated by von Neumann: In *Mathematical Foundations* it was shown that the peculiarity of wave mechanics and matrix mechanics consists in the algebraic structure of their physical magnitudes. The solution to the imbedding problem shows that this algebraic structure occurs essentially, and therefore cannot be regarded as a property of the theory's formulation.

5. IDEMPOTENTS AS PROPOSITIONS

To begin with, let us consider the relationship between the properties of a physical system and quantities taking values in R. Let Ω be a subset of n-dimensional Euclidian space. In classical particle mechanics a physical quantity is represented by a function in R^{Ω}. Take a quantity A and real number λ in the range of $f_A \in R^{\Omega}$. Then $f_A = \lambda$ (this is read 'the value of f_A is λ') represents a property of the physical system S. More generally, given A and a subset U of R, $f_A \in U$ (the value of f_A lies in U) represents a property of S.

To define the holding of a property we shall require the notion of a state of S. This must not be confused with a statistical state. A state is simply an event in the history of S. In classical mechanics an event is represented by a point ω in Ω. As is well-known, an event represented by ω is associated with a pure statistical state: the two-valued measure on $\mathscr{F}(\Omega)$ determined by ω; but the concept of an event is not a statistical concept.

The property $f_A \in U$ holds for S if and only if S is in a state such that

$f_A(\omega) \in U$. Notice, in von Neumann's terminology $f_A \in U$ is then said to be a property of the *state* ω ([13] p. 249). This is misleading, as will be shown in connection with quantum mechanics.

Let us now consider the representation of properties of S by idempotent magnitudes. Let Γ denote the subset $f_A^{-1}(U)$ of Ω. It is clear that S has the property $f_A \in U$ if and only if the state ω of S lies in Γ. The property $f_A \in U$ is said to be *associated with* Γ. In general there are many properties $f_{A_i} \in U_j$ such that $f_{A_i}^{-1}(U_j) = \Gamma$ for some $U_j \subseteq R$. Now let χ_Γ be the characteristic function of Γ, and let P be a property associated with Γ. By the correspondence between properties of S and subsets of Ω, it follows that every property P is represented by the characteristic function χ_Γ, in the sense that P holds if and only if S is in a state ω such that $\chi_\Gamma(\omega) = 1$. Since χ_Γ is two-valued this is equivalent to $\chi_\Gamma(\omega) \neq 0$. This is the formulation employed by von Neumann ([13] Ch. III. 5).

Now the characteristic functions of the subsets of Ω are just the subset of idempotent elements in R^Ω. The idempotents form a Boolean ring with unit $1 = \chi_\Omega$, i.e. a Boolean algebra. To simplify the notation, let B denote the Boolean subalgebra of idempotents in R^Ω. Elements of B will be denoted by $a, b, c, \dots$. Whenever lattice operations are used, it is assumed that they have been defined in terms of the ring operations in the usual way.

To summarize, we have seen that every magnitude may be replaced by a set of properties, and that every property corresponds to a two-valued quantity, i.e. idempotent magnitude in B. The correspondence is not one-to-one, since very many properties are associated with the same subset of Ω, and therefore represented by the same idempotent magnitude. Since a is also a magnitude in R^Ω, $a = 1$ (or $a \neq 0$) is also a property of S just as $f_A = \lambda$ is a property of S. Here the property $a = 1$ represents a whole class of properties of the form $f_A \in U$.

That idempotents may be regarded as propositions is justified by the following considerations. For each a in B we may define: a is *true* (i.e. $a = 1$ or $a \neq 0$) if and only if S is in a state ω such that $a(\omega) = 1$. (Since a is two valued, this is equivalent to $a(\omega) \neq 0$.) I.e. a is true if and only if S has any (and therefore, *all*) of the properties represented by a. Also,

$$a' \text{ is true iff } 1 - a(\omega) = 1$$
$$a \vee b \text{ is true iff } a(\omega) + b(\omega) - a(\omega)\,b(\omega) = 1,$$

so that the lattice operations $'$ and $\vee$ in B represent the operations of negation and disjunction of classical logic. In a similar way the other propositional connectives may be identified with the corresponding Boolean operations.

[Strictly speaking B should be regarded as the Lindenbaum-Tarski algebra of a suitable formal language $\mathscr{L}$, and truth then defined for sentences of $\mathscr{L}$. For our purposes, this would introduce an unnecessary complication.]

The distinction drawn between states and statistical states is expressed notationally as follows. Let $a \in B$. If I write $\omega(a)$, this denotes the probability of the proposition a in the pure state determined by ω. But $a(\omega)$ denotes the truth value of a for the state ω. In other words, if I write $\omega(a)$, i.e. if ω appears as a function, then it denotes a probability measure; but when ω appears as an argument, it denotes a state.

Notice, in classical mechanics we always have
$$\omega(a) = a(\omega).$$

This depends on the fact that the pure states, like the propositions are two-valued. For this reason it is possible to define the truth of a proposition a in B by writing

a is true iff S is in a state ω such that $\omega(a) = 1$.
a' is true iff $1 - \omega(a) = 1$.
$a \vee b$ is true iff $\omega(a) + \omega(b) - \omega(a)\,\omega(b) = 1$.

This definition is formally equivalent to the one given earlier. But the conception of truth which underlies the two definitions is very different. This definition identifies truth with probability equal to 1, so that a proposition is true only if the statistical state of S assigns it probability 1. That is to say, for a proposition a to be true, the system must be in a pure *statistical* state ω such that $\omega(a) = 1$.

In classical mechanics each ω in Ω determines a two-valued homomorphism $h: B \to Z_2$. Each h corresponds biuniquely to a two-valued measure ω on $\mathscr{F}(\Omega)$. Substituting h for the probability measure determined by ω yields a formally equivalent definition of truth. This definition is related to the one given in van Fraassen [12] as follows. A possible world is a classical truth value assignment to the propositions of B. Each such world is represented by a two-valued homomorphism. A proposition is true only if it is true in some possible world, i.e. only if $h(a) = 1$ for some $h: B \to Z_2$. This is a necessary condition for the truth of a. (a is true if this truth-value assignment is determined by the actual world.) The mistake underlying the identification of truth with probability equal to 1 is transparent. It is less obvious that exactly the same misconception underlies this definition.

First, notice that if a possible world is represented by a state or event (rather than a two-valued homomorphism), the resulting definition coincides with the one given here, i.e. with $a(\omega)=1$. It is not the concept of a possible world which poses a problem, but the interpretation of a possible world as a two-valued homomorphism. For this has the consequence that the truth of an atomic proposition is defined only if the truth or falsity of every *other* proposition is also specified. But this is cerainly not required by the correspondence theory of truth. To put this very simply, on any reasonable definition, the truth of the proposition, (a) 'It is raining', depends, not on the truth or falsity of every other proposition, but just on the state of the weather. This is independent of whether or not our knowledge of the truth of a depends on our knowledge of the truth of other propositions. It is this simple insight which is preserved in the correspondence theory, and which is given up when, in the *definition* of the truth of a, it is required that $h(a)=1$.

We may summarize this discussion of the definition of 'truth' in classical mechanics. Classically a state is associated with a two-valued measure and a two-valued homomorphism. Because the Boolean algebra of subsets of Ω is perfect and reduced, this association is biunique. There are therefore three formally equivalent definitions of 'a is true': (A) $a(\omega)=1$, (B) $\omega(a)=1$ and (C) $h(a)=1$. In the first definition the truth of a is exclusively determined by the state of S: A proposition a is true if and only if the system has (any) one of the properties represented by a. Each of the other two definitions imposes an additional requirement on the truth of a. In the case of (B) a must have a probability equal to 1. If the definition is $h(a)=1$, then the truth of a requires that the truth or falsity of every other proposition in B is also given. The formal equivalence, which holds classically, does not mean that (A), (B), and (C) are explications of equivalent conceptions of truth. The conception underlying (B) is remarkably like the pragmatic theory of truth, while (C) is similar to the doctrine of internal relations of the coherence theory. Both conceptions of truth confuse the meaning or reference of the proposition 'a is true' with considerations that are strictly evidential in character.

Thus far we have concentrated on classical mechanics, but the situation in quantum mechanics is exactly analogous. The idempotent magnitudes, i.e. the propositions a in the partial Boolean algebra N are projection operators acting on a suitable Hilbert space H. A state or event of a system S is represented by a (unit) ray $\mathscr{K}$ in H. Each event $\mathscr{K}$ is associated with a pure statistical state. In quantum mechanics, statistical states are given by measures on the closed linear subspaces of H. The pure state associated with $\mathscr{K}$ is determined by taking the square of the norm of the projection of a unit vector lying in $\mathscr{K}$ onto each subspace of H. Since by Theorem 12 of von Neumann [13], there is a one-to-one correspondence which associates each projection operator with the subspace in H which is its range, this determines a probability measure on N. Recall, in classical mechanics a statistical state is a measure on the field $\mathscr{F}(\Omega)$ of subsets of Ω. There the correspondence between subsets and propositions is trivial. Note, atoms in B are the characteristic functions associated with singleton subsets $\{\omega\}$ of $\mathscr{F}(\Omega)$. N is also atomic. An atom in N is a projection operator onto a one-dimensional subspace of H. Thus in each theory there is a one-to-one correspondence between events and atomic propositions.

Quantum mechanics is probabilistic in the sense that the set S of statistical states does not include two-valued measures. This means that the expectation (or average) value is never dispersion-free for all magnitudes – even in the case of pure statistical states. But exactly the same magnitudes, and therefore, exactly the same propositions occur in both classical and quantum mechanics; that is the propositions of both B and N make assertions about properties of physical systems, not ensembles of such systems. In quantum mechanics there are no statistical states which determine a probability of 1 or 0 for every a in N, and which may therefore be regarded as two-valued truth value assignments to the propositions of N. Although a statistical state determines the probability of every a in N, the corresponding event does not determine the truth values of all propositions.

Suppose that the event represented by $\mathscr{K}$ determines the truth or falsity of a. Then the situation is exactly as described for classical mechanics, and the truth of a' and $a \vee b$ is defined by writing

a' is true iff $1 - a(\mathscr{K}) = 1$
$a \vee b$ is true iff $a(\mathscr{K}) + b(\mathscr{K}) - a(\mathscr{K}) b(\mathscr{K}) = 1$.

That is, the partial operations $'$, $\vee$ of N represent the logical operations of negation and disjunction of classical logic. (Recall that in a partial Boolean algebra $a \vee b$ exists iff a and b are compatible.)

Of course, the identity

$$a(\mathcal{K}) = \mathcal{K}(a)$$

cannot hold in quantum mechanics. It is possible to *make* it hold by identifying the truth value of a in the state $\mathcal{K}$ with the probability assigned to a by the statistical state determined by $\mathcal{K}$, i.e. by stipulating that $a(\mathcal{K}) = \mathcal{K}(a)$. But there is no more justification for identifying truth with probability in quantum mechanics, than there is in classical mechanics.

It follows from what has been said so far that an event does not determine all properties of S. Here it is important to be extremely clear. Let us consider a specific property P. Then there are states $\mathcal{K}$ such that $\mathcal{K}$ does not determine whether P holds or fails to hold. But P is a property of S and it is always determinate whether or not P holds for S: The answer to this question is contained in S, though not in every event in the history of S. The determinateness of the holding of P is completely independent of whether or not the holding of P is determined by every state of S. I regard this claim as central to the logical interpretation of quantum mechanics. This is obscure if it is assumed that P is a property of a state rather than a property of S and that S has only a single state $\mathcal{K}$.

In quantum mechanics a system S is characterized by a single *statistical* state. But S has many states – enough to determine the truth value of each a in N. In both classical mechanics and quantum mechanics, every a in N or B is true or false, and if a is false, then a' is true. This is a consequence of the fact that both algebras are idempotent, hence every a in N or B takes only the values 0 (false) and 1 (true). But B is also semi-simple, and therefore admits two-valued measures. The correspondence between two-valued measures and events means that each event determines a two-valued truth value assignment to all the propositions of B. This is to be contrasted with N which is not semi-simple (Theorem 1 of [9]), hence there is no extension of N which recovers the correspondence between events and two-valued measures.

The structure of N makes it necessary to distinguish an event from a possible world since, intuitively, a possible world should determine all properties of S. But S has many more properties than are represented by the propositions whose truth is determined by $\mathscr{K}$. Hence $\mathscr{K}$ cannot be regarded as a possible world in this sense. The situation is rather as follows: In classical mechanics a single point ω in Ω represents a possible world, since a single event determines *all* properties of S. In quantum mechanics, a possible world is represented only by the whole logical space N, since no one event determines all properties of S. This suggests that the usefulness of the concept of a possible world is restricted to the classical case.

In quantum mechanics a pure statistical state of S is significantly probabilistic in the sense that pure states are not degenerate statistical states as in classical mechanics. But unlike classical statistical mechanics, this does not arise from an incompleteness in the theory, since it is impossible to introduce two-valued measures given the logical structure of N. In classical statistical mechanics the degenerate statistical states, i.e. the two-valued measures, are recoverable by imbedding the algebra of idempotent *macroscopic* magnitudes into an atomic Boolean algebra. But N is atomic, and there are no (proper) extensions of N; in particular there are no Boolean extensions.

So far it has been shown that the classical concepts of truth and logical structure are largely independent, and that the concept of truth is the same in both classical and quantum mechanics. In particular, any formal language $\mathscr{L}$, which is based on N, i.e. for which N is the Lindenbaum-Tarski Algebra, is bivalent. $\mathscr{L}$ differs from a classical language in the following respect. A sentence ϕ of $\mathscr{L}$ corresponds to an element a of the logical structure N. This is exactly as in classical logic. But unlike the classical case, a is never associated with a two-valued homomorphism on N. To put this slightly differently: A Boolean representation of the fact that every sentence ϕ is true or false requires that the corresponding a in B is representable by the sequence $k(a)$ of its truth values under all possible truth value assignments. Semi-simplicity insures that this is always the case. Now every sentence ϕ of $\mathscr{L}$ is true or false, and only true or false. For $\mathscr{L}$ is bivalent if N is idempotent, i.e. if for every a in N, $a \wedge a = a$. But the failure of semi-simplicity means that there is no Boolean representation of this fact. Whether every proposition a in N (and hence, every sentence ϕ in $\mathscr{L}$) is true or false depends exclusively on a. The bivalence of $\mathscr{L}$ is independent of how the corresponding propositions in N

are interrelated. This is obviously not true if bivalence is represented by semi-simplicity.

It has been maintained (e.g. by van Fraassen [12] and Friedman and Glymour [4] that there is a problem with applying the classical concept of truth to elements of N. This problem does not arise for propositions in B or in a maximal Boolean subalgebra B_i of N, since B and B_i each admit two-valued homomorphisms. If the discussion of this section is correct, semi-simplicity is irrelevant to the classical concept of truth, so that new 'semantic analyses' of quantum mechanics are completely ancillary.

6. 'ANOMALIES'

I shall now briefly consider the bearing of this discussion on the paradoxes or anomalies of quantum mechanics. (A complete discussion is contained in a forthcoming paper with Jeffrey Bub.) It seems likely that all of the paradoxes have essentially the following form. There exist two statistical states, one pure, the other a mixture, which are the same for a given class of idempotents, but which are generally distinct. The pure state correctly characterizes the system (i.e. it is confirmed experimentally). Such a state generates a collection of propositions asserting the probability that the system has a certain property. A mixed state gives the probability that the system is in a given pure state, and from this the probability that S has a certain property is inferred. For example suppose we are interested in a property P but that the pure state of S is neither 0 nor 1 for the proposition a in N representing P. One might suppose that S is really characterized by a mixture, so that S is in a pure state $\mathcal{K}$ with a certain weight w such that $\mathcal{K}$ assigns a a probability of 1 or 0. But this is excluded theoretically (by the fact that pure states are not reducible to mixtures) as well as experimentally.

The situation just described arises in the two slit experiment. (This is the only case I shall explicitly consider.) Recall that the statistical state of the electron is experimentally determined by examining the diffraction pattern which appears on the emulsion opposite the screen after very many electrons have been emitted by the source. The electrons are emitted one at a time and at intervals of any length. The statistical state $\mathcal{K}$ associated with both slits open is not the weighted sum of the pure statistical states $\mathcal{K}_{\alpha_i}$ which assign a probability of 1 to the propositions a_i: "The

electron passes through slit i" $(i=1, 2)$. The pure state exhibits interference, while the mixed state does not. Now the fact that the statistical
state is not the mixture but another pure state is not paradoxical. By itself this is no more puzzling than the relativistic replacement of the classical addition theorem for relative velocities. It is clear that an anomaly
arises only if there is some reason to suppose that the statistical state must
be represented by a mixture of the $\mathscr{K}_{\alpha_i}$.

The basic idea seems to be that if the probability of a_i is neither 1 nor 0
in the state $\mathscr{K}$, then the electron is in some sense indeterminate with respect to the property $a_i = 1$ (or $a_i \neq 0$). This means that neither a_1 nor a_2 is
true or false. On this basis it is often suggested that quantum mechanics
requires some thorough-going revision in our space-time concepts: the
two-slit experiment is anomolous given our classical and relativistic conceptions of space-time. But how seriously this suggestion should be considered is unclear since it has never been seriously developed. In any case
it overlooks the fact that quantum mechanics, like classical mechanics and
relativity, assumes that the symmetry group of all physical systems is a
subgroup of the manifold mapping group, and that therefore, the theory
makes precisely the same continuity and differentiability assumptions as
these theories. Hence on this suggestion, quantum mechanics is a fundamentally incoherent theory. But the theoretical and experimental success
of quantum mechanics is simply too great for this conclusion to be
seriously considered.

That the whole problem is misconceived, is immediate from the analysis
of this paper. The statistical state of the electron is indeed the pure state.
This state exhibits interference, and is not to be replaced by a mixture.
The pure state like all of the statistical states of the theory, is significantly
probabilistic: i.e. it assigns a probability which is not dispersion-free on
very many propositions in N. In particular, it is not 0 or 1 for a_i. But
each a_i is true or false. Moreover, this holds for every proposition in N. A
difficulty arises when one attempts to express this fact by a simultaneous
truth value assignment to all propositions in N, since this is possible only
if N is imbeddable into a Boolean algebra.

More generally, quantum mechanics is indeterministic in the sense that
the pure statistical states of the theory are not degenerate measures concentrated on 0 and 1 as in classical mechanics; hence the maximal amount
of information concerning a physical system is significantly probabilistic.

This arises from the fact that certain properties are independent, as are the idempotents which represent them. More exactly, the properties are *strongly independent* in the sense that they are stochastically related to other properties in a way which excludes their being stochastically related to each other. This is the significance of incompatibility.

Indeterminism in this sense must not be confused with the very different concept of indeterminateness. The theory is indeterministic or significantly statistical in the sense that the pure states take values in the open interval $(0, 1)$. The thesis that the theory is indeterminate holds that there are properties P such that P neither holds nor fails to hold of S. This is not implied by indeterminism nor is it in any way required by the view that the theory provides a maximal amount of information concerning the system. Rather, indeterminateness is suggested by essentially two mistaken ideas. The first of these is that incompatible propositions are somehow inconsistent. But just the opposite is the case: since a pair of propositions are incompatible, they *cannot* be inconsistent.

The second mistake concerns the definition of the truth of atomic propositions. According to the correspondence theory of truth an atomic proposition a in N is true if and only if the properties represented by a hold of S. This definition is independent of the semi-simplicity of N, so that at any given instant exactly one proposition in each $B_i \subset N$ is true of S. The essential point is that the absence of a simultaneous truth value assignment does not imply that the properties of S which, on the account given here, are supposed to obtain, cannot obtain simultaneously. The opposite view rests on a simple equivocation. A simultaneous truth value assignment is a two-valued homomorphism. That simultaneous truth value assignments do not exist is a fact about the structure of N which has nothing to do with what occurs simultaneously. The properties of S which obtain simultaneously include *incompatible* properties. But their logical structure excludes the existence of a two-valued homomorphism, and hence, of a simultaneous truth value assignment to the corresponding idempotents. At any one instant the system is characterized by exactly one class of properties from each $B_i \subset N$, and all such classes of properties obtain at the same time. But there is no Boolean representation of this fact.

To summarize this part of the discussion: There are two different accounts of indeterminism which are historically important. The first, which apparently goes back to Aristotle, rejects bivalence: A theory is indeterministic if it assumes that there are propositions whose truth value is indeterminate. The second, represented by the quantum theory, retains bivalence while rejecting semi-simplicity. An indeterministic theory is then characterized by the absence of two-valued homomorphisms, and therefore, of two-valued measures. The coherence of indeterminateness seems to rest on the Aristotelian metaphysic of act and potency. But nothing of this sort is required by the indeterminism of quantum mechanics. This form of indeterminism implies that there is no Boolean representation of the properties obtaining at a given time; yet for any property P it is completely determinate whether or not P holds.

The anomalous character of the two-slit experiment depends on the assumption that the system is indeterminate with respect to the property $a_i = 1$, if the statistical state is $\mathscr{K} \neq \mathscr{K}_{a_i}$. This assumes that the usual notions of truth and falsity make sense only in the case of propositions which form a Boolean algebra. This view lies at the basis of both the Copenhagen and hidden variable interpretations of the quantum theory. According to the Copenhagen interpretation, at each instant the system 'projects' exactly one maximal Boolean subalgebra of N; in a hidden variable interpretation all Boolean subalgebras are represented but their structure is Boolean. The difference is that the Copenhagen interpretation is willing to consider systems with properties corresponding to at most *one* maximal Boolean subalgebra in the logical structure associated with N. Now the implicit restriction of $\{B_i : i \in I\}$ to maximal Boolean subalgebras has an interesting consequence. If B_i, B_j are maximal Boolean subalgebras, then $B_i \subseteq B_j$ implies $B_i = B_j$, i.e. the logical structure $\{B_i : i \in M\}$ consisting of all maximal Boolean subalgebras is totally unordered by $\subseteq$. In this case condition (ii) of Section 4 is trivially satisfied, so that the direct limit of the B_i coincides with the direct product, which is a Boolean representation of $\{B_i : i \in M\}$.

Thus both the Copenhagen and hidden variable interpretations are committed to representations of $\{B_i : i \in I\}$ which are semi-simple: In the hidden variable interpretation this requires dropping condition (ii), while in the Copenhagen interpretation this is accomplished by replacing $\{B_i : i \in I\}$ with $\{B_i : i \in M\}$. In effect both views fail to consider the possibility that the properties of physical systems exemplify the logical structure of N. I.e. both views completely fail as accounts of the significance of the transition from classical mechanics to quantum mechanics.

It should be remarked that the hidden variable interpretation is at least coherent. The idea that a system projects a single B_i at each instant has the absurd consequence that the system must somehow anticipate the decision of the experimenter to measure a magnitude associated with B_i. This consequence is avoidable only if measurements are regarded as a theoretically opaque subclass of physical interactions. It is a strange comment on current investigations in foundations of physics that both possibilities are seriously considered and widely entertained.

[The possibility of a classical theory of the maximal magnitudes was noted by Wiener and Siegel ([14], Appendix), and independently, by Gudder [5], who proved this theorem in a more general context. The discussion here follows the very elegant presentation of Macyznski.]

In conclusion, I wish to compare the discussion in Section 5 with von Neumann [13] Ch. III.5, 'Projections as Propositions'. *Prima facie* there is only the slightest difference between the conception of truth presented here and the one implicitly assumed by von Neumann. But the difference has important consequences. Adopting von Neumann's approach, one is led to propose an additional class of non-unitary time transformations. This is the content of the projection postulate, which may be simply explained as follows: Let us assume that a system S is in a pure state represented by a unit ray $\mathcal{K}_\psi$ in H (the Hilbert space associated with S). Now suppose we find that the value of a magnitude A is a_i. The value a_i is associated with a ray $\mathcal{K}_{\alpha_i}$ in H. $\mathcal{K}_{\alpha_i}$ represents the pure statistical state which assigns the property $A = a_i$ a probability equal to one. The projection postulate requires that the statistical state of S undergo a transition, $\mathcal{K}_\psi \mapsto \mathcal{K}_{\alpha_i}$, which is generally discontinuous. Since the dynamics of the theory considers only continuous transitions, the projection postulate represents an additional hypothesis.

Essentially the same idea underlies the characterization of the probabilities of quantum mechanics as 'transition' probabilities. The probability $|(\psi, \alpha_i)|^2$ which $\mathcal{K}_\psi$ assigns to $A = a_i$ is not the probability that the property $A = a_i$ obtains, but rather, the probability that it will obtain. This requires that S undergo a transition from the state $\mathcal{K}_\psi$ to $\mathcal{K}_{\alpha_i}$. The problem of finding a theoretical account for such stochastic transitions has come to be known as the 'measurement problem', since transitions of this type are supposed to occur whenever a measurement is performed. The projection postulate is simply a precise characterization of this class of transitions. (See Jeffrey Bub's contribution to this volume.)

If the analysis of this paper is correct, the projection postulate results from a misconception of the logical structure of the theory: there is nothing about the logical structure which requires that a proposition is true only in certain statistical states. The projection postulate is therefore quite clearly ancillary to an understanding of the theory. Similarly, since the measurement problem requires the occurrence of transitions of the kind described by the projection postulate, it follows that this cannot be a real difficulty for the theory.

University of New Brunswick and
University of Western Ontario

BIBLIOGRAPHY

[1] Bub, J., *The Interpretation of Quantum Mechanics*, Reidel, 1974.
[2] Bub, J. and Demopoulos, W., 'The Interpretation of Quantum Mechanics', in *Boston Studies in the Philosophy of Science* vol. XIII (ed. by R. S. Cohen and M. J. Wartofsky), Reidel, 1974.
[3] Finch, P. D., 'On the Structure of Quantum Logic', *Journal of Symbolic Logic* **34** (1969), 275–282.
[4] Friedman, M. and Glymour, C., 'If Quanta Had Logic', *Journal of Philosophical Logic* **1** (1972), 16–28.
[5] Gudder, S., 'On Hidden-Variable Theories', *Journal of Mathematical Physics* **11** (1970), 431–436.
[6] Gudder, S., 'Partial Algebraic Structures Associated with Orthomodular Posets', *Pacific Journal of Mathematics* **41** (1972), 717–730.
[7] Gudder, S. and Schelp, R., 'Coordinatization of Orthocomplemented and Orthomodular Posets', *Proceedings of the American Mathematical Society* **25** (1970), 229–237.
[8] Kochen, S. and Specker, E. P., 'Logical Structures Arising in Quantum Theory', *The Theory of Models, 1963 Symposium at Berkeley* (compiled by J. Addison *et al.*), North-Holland, 1965.
[9] Kochen, S. and Specker, E. P., 'The Problem of Hidden Variables in Quantum Mechanics', *Journal of Mathematics and Mechanics* **17** (1967), 59–87.
[10] Maczynski, M. J., 'Boolean Properties of Observables in Axiomatic Quantum Mechanics', *Reports on Mathematical Physics* **2** (1971), 135–150.
[11] Putnam, H., 'Is Logic Empirical?', in *Boston Studies in the Philosophy of Science*, vol. V (ed. by R. S. Cohen and M. J. Wartofsky), Reidel, 1969.
[12] van Fraassen, B., 'Semantic Analysis of Quantum Logic', in *Contemporary Research in the Foundations and Philosophy of Quantum Theory* (ed. by C. A. Hooker), Reidel, 1973.

[13] von Neumann, J., *Mathematical Foundations of Quantum Mechanics*, Princeton University Press, 1955.

[14] Wiener, N. and Siegel, A., 'The Differential-Space Theory of Quantum Systems', *II Nuovo Cimento*, supplement to vol II, series X (1955), 982–1003.

P. D. FINCH

QUANTUM MECHANICAL PHYSICAL QUANTITIES
AS RANDOM VARIABLES

1. INTRODUCTION

The extensive development of probability theory during the past thirty five years is largely due to the impetus given it by the axiomatic formulation of Kolmogorov (1933). In this formulation the basic concept is that of a probability space, namely an ordered triplet $\{\mathscr{X}, \mathscr{A}, \mu\}$ where $\mathscr{X}$ is a non-empty set, $\mathscr{A}$ is a Boolean σ-algebra of subsets of $\mathscr{X}$ and μ is a probability measure on $\mathscr{A}$. A real-valued function X on $\mathscr{X}$ is said to be $\mathscr{A}$-measurable when, for any Borel subset B of the real line, the set

$$X^{-1}B = \{x : X(x) \in B\}$$

is in $\mathscr{A}$. A random variable is just an $\mathscr{A}$-measurable function X with associated probabilities

$$\Pr\{X \in B\} = \mu(X^{-1}B).$$

It is well-known that one can interpret the elements of $\mathscr{A}$ as propositions and obtain, in this way, a Boolean logic of propositions in which the logical operations of disjunction, conjunction and negation correspond to the Boolean lattice operations of join, meet and orthocomplementation respectively.

The Kolmogorov formulation of probability theory has achieved a striking success in its application to many fields of scientific and mathematical research and yet, in spite of this, it seems to be inadequate as a mathematical framework in which to formulate the problems of quantum mechanics. This inadequacy has sometimes been described by saying that the classical laws of probability breakdown in the quantum mechanical situation, for example by Feynman (1951), although the validity of such a description has been questioned by Koopman (1957) and Suppes (1961).

In quantum mechanics the possible values of certain physical quantities seem to arise as the eigenvalues of self-adjoint operators in separable

Harper and Hooker (eds.), Foundations of Probability Theory, Statistical Inference, and Statistical Theories of Science, Vol. III, 81–103. *All Rights Reserved. Copyright* © 1976 *by D. Reidel Publishing Company, Dordrecht-Holland.*

Hilbert space, a circumstance which is sometimes described by saying that these physical quantities correspond to or are represented by certain operators in Hilbert space. Following von Neumann (1932) and Birkhoff and von Neumann (1936) one is lead to a quantum logic of propositions which has the structure of the lattice of subspaces of Hilbert space, see for example Mackey (1963), Jauch (1968) and Varadarajan (1968). This quantum logic is an orthomodular lattice in which the lattice operations of join, meet and orthocomplementation correspond to logical operations in a way which is somewhat similar to the case of a Boolean logic mentioned above. However one meets a difficulty in this new situation when one comes to define the analogue of a random variable on a quantum logic because there are no points on which to define a random variable as a real-valued function in analogy to the Kolmogorov formulation of probability theory.

This difficulty can be overcome by observing that if $\{\mathcal{X}, \mathcal{A}, \mu\}$ is a probability space and X is a random variable then to each Borel subset B of the real line is associated the set $X^{-1}B$ in $\mathcal{A}$. Thus to each random variable X there is associated a mapping $\xi: B \to X^{-1}B$ which maps the Boolean algebra $\mathcal{B}$ of Borel subsets of the real line into the Boolean algebra $\mathcal{A}$. It turns out that the random variables are characterised as the σ-homomorphisms of $\mathcal{B}$ into $\mathcal{A}$, see for example Varadarajan (1962). This characterisation of random variables in the classical case suggests that in a quantum logic $\mathcal{L}$ one could *define* a random variable to be a σ-homomorphism of the Boolean algebra $\mathcal{B}$ into the logic $\mathcal{L}$. It is this procedure which is usually followed in abstract discussions of quantum logic. In such discussions one has a quantum logic $\mathcal{L}$ whose elements are propositions and a set of σ-homomorphisms of $\mathcal{B}$ into $\mathcal{L}$. If ξ is one of these σ-homomorphisms it is thought of as representing a physical quantity X such that

$$\Pr\{X \in B\} = \mu(\xi B)$$

where μ is the analogue of a probability measure and specifies the state of the quantum logic $\mathcal{L}$. For the development of these ideas we refer to Mackey (1963), Varadarajan (1962), Bodiov (1964) and, more recently, Gunson (1967), Varadarajan (1968).

The representation of physical quantities by means of σ-homomorphisms ties in with the more familiar representation by operators in

Hilbert space in the following way. Let $\mathscr{X}$ be separable Hilbert space and by an operator mean a closed self-adjoint transformation R in $\mathscr{X}$ whose domain is a linear manifold which is dense in $\mathscr{X}$ and which has a spectral representation

$$R = \int_{-\infty}^{+\infty} \lambda \pi\,(d\lambda),$$

where $\{\pi(\lambda)\}$ is the spectral resolution of the identity associated with R. In the quantum mechanical situation $\mathscr{X}$ is the Hilbert space of certain solutions to the Schrödinger equation of a physical system and certain of the physical quantities associated with the physical system correspond in a natural way to operators. Those operators which do correspond to physical quantities are often called observables. If R is an observable and if X is the physical quantity to which it corresponds then, for ψ in $\mathscr{X}$ with $\|\psi\|=1$

$$\text{Exp}\,\{X \mid \psi\} = (R\psi, \psi)$$

is the conditional expectation of the physical quantity X when a measurement of it is made at a time when the system is known to be in the pure state specified by ψ. For each Borel set B we have

$$\text{Pr}\,\{X \in B \mid \psi\} = \text{Exp}\,\{\chi_B(R) \mid \psi\},$$

where

$$\chi_B(R) = \int_{\infty-}^{\infty+} \chi_B(\lambda)\,\pi\,(d\lambda)$$

and $\chi_B(\lambda)$ is 1 or 0 according as λ is or is not in B. Thus we may associate with the observable R the σ-homomorphism ξ defined by

$$\xi B = \int_B \pi\,(d\lambda).$$

The associated probability measure on the lattice of subspaces of $\mathscr{X}$ which corresponds to the pure state ψ is

$$\mu^\psi\,(\xi B) = \int_B (\pi\,(d\lambda)\,\psi, \psi).$$

The procedures outlined above provide legitimate mathematical constructs to play the role of physical quantities, however they suffer the disadvantage that in using them one loses the idea of a physical quantity as a random variable in the sense of the classical theory of probability. Because of this the physical quantities of quantum mechanics have often been thought of as being essentially different from the physical quantities of classical mechanics. This supposed essential difference is emphasised by the fact that the formal application of certain standard mathematical procedures of classical probability theory to quantum mechanical physical quantities can lead to paradoxical results. For example the formal derivation of the joint distribution function of momentum and position can lead to negative or even complex-valued probabilities, for details about this problem one can refer to Suppes (1961) where further references are given. It should be noted that in the formulation of Mackey (1963) one cannot talk of the joint distribution of quantum mechanical physical quantities if these are not simultaneously measurable, in this context one should refer also to Varadarajan (1962) and Ramsay (1966).

In this paper we introduce an alternative description of the physical quantities of quantum mechanics in which there are effectively (equivalence classes of) random variables in the usual sense of probability theory and where the quantum logic is thought of as a family of discrete probability spaces related in a way discussed below and treated in detail in Finch (1969a). However the description we propose is not so much a new mathematical framework for quantum mechanics as a reinterpretation of the usual formulation in terms of Hilbert space and, for this reason, it is not to be regarded as a competitor seeking to oust the usual formulations. Its purpose is to clarify certain of the concepts involved in the logic of quantum mechanics and to relate them to concepts of the classical theory of probability. For this reason we do not introduce our model in a full abstract setting but consider in some detail the case of physical quantities which take on at most a countable number of values. We then indicate how our procedure must be modified to take into account those physical quantities whose values form an uncountable Borel subset of the real line.

However our procedure applies in a setting more general than that of the lattice of subspaces of Hilbert space. It seems worthwhile taking advantage of this fact, firstly because it gives emphasis to the results which do not depend on the Hilbert space structure and secondly because it leads us to indicate some interesting questions which we do not attempt to answer here. Throughout the paper we use the terminology of Finch (1969a) to which we refer for the relevant definitions.

2. PHYSICAL SYSTEMS AND THEIR STATES

Throughout this section $\mathscr{L}$ is a separable logical σ-structure and L is its associated logic. If $\{F_\gamma : \gamma \in \Gamma\}$ is the set of frames of L then $\mathscr{L} = \{L_\gamma : \gamma \in \Gamma\}$ and $L = \bigcup \{L_\gamma : \gamma \in \Gamma\}$ where L_γ is the Boolean subalgebra of L which is generated by the frame F_γ. The Boolean logic L_γ is isomorphic to the Boolean algebra of all subsets of the countable set F_γ.

For each F_γ we write $\mathscr{R}_\gamma = \mathscr{R}(F_\gamma)$ for the set of all real-valued functions defined on F_γ. We call the ordered pair $\{F_\gamma, \mathscr{R}_\gamma\}$ a Boolean physical system associated with $\mathscr{L}$ and we call the elements of $\mathscr{R}_\gamma$ the measurable quantities of that physical system. By a state of the Boolean physical system $\{F, \mathscr{R}(F)\}$ we mean a probability measure μ defined on the set of all subsets of the frame F. Thus if A is a non-empty subset of F we have

$$\mu(A) = \sum_{f \in A} \mu(f),$$

where $\mu(f)$ is the measure attaching to the one element set $\{f\}$ and $\mu(f) \geqslant 0$, $\sum_{f \in \Gamma} \mu(f) = 1$. The ordered pair $\{F, \mu\}$ is a discrete probability space and so a Boolean physical system in a given state is an ordered triplet $\{F, \mathscr{R}(F), \mu\}$ where $\{F, \mu\}$ is a discrete probability space and, in the language of probability theory, the elements of $\mathscr{R}(F)$ are just its random variables with probability distributions given by

$$\Pr\{X \in B \mid \mu\} = \sum_{X^{-1}B} \mu(f)$$

for each X in $\mathscr{R}(F)$ and any subset B of the real line.

By the physical system associated with the separable logical σ-structure $\mathscr{L}$ we mean the set

$$\mathscr{G} = [\{F_\gamma, \mathscr{R}_\gamma\} : \gamma \in \Gamma]$$

of all the Boolean physical systems associated with $\mathscr{L}$. A measurable quantity of $\mathscr{G}$ is just a measurable quantity of one of its component Boolean physical systems. A set of measurable quantities of $\mathscr{G}$ is said to be strictly compatible when they are measurable quantities of the same component Boolean physical system. If $\{X_t:t\in T\}$ is a set of strictly compatible measurable quantities, if each X_t is in $\mathscr{R}(F)$ and $\{x_t:t\in T\}$ is a set of real numbers we write

$$\Pr\{X_t \leqslant x_t, t\in T\} = \sum \mu(f),$$

where the summation is over all f in F for which $X_t(f)\leqslant x_t$ for each t in T, and regarding the left-hand side as a function defined for all sets of real numbers $\{x_t:t\in T\}$ we refer to it as the simultaneous probability distribution of the strictly compatible measurable quantities X_t.

In order to make some important distinctions we introduce the following terminology. Let P be a separable completely orthomodular poset, by a normed σ-orthovaluation on P we mean a real-valued function μ on P such that (i) $\mu(x)\geqslant 0$ for each x in P, (ii) $\mu(1)=1$ and (iii) for any orthogonal subset $\{x_j\}$ (which must be finite or countably infinite since P is separable) one has

$$\sum_j \mu(x_j) = \mu(x)$$

where $x=x_j$. By a result of Finch (1969a) every completely orthomodular poset P is the logic associated with a logical σ-structure and in that context we often call a normed σ-orthovaluation on the logic P a state of that logic.

By a state of the physical system $\mathscr{G}$ we mean a set $\mathscr{M}=\{\mu_\gamma:\gamma\in\Gamma\}$ of states of the Boolean physical systems comprising $\mathscr{G}$. Any state of the logic L associated with L determines a state of the physical system $\mathscr{G}$ in the following way. Let μ be a state of L and define the probability measure μ_γ on the Boolean physical system $\{F_\gamma, \mathscr{R}_\gamma\}$ by $\mu_\gamma(f)=\mu(f)$ for each f in F_γ. We say that the resulting state $\mathscr{M}$ of $\mathscr{G}$ is induced by the state μ of L. Not all states of $\mathscr{G}$ arise in this way, to characterise those that do we need some preliminary definitions.

Let F be a frame of L and let X be in $\mathscr{R}(F)$. Denote the range of X by $\{x_k:k\in K\}$ and write

$$f_k^X = \vee \{f:f\in F, X(f) = x_k\}, \quad k\in K,$$

the lattice join on the right existing in L since L is a completely orthomodular poset and the elements of any frame are mutually orthogonal.

Then

$$F^X = \{f_k^X : k \in K\}$$

is a frame of L, we define X^F in $\mathscr{R}(F^X)$ by the equations

$$X^F(f_k^X) = x_k, \quad k \in K.$$

Note that we have $F^X = F$, and then also $X^F = X$, if and only if

$$f, f' \in F \& X(f) = X(f') \Rightarrow f = f'.$$

Now let F and G be any two frames of L and let X and Y be measurable quantities in $\mathscr{R}(F)$ and $\mathscr{R}(G)$ respectively. We say that X and Y are similar, and then write $X \sim Y$, when $F^X = G^Y$ and $X^F = Y^G$. The relationship of similarity between measurable quantities is an equivalence relation and for X in $\mathscr{R}(F)$ one has always $X^F \sim X$. We say that X in $\mathscr{R}(F)$ is irreducible when $F^X = F$, and hence also $X^F = X$. Thus X^F is irreducible and each equivalence class of similar measurable quantities contains exactly one irreducible element, namely the equivalence class containing X in $\mathscr{R}(F)$ has X^F as its irreducible element. We often write $s(X)$ for the equivalence class of measurable quantities which are similar to X and write $X^{(i)}$ for the irreducible element of $s(X)$. If $X \sim Y$ and c is a real number then $cX \sim cY$ and so we define $cs(X)$ to be the equivalence class $s(cX)$.

To characterise those states of the physical system $\mathscr{G}$ which are induced by states of the logic L we introduce the idea of a congruent state of $\mathscr{G}$ as one in which similar measurable quantities have the same probability distribution, we formalise this concept in the

DEFINITION. *A state $\mathscr{M}$ of the physical system $\mathscr{G}$ is said to be congruent when for γ, δ in Γ, X_γ in $\mathscr{R}(F_\gamma)$ and X_δ in $\mathscr{R}(F_\delta)$ one has*

$$X_\gamma \sim X_\delta \Rightarrow \Pr\{X_\gamma \in B \mid \mu_\gamma\} = \Pr\{X_\delta \in B \mid \mu_\delta\}$$

for every subset B of the real line.

We are now in a position to prove

THEOREM (2.1) *A state of the physical system $\mathscr{G}$ is congruent if and only if it is induced by a state of the logic L.*

Proof. Let $\mathscr{M} = \{\mu_\gamma : \gamma \in \Gamma\}$ be the state of $\mathscr{G}$ induced by the state μ of L.

Suppose that X_γ in $\mathscr{R}(F_\gamma)$ and X_δ in $\mathscr{R}(F_\delta)$ are similar measurable quantities. Then X and X_δ have the same range, let it be $\{x_k : k \in K\}$. Using the notation introduced above we have

$$\Pr\{X_\gamma = x_k \mid \mu_\gamma\} = \mu(f_k^{X_\gamma})$$

and

$$\Pr\{X_\delta = x_k \mid \mu_\delta\} = \mu(g_k^{X_\delta})$$

where

$$f_k^{X_\gamma} = \vee \; \{f : f \in F_\gamma, \; X_\gamma(f) = x_k\},$$
$$g_k^{X_\delta} = \vee \; \{g : g \in F_\delta, \; X_\delta(g) = x_k\}.$$

Since X_γ and X_δ are similar we have $F_\gamma^{X_\gamma} = F_\delta^{X_\delta}$ and $X_\gamma^{F_\gamma} = X_\delta^{F_\delta}$, thus $f_k^{X_\gamma} = g_k^{X_\delta}$ for each k in K. This shows that $\mathscr{M}$ is a congruent state of $\mathscr{G}$.

Conversely suppose that $\mathscr{M} = \{\mu_\gamma : \gamma \in \Gamma\}$ is a congruent state of $\mathscr{G}$. Let f, $0 < f < 1$ be in L and let $F_\gamma = \{f, f_2, f_3, \dots\}$ and $F_\delta = \{f, g_2, g_3, \dots\}$ be any two frames of L which contain the element f. Then

$$\overset{\infty}{\underset{j=2}{\vee}} \, f_j = f^\perp = \overset{\infty}{\underset{k=2}{\vee}} \, g_k.$$

Let X_γ in $\mathscr{R}(F_\gamma)$ be defined by $X_\gamma(f) = 1$ and $X_\gamma(f_j) = 0$ for $j \geqslant 2$, similarly let X_δ in $\mathscr{R}(F_\delta)$ be defined by $X_\delta(f) = 1$ and $X_\delta(g_j) = 0$ for $j \geqslant 2$. Then

$$F_\gamma^{X_\gamma} = \{f, f^\perp\} = G_\delta^{X_\delta}$$

and

$$X_\gamma^{F_\gamma}(f) = X_\delta^{F_\delta}(f) = 1, \quad X_\gamma^{F_\gamma}(f^\perp) = X_\delta^{F_\delta}(f^\perp) = 0.$$

Thus X_γ and X_δ are similar measurable quantities and so, since $\mathscr{M}$ is a congruent state,

$$\mu_\gamma(f) = \Pr\{X_\gamma = 1 \mid \mu_\gamma\} = \Pr\{X_\delta = 1 \mid \mu_\delta\} = \mu_\delta(f).$$

It follows that we can define a real-valued function μ on L by writing $\mu(0) = 0$, $\mu(1) = 1$ and, for $0 < f < 1$, decreeing that $\mu(f) = \mu_\gamma(f)$ for any γ in Γ such that F_γ contains f.

Now let $\{\xi_j : j \in J\}$ be an orthogonal subset of L with $0 <$, $\xi_j < 1$ for each j in J. In what follows we suppose that $\xi = \{\xi_j : f \in J\} < 1$, the case $\xi = 1$ requiring only a few obvious modifications of the argument. There are γ and δ in Γ such

that
$$F_\gamma = \{\xi^\perp\} \cup \{\xi_j : j \in J\}$$
and
$$F_\delta = \{\xi^\perp, \xi\}.$$

Let X_γ in $\mathscr{R}(F_\gamma)$ be defined by $X_\gamma(\xi^\perp)=0$ and $X_\gamma(\xi_j)=1$ for each j in J, similarly let X_δ in $\mathscr{R}(F_\delta)$ be defined by $x_\delta(\xi^\perp)=0$ and $X_\delta(\xi)=1$, then defining μ on L as above we have

$$\Pr\{X_\gamma = 1 \mid \mu_\gamma\} = \sum_J \mu_\gamma(\xi_j) = \sum_J \mu(\xi_j)$$
$$\Pr\{X_\delta = 1 \mid \mu_\delta\} = \mu_\delta(\xi) = \mu(\xi).$$

But $F_\delta = F_\gamma^{X_\gamma}$ and $X_\delta = X_\gamma^{F_\gamma}$ and so X_γ and X_δ are similar measurable quantities. Since $\mathscr{M}$ is congruent we have

$$\mu(\xi) = \sum_J \mu(\xi_j)$$

and this shows that μ is a state of the logic L. Moreover, as indicated by the definition of μ, the state $\mathscr{M}$ of $\mathscr{G}$ is that induced by the state μ of L.

3. COMPATIBLE MEASURABLE QUANTITIES

In this section we define compatibility between equivalence classes of similar measurable quantities of the physical system $\mathscr{G}$ associated with a separable logical σ-structure $\mathscr{L}$. We show how one can define addition and multiplication of compatible equivalence classes of similar measurable quantities. Later we look at the case when L, the logic associated with $\mathscr{L}$, is the lattice of subspaces of separable Hilbert space, this is the model used for the standard formulation of quantum mechanics and, for this case, we will show that equivalence classes of similar measurable quantities can be represented by self-adjoint operators in Hilbert space, that compatibility in our-self sense corresponds to the usual concept with that name in quantum mechanics, and that addition of compatible equivalence classes of similar measurable quantities corresponds to the addition of their representative operators.

Let $\mathscr{F}$ be the set of all frames of the logic L. For F and G in $\mathscr{F}$ we say that F is finer than G, or that F is a refinement of G, in which case we write $F \leqslant G$, when (i) to each f in F there is an element g in G such that $f \leqslant g$ and (ii) to each g in G there is at least one element f in F such that

$f \leqslant g$. Note that, in fact, (i) implies (ii) but (ii) does not imply (i). Refinement is clearly a partial ordering of $\mathscr{F}$, we prove first

LEMMA (3.1) *Let* $F = \{f_j : j \in J\}$ *and* $G = \{g_k : k \in K\}$, *then* $F \leqslant G$ *if and only if to each* k *in* K *there is a non-empty subset* J_k *of* J *such that*

$$\vee \{f_j : j \in J_k\} = g_k.$$

Proof. Suppose there exist non-empty sets J_k with the property stated above. Since, in that case,

$$\underset{k \in K}{\vee} [\vee \{f_j : j \in J_k\}] = \underset{k \in K}{\vee} g_k = 1$$

we see that each f in F belongs to one of the sets J_k. Thus to each f in F there is a g in G with $f \leqslant g$ similarly, since no J_k is empty, to each g in G there is an f in F with $f \leqslant g$, it follows that $F \leqslant G$. Now suppose that $F \leqslant G$, let J_k be the set of those j in J for which $f_j \leqslant g_k$. Then J_k is not empty and

$$\vee \{f_j : j \in J_k\} \leqslant g_k.$$

But on the other hand we have

$$\begin{aligned}
[\vee \{f_j : j \in J_k\}]^{\perp} &= \vee \{f_j : j \in J \setminus J_k\} \\
&\leqslant \vee \{g_h : h \in K \setminus k\} \\
&\leqslant g_k^{\perp},
\end{aligned}$$

thus

$$\vee \{f_j : j \in J_k\} \geqslant g_k,$$

and this, together with the reverse ordering above, establishes the desired result.

Let F and G be frames with $F \leqslant G$, to each f in F there corresponds exactly one g in G, $g(f)$ say, such that $f \leqslant g(f)$. Thus we can define a map $X \to XF^*$ of $\mathscr{R}(G)$ into $\mathscr{R}(F)$ by writing

$$(XF^*)(f) = X\{g(f)\},$$

for each X in $\mathscr{R}(G)$ and each f in F. Some important properties of the map F^* are listed below as lemmas for future reference. Since the proofs of these lemmas are routine verifications of the properties stated we omit them.

LEMMA (3.2) *If $F \leq G$ and X is in $\mathcal{R}(G)$ then X and XF^* are similar measurable quantities.*

LEMMA (3.3) *If $F_1 \leq F_2 \leq G$ and X is in $\mathcal{R}(G)$ then*

$$s(XF_1^*) = s(XF_2^*) = s(X)$$

LEMMA (3.4) *If F is a frame and Y is in $\mathcal{R}(F)$ then $F \leq F^Y$ and $Y^F F^* = Y$.*

LEMMA (3.5) *Let F, G be frames with $F \leq G$. The map $F^*: \mathcal{R}(G) \to \mathcal{R}(F)$ has the properties that for any real c and any X_1, X_2, ..., X_n in $\mathcal{R}(G)$*

$$(cX_1)F^* = c(X_1F^*)$$
$$(X_1 X_2 \dots X_n)F^* = (X_1F^*)(X_2F^*)\dots(X_nF^*)$$
$$(X_1 + X_2 + \cdots + X_n)F^* = X_1F^* + X_2F^* + \cdots + X_nF^*.$$

A set $\{X_t : t \in T\}$ of measurable quantities, where $X_t \in \mathcal{R}(F_t)$, is said to be compatible when the frames $F_t^{X_t}$, $t \in T$, have a common refinement. If $\{X_t : t \in T\}$ is a compatible set of measurable quantities and $\{Y_t : t \in T\}$ is another set of measurable quantities with $Y_t \sim X_t$ for each t in T then the Y_t are also compatible since $G_t^{Y_t} = F_t^{X_t}$. We can therefore define the compatibility of equivalence classes of similar measurable quantities. We say then that a set $\{s_t : t \in T\}$ of equivalence classes of similar measurable quantities is compatible when the set of frames which are the domains of the irreducible elements of these classes has a common refinement.

Let $X_1, X_2, ..., X_n$ be n measurable quantities and for each $j = 1, 2, ..., n$ let $X_j^{(i)}$ be the irreducible element of the equivalence class $s(X_j)$. Suppose that X_j is in $\mathcal{R}(F_j)$ and write $F_j^{(i)} = F_j^{X_j}$ for the domain on which $X_j^{(i)} = X_j^{F_j}$ is defined. If the X_j are compatible there is a frame F which is a common refinement of the $F_j^{(i)}$, that is there is a frame F with $F \leq F_j^{(i)}$ for each $j = 1, 2, ..., n$. In this case we define the sum and product of the compatible equivalence classes $s(X_j)$ by the equations

$$\prod_{j=1}^{n} s(X_j) = s\left(\prod_{j=1}^{n} X_j^{(i)} F^* \right),$$

and

$$\sum_{j=1}^{n} s(X_j) = s\left(\sum_{j=1}^{n} X_j^{(i)} F^* \right).$$

It is a consequence of Lemmas (3.3) and (3.5) that the right-hand sides of these equations do not depend on the choice of the common refinement F of the $F_j^{(i)}$.

Addition and multiplication of compatible equivalence classes of measurable quantities is associative, that is

$$s(X) + (s(Y) + s(Z)) = (s(X) + s(Y)) + s(Z)$$

and

$$s(X)\{s(Y)s(Z)\} = \{s(X)s(Y)\}s(Z)$$

whenever X, Y and Z are compatible measurable quantities. This is a consequence of the following

LEMMA (3.6) *If F is a frame and X, Y belong to $\mathcal{R}(F)$ then X and Y are compatible and*

$$s(X) + s(Y) = s(X + Y)$$

Proof. F is a common refinement of F^X and F^Y and so X and Y are compatible. By the definition of addition

$$s(X) + s(Y) = s(X^{(i)}F^* + Y^{(i)}F^*),$$

but $X^{(i)} = X^F$, $Y^{(i)} = Y^F$ and so, by Lemma (3.4), we obtain the desired result.

COROLLARY. *Addition and multiplication of compatible equivalence classes of similar measurable quantities are associative.*

Proof. We establish the associativity of addition, that of multiplication is proved by a similar argument. Let X, Y and Z in $\mathcal{R}(A)$, $\mathcal{R}(B)$ and $\mathcal{R}(C)$ respectively be irreducible measurable quantities which are compatible. Let D be a common refinement of the frames A, B and C, then

$$s(Y) + s(Z) = s(YD^* + ZD^*).$$

Noting that XD^* and YD^* are both in $\mathcal{R}(D)$ we obtain, by use of the lemma,

$$\begin{aligned}
s(X) + (s(Y) + s(Z)) &= s(XD^*) + s(YD^* + ZD^*) \\
&= s(XD^* + YD^* + ZD^*).
\end{aligned}$$

Similarly

$$(s(X) + s(Y)) + s(Z) = s(XD^* + YD^* + ZD^*).$$

This establishes the corollary.

Remark. We remark that there is no difficulty in extending the preceding results to infinite sums of compatible equivalence classes of similar measurable quantities since, however, we have no occasion to these here we omit the details.

We conclude this section by noting that one can define a simultaneous distribution function for a set of compatible equivalence classes of similar measurable quantities, or equivalently of a set of compatible measurable quantities. To see this let $\{X_t : t \in T\}$ be a set of compatible measurable quantities, let $X_t^{(i)}$ be the irreducible element of the equivalence class $s(X_t)$ and let F be a common refinement of the domains of the $X_t^{(i)}$. Then the $X_t^{(i)}F^*$ are all in $\mathscr{R}(F)$, that is the $X_t^{(i)}F^*$ are strictly compatible in the sense of the definition in the preceding section. We define the simultaneous distribution function of the X_t, or equivalently of the $s(X_t)$, to be that of the strictly compatible measurable quantities $X_t^{(i)}F^*$, one verifies easily that this distribution does not depend on the choice of the common refinement F.

4. MEASURABLE QUANTITIES IN THE HILBERT MODEL OF QUANTUM THEORY

In this section we take another look at some of our earlier results in the case the logic L associated with our separable logical σ-structure $\mathscr{L}$ is the lattice of subspaces of separable Hilbert space $\mathscr{X}$, that this is so is assumed throughout the section. Let F be a frame of L and to X in $\mathscr{R}(F)$ associate the linear operator in given by

$$R^X = \sum_{f \in F} X(f) P_f$$

where P_f is the projection onto the subspace f of $\mathscr{X}$. Such linear operators are self-adjoint and have a dense domain in $\mathscr{X}$, for if $\Phi = \{\phi_j\}_{j=1}^{\infty}$ is an orthonormal basis of $\mathscr{X}$, such that each f in F is generated by a subset of Φ, then R^X is defined on the dense linear manifold generated by Φ. We prove

LEMMA (4.1) *If F and G are frames of L, if X in $\mathscr{R}(F)$ and Y in $\mathscr{R}(G)$ are irreducible then $R^X = R^Y$ (if and) only if F = G and X = Y.*

Proof. Let $F = \{f_j : j \in J\}$ and $G = \{g_k :: k \in K\}$. Assume that X in $\mathscr{R}(F)$ and Y in $\mathscr{R}(G)$ are irreducible and that $R^X = R^Y$. For $\theta \neq 0$ in g_k we have

$$\sum_J X(f_j) P_j \theta = R^X \theta = R^Y \theta = Y(g_k) \theta = \sum_J Y(g_k) P_{f_j} \theta,$$

thus

$$\{X(f_j) - Y(g_k)\} P_{f_j} \theta = 0, \quad j \in J.$$

We cannot have $P_{f_j} \theta = 0$ for each j in J for this would imply $\theta = 0$ contrary to assumption, thus there is at least one j in J such that $X(f_j) = Y(g_k)$ and, since X is irreducible there is exactly one such j. Reversing the roles played by X and Y we establish a bijection between J and K such that X and Y take the same value at corresponding points of their domains. We may suppose therefore that $K = J$ and that $Y(g_j) = X(f_j)$ for each j in J.

For j' in J and $\phi \neq 0$ in $g_{j'}$ an argument like that just used shows that

$$\{X(f_j) - Y(g_{j'})\} P_{f_j} \phi = 0$$

for all j in J. Since X is irreducible we must have $p_{f_j} \phi = 0$ for each $j \neq j'$ and so ϕ is in $f_{j'}$. Thus $g_{j'} \leqslant f_{j'}$, a symmetry argument shows that $f_{j'} \leqslant g_{j'}$ and so $g_{j'} = f_{j'}$. This means that $G = F$ and $Y = X$, this is the desired result.

We are now in a position to establish

THEOREM (4.1) *Let $\mathscr{G}$ be the physical system associated with the logic of the lattice of subspaces of separable Hilbert space. If X and Y are measurable quantities of the physical system $\mathscr{G}$ then $R^X = R^Y$ if and only if X and Y are similar measurable quantities.*

Proof. Suppose that X is in $\mathscr{R}(F)$ and that Y is in $\mathscr{R}(G)$. Write $A = X^F$ and $B = Y^G$. If $X \sim Y$ then $A = B$ and $F^X = G^Y$, thus

$$R^X = R^A = R^B = R^Y.$$

Conversely if $R^X = R^Y$ then $R^A = R^B$, but A and B are irreducible and so by the lemma, $F^X = G^Y$ and $X^F = Y^G$, that is X and Y are similar measurable quantities.

Theorem (4.1) asserts that there is a one-to-one correspondence between equivalence classes of similar measurable quantities of and certain linear operators acting in $\mathscr{X}$, for this reason we sometimes write $R^{s(X)}$ instead of R^X. It must be emphasized, however, that this 'representation' of measurable quantities by operators is nothing more than this one-to-one correspondence, the fact that it exists does not imply that it preserves, in a meaningful way, any additional algebraic structure carried by one or the other of the two sets in question. Thus operators can be added and multiplied and it is tempting to try to transfer these algebraic operations to the set of measurable quantities through the one-to-one correspondence of Theorem (4.1). For instance one verifies easily that $R^{X^2} = (R^X)^2$ and, for real c, $R^{cX} = cR^X$. Again if F is a frame and X, Y are measurable quantities which belong to $\mathscr{R}(F)$ then

$$R^{X \pm Y} = R^X \pm R^Y \tag{4.1}$$

and hence, since

$$4XY = (X + Y)^2 - (X - Y)^2$$

we obtain

$$R^{XY} = (R^X R^Y + R^Y R^X)/2. \tag{4.2}$$

The operator additions and multiplications in the right-hand side of Equations (4.1) and (4.2) would still make sense even if X belonged to $\mathscr{R}(F)$ and Y belonged to $\mathscr{R}(G)$ if $F \neq G$. In such circumstances, however, one cannot define $X + Y$ and XY as function addition and multiplication since the functions X and Y are defined on different domains. It seems plausible therefore to define new operations '$\oplus$', '$\ominus$' and '$\otimes$' between measurable quantities through the equations,

$$R^{X \oplus Y} = R^X + R^Y,$$
$$R^{X \ominus Y} = R^X - R^Y,$$
$$R^{X \otimes Y} = (R^X R^Y + R^Y R^X)/2,$$

thinking that we are thereby defining, in some sense, a sum, difference and product of measurable quantities. Of course such definitions are effective only if these equations remain invariant when X and Y are replaced by similar measurable quantities and only if the right-hand sides of these defining equations do, in fact, determine operators which correspond to equivalence classes of similar measurable quantities in the

way described above. To shorten our discussion we assume the effectiveness of these definitions at least over some subset of the set of measurable
quantities.

A procedure such as this is often suggested, for example, by Temple
(1934), but its interpretation is somewhat obscure. For instance a short
calculation shows that

$$R^{(X \otimes Y) \otimes Z} - R^{X \otimes (Y \otimes Z)} = [Y[XZ]]/4$$

where, for operators A and B, $[AB]$ denotes the commutator $AB - BA$.
Thus in general

$$(X \otimes Y) \otimes Z \sim X \otimes (Y \otimes Z)$$

and the binary multiplication operation '$\otimes$' is not associative.

From the point of view adopted in this paper there is, of course, no
obvious phenomenological interpretation attached to the operations
defined above. The primary objects of study are the measurable quantities, their representation as operators comes about afterwards because
of the assumed Hilbert space structure of the logic associated with the
logical σ-structure under consideration. In general the addition of
measurable quantities has no meaning for us except when these can be
replaced by similar measurable quantities which are defined on a common domain. This lack of meaning corresponds to the fact that in order
to give meaning to the addition of random variables they must be defined
on the same probability space. This is, of course, the case with compatible measurable quantities and it is not surprising therefore that the
addition of equivalence classes of similar measurable quantities corresponds to the addition of their representing operators. To show this
we start with the following observation. Let $G = \{g_k : k \in K\}$ be a frame
and let $\Phi = \{\phi\}_{j=1}^{\infty}$ be an orthonormal basis of $\mathscr{X}$ such that each g_k is
generated by a subset of Φ. Let f_j be the one-dimensional subspace
generated by ϕ_j, then $F = \{f_j\}_{j=1}^{\infty}$ is a refinement of G which is minimal
in the sense that $F_1 \leqslant F$ implies $F_1 = F$. Conversely any minimal refinement
of a frame is generated by an orthonormal basis of $\mathscr{X}$.

LEMMA (4.2) *Let* $A = \{a_i : i \in I\}, B = \{b_j : j \in J\}$ *be in* $\mathscr{F}$. *Let* $G = \{g_k : k \in K\}$
be the set of non-trivial subspaces among the subspaces $a_i \wedge b_j$, $i \in I$, $j \in J$.
If A *and* B *do have a common refinement then* G *is their greatest common*

refinement, that is G is a common refinement of A and B and if F is any other common refinement of A and B then $F \leqslant G$.

Proof. Let F be a common refinement of A and B. Let $C = \{c_t : t \in T\}$ be a minimal refinement of both A and B, for instance a minimal refinement of F. Then

$$a_i = \bigvee (c_t : t \in P_i)$$
$$b_j = \bigvee (c_s : s \in Q_j)$$

where P_i and Q_j are non-empty subsets of T. For fixed i and j write

$$x = \bigvee (c_u : u \in P_i \cap Q_j)$$
$$y = \bigvee (c_u : u \in P_i \setminus Q_j)$$
$$z = \bigvee (c_u : u \in Q_j \setminus P_i).$$

Then $x \vee y \leqslant z^{\perp}$ and so, by the orthomodularity of L,

$$x \leqslant (x \vee y) \wedge (x \vee z) \leqslant z^{\perp} \wedge (x \vee z) = x$$

Thus $(x \vee y) \wedge (x \vee z) = x$, that is

$$a_i \wedge b_j = (c_u : u \in P_i \cap Q_j).$$

This shows that G is a common refinement of A and B. It follows easily that G is the greatest common refinement.

When frames F and G do have a common refinement we denote their greatest one by $F \wedge G$. Note that one can define the concept of a minimal refinement in the general case provided the poset L is atomic in the sense that atoms exist and each element is the join of the atoms it contains. In this case a minimal refinement is just a frame all of whose elements are atoms. If, in addition, to being atomic the logic L is, in fact, a lattice then Lemma (4.2) and its proof remain valid in this more general context.

LEMMA (4.3) *Let P_x denote the projection onto the subspace x of $\mathcal{X}$. If F, G are frames of L then they have a common refinement if and only if*

$$P_f P_g = P_g P_f$$

for each f in F and each g in G.

Proof. If F and G do have a common refinement they have a minimal one and it follows that

$$P_f P_g = P_{f \wedge g} = Pg P_f$$

for each f in F and each g in G. Conversely suppose that P_f and P_g commute for each f in F and each g in G. Suppose that ϕ in belongs to f in F. If ϕ is in $f \wedge g$ for some g in G then ϕ belongs to $\vee \{f \wedge g : g \in G\}$. On the other hand if ϕ is not in $f \wedge g$ then

$$P_f P_g \phi = P_g P_f \phi = Pg \phi$$

and so $Pg \phi$ is in $f \wedge g$. Thus if ϕ belongs to f we have

$$\phi = \sum_G P_g \phi \in \vee \{f \wedge g : g \in G\}.$$

It follows that

$$f = \vee \{f \wedge g : g \in G\}.$$

Similarly

$$g = \vee \{f \wedge g : f \in F\}.$$

Thus the non-trivial subspaces among the $f \wedge g$ form a frame which is, in fact, the greatest common refinement of F and G.

We are now able to establish

THEOREM (4.2) *Let X in $\mathscr{R}(F)$ and Y in $\mathscr{R}(G)$ be compatible measurable quantities, then*

$$R^{s(X)+s(Y)} = R^{s(X)} + R^{s(Y)}$$

Proof. There is no loss of generality in suppose that X and Y are irreducible. In this case F and G have a common refinement and

$$P_f P_g = P_{f \wedge g} = P_g P_f$$

for each f in F and each g in G. The measurable quantity $X(F \wedge G)^* +$ $+ Y(F \wedge G)^*$ is defined on the frame $F \wedge G$ and so we have

$$R^{s(X)+s(Y)} = \sum_{f \in F, g \in G} (X(f) + Y(g)) P_{f \wedge g} = R^{s(X)} + R^{s(Y)}.$$

This is the desired result.

5. CONTINUOUS PHYSICAL QUANTITIES

In this section we indicate, briefly and in a non-rigourous way, how the discussion above must be modified to bring within its scope physical quantities which can take values on a noncountable Borel subset of the real line. There are at least two possible modifications, one of these we mention in the next section, but here we look at a procedure which mimics the one of the standard formulation of quantum mechanics. For this reason we retain the assumptions of the last section, namely that the logic L associated with the separable logical σ-structure has the structure of the lattice of subspaces of separable Hilbert space. We postpone for a later publication a detailed analysis of the matters we discuss here, within the broader framework of a general logical σ-structure.

Suppose then that $\mathscr{X}$ is separable Hilbert space and let R be a self-adjoint operation with spectral representation

$$R = \int_{-\infty}^{+\infty} \lambda \pi(d\lambda).$$

To each Borel subset B of the real line we can associate the projection P_b onto a subspace b given by

$$P_b = \int_B \pi(d\lambda).$$

Since

$$\int_{-\infty}^{+\infty} \chi_{B_1}(\lambda) \, \pi(d\lambda) \int_{-\infty}^{+\infty} \chi_{B_2}(\lambda) \, \pi(d\lambda) = \int_{-\infty}^{+\infty} \chi_{B_1}(\lambda) \, \chi_{B_2}(\lambda) \, \pi(d\lambda)$$

$$= \int_{-\infty}^{+\infty} \chi_{B_1 \wedge B_2}(\lambda) \, \pi(d\lambda)$$

we see that

$$P_{b_1} P_{b_2} = P_{b_2} P_{b_1} = P_{b_1 \wedge b_2}$$

and

$$P_{b_1 \vee b_2} = P_{b_1} \vee P_{b_2} = P_{b_1} + P_{b_2} - P_{b_1 \wedge b_2}.$$

Thus the mapping $B \to B^{\tau} = b$ has the properties

$$(B_1 \cup B_2)^{\tau} = B_1^{\tau} \cap B_2^{\tau},$$
$$(B_1 \cap B_2)^{\tau} = B_1^{\tau} \wedge B_2^{\tau},$$
$$(B')^{\tau} \quad = (B^{\tau})^{\perp},$$

here B' is the set complement in the real line of the Borel set B. Since

$$\begin{aligned}
(B_1^{\tau} \vee B_2^{\tau}) \wedge B_3^{\tau} &= \{(B_1 \cup B_2) \cap B_6\}^{\tau} \\
&= \{(B_1 \cap B_3) \cup (B_2 \cap B_3)\}^{\tau} \\
&= (B_1^{\tau} \wedge B_3^{\tau}) \vee (B_2^{\tau} \wedge B_3^{\tau})
\end{aligned}$$

we see that the subspace B^{τ} form a Boolean algebra of subspaces of $\mathscr{X}$. In fact this Boolean algebra is up to isomorphism, just the factor algebra of $\mathscr{B}$, the Boolean algebra of Borel subsets of the real line, modulo the sets of 'spectral content' zero, for if

$$\int_{-\infty}^{+\infty} \chi_{B_1}(\lambda) \, \tau(d\lambda) = \int_{-\infty}^{+\infty} \chi_{B_2}(\lambda) \, \pi(d\lambda)$$

then

$$\int_{-\infty}^{+\infty} \chi_{B_1 \cap B_2}(\lambda) \, \pi(d\lambda) = \int_{-\infty}^{+\infty} \chi_{B_1 \cup B_2}(\lambda) \, \pi(d\lambda)$$

and so

$$\int_{-\infty}^{+\infty} \lambda_{B_1 \ominus B_2}(\lambda) \, \pi(d\lambda) = 0$$

where

$$B_1 \ominus B_2 = (B_1 \cup B_2) \setminus (B_1 \cap B_2)$$

is the symmetric difference of the sets B_1, B_2.

If X is a real-valued Borel measurable function on the real line we can associate with it the self-adjoint operator

$$X(R) = \int_{-\infty}^{+\infty} X(\lambda) \, \pi(d\lambda),$$

in this way operators become replaced by real-valued functions, in particular R itself becomes associated with the identity function $X(\lambda)=\lambda$. It is then possible, using the results above, to reformulate the model in such a way that an operator is represented by a measurable function on a Boolean σ-algebra of sets which is, effectively, a Boolean algebra of subspaces of the lattice L.

6. Some further questions

It should be noted that Theorem (2.1) does not establish the existence of congruent states on the physical system associated with a separable logical σ-structure. All that the theorem does establish is that when such states do exist they are equivalent to states of the associated logic L. This leads one to ask

QUESTION 1. *Does the logic associated with every separable logical σ-structure have at least one state?*

Because of a result in Finch (1969a) this question is equivalent to asking if every separable completely orthomodular poset has at least one normed σ-orthovaluation.

It is, of course, true that a physical system $\mathcal{G}$, as defined above, always admits states because if F_γ is a frame of L we can define μ_γ arbitrarily on F_γ provided only that it defines a probability measure on its component Boolean physical system. In particular $\mathcal{G}$ admits deterministic states, that is those for which the μ_γ take on the values 1 and 0 only. There are cases in which these deterministic states are not congruent. For instance, when L is the lattice of subspaces of separable Hilbert space it follows from a theorem of Gleason (1957) and a result of von Neumann (1932) that, excluding the two dimensional case, L admits no deterministic σ-orthovaluations. A simple and direct proof of this result is given in Bell (1966). It follows from Theorem (2.1) that, in this case, there can be no congruent deterministic states of $\mathcal{G}$. A similar result holds when L is a lattice and not just a poset, at least if one restricts discussion to normed σ-orthovaluations on L with the additional property

$$\mu(f) = \mu(g) = 1 \Rightarrow \mu(f \wedge g) = 1$$

This follows from a result of Jauch and Piron (1963). However there do exist orthomodular posets which admit deterministic orthovaluations, I

am indebted to Mr D. H. Adams for this comment. An example is provided by the orthomodular poset constructed in Adams (1969). Thus let $S = \{1, 2, 3, 4, 5, 6\}$ and let L be the set of all subsets of S which have an even number of elements. For X in L let $X^\perp = S \setminus X$, then $\perp$ is an orthocomplementation of L and, as is easily verified, L is an orthomodular poset. For X in L define $\mu(X) = 1$ if X contains 1 and $\mu(X) = 0$ otherwise, then μ is a deterministic orthovaluation on the orthoposet L. This leads us to ask

QUESTION 2. *What separable completely orthomodular posets admit deterministic σ-orthovaluations?*

Gleason's theorem referred to above determines all the normed σ-orthovaluations on the lattice of subspaces of separable Hilbert space, however very little is known about the more general situation discussed in this paper, this leads us to ask

QUESTION 3. *What is the set of states (if any) of the logic associated with a separable logical σ-structure?*

We remark too that little is known both about the structure of ortho-modular posets which are not lattices and about the structure of ortho-modular lattices. Recently Finch (1969a) has shown that if a completely orthomodular poset has completion by cuts which is orthomodular then the poset is, in fact, a complete orthomodular lattice.

Throughout the paper we have restricted our discussion to *separable* logical σ-structures, there is however not much difficulty in extending the discussion to non-separable logical σ-structures. The restriction of separability has been made here because we had in mind the quantum mechanical situation where the associated logic, being the lattice of sub-spaces of separable Hilbert space, is a separable completely orthomodular lattice. From the point of view of the probabilist however, the natural object of study would, perhaps, be the physical system associated with a non-separable logical σ-structure. Such a physical system in a given state would be just a set of probability spaces and the measurable quantities, which would be the random variables associated with these prob-ability spaces, could take on a non-countable number of values. The study of such a physical system would have an interest of its own, but the point we wish to emphasize here is that it provides an alternative to the procedure indicated in the last section. With this in mind we conclude with the very vague

QUESTION 4. *Does the physical system associated with a non-separable logical σ-structure have any relevance for quantum mechanics?*

Monash University

BIBLIOGRAPHY

Adams, D. H.: 'A Note on a Paper by P. D. Finch', *Journ. of Austral. Math. Soc.* **9** (1970), 63–65.

Bell, J. S.: 'On the Problem of Hidden Variables in Quantum Mechanics', *Rev. Mod. Phys.* **38** (1966), 447–452.

Birkhoff, G. and von Neumann, J.: 'The Logic of Quantum Mechanics', *Ann. Math.* **37** (1936), 823–843.

Bodiou, G.: *Théorie dialectiques des probabilités*, Gauthier-Villars, Paris, 1964.

Feynman, R. P.: *The Concept of Probability in Quantum Mechanics*, Proc. 2nd Berkeley Symp., Univ. of Calif. Press, 1951.

Finch, P. D.: 'On the Structure of Quantum Logic', *Journ. Symb. Logic* **34** (1969), 275–282.

Finch, P. D.: 'On Orthomodular Posets', *Journ. of Austral. Math. Soc.* **9** (1970), 57–62.

Gleason, A. M.: 'Measures on the Closed Subspaces of Hilbert Spaces', *Journ. of Math. and Mech.* **6** (1957), 885–894.

Gunson, J.: 'On the Algebraic Structure of Quantum Mechanics', *Commun. math. Phys.* **6** (1967), 267–285.

Jauch, J. M., *Foundations of Quantum Mechanics*, Addison-Wesley Publishing Company, 1968.

Jauch, J. M. and Piron, C., 'Can Hidden Variables be Excluded in Quantum Mechanics?' *Helv. Phys. Acta* **36** (1963), 827–837.

Kolmogorov, A., 'Grundbegriffe der Wahrscheinlichkeitsrechnung', *Erg. Mat.* **2** (1933), No. 3.

Koopman, B. O., 'Quantum Theory and the Foundations of Probability', *Proc. Symp. App. Math.* vol. VII *Applied Probability*, Mc Graw-Hill, 1957, pp. 97–102.

Mackey, G. W., The Mathematical Foundations of Quantum Mechanics Benjamin Inc., New York, 1963.

Ramsay, A., 'A Theorem on Two Commuting Observables', *Journ. of Math and Mech.* **15**, (1966), 227–234.

Suppes, P., 'Probability Concepts in Quantum Mechanics', *Philosophy of Science* **28** (1961), 378–389.

Temple, G., *The General Principles of Quantum Theory*, Methuen & Co. Ltd., London, 1934.

Varadarajan, V. S., 'Probability in Physics and a Theorem on Simultaneous Observability', *Commun. in Pure and Appl. Math.* **15** (1962), 189–217; correction, *loc. cit*, **18** (1965).

Varadarajan, V. S., *Geometry of Quantum Mechanics*, volume 1. Van Nostrand. Inc., Princeton. New Jersey, 1968.

von Neumann, J., *Mathematische Grundlagen der Quantenmechanik*. Springer, Berlin, 1932.

P. D. FINCH

ON THE INTERFERENCE OF PROBABILITIES

1. A PRELIMINARY LEMMA

LEMMA. *Let ρ be a positive real number. In order that there exist complex numbers ψ_0 and ψ_1 such that*

$$|\psi_0 + \psi_1|^2 = 1 \tag{1}$$

and

$$\psi_0\psi_1^* + \psi_0^*\psi_1 = 1 - \rho \tag{2}$$

it is necessary and sufficient that $2\rho \geqslant 1$. Moreover if $2\rho \geqslant 1$ and ρ_0, ρ_1 are non-negative quantities such that $\rho_0 + \rho_1 = \rho$ then there are solutions ψ_0, ψ_1 to (1) and (2) with $|\psi_0|^2 = \rho_0$, $|\psi_1|^2 = \rho_1$ if and only if

$$|\rho_0 - \rho_1| \leqslant (2\rho - 1)^{1/2} \tag{3}$$

Proof. If $\psi_s = |\psi_s| e^{i\beta_s}$, $s = 0, 1$, satisfy (1) and (2) then so do $\theta_0 = |\psi_0|$ and $\theta_1 = |\psi_1| e^{i(\beta_1 - \beta_0)}$. Thus there are solutions if and only if there are θ_0, θ_1 satisfying (1) and (2) with θ_0 real and positive. Moreover, when solutions exist, any solution is of the form $\psi_s = \theta_s e^{i\alpha}$, $s = 0, 1$, where α is real, θ_0 is real and positive and θ_0, θ_1 also satisfy (1) and (2).

Suppose then that θ_0, θ_1 satisfy (1) and (2) and that θ_0 is real and positive. From (1) there is a real β such that $\theta_1 = e^{i\beta} - \theta_0$ and substitution in (2) gives

$$\theta_0 [e^{i\beta} + e^{-i\beta} - 2\theta_0] = 1 - \rho. \tag{4}$$

This leads to a quadratic equation for θ_0 with roots

$$\tfrac{1}{2} [\cos\beta \pm \{\cos^2\beta - 2(1 - \rho)\}^{1/2}].$$

Since θ_0 is real we must have $2(1 - \rho) \leqslant \cos^2\beta \leqslant 1$, that is $2\rho \geqslant 1$, and this establishes necessity. To establish sufficiency one need only note that when $2\rho \geqslant 1$ a particular solution to (1) and (2) is given by

$$\theta_0 = \tfrac{1}{2} [1 + (2\rho - 1)^{1/2}], \quad \theta_1 = [1 - (2\rho - 1)^{1/2}].$$

Finally suppose that $2\rho \geqslant 1$ and that ρ_0, ρ_1 are non-negative with

Harper and Hooker (eds.), Foundations of Probability Theory, Statistical Inference, and Statistical Theories of Science, Vol. III, 105–109. All Rights Reserved. Copyright © 1976 by D. Reidel Publishing Company, Dordrecht-Holland.

$\rho_0 + \rho_1 = \rho$. There exist solutions ψ_0, ψ_1 to (1) and (2) satisfying $|\psi_0|^2 = \rho_0$, $|\psi_1|^2 = \rho_1$ if and only if there is a solution θ_0, θ_1 with $\theta_0 = \rho_0^{1/2}$ and $|\theta_1|^2 = \rho_1$. If such a solution exists then substitution for θ_0 in (4) gives

$$\cos \beta = (1 - \rho + 2\rho_0)/2\rho_0^{1/2} \tag{5}$$

But this implies that

$$(1 - \rho + 2\rho_0)^2 \leqslant 4\rho_0$$

and a simple rearrangement of this inequality gives (3). Conversely if (3) holds then (5) determines β. Since $\theta_1 = e_1^{\beta} - \rho_0^{1/2}$ we find that $|\theta_1|^2 = \rho_1$. This concludes the proof of the lemma.

2. THE PHENOMENON OF INTERFERENCE

The essential features of the phenomenon of interference of probabilities due to measurement can be discussed within a framework relating to two measurement procedures, A and B respectively, where the response to A can be either of only two possible results x_0, x_1 and the response to B can be any one of m possible results $y_1, y_2, ..., y_m$, $m \geqslant 2$.

The experimenter can carry out either of two sequences of measurements. On the one hand he may perform a sequence of n distinguishable applications of the measurement procedure B yielding a corresponding sequence of results $R_B = (b_1, b_2, ..., b_n)$ where, for each $k = 1, 2, ..., n$, b_k denotes that one of $y_1, y_2, ..., y_m$ which results at the kth application of the measurement procedure B. On the other hand the experimenter may perform a sequence of n distinguishable pairs of applications of the measurement procedures A and B, yielding a corresponding sequence of results $R_{AB} = ((a_1, b_1'), (a_2, b_2'), ..., (a_n, b_n'))$, where, for each $k = 1, 2, ..., n$, the ordered pair (a_k, b_k') denotes the result of the kth application of the pair (A, B), a_k is either x_0 or x_1 and b_k is one of $y_1, y_2, ..., y_m$. We write $R_{B'}$ for the sequence $(b_1', b_2', ..., b_m')$.

For each $t = 1, 2, ..., m$ let $N_B(y_t)$ be the number of times y_t occurs in the sequence R_B and, for each $s = 0, 1$ and each $t = 1, 2, ..., m$ let $N_{AB}(x_s, y_t)$ be the number of times the pair (x_s, y_t) occurs in the sequence R_{AB}. Then

$$N_{AB}(y_t) = N_{AB}(x_0, y_t) + N_{AB}(x, y_t)$$

is the number of times y_t occurs in the sequence $R_{B'}$.

The quantities $n^{-1}N_B(y_t)$, $n^{-1}N_{AB}(x_s, y_t)$ and $n^{-1}N_{AB}(y_t)$ are the corresponding relative frequencies of occurrence within the sequences R_B, R_{AB} and $R_{B'}$ respectively. Under suitable assumptions about the nature of the sequences in question we may suppose that as $n \to \infty$ these relative frequencies converge, in an appropriate measure theoretic sense, to corresponding probabilities $P_B(y_t)$, $P_{AB}(x_s, y_t)$ and $P_{AB}(y_t)$. Write

$$\Delta_{AB}(y_t) = P_B(y_t) - P_{AB}(y_t). \tag{6}$$

The content of the phenomenon of the interference of probabilities is that in general

$$\Delta_{AB}(y_t) \not\equiv 0.$$

This expression exhibits the fact that the A-measurements interfere with the B-measurements to the extent that the distribution of the results of the B-measurements depends on the presence or absence of the A-measurements.

3. THE WAVE ANALOGY

In some physical experiments it is claimed that the interference which occurs is like that known in the interference of wave phenomena. In other words the result of the interference of A on B is alleged to be *as if* there were, for each $t = 1, 2, \ldots, m$ complex quantities $\phi_0(y_t)$, $\phi_1(y_t)$ such that

$$P_{AB}(x_0, y_t) = |\phi_0(y_t)|^2 \tag{7}$$

$$P_{AB}(x_1, y_t) = |\phi_1(y_t)|^2 \tag{8}$$

and

$$P_B(y_t) = |\phi_0(y_t) + \phi_1(y_t)|^2 \tag{9}$$

In this paper we ask to what extent, if any, does the existence of such so-called probability amplitudes restrict the corresponding probabilities P_{AB}, P_B. Could it be, for instance, that there are, at least conceptually, cases in which the A-measurement interferes with the B-measurement in such a way that there cannot exist probability amplitudes ϕ_0, ϕ_1 satisfying (7), (8), and (9)?

To answer this question observe that (7), (8) and (9) are together equivalent to (7), (8) and

$$\phi_0(y_t)\phi_1^*(y_t) + \phi_0^*(y_t)\phi_1(y_t) = \Delta_{AB}(y_t), \tag{10}$$

where $\varDelta_{AB}(y_t)$ is given by (6). Assume now that $P_B(y_t)>0$ for each $t = 1, 2, ..., m$ and write

$$\rho(y_t) = P_{AB}(y_t)/P_B(y_t), \quad 1 \leqslant t \leqslant m,$$
$$\rho_s(y_t) = P_{AB}(x_s, y_t)/P_B(y_t), \quad s = 0, 1; \quad 1 \leqslant t \leqslant m$$

and

$$\psi_s(y_t) = \{P_B(y_t)\}^{-1/2} \phi_s(y_t), \quad s = 0, 1; \quad 1 \leqslant t \leqslant m,$$

Then (9) and (10) become

$$|\psi_0(y_t) + \psi_1(y_t)|^2 = 1, \quad 1 \leqslant t \leqslant m \tag{9'}$$

and

$$\psi_0(y_t) \psi_1^*(y_t) + \psi_0^*(y_t) \psi_1(y_t) = 1 - \rho(y_t), \tag{10'}$$

respectively. Moreover $0 \leqslant \rho_s(y_t) \leqslant \rho(y_t)$, $s = 0, 1, t = 1, 2, ..., m$,

$$\rho_0(y_t) + \rho_1(y_t) = \rho(y_t), \tag{11}$$

and (7) and (8) take the form

$$|\psi_0(y_t)|^2 = \rho_0(y_t) \,\&\, |\psi_1(y_t)|^2 = \rho_1(y_t). \tag{12}$$

Thus if probability amplitudes $\phi_0(y_t)$, $\phi_1(y_t)$ exist we have solutions to (9'), (10') and (12). From the preliminary lemma we must have

$$P_B(y_t) \leqslant 2P_{AB}(y_t), \quad 1 \leqslant t \leqslant m \tag{13}$$

and

$$[P_{AB}(x_0, y_t) - P_{AB}(x_1, y_t)]^2 \leqslant$$
$$\leqslant P_B(y_t) [2P_{AB}(y_t) - P_B(y_t)], \quad 1 \leqslant t \leqslant m. \tag{14}$$

Conversely if the probabilities P_B, P_{AB} satisfy (13) and (14) then there exist complex $\psi_s(y_t)$ satisfying (9'), (10') and (12), thus the desired probability amplitudes are given by

$$\phi_s(y_t) = \{P_B(y_t)\}^{1/2} \psi_s(y_t).$$

Thus in order that there exist probability amplitudes $\phi_0(y_t)$, $\phi_1(y_t)$ satisfying (7), (8) and (9) it is necessary and sufficient that the probabilities in question satisfy the inequalities (13) and (14) for each $t = 1, 2, ..., m$. It is, of course, quite easy to construct examples of probabilities which do not satisfy (13) and (14).

4. CONCLUSION

It is clear from the preceding discussion that one can formulate, at least at the conceptual level, measurement problems which violate the conditions derived from the preliminary lemma. For such problems the customary quantum mechanical formulation in terms of wave functions is inadmissible because the wave functions in question do not exist. It could be, of course, that the actual measurement procedures of physics are such that the conditions in question are never violated in practice. However it seems difficult to argue either that this must be so on a priori grounds or that, even though such a situation may be true now, it is likely to hold in all future experimental situations.

At any rate the import of the preceding discussion is that one cannot sustain a claim that the current formulation of quantum theory has *universal* application to measurement problems.

Monash University

DAVID FINKELSTEIN

CLASSICAL AND QUANTUM PROBABILITY AND SET THEORY

I have been trying to make quantum logical models of the physical world in the way McCulloch and Pitts [1] and von Neumann [2] made classical logical models of nervous systems. As a result my ideas about quantum logic and about the physical world have undergone a process of mutual adaptation.

My quantum logic has become (to put it in three words which will require several paragraphs each of explanation) relativistic, hierarchic and existential. My physical world is not one of objects or fields in space-time but one of actions, and not a plenum but a plexus.

1. RELATIVISTIC LOGIC

The symmetry of the elementary constituent of a network limits the symmetry of the network. For example the binary decision or flipflop whose lattice has the form of a diamond

is adapted for the construction of a checkerboard, which has the same symmetries, but not for the construction of a Chinese-checkerboard, which has the symmetry of a hexagon and is suited to a 3- or 6-fold decision, not a binary. Accordingly I seek a quantum logical element having the symmetry of the Lorentz group and a further element of logical structure reducing this to the rotation group in the way that the time-axis reduces the Lorentz group of space-time.

Mathematically the problem is trivial to solve. A quantum binary system with a 2-dimensional unitary space has the elements of structure of inclusion $\subset$ and complement $\sim$. The group of the inclusion relation

Harper and Hooker (eds.), Foundations of Probability Theory, Statistical Inference, and Statistical Theories of Science, Vol. III, 111–119. *All Rights Reserved. Copyright © 1976 by D. Reidel Publishing Company, Dordrecht-Holland.*

alone is essentially the Lorentz group. The additional element of structure of complement reduces this to the rotation group. This is much the justification that Weizsäcker [3] gave for building the world out of quantum binary elements.

Operationally this resolution is still implausible. It would seem that the operations required to verify the inclusion relation (production, detection, and comparison of counts) more than suffice already to verify the complement relation with no further physical agent.

But in fact this argument overlooks an important duality, that between production and detection. I call production processes channels)| and detection processes cochannels) |. The most primitive operational relation is then exclusion $|1)\perp)2|$, none of the systems from $|1)$ pass $)2|$; which requires no calibration of either channel. Only when calibration is provided is it possible to verify when all the systems from $|1)$ pass $)2|$, and indeed to establish an identification of channels with cochannels, $|1)=)1|*$. It is easy to see that the group of the exclusion relation is essentially the Lorentz group, and that the * relation reduces this to the rotation group. Moreover the addition of a clock defines both a time axis and, by permitting a calibration of the channels, a *.

Therefore I take the primitive logical element to be a system of channels and cochannels with an exclusion relation. The * relation is left relative. Since propositions are represented by normal projections (a projection obeys $P^2 = P$, a normal operator obeys $[P, P^*] = 0$) the concept of proposition too is relative. Insofar as the elementary decision is binary, time is as a child playing checkers (Herakleitos, Feynman).

2. Hierarchic Logic

The name quantum logic is widely used for what is only the quantum propositional calculus. The propositional calculus is the poorest part of logic. Any argument which involves counting or mappings or arithmetic uses the predicate calculus or set theory, which is hierarchic in that it describes entities of many orders of abstraction: elementary entities, sets of elementary entities, sets of sets, and so on, in a non-linear hierarchy.

The formulation of any theory of interaction likewise requires a hierarchic logic, dealing at least with pairs. Not all the apparatus of classical set theory seems necessary. For any finite number of entities the existential

∃ and universal ∀ quantifiers can be replaced by finite sums $\sum$ and products $\prod$, and this seems enough for physics. Because of this finiteness it seems appropriate to call this higher part of quantum logic a combinatorial calculus. Remarkably, all the combinatorial processes used in quantum many-body theory are already invariant under the relativistic transformations of the previous heading. The usual appearance of the * in the various commutation relations of quantum statistical mechanics is spurious. I have given a simple category algebra construction for quantizing the classical combinatorial calculus, suggested by work of Giles and Kummer [4].

3. EXISTENTIAL LOGIC

The propositions of the logic I have had to use concern actions not things.

Existence (process, morphism, becoming) is prior to essence (thing, object, being). Herakleitos saw deeper than Epikouros, Leibniz than Newton.

Here is one of the paths that took me to this decision. The theory of a field of F's distributed over a space of X's uses the logical exponential F^X (an F at every X). I tried, following Snyder's [5] important insight, to do quantum fields over a quantum space, an exponential of the kind Q^Q. It is easy to do C^C (classical field theory), Q^C (quantum field in classical space) and 2^Q (Fermi-Dirac ensemble or quantum set). But I am still unable to do Q^Q, and in this work anything possible at all has always been transparent. At present the quantum combinatorial calculus has sum and product but not the exponential, for which the quantization process fails. (I would welcome a theorem.)

Therefore I regressed from field theory to particle theory. But the same exponential arises there as a mapping of a quantum system on itself, a quantum dynamical process or action. Since actions exist, and I could not express them in terms of quantum objects, I had to give them at least equal status with objects. Then unity urged the elimination of primitive objects altogether.

In retrospect however an action physics is so suited to quantum theory and relativity, has been so clearly foreshadowed by so many philosophers, and is so much more unified than the object/spacetime formulation, that it seems odd it has not been tried before, if it has not.

Consider for example the process of measurement. In one and the same work von Neumann [6] proves the non-existence of one kind of hidden variable and the existence of another kind. The kind that does not exist sits out alongside the usual variables as a factor in a tensor or outer product; out in full view, so to speak. A more hidden variable would be more intricately twined with the other variables, so that the imbedding was only of the poset of propositions, not of the lattice. Thus the quantum poset for photon experiments with linear polarizers at multiples of $\pi/4$

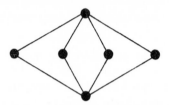

is imbeddable in the classical poset 2^4 of an object with four states.

The description of quantum mechanics in terms of a more hidden variable V of this kind is as follows: Although we observe $x, p, \ldots$ these do not exist. What exists is really V; but this is not observed. The variable V evolves deterministically between measurements. Measurement forces V into one of several sets. The seeming observables $x, p, \ldots$ are merely labels of these sets, and are thus created by the very act we inappropriately call measurement.

Such is my impression of von Neumann not Bohr-Heisenberg quantum mechanics. The poset of Hilbert subspaces is a subposet of the poset of Hilbert space subsets. Ψ is the more hidden variable. This creates the problem of measurement: how can the radically different measurement process be expressed as a dynamical evolution? It is easy to see that this elimination of measurement is not possible, and von Neumann instead pushed measurement back to a final irreducible measurement performed by the psychic person on the physical, the mind on the body.

This problem of measurement is peculiar to the forms of quantum mechanics which use Ψ as a more hidden variable with two evolutionary principles. In the form I use the question of how a production process affects Ψ is ill-formed. Ψ *is* the production process, Φ^* *is* the detection process. The wave function e^{ikx} describes not the electron but the whole process of production that makes an electron of momentum $\hbar k$. (It even looks more like a periodic diffraction grating than a point electron.)

The entities that exist are the entities that are observed: the electron and its x, p, ... The Ψ's are morphisms linking observer and system in a measurement just as the vectors of relativity are morphisms linking receiver and transmitter of signals. Ψ can be factored into simpler processes but not expressed in terms of objects. Objects are expressed in terms of Ψ's: the electron is that which is produced in a certain kind of process.

4. PHYSICAL PROCESSES

I am exploring a quantum dynamics in which any process is described by a network of elementary quantum processes or actions bearing a fundamental time $\tau \sim \hbar/40$ GeV and the fundamental action $\hbar$. The dynamical law is given by a single state vector for the network. The concept of time does not exist at the elementary level except in the pre-Newtonian sense of the occasion for action (Ecclesiastes 3). The Feynman amplitude for a process, and thus classical quantum mechanics, emerges in the first limit of long processes (many actions in sequence). This is the limit $\tau \to 0$, the limit of classical time. The Hamilton action principle, and thus classical mechanics, emerges in the second familiar limit of thick processes (many actions in parallel). This is the limit $\hbar \to 0$, the limit of classical action. The first limit has been carried out on a simple model to obtain Dirac's equation, and Maxwell's equation has a similar model. [7]

At present my assessment of the probability of this world picture is based on the qualitative features I have sketched and is not supported by any quantitative prediction. We still do not know how to compute cross sections or energy levels in this language. Before the problem was to bring relativity and quantum mechanics together. Now it is to get them apart. [8]

5. PROBABILITY

In view of the subjects of this conference I add a remark on how to go from Ψ as a production process to the more familiar use of Ψ as a probability amplitude. In experimental practice, calculations of theoretical probabilities are compared to reproducible and accurate measurements of currents, photographic exposures or other indicators of frequency of occurrence. Since these measurements are predictable and repeatable they are measurements of the eigenvalue of some dynamical variable or coordinate and are thus part of the yes-or-no logic of the theory. However these coordinates are ensemble coordinates and cannot be constructed in the propositional calculus alone. They can be constructed in the predicate or combinatorial calculus. Intrinsic probability amplitudes are only a poor man's combinatorial calculus. With an adequate logic there is exactly as little need for intrinsic probability in quantum as in classical mechanics. The statistical formula of quantum mechanics is a theorem, not an independent axiom. The kind of dispersion peculiar to quantum mechanics is already fully specified by the logical axioms: the properties of the exclusion and inclusion relations and the combinatorial process.

Yeshiva University

BIBLIOGRAPHY

[1] McCulloch, W. S. and Pitts, W. H., *Bull. Math. Biophys.* **5** (1943) 115–133.
[2] von Neumann, J., *The Computer and the Brain*, Yale Univ. Press, 1958.
[3] von Weizsäcker, C. F., *Naturwiss.* **20** (1955) 545.
[4] Giles, R. and Kummer, H., *Indiana U. Math. J.* **21** (1971), 91.
[5] Snyder, H., *Phys. Rev.* **71**, (1947), 38.
[6] von Neumann, J., *Mathematical Foundations of Quantum Mechanics*, Princeton Univ. Press, 1955.
[7] Finkelstein, D., Frye, G., and Susskind, L., *Phys. Rev.* D, **9** (1974), 2231.
[8] Note added in proof: For cross sections see Finkelstein, D. and McCollum, G., 'Space-Time Code. VI', (submitted to *The Physical Review*).

DISCUSSION

COMMENTATOR: Bunge: You seem to me to be adopting a process ontology of a most extreme sort. Can you really mean to say that the fundamental elements are processes, or changes, and not things? Surely when there is a change it is a change in some *thing*.

Finkelstein: Of course the theory must ultimately make room for the construction of objects. What matters here, however, are the basic entities from which one begins. In the past, we have always begun from things, and processes were regarded as mappings of things. Since the invention of categorical algebra, however, for which we shall be eternally grateful, we see that it is possible to begin from mappings (processes) and construct things. The basic elements in my scheme are processes, and things are interacting patterns of processes.

Bunge: But surely you are aware that in the standard interpretation of the predicate calculus one reads (x) Fx as 'Every object (e.g. thing), of kind K, has the property F (is F)'.

Finkelstein: Actually, nothing could be simpler than to offer a reformulation in the English language of sentences formulated in terms of objects as sentences formulated in terms of processes: after every noun word add '-process'. This is not a microphone, it is a microphone-process. Of course all such additions appearing uniformly throughout the language can be dropped: this is, after all, a microphone. Similarly, every physical law has an object formulation and a process formulation. The real question is: which is simpler? Now so long as both systems are infinite, it hardly pays to discuss the issue. But as soon as you get into finite cases then it is worthwhile considering the question. For example, are the natural numbers really multiplicative morphisms of the real numbers (i.e. do they come from the 'n' in 'x^n'?) or are the real numbers Dedekind cuts in ratios of differences of natural numbers? In one way you have reduced an infinite structure, in fact a continuum, to the process of adding one; and in the other way you have taken the process of adding one and explained it in terms of the infinite continuum. Both descriptions are perfectly legitimate, the only question in this case is which is the simpler, more perspicuous formulation of the system. In addition, for physical theories there is the further question of which formulation is in the closest correspondence with processes in the physical world. $(x)F(x)$ can also be used for "Every *process* of kind K has property F".

Caffentzis: I should like to put two questions. The first is this, although you have not explored here the formal development of your theory of logic and set theory, two things are clear: On the one side they would have a non-standard structure and on the other side your approach thus far has been heavily operationally oriented. This leads me to believe that you might well want to reject the notion of infinity. But at present there is simply no way to reconstruct the larger part of mathematics without recourse to this non-operational notion and so my first question is: What does happen to the reconstruction of classical mathematics within your non-standard, operational system? A second question is closely related: It seems to me that if you were going to alter quantification theory in the fashion you have suggested then the theory of relations will have to undergo substantial changes and I wonder whether you have explored what those changes are?

Finkelstein: They are two very good questions and rather than giving my answer in detail here, let me sketch a recipe from which you can reconstruct my answer at your leisure. I am struck by the analogy between the historical development of geometry and the historical development of logic. Both disciplines began as separate, well-defined subjects. And then geometry branched. We discover already by the time of Gauss that there is a mathematical geometry and there is physical geometry. And thereafter the mathematical theories of geometry proliferated into all of the mathematical theories which we have today. We came to see that the original development of our geometry was in fact based on our perception of the laws of *physical* geometry that happened to operate at the macroscopic, mansize level. These laws never turn out to be false, as long as they are formulated carefully with specified limits of validity. Even within mathematical geometry those original concepts never lose their importance: manifolds are built up out of tangent spaces, the flat spaces of our original euclidean perceptions. Likewise with logic: our original conceptions of logical operations were derived from our immediate experience at the macroscopic, mansize level. The objects in mathematics can be regarded as infinite masses in a certain constructive sense. Von Neumann pointed out how, if you begin with a finite computer subject to error, you will of course not verify the laws of arithmetic – we approach the laws of arithmetic by letting the size of our computer go to infinity, by multiplexing. And mathematics is a collection of statements of the form: What would happen if the following processes could occur? So there will never be a question of overthrowing a theorem in mathematical logic – that corresponds to the tangent space in geometry. For quantum logic also you can construct inner models and outer models, i.e. you can regard quantum logic as a bundle of classical logics each of limited domain, or you can imbed quantum logic in a richer classical logical structure and regard the quantum logic as a restricted portion of it.

About the theory of quantum relations: This is set up in 'Space-Time Code', *Phys. Rev.* **184** (1969), 126. The dramatic change is in the properties of the relation '$=$' (equality, identity) among quanta. Equality is represented by the symmetrizing projection in the tensor or Kronecker square. Equality is still symmetric and transitive but the meaning of reflexive is not as obvious for quanta, and the probability of the relation $a = b$, where a and b are similar quanta of multiplicity N, is not $1/N$ but $(N+1)/2N$.

S. GUDDER

A GENERALIZED MEASURE AND PROBABILITY THEORY FOR THE PHYSICAL SCIENCES

ABSTRACT. It is argued that a reformulation of classical measure and probability theory is necessary if the theory is to accurately describe the measurements of physical phenomena. The postulates of a generalized theory are given, the fundamentals of this theory are developed and possible applications and open questions are discussed. Specifically, generalized measure and probability spaces are defined, integration theory is considered, the partial order structure is studied and applications to hidden variables and the logic of quantum mechanics are given.

1. INTRODUCTION

Measure and integration theory lies at the cornerstone of modern mathematical analysis. It is no accident that the birth of modern analysis took place about the beginning of the 20th century, at the same time that Lebesgue's work on measure and integration originated [19, 17]. In the 1930's Kolmogorov [16] showed that probability theory is a special case of measure theory. Measure and integration theory has proved to be an important tool, not only in pure but also in applied mathematics. One need cite only a few examples – probability theory and statistics, communication and information theory, partial differential equations and quantum mechanics – to make a convincing case. As important as modern measure and probability theory is, there are indications that a re-examination of its basic postulates are in order. If measure theory is to describe accurately the processes taking place in finding lengths, areas, volumes, mass, charge, averages, etc., in practical situations and under conditions demanded by nature, its present structure must be generalized to include a wider class of phenomena than is currently applicable. In this introduction we will attempt to illustrate this contention.

Suppose we are making length measurements with a micrometer and that this micrometer is accurate to within 10^{-4} cm and can measure lengths up to one cm. Since we must round-off measurements to the nearest 10^{-4} cm, the micrometer in effect is able to give lengths only of the form $n10^{-4}$ cm, where n is an integer between 1 and 10^4. Let Ω be the interval $[0, 1]$ and let C be the class of subsets of Ω to which we can at-

Harper and Hooker (eds.), Foundations of Probability Theory, Statistical Inference, and Statistical Theories of Science, Vol. III, 121–141. All Rights Reserved. Copyright © 1976 by D. Reidel Publishing Company, Dordrecht-Holland.

tribute definite lengths. Now any interval of the form $[m10^{-4}, n10^{-4}]$, $m \leqslant n$, m, $n = 1, 2, ..., 10^4$ has the definite length $(n-m)10^{-4}$ so such intervals are in C. In the same way any interval of the form $[\alpha + m10^{-4}, \alpha + n10^{-4}]$, $0 \leqslant \alpha \leqslant 1$, $\alpha + n10^{-4} \leqslant 1$, $m \leqslant n = 1, 2, ..., 10^4$ is in C and has length $(n-m)10^{-4}$. We can also admit non-interval sets in C. For example, the set $[0, 10^{-4}] \cup [2 \times 10^{-4}, 3 \times 10^{-4}]$ is in C and has definite length 2×10^{-4}. Although the length of the set $A = [0, 1/2 \times 10^{-4}] \cup \cup [3/2 \times 10^{-4}, 2 \times 10^{-4}]$ cannot be accurately measured directly, we can measure its complement $[1/2 \times 10^{-4}, 3/2 \times 10^{-4}] \cup [2 \times 10^{-4}, 1]$ (we assume the length of a point is zero) and conclude the length of A is one. Thus $A \in C$. We thus conclude that C contains all intervals of the form $[\alpha + m10^{-4}, \alpha + n10^{-4}]$ as above together with all sets that can be obtained from these using the operations of finite disjoint unions (ignoring points) and complementations. Notice that C is not closed under formations of unions or intersections of two arbitrary sets of C. The length of any member of C must have the form $n10^{-4}$, $n = 1, ..., 10^4$.

Notice that if the length is to have decent properties we are forced to assume that C has the above structure. For example, suppose we were to assume that any subinterval of $[0, 1]$ is in C and that the length of a subinterval is that measured by the micrometer rounded off to the nearest 10^{-4} cm. We would then conclude that the length of the interval $[0, 1/3 \times 10^{-4}]$ is zero, for example. Similarly the lengths of $[1/3 \times 10^{-4}, 2/3 \times 10^{-4}]$ and $[2/3 \times 10^{-4}, 10^{-4}]$ are zero. If the length is to have the eminently reasonable property of additivity we would then be faced with the contradictory conclusion that the length of $[0, 10^{-4}]$ is zero. As another example of what can go wrong in this case, suppose we assume the length of $[0, 1/2 \times 10^{-4}]$ is one. Using additivity we would conclude that the length of $(1/2 \times 10^{-4}, 1]$ is zero and similarly the length of $[0, 1/2 \times 10^{-4})$ is zero so that the length of the point $1/2 \times 10^{-4}$ is one!

One might argue that the situation we have considered is unrealistic in that we have unduly restricted ourselves. We do not have to use micrometers with an accuracy of only 10^{-4} cm. We can, in principle, construct length measuring apparata with increasingly fine accuracy. We can then attribute to any interval an arbitrarily precise length, go through a similar construction as before (using countable unions instead of finite disjoint unions) and obtain the Lebesque measurable sets and Lebesgue measure on $[0, 1]$. Our answer to this argument is two-old. First, if we are to describe a particular measuring apparatus, we must be content with its inherent accuracy. Second, it is possible that nature has forced upon us an intrinsic limit to accurate length measurement. There is experimental as well as theoretical evidence [1, 3, 9, 13] pointing toward the existence of an elementary length. This would be a length λ (about 10^{-15} cm) such that no smaller length measurement is attainable and all length measurements must be an integer multiple of λ. If an 'ultimate' apparatus could be constructed which can measure this length then upon replacing 10^{-4} cm by λ we would be forced to a construction similar to the above.

There are, in fact, instances in nature in which an ultimate accuracy is known to obtain. It is accepted that the charge on the electron is the smallest charge obtainable. All charge measurements must give an integer multiple of e. If we think, for example, of a charge of $10^4 e$ as uniformly distributed over the interval $[0, 10^4 e]$ then a description of a charge measurement would begin with a construction similar to the above.

There are important situations in which the apparatus under consideration has inherent accuracy limitations. For example, all high speed computers have such limitations. The computer will accept only a certain quantity of significant digits and all numbers must be rounded-off to this quantity. Numbers are rounded-off with each internal operation performed by the computer which sometimes results in considerable round-off error. This type of phenomena also occurs in pattern recognition studies [24, 25, 26].

Another example of the above phenomena is motivated by quantum mechanics. Suppose we are considering a particle which is constrained to move along the x axis. According to classical mechanics, if we form a two-dimensional phase space Ω with coordinate axes x, p where p is the x-momentum of the particle, then the mechanics of the particle are completely described by a point in Ω. If we want to describe quantum mechanical effects, however, we would have to contend with the Heisenberg uncertainty principle [14, 13]. (This principle also occurs in wave propagation studies). This principle states that position and momentum measurements cannot be made simultaneously with arbitrary precision. In fact, if Δx, Δp are the errors made in an x and p measurement respectively, then $\Delta x\, \Delta p \geqslant \hbar/2$ where $\hbar$ is Planck's constant h divided by 2π. For this reason a point in Ω is physically meaningless since one can never determine whether the phase space coordinates (x, p) of a particle are at a particular point. The best one can do is determine if (x, p) is contained in a rectangle with sides of length Δx, Δp where $\Delta x \, \Delta p = \hbar/2$. Let us suppose our measuring instruments have ultimate precision so we can determine if (x, p) is in a rectangle of area $\hbar/2$. Physically these elementary rectangles in Ω become the basic elements of the theory instead of the points in Ω. Generalizing this slightly, we say that a set E is *admissible* if the area of E (strictly speaking, we mean the Lebesgue measure of E) is an integer multiple of $\hbar/2$. An admissible set E is one for which it is physically meaningful to say that $(x, p) \in E$. For simplicity, let us assume that Ω is a large rectangle of area $n\hbar/2$ where n is a large integer. Let us now consider the mathematical structure of the class C of admissible sets. First, it is clear that $\Omega \in C$ and also $\emptyset \in C$. It is clear that if $E \in C$ then the complement $E' \in C$. Further if E, $F \in C$ are disjoint then $E \cup F \in C$. Note, however, that in general if E, $F \in C$, then $E \cap F$ and $E \cup F$ need not be in C.

We hope it is now clear that to study certain diverse practical situations the basic framework of measure and probability theory should be generalized. This contention seems to be supported in the recent book by Terrance Fine [6] from which we quote:

The time is at hand for those concerned about the characterization of change and uncertainty and the design of inference and decision making systems to reconsider their long-standing dependence on the traditional statistical and probabilistic methodology.

Instead of considering measure spaces $(\Omega, \mathscr{A}, \mu)$ in which $\mathscr{A}$ is a σ-algebra of subsets of a set Ω and μ is a measure on $\mathscr{A}$, it may be useful to study structures (Ω, C, μ) where C is a more general class of subsets of Ω than a σ-algebra.

In this article we develop some of the fundamentals of this generalized measure and probability theory and introduce the reader to some open questions and possible applications.

2. GENERALIZED MEASURE SPACES

Let Ω be a nonempty set. A *σ-class* C of subsets of Ω is a collection of subsets which satisfy

(i) $\Omega \in C$;

(ii)   if $a \in C$, then $a' \in C$;

(iii)   if $a_i \in C$ are mutually disjoint then $\cup a_i \in C$, $i = 1, 2, \dots$;

where we denote the complement of a set by a'. A *measure* μ on C is a nonnegative set function on C such that $\mu(\emptyset)=0$ and $\mu(\cup a_i)=\sum_1^\infty \mu(a_i)$ if a_i are mutually disjoint elements of C. A *generalized measure space* is a triple (Ω, C, μ) where C is a σ-class of subsets of Ω and μ is a measure on C. If $\mu(\Omega)=1$, then (Ω, C, μ) is called a *generalized probability space*. The germ of this idea may be traced to P. Suppes [22]. Further studies are carried out in [10, 21].

We say that two sets $a, b \in C$ are *compatible* (written $a \leftrightarrow b$) if $a \cap b \in C$. A collection of sets A in C is said to be *compatible* provided any finite intersection of sets in A belongs to C. Compatibility is an important concept of this theory. Compatible sets correspond to non-interfering events in quantum mechanics.

Recall that a *measure space* is a triple $(\Omega, \mathscr{A}, \mu)$ where $\mathscr{A}$ is a σ-algebra of subsets of Ω, that is,

(i) $\Omega \in \mathscr{A}$:
(ii)   if $a \in \mathscr{A}$ then $a' \in \mathscr{A}$;
(iii)   if a_i is a sequence in $\mathscr{A}$ then $\cup a_i \in \mathscr{A}$; and μ is a measure on $\mathscr{A}$.

It is shown in [10] that a σ-class is a σ-algebra if and only if all its elements are pairwise compatible. We now give some examples of σ-classes that are not σ-algebras. By placing a measure on these (which can always be done in a non-trivial way) we obtain generalized measure spaces which are not measure spaces.

Example 1. The simplest σ-class that is not a σ-algebra is given as follows. Let $\Omega = \{1, 2, 3, 4\}$ and let C be the class of subsets of Ω with an even number of elements. Then C is a σ-class but $\{1, 2\} \cap \{2, 3\} = \{2\} \notin C$ so C is not a σ-algebra. It is easy to see that any pairwise compatible collection of sets in C is compatible.

Example 2. Let $\Omega = \{1, 2, \ldots 8\}$ and let C be the class of subsets of Ω with an even number of elements. Again C is a σ-class but is not a σ-algebra. In this example there are pairwise compatible collections which are not compatible; for instance $\{1, 2, 3, 4\}$, $\{1, 2, 5, 6\}$, $\{1, 3, 6, 8\}$ is such a collection.

Example 3. A generalization of Examples 1 and 2 is the collection of Lebesgue measurable subsets of the real line R with even measure. More generally let $\lambda > 0$ and let $\Omega = [0, n\lambda]$ where n is a positive integer. If C is the collection of Lebesgue measurable subsets of Ω whose Lebesgue measures are an integer multiple of λ then C is a σ-class but not a σ-algebra.

Example 4. Let $(\Omega_1, \mathscr{A}_1)$ and $(\Omega_2, \mathscr{A}_2)$ be (generalized) measurable spaces (i.e., $\mathscr{A}_1$ and $\mathscr{A}_2$ are (σ-classes) σ-algebras in Ω_1 and Ω_2 respectively). Let $\Omega_3 = \Omega_1 \times \Omega_2$ and let $C = \{A_1 \times \Omega_2, \Omega_1 \times A_2 : A_1 \in \mathscr{A}_1, A_2 \in \mathscr{A}_2\}$. Then C is a σ-class which is not a σ-algebra if $(\Omega_1, \mathscr{A}_1)$ and $(\Omega_2, \mathscr{A}_2)$ are non-trivial. We call (Ω_3, C) the *σ-class product* of $(\Omega_1, \mathscr{A}_1)$ and $(\Omega_2, \mathscr{A}_2)$. The construction can be carried through for any number of measurable spaces or generalized measurable spaces.

We say that two sub σ-algebras $\mathscr{A}_1$, $\mathscr{A}_2$ of a σ-class C are *completely noncompatible* if $A_1 \leftrightarrow A_2$ for every nontrivial $A_1 \in \mathscr{A}_1, A_2 \in \mathscr{A}_2$. The following theorem results from a simple application of Example 4:

THEOREM 2.1. (1) If $(\Omega_1, \mathscr{A}_1)$, $(\Omega_2, \mathscr{A}_2)$ are (generalized) measurable spaces there exists a generalized measurable space (Ω, C) and (σ-classes) σ-algebras B_1, B_2 in C such that B_1, $\mathscr{A}_1$ and B_2, $\mathscr{A}_2$ are isomorphic and $C = B_1 \cup B_2$. (2) If $\mathscr{A}_1$ and $\mathscr{A}_2$ are completely non-compatible in (Ω, C) and if $\mathscr{D}$ is the σ-class generated by $\mathscr{A}_1$ and $\mathscr{A}_2$ then $\mathscr{D} = \mathscr{A}_1 \cup \mathscr{A}_2$. Furthermore, if $(\Omega \times \Omega, C)$ is the σ-class product space of $(\Omega, \mathscr{A}_1)$ and $(\Omega, \mathscr{A}_2)$ then C is isomorphic to $\mathscr{D}$.

Theorem 2.1 does not hold for the usual measurable product of two measurable spaces. In that case the σ-algebra C is much more complicated than $B_1 \cup B_2$; in fact, C is the σ-algebra generated by the 'measurable rectangles' [12].

The sub σ-algebras of a σ-class are extremely important because they correspond to conventional measurable spaces and in quantum mechanics they represent classical experiments and single quantum mechanical quantities. It is important to know when a collection of sub σ-algebras is contained in a single sub σ-algebra. The next two results (Lemma 2.2 and Theorem 2.3) are due to Peter Warren. Theorem 2.3 is an improvement upon Theorem 3.1 [10].

LEMMA 2.2. If $A_1, A_2, ..., A_N$ is a finite compatible collection of sets in a σ-class C, then any set of the form $A_1' \cap ... \cap A_m' \cap A_{m+1} \cap ... \cap A_N$ where $1 \leqslant m \leqslant N$ belongs to C.

Proof. For $1 \leqslant m \leqslant N$ we have $A_1' \cap ... \cap A_m' \cap ... \cap A_N = (\bigcup_1^m A_i)' \cap (\bigcap_{m+1}^N A_i)$ (take $\bigcap_{m+1}^N A_i = \emptyset$ if $m = N$). Now $A_i \cup A_2 \in C$ by Lemma

2.3(i) [9]. Since $A_1 \cap A_3 \leftrightarrow A_2 \cap A_3$, applying Lemma 2.3(i) [9] again $A_3 \cap (A_1 \cup A_2) = (A_3 \cap A_1) \cup (A_3 \cap A_2) \in C$, so $A_3 \leftrightarrow A_1 \cup A_2$ and $A_1 \cup \cup A_2 \cup A_3 \in C$. By induction $\bigcup_{i=1}^{m} A_i \in C$. Applying Lemma 2.3(i) [9] again, it suffices to show that $\bigcup_1^m A_i \leftrightarrow \bigcap_{m+1}^N A_i$. Thus $(\bigcup_1^m A_i) \cap \cap (\bigcap_{m+1}^N A_i) = \bigcup_{i=1}^m (A_i \cap A_{m+1} \cap ... \cap A_N)$ which by a similar argument as above belongs to C.

THEOREM 2.3. If $\{A_\alpha : \alpha \in L\}$ is any compatible collection of sets belonging to a σ-class C, then this collection is contained in a sub σ-algebra of C.

Proof. For any positive integer n and any collection of indices $\alpha(1)...,$ $\alpha(n) \in L$ define $F_{\alpha(1),...\alpha(n)}$ to be the finite sub σ-algebra generated by the collection of sets $\{A_{\alpha(1)} \cap ... \cap A_{\alpha(m)} \cap A_{\alpha(m+1)} \cap ... \cap A_{\alpha(n)}: 0 \leq m \leq n\}$. Define $G_n = \{F_{\alpha(i_1),...,\alpha(i_n)} : \alpha(i_1),..., \alpha(i_n) \in L\}$. Note that $G_n \subseteq G_{n+1}$ and let $G = \bigcup_1^\infty G_n$. Clearly, $\emptyset$ and Ω belong to G and if $A \in G$, then $A' \in G$. Furthermore if $A, B \in G$, then for some m and n, $A \in G_n$ and $B \in G_m$. Let $p = \max\{m, n\}$. It follows that $G_m, G_n \subseteq G_p$ so that $A \cup B \in G_p$. Hence $A \cup B \in G$. Thus G is a subalgebra of C. Now let $M(G)$ denote the smallest monotone class of sets containing G. Applying Lemma 2.1 [10], $M(G)$ is included in C so $M(G)$ is a sub σ-algebra [12].

COROLLARY 2.4. Let $\mathscr{A}_1, \mathscr{A}_2$ be sub σ-algebras of a σ-class C. If $A_1 \leftrightarrow A_2$ for every $A_1 \in \mathscr{A}_1$, $A_2 \in \mathscr{A}_2$ then $\mathscr{A}_1 \cup \mathscr{A}_2$ is contained in a sub σ-algebra of C.

Let μ be a measure on a σ-class C. Let us briefly compare some of the properties of μ to those of a measure on a σ-algebra. Now a σ-algebra measure ν always satisfies $\nu(A \cup B) + \nu(A \cap B) = \nu(A) + \nu(B)$. Our measure μ also satisfies this condition when the left-hand side is defined. Indeed, we would then have $A \cap B \in C$, so by Theorem 2.3, A and B are contained in a sub σ-algebra $\mathscr{A}$ of C and the restriction of μ to $\mathscr{A}$ is an ordinary measure. Now a measure ν on a σ-algebra $\mathscr{A}$ is always subadditive; that is, $\nu(\bigcup_1^\infty A_i) \leq \sum_1^\infty \nu(A_i)$, for any $A_i \in \mathscr{A}$. We now show that μ does not necessarily have this property when the left-hand side is defined. Consider the following subsets of the real line: $A = [0, 4]$, $B = [2, 5]$, $D = [0, 1] \cup \cup [2, 3] \cup [5, 6]$. Let $C = \{\emptyset, [0, 6], A, B, D, A', B', D'\}$. Then C is a σ-class of subsets of $[0, 6]$. Define the measure μ on C as follows: $\mu(\emptyset) = 0$, $\mu(A) = \mu(B) = \mu(D) = 1$, $\mu(A') = \mu(B') = \mu(D') = 3$, $\mu([0, 6]) = 4$. Now

$A \cup B \cup D = [0, 6] \in C$ and yet $\mu([0, 6]) = 4 > 3 = \mu(A) + \mu(B) + \mu(D)$. A measure μ on a σ-class C is always sub-additive on two sets; that is, $\mu(A \cup B) \leqslant \mu(A) + \mu(B)$ for all A, $B \in C$ for which $A \cup B \in C$. Indeed, if $A \cup B \in C$ then $A' \cap B' = (A \cup B)' \in C$ so $A' \leftrightarrow B'$. It follows (Lemma 2.3(i) [10]) that $A \leftrightarrow B$ and so by Theorem 2.3 A, B are contained in a sub σ-algebra of C.

It follows from the non-subadditivity of the previous paragraph that a measure μ on a σ-class C cannot in general be extended to the σ-algebra generated by C.

3. INTEGRATION THEORY

In this section (Ω, C, μ) will be a generalized measure space, R the real line and $B(R)$ the Borel σ-algebra on R. A function $f: \Omega \to R$ is *measurable* if $f^{-1}(E) \in C$ for every open set $E \subseteq R$. If (Ω, C, μ) is a generalized probability space, measurable functions are usually called random variables. It is shown in [21] that the σ-class generated by the open sets of any topological space is a σ-algebra. It follows that the σ-class generated by the open sets of R is $B(R)$. One can then conclude that if f is measurable $f^{-1}(E) \in C$ for every $E \in B(R)$. If f is measurable we use the notation $A_f = = \{f^{-1}(E) : E \in B(R)\}$. It is easily seen that A_f is a sub σ-algebra. We say that two measurable functions f and g are *compatible* (written $f \leftrightarrow g$) if $A_f \cup A_g$ is compatible. It follows from Corollary 2.4 that $f \leftrightarrow g$ if and only if $f^{-1}(E) \leftrightarrow g^{-1}(F)$ for every E, $F \in B(R)$. A beautiful theorem due to Varadarajan [23] states that $f \leftrightarrow g$ if and only if there exists a measurable function h and two real Borel functions u, v such that $f = u \circ h$ and $g = v \circ h$; that is, both f and g are functions of the same function h. This theorem shows that compatible measurable functions correspond to simultaneously observable (or testable) quantities since to measure these two quantities one need measure only a single quantity. It is well-known that in measure spaces the sum of any two measurable functions is measurable. It follows that in a generalized measure space the sum of two compatible measurable functions is measurable. However, the sum of two noncompatible measurable functions need not be measurable. This follows from the general fact that C is a σ-algebra if and only if the sum of any two measurable functions is measurable [10]. One can show that the sum of two noncompatible measurable characteristic functions is never measurable [10]. However, there are noncompatible measurable functions whose sum is

measurable. For instance, two such functions would be $f(1)=f(2)=$
$=f(7)=f(8)=0, f(3)=f(4)=1, f(5)=f(6)=2; g(1)=g(6)=1, g(2)=$
$=g(4)=2, g(3)=g(5)=g(7)=g(8)=0$ in Example 2. The fact that the
sum of noncompatible measurable functions may be measurable could
be important if this theory is to describe situations that arise in quantum
mechanics. For example, in this case the total energy is a measurable quantity
which is the sum of the kinetic and potential energies the latter, in general,
being noncompatible measurable quantities.

If f is measurable then μ restricted to A_f is a measure on a σ-algebra.
Thus (Ω, A_f, μ) becomes a measure space and we define the integral
$\int f \, d\mu$ in the usual way. Let us discuss the basic properties of this integral.
It is clear that $\int f \, d\mu \geqslant 0$ if $f \geqslant 0$ and $\int \alpha f \, d\mu = \alpha \int f \, d\mu$ for any $\alpha \in R$. Also
if $f \leftrightarrow g$ then $\int (f+g) \, d\mu = \int f \, d\mu + \int g \, d\mu$. Of course, in ordinary integration theory on a σ-algebra the integral is always additive (unless $\int f \, d\mu =$
$=\infty, \int g \, d\mu = -\infty$ or *vice versa*). We now inquire whether this property
holds for our generalized integral.

We say that two measurable functions f and g are *summable* if $f+g$ is
measurable. We say that the integral is *additive* on summable functions
f and g if $\int (f+g) \, d\mu = \int f \, d\mu + \int g \, d\mu$ (unless $\int f \, d\mu = \infty, \int g \, d\mu = -\infty$
or *vice versa*). Now it is clear that if g is a constant and f is measurable
then the integral is additive on f and g since $f \leftrightarrow g$. As usual, a measurable
function is *simple* if it has only a finite number of values.

LEMMA 3.1 Suppose f is a simple function and g is a simple function
with two distinct values. If f and g are summable then $f \leftrightarrow g$ so the integral
is additive on f and g.

Proof. Suppose the values of g are β_1, β_2 and the distinct values of f
are $\alpha_1, \ldots, \alpha_n$. It suffices to show that $f^{-1}\{\alpha_1\} \leftrightarrow g^{-1}\{\beta_1\}$ since the general
case would follow from a reordering of the values. Since the values are
distinct $\alpha_1 + \beta_1 \neq \alpha_i + \beta_1$, $i \neq 1$ and $\alpha_1 + \beta_1 \neq \alpha_1 + \beta_2$. If $\alpha_1 + \beta_1 \neq \alpha_i + \beta_2$,
$i = 2, 3, \ldots, n$ then $f^{-1}\{\alpha_1\} \cap g^{-1}\{\beta_1\} = (f+g)^{-1}\{\alpha_1 + \beta_1\} \in C$ so $f^{-1} \times$
$\times \{\alpha_1\} \leftrightarrow g^{-1}\{\beta_1\}$ and we are finished. We can hence assume that $\alpha_1 +$
$+ \beta_1 = \alpha_{i_1} + \beta_2$ for some $i_1 \neq 1$ and $\alpha_1 + \beta_1 \neq \alpha_j + \beta_2$, $j \neq 1, i_1$. Again
$\alpha_1 + \beta_2 \neq \alpha_i + \beta_2$, $i \neq 1$ and also $\alpha_1 + \beta_2 \neq \alpha_{i_1} + \beta_1$ since otherwise $\beta_1 = \beta_2$.
Suppose $\alpha_1 + \beta_2 \neq \alpha_j + \beta_1$ for any $j = 1, \ldots, n$. Then $f^{-1}\{\alpha_1\} \cap g^{-1}\{\beta_2\} =$
$= (f+g)^{-1}\{\alpha_1 + \beta_2\} \in C$. It then follows that $f^{-1}\{\alpha_1\} \cap g^{-1}\{\beta_1\} =$
$= f^{-1}\{\alpha_1\} - f^{-1}\{\alpha_1\} \cap g^{-1}\{\beta_2\} \in C$ and again we are finished. Continu-

ing, we are finished unless $\alpha_1 + \beta_1 = \alpha_{i_1} + \beta_2, i \neq 1, \alpha_1 + \beta_2 = \alpha_{i_2} + \beta_1, i_2 \neq 1,$ $i_1, \alpha_2 + \beta_1 = \alpha_{i_3} + \beta_2, i_3 \neq 1, 2, i_1, i_2, \dots.$

Now it can be shown that the only solution of these n equations is $\beta_1 = \beta_2, \alpha_i = \alpha_j, i, j = 1, \dots, n$ so the proof is complete.

We thus see that the integral is additive on two summable functions if one of the functions has one or two values. The author has not been able to solve this problem in general. Thus it is not known, in general, whether the integral is additive on summable functions. However, we will later give a sufficient condition for this result to hold. Although it would be an important mathematical result if it were true that the integral is additive on summable functions, from a physical point of view it would not be so surprising if this result did not hold in general. Indeed, measurable functions correspond to observable operations. Now if two observable operations f and g are interfering, then even though the sum $f + g$ may be observable it will have no relationship to the original observations. Thus there is no physical reason to expect the average of $f + g$ to be the average of f plus the average of g.

Another basic question one may ask about the generalized integral is the following: If f and g are measurable and $f \leqslant g$ is $\int f \, d\mu \leqslant \int g \, d\mu$? Notice, even if $g - f$ is measurable and hence $\int (g - f) \, d\mu \geqslant 0$, since the integral may not be additive, we cannot yet conclude that $\int g \, d\mu \geqslant \int f \, d\mu$. The answer to this question is unknown. Nevertheless, if f, g are measurable, $f(\omega_1) \leqslant g(\omega_2)$ for all $\omega_1, \omega_2 \in \Omega$ and $\mu(\Omega) < \infty$ then we do have $\int f \, d\mu \leqslant \int g \, d\mu$. Indeed we then have:

$$\int f \, d\mu \leqslant (\sup f) \, \mu(\Omega) \leqslant (\inf g) \, \mu(\Omega) \leqslant \int g \, d\mu.$$

We now give sufficient conditions for the integral to be additive for two summable simple functions. Let f, g be summable simple functions with values $\alpha_1, \dots, \alpha_n, \beta_1, \dots, \beta_m$ respectively. If $\alpha_i + \beta_j = \alpha_k + \beta_l$ for $i \neq k, j \neq l$ then we call $(\alpha_i, \beta_j; \alpha_k, \beta_l)$ a *degeneracy* for f, g. If the values of f, g can be reordered in such a way that whenever $(\alpha_i, \beta_j; \alpha_k, \beta_l)$ is a degeneracy we have $i = l, j = k$ then f, g are called *symmetric*.

LEMMA 3.2. If f, g have no degeneracies then the integral is additive on them.

Proof. $f^{-1}\{\alpha_i\} \cap g^{-1}\{\beta_j\} = (f + g)^{-1}\{\alpha_i + \beta_j\} \in C, \quad i = 1, \dots, n, \quad j = 1, \dots, m$ so $f \leftrightarrow g$.

Although, as we have shown in Lemma 3.2, nondegenerate summable simple functions are compatible, symmetric functions need not be compatible. For example, let $\Omega = \{1, 2, \ldots 9\}$, $F_1 = \{1, 4, 7\}$, $F_2 = \{2, 5, 8\}$, $F_3 = \{3, 6, 9\}$, $G_1 = \{1, 2, 3\}$, $G_2 = \{4, 5, 6\}$, $G_3 = \{7, 8, 9\}$, $H_1 = \{2, 4\}$, $H_2 = \{3, 7\}$, $H_3 = \{6, 8\}$, and let C be the σ-class generated by these subsets together with the subsets $\{1\}$, $\{5\}$, $\{9\}$. Define the functions f, g by $f(1) = f(4) = f(7) = 0$, $f(2) = f(5) = f(8) = 1$, $f(3) = f(6) = f(9) = 2$, $g(1) = g(2) = g(3) = -1$, $g(4) = g(5) = g(6) = 0$, $g(7) = g(8) = g(9) = 1$. If we let $\alpha_1 = 0$, $\alpha_2 = 1$, $\alpha_3 = 2$, $\beta_1 = -1$, $\beta_2 = 0$, $\beta_3 = 1$, then $\alpha_1 + \beta_2 = \alpha_2 + \beta_1$, $\alpha_1 + \beta_3 = \alpha_3 + \beta_1$, $\alpha_2 + \beta_3 = \alpha_3 + \beta_2$. It is easily seen that f, g are measurable and summable so f, g are symmetric. However, $f \leftrightarrow g$ since $f^{-1}\{0\} \cap \cap g^{-1}\{0\} \notin C$, for example. It would be interesting to test the additivity of the integral in this case so let us place a measure on C. Define the set function μ_0 by $\mu_0\{1\} = \mu_0\{5\} = \mu_0\{9\} = 0$, $\mu_0(F_1) = 2$, $\mu_0(F_2) = 0$, $\mu_0(F_3) = 5$, $\mu_0(G_1) = \mu_0(G_2) = 3$, $\mu_0(G_3) = 1$, $\mu_0(H_1) = 1$, $\mu_0(H_2) = 4$, $\mu_0(H_3) = 2$ and extend μ_0 to μ on C. We then see that $\int (f + g)\, d\mu = 8 = \int f\, d\mu + \int g\, d\mu$ so we have additivity. Our next theorem shows that this always happens.

THEOREM 3.3. If f, g are symmetric then $\int (f + g)\, d\mu = \int f\, d\mu + \int g\, d\mu$.

Proof. We shall prove this theorem for the case in which f and g have four values $\alpha_1, \ldots, \alpha_4$, $\beta_1, \ldots, \beta_4$. The proof in the general case is similar but is encumbered by more indices. We can assume that $\alpha_i + \beta_j = \alpha_j + \beta_i i$, $j = 1, 2, 3, 4$ since if the functions have less degeneracy the proof is actually easier. Let $F_i = f^{-1}\{\alpha_i\}$, $G_i = g^{-1}\{\beta_i\}$, $H_{ij} = (f + g)^{-1}\{\alpha_i + \beta_j\}$, i, $i = 1, 2, 3, 4$.

$$\int f\, d\mu + \int g\, d\mu = \sum_1^4 \alpha_i \mu(F_i) + \sum_1^4 \beta_i \mu(G_i)$$

$$= \alpha_1 \mu(F_1) + (\beta_2 + \alpha_1 - \alpha_2)\, \mu(G_1) + \beta_2 \mu(G_2) +$$
$$+ (\alpha_1 + \beta_2 - \beta_1)\, \mu(F_2) + \alpha_3 \mu(F_3) + (\alpha_3 + \beta_1 - \alpha_1) \times$$
$$\times \mu(G_3) + \beta_4 \mu(G_4) + (\alpha_1 + \beta_4 - \beta_1)\, \mu(F_4)$$

$$= \alpha_1 [\mu(F_1) + \mu(G_1)] + (\beta_2 - \alpha_2)\, \mu(G_1) +$$
$$+ \beta_2 [\mu(G_2) + \mu(F_2)] + (\alpha_1 - \beta_1)\, \mu(F_2) +$$
$$+ \alpha_3 [\mu(F_3) + \mu(G_3)] + (\beta_1 - \alpha_1)\, \mu(G_3) +$$
$$+ \beta_4 [\mu(G_4) + \mu(F_4)] + (\alpha_1 - \beta_1)\, \mu(F_4)$$

$$= \alpha_1 [\mu(H_{12}) + \mu(H_{13}) + \mu(H_{14})] + (\beta_2 - \alpha_2)\, \mu(G_1) +$$

$$+ \beta_2 \left[\mu(H_{12}) + \mu(H_{32}) + \mu(H_{42})\right] + (\alpha_1 - \beta_1)\,\mu(F_2) +$$
$$+ \alpha_3 \left[\mu(H_{13}) + \mu(H_{32}) + \mu(H_{43})\right] + (\beta_1 - \alpha_1)\,\mu(G_3) +$$
$$+ \beta_4 \left[\mu(H_{41}) + \mu(H_{42}) + \mu(H_{43})\right] + (\alpha_1 - \beta_1)\,\mu(F_4) +$$
$$+ 2\left[\alpha_1\mu(H_{11}) + \beta_2\mu(H_{22}) + \alpha_3\mu(H_{33}) + \alpha_4\mu(H_{44})\right]$$
$$= (\alpha_1 + \beta_2)\,\mu(H_{12}) + (\alpha_3 + \beta_4)\,\mu(H_{43}) +$$
$$+ (\alpha_1 + \beta_4)\,\mu(H_{41}) + (\alpha_3 + \beta_2)\,\mu(H_{32}) +$$
$$+ (\alpha_1 + \alpha_3)\,\mu(H_{13}) + (\beta_2 + \beta_4)\,\mu(H_{42}) + (\beta_2 - \alpha_2) +$$
$$+ \left[\mu(G_1) - \mu(F_2) + \mu(G_3) - \mu(F_4)\right] +$$
$$+ 2\left[\alpha_1\mu(H_{11}) + \beta_2\mu(H_{22}) + \alpha_3\mu(H_{33}) + \beta_4\mu(H_{44})\right]$$
$$= \sum_{i<j} (\alpha_i + \beta_j)\,\mu(H_{ij}) + (\beta_2 - \alpha_2) \times$$
$$\times \left[\mu(G_1) - \mu(F_2) + \mu(G_3) - \mu(F_4)\right] + (\alpha_3 - \beta_3) \times$$
$$\times \mu(H_{13}) + (\beta_2 - \alpha_2)\,\mu(H_{42}) + (\alpha_1 - \beta_1)\,\mu(H_{11}) +$$
$$+ (\beta_2 - \alpha_2)\,\mu(H_{22}) + (\alpha_3 - \beta_3)\,\mu(H_{33}) + (\beta_4 - \alpha_4) \times$$
$$\times \mu(H_{44})$$
$$= \int (f + g)\,\mathrm{d}\mu - (\beta_2 - \alpha_2) \times$$
$$\times \left[\mu(F_2) + \mu(F_4) + \mu(H_{13}) + \mu(H_{11}) + \mu(H_{33})\right] +$$
$$+ (\beta_2 - \alpha_2)\left[\mu(G_1) + \mu(G_3) + \mu(H_{42}) + \mu(H_{22}) +\right.$$
$$\left. + \mu(H_{44})\right].$$

However, $F_2 \cup F_4 \cup H_{13} \cup H_{11} \cup H_{33} = G_1 \cup G_3 \cup H_{42} \cup H_{22} \cup H_{44}$ so the proof is complete.

Let us note that although the integral may not be additive, in general, on summable functions there are interesting, special situations in which it is. For instance, in Example 4, Section 2, it can be shown that two simple functions are summable if and only if they are compatible. As another example, let μ be a *point measure* on a σ-class C; that is, there is a point $\alpha \in \Omega$ such that $\mu(A) = 1$ if $\alpha \in A$, $\mu(A) = 0$ if $\alpha \notin A$ for all $A \in C$. Then the integral with respect to μ is always additive for summable functions. This same conclusion also holds if μ is a convex combination (finite or infinite) of point measures.

There is a simple basic property that breaks down as far as the generalized integral is concerned. Suppose f and g are measurable functions in the generalized measure space (Ω, C, μ) which are equal almost everywhere; that is, $\{\omega : f(\omega) \neq g(\omega)\} \in C$ and $\mu\{\omega : f(\omega) \neq g(\omega)\} = 0$. Is $\int f\,\mathrm{d}\mu = \int g\,\mathrm{d}\mu$? The following example shows that the answer can be no.

Let $\Omega = \{1, 2, 3, 4\}$, $A_1 = \{1, 2\}$, $A_2 = \{3, 4\}$, $B_1 = \{1, 3\}$, $B_2 = \{2, 4\}$, $H_1 = \{1, 4\}$, $H_2 = \{2, 3\}$. Then these sets and $\emptyset$ form a σ-Class in Ω. Define a measure μ on C by $\mu(A_1)=\mu(B_2)=1$, $\mu(A_2)=\mu(B_1)=2$, $\mu(H_1)=3$, $\mu(H_2)=0$. Then the characteristic functions χ_{A_2}, χ_{B_2} are equal almost everywhere but $\int \chi_{A_2}\,d\mu=2\neq1=\int \chi_{B_2}\,d\mu$.

We close this section by noting that quantization effects seem to occur naturally in this theory. For instance, consider our quantum mechanical example in Section 1. If f is a measurable function and α a value of f then $f^{-1}(\{\alpha\})$ has area $n\hbar/2$ where n is a nonzero integer. Thus f can have only finitely many values. Suppose now that the particle is not constrained to a rectangle in phase space, then if f has finite expectation, we would conclude that f has finitely many values or a countable number of values which converge to 0.

4. Partial Order Structure of σ-classes

If $C=\{a,b,c,\dots\}$ is a σ-class then C is a partially ordered set (poset) under the natural order $a\leqslant b$ if $a\subseteq b$. Also C has first and last elements $\emptyset$, Ω which we denote by 0, 1 respectively. As in any poset we define the greater lower bound (denoted $a\wedge b$) and the least upper bound (denoted $a\vee b$) of a and b in the usual way. Now $a\wedge b$ and $a\vee b$ need not exist; however, if $a\cap b\in C$ or $a\cup b\in C$ it is easily seen that $a\wedge b=a\cap b$ and $a\vee b=a\cup b$. If $a\cap b\notin C$ (or $a\cup b\notin C$) we still may have $a\wedge b$ (or $a\vee b$) existing. For instance, in Example 1, Section 2, $\{1,2\}\cap\{2,3\}=\{2\}\notin C$ but $\{1,2\}\wedge\{2,3\}=\emptyset$. We say that a and b are orthogonal (denoted $a\perp b$) if $a\leqslant b'$. Notice if $a\perp b$ then $b\perp a$, and $a\cap b=a\wedge b=\emptyset$. However, $a\wedge b=\emptyset$ does not imply $a\perp b$. Indeed, in Example 1, $\{1,2\}\wedge\{2,3\}=\emptyset$ yet $\{1,2\}\not\perp \{2,3\}$.

If we let $'$ denote the usual complement then $(C,\leqslant,')$ becomes a σ-orthocomplemented poset [2]. That is, (1) $a\leqslant b$ implies $b'\leqslant a'$, (2) $a''=a$, (3) $a\vee a'=1$, (4) if $a_i\perp a_j$, $i\neq j=1,2,\dots$, then $\bigvee a_i$ exists. Furthermore, we have the following result

LEMMA 4.1 $(C,\leqslant,')$ is a σ-orthomodular poset, that is, if $a\leqslant b$ then $b=a\vee(b\wedge a')$.

Proof. If $a\leqslant b$ then $a\cap b'=\emptyset$ so $a\cup b'\in C$. Hence $b\cap a'=(a\cup b')'\in C$ so $b\wedge a'=b\cap a'$. Since $a\cap(b\cap a')=\emptyset$ we have $a\cup(b\cap a')\in C$ so $a\vee(b\wedge a')=a\cup(b\cap a')=b$.

Now it seems that a σ-class C has, in general, no further partial order properties than its being a σ-orthomodular poset. For example, C need not be a lattice (a poset in which $a \wedge b$ and $a \vee b$ always exist). Even σ-classes which are lattices need not be distributive and hence cannot be Boolean algebras [2]. Indeed, Example 1 is a lattice, but $\{1, 2\} \vee (\{1, 3\} \wedge \wedge \{3, 4\}) = \emptyset$ and $(\{1, 2\} \vee \{1, 3\}) \wedge (\{1, 2\} \vee \{3, 4\}) = \{1, 2, 3, 4\}$. Also σ-classes that are lattices need not have the weaker property of modularity [2]. For example, let $\mathscr{A}_1$, $\mathscr{A}_2$ be the σ-algebras of all subsets of $\{1, 2, 3\}$ and $\{1, 2\}$ respectively and let C be the σ-class product $\mathscr{A}_1 \times \mathscr{A}_2$. Let

$$a = \{(1, 1), (1, 2)\}, \, b = \{(1, 1), (2, 1), (3, 1)\}$$
$$c = \{(1, 1), (1, 2), (2, 2)\}. \text{ Then } a \leqslant c, \text{ but}$$
$$a \vee (b \wedge c) = a \neq c = (a \vee b) \wedge c.$$

In the next section we shall give an example of a σ-orthomodular poset which is not isomorphic to a σ-class. We now give an answer to the question of when a σ-orthomodular poset is (isomorphic to) a σ-class. A *state* on a σ-orthomodular poset P is a map m from P to the real unit interval $[0, 1]$ that satisfies (1) $m(1) = 1$, (2) $m(\vee a_i) = \sum m(a_i)$ if $a_i \leqslant a_j'$, $i \neq j = 1, 2, \ldots$. A state is *dispersion-free* if its only values are 0 and 1. A set of states M on P is *order determining* if $m(a) \leqslant m(b)$ for all $m \in M$ implies $a \leqslant b$.

THEOREM 4.2. A σ-orthomodular poset P is isomorphic to a σ-class if and only if the set S of dispersion-free states on P is order determining. In this case P is isomorphic to a σ-class of subsets of S.

Proof. Suppose P is isomorphic to a σ-class C of subsets of Ω under the isomorphism $\phi : P \to C$. Suppose $a, b \in P$ and $m(a) \leqslant m(b)$ for all $m \in S$. In particular if $\omega \in \phi(a)$ and μ_ω is the point of measure at ω then $c \to \mu_\omega(\phi(c))$ is a dispersion-free state so $\mu_\omega(\phi(a)) \leqslant \mu_\omega(\phi(b))$. Hence $\omega \in \phi(b)$ and $\phi(a) \leqslant \phi(b)$. It follows that $a \leqslant b$ so S is order-determining. Conversely, suppose S is order-determining. Let h be the map from P to the collection of subsets of S defined by $h(a) = \{m \in S : m(a) = 1\}$ and let C be the range of h. We first show C is a σ-class. Now $S = h(1)$ and $\phi = h(0)$ so S, $\emptyset \in C$. For $h(a) \in C$ we have $h(a)' = h(a') \in C$. Also if $h(a_i)$ are mutually disjoint we have $\bigcup_1^\infty h(a_i) = h(\vee a_i) \in C$. Now we already have that h preserves $'$. If $a \leqslant b$ then clearly $h(a) \leqslant h(b)$. To show h is one-one suppose $a \neq b$. Since S is order-determining, there is an $m \in S$ such that $m(a) \neq m(b)$. Thus

$m(a)=1$, $m(b)=0$, or *vice versa*, so $h(a)\neq h(b)$. Finally, if $h(a)\leqslant h(b)$, then $m(a)\leqslant m(b)$ for all $m\in S$ and hence $a\leqslant b$.

If S is not order-determining (in the next section we give an example in which $S=\emptyset$; there are even examples of σ-orthomodular lattices with no states [8]), then P cannot be isomorphic to a σ-class. However, we now give a weaker result that is the analogue of Loomis' theorem [18] which states that a Boolean σ-algebra is a σ-homomorphic image of a σ-algebra of subsets.

THEOREM 4.3. *A σ-orthocomplemented poset P is a one-one σ-homomorphic image of some σ-class of subsets.*

Proof. Let Ω be the collection of all maps from P into $\{0,1\}$ R such that $\omega(a')=1-\omega(a)$ for all $a\in P$. Let $\phi(a)=\{\omega\in\Omega:\omega(a)=1\}$, $a\in P$. The family C consisting of Ω, $\emptyset$ and $\{\phi(a):a\in P\}$ is a σ-class. Indeed, $\phi(a)'=\phi(a')\in C$ for all $a\in P$. Now $\phi(a)\cap\phi(b)=\emptyset$ if and only if $a=b'$. Therefore, $\phi(a_i)$ $i=$ $=1,2,...$, are mutually disjoint if and only if i runs through the set $\{1,2\}$ with $a_1=a_2'$. Thus $\bigcup\phi(a_i)=\phi(a_1)\cup\phi(a_2)=\Omega\in C$. Now define $h:C\to P$ by $h(\Omega)=1$, $h(\emptyset)=0$, $h(\phi(a))=a$, $a\in P$. It is easy to check, that ϕ is a one-one σ-homomorphism.

5. APPLICATIONS TO QUANTUM MECHANICS

In general axiomatic quantum mechanics the set of propositions for a quantum system is taken to be a σ-orthomodular poset or lattice [14, 20, 23] $P=\{a,b,c,...\}$. The quantum states on P are states as defined in the previous section. The quantum observables are defined to be σ-homomorphisms from the real Borel sets $B(R)$ to P. Two propositions a, $b\in P$ are said to be *compatible* if there are mutually disjoint elements a_1, b_1, c such that $a=a_1\vee c$, $b=b_1\vee c$. Now we see that a σ-class C is a special case of a quantum propositional system and that quantum states correspond to probability measures on C. Furthermore it can be shown [10] that the two definitions of compatibility are equivalent on C. Finally, it follows from a theorem due to Sikorsky-Varadarajan [23] that if $x:B(R)\to C$ is an observable then there is a unique measurable function $f:\Omega\to R$ such that $x(E)=f^{-1}(E)$ for all $E\in B(R)$. Thus our generalized probability theory can be viewed as a particular instance of a quantum propositional system and all our measure theoretic constructs such as measures, compatibility, measurable functions, correspond to important quantum mechanical notions. Now the distinguishing feature of σ-classes among the general σ-orthomodular posets is that σ-classes have an order-determining set of dispersion-free states. This might be interpreted as corresponding to the existence of 'hidden variables' in the theory [4, 11, 14, 15]. This corresponds to what hidden variable proponents seem to be advocating. In this theory the existence of many dispersion-free states means that there is determinism in the sense that exact predictions can be made. On the other hand interference effects and noncompatibility are still possible. We feel that a generalized probability theory may give a useful model for quantum mechanics. For instance a measurable function in Example 3 must have discrete values so a 'quantization' effect already appears.

Now conventional quantum mechanics is also a special case of a quantum propositional system. In conventional quantum mechanics [14, 20 23] the quantum propositions are taken to be the σ-orthomodular lattice $L(H)$ of closed subspaces (or equivalently, orthogonal projections) of a separable complex Hilbert space H. The order is defined as subspace inclusion and the complement is taken to be the orthogonal complement. An observable is now a projection-value measure $x: B(R) \to L(H)$ which by the spectral theorem [5] corresponds to a unique self-adjoint operator $A = \int \lambda x(d\lambda)$. It follows from a theorem due to A. Gleason [7] that corresponding to every state m on $L(H)$ (if $\dim H > 2$) there is a unique positive trace class operator T on H such that $m(P) = \mathrm{tr}(TP)$ for all $P \in L(H)$.

Probably the simplest quantum system is a photon. This system, in conventional quantum theory, is represented by a two-dimensional Hilbert space H_2. It is easily seen that $L(H_2)$ is isomorphic to a σ-class product $\Pi\{C_i : i \in [0, 1]\}$ where C_i is the 4 element Boolean algebra $i \in [0, 1]$. For dimensions greater than 2, however, $L(H)$ is not isomorphic to a σ-class.

THEOREM 5.1. If $\dim H > 2$ then $L(H)$ is not isomorphic to a σ-class.

Proof. If $L(H)$ were isomorphic to a σ-class then by Theorem 4.2 there is a dispersion-free state m on $L(H)$. By Gleason's theorem there is a trace class operator T such that $m(P) = \mathrm{tr}(PT)$ for all $P \in L(H)$. If λ_i and ϕ_i are the eigenvalues and orthonormal eigenvectors of T it follows that $m(P) = \sum \lambda_i \langle \phi_i, P\phi_i \rangle$ for all $P \in L(H)$. If P_{ϕ_j} is the one-dimensional pro-

jection on ϕ_j we have $\lambda_j = \lambda_j |\langle \phi_j, \phi_j \rangle|^2 = \sum \lambda_i \langle \phi_i P_{\phi_j} \phi_i \rangle = m(P_{\phi_j}) = 0$ or
1. Since $1 = m(T) = \sum \lambda_i$ we see that all the λ_i's are zero except one, so T
is itself a one-dimensional projection P_ϕ. Now if ψ is a unit vector we have
$|\langle \phi, \psi \rangle|^2 = \mathrm{tr}(P_\phi P_\psi) = m(P_\psi) = 0$ or 1. This is clearly impossible.

We can summarize some of our results by the following diagram.

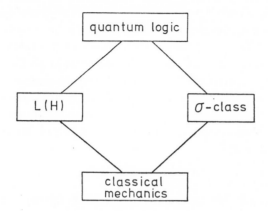

Thus, both the Hilbert space formulation of quantum mechanics and
our σ-class structure are special cases of quantum logics while classical
mechanics is a special case of both $L(H)$ and the σ-class structure. Also
$L(H)$ is not isomorphic to a σ-class unless dim $H = 2$. We can physically
characterize σ-classes and classical mechanics among all the quantum
logics. The σ-classes are precisely those quantum logics that admit hidden
variables while classical mechanics is precisely those quantum logics in
which all propositions are compatible. In this latter case the logic of classical mechanics is isomorphic to a σ-algebra of subsets of a phase space.
It is a major unsolved problem to find physical conditions that characterize $L(H)$ among all quantum logics.

Let us briefly consider integration theory in conventional quantum
mechanics. If A is a self-adjoint operator with spectral resolution $P^A(\cdot)$
and m is a state on $L(H)$ the *integral* of A *relative to* m is defined as $I(A) =$
$= \int \lambda m(P^A(d\lambda))$ when this quantity exists. Now unlike the σ-class case
two bounded self-adjoint operators are always summable. This is because
the sum of bounded self-adjoint operators is self-adjoint. Now there is no
physical reason for this to be the case. This happens only as a result of the

rich Hilbert space structure and we feel this is an accident of the particular theory of conventional quantum mechanics. We now ask whether the integral I is additive; that is, does $I(A+B)=\int \lambda m(P^{A+B}(d\lambda))=\int \lambda m \times \times (P^A(d\lambda))+\int \lambda m(P^B(d\lambda))=I(A)+I(B)$ for any bounded self-adjoint operators A, B (we consider only bounded operators to avoid tedious problems of domains and existence)? Now it is not at all obvious whether this is the case. However, using the deep theorem of Gleason cited above, we can show that this holds. Indeed, there is a trace class operator T such that $m(P)=\text{tr}(TP)$ for all $P \in L(H)$ so $I(A)=\int \lambda \text{tr}(TP^A(d\lambda))= =\text{tr}(T\int \lambda P^A(d\lambda))=\text{tr}(TA)$. Hence $I(A+B)=\text{tr}(T(A+B))= =\text{tr}(TA+TB)=\text{tr}\,TA+\text{tr}\,TB=I(A)+I(B)$. Again there is no intrinsic physical reason for this to occur and we feel it is an accident of the particular theoretical model. It may be that a more appropriate model for quantum mechanics might be formulated within a generalized measure theoretic framework.

ACKNOWLEDGMENT

The author would like to thank Loren Haskins for reading a previous version of this manuscript and correcting a number of errors. The author is also grateful to D. Schadach for pointing out some relevant literature.

University of Denver

BIBLIOGRAPHY

[1] Atkinson D. and Halpern, M., 'Non-Usual Topologies on Space-Time and High-Energy Scattering', *J. Math. Phys.* **8** (1967), 373–387.
[2] Birkhoff, G., *Lattice Theory*, A.M.S. Coll. Publ. XXV, Providence, R.I. 1967.
[3] Blumenthal, R., Ehn, D., Faissler, W., Joseph, P., Langerotti, L., Pipkin, F., and Stairs, D., 'Wide Angle Electron-Pair Production', *Phys. Rev.* **144** (1966), 1199–1223.
[4] Bohm, D. and Bub, J., 'A Proposed Solution of the Measurement Problem in Quantum Mechanics by Hidden Variables', *Rev. Mod. Phys.* **38** (1966), 453–469.
[5] Dunford, N. and Schwartz, J., *Linear Operators*, Part II, Interscience, New York, 1963.
[6] Fine, T., *Theories of Probability: An Examination of Foundations*, Academic Press, New York, 1973.
[7] Gleason, A., 'Measures on Closed Subspaces of a Hilbert Space', *J. Rat. Mech. Anal.* **6** (1957), 885–893.
[8] Greechie, R., 'Orthomodular Lattices Admitting no States', *J. Comb. Theory* **10** (1971), 119–132.

[9] Gudder, S., 'Elementary Length Topologies in Physics', *SIAM J. Appl. Math.* **16** (1968), 1011–1019.

[10] Gudder, S., 'Quantum Probability Spaces', *Proc. Amer. Math. Soc.* **21** (1969), 296–302.

[11] Gudder, S., 'On Hidden-Variable Theories', *J. Math. Phys.* **11** (1970), 431–436.

[12] Halmos, P., *Measure Theory*, Van Nostrand and Co., Princeton, N.J., 1950.

[13] Heisenberg, W., *The Physical Principles of Quantum Mechanics*, Univ. of Chicago Press, Chicago, Ill., 1930.

[14] Jauch, J. M., *Foundations of Quantum Mechanics*, Addison-Wesley, Reading, Mass., 1968.

[15] Jauch, J. M. and Piron, C., 'Can Hidden Variables be Excluded from Quantum Mechanics?', *Helv. Phys. Acta* **36** (1963), 827–837.

[16] Kolmogorov, A., *Foundations of the Theory of Probability*, Chelsea, 1950.

[17] Lebesgue, H., 'Sur les fonctions répresentable analytiquement', *J. Math. Ser.* **16**, 1, (1905), 139–216.

[18] Loomis, L., 'On the Representation of σ-Complete Boolean Algebras', Bull. *Amer. Math. Soc.* **53** (1947), 757–760.

[19] Lorch, E., 'Continuity and Baire Functions', *Amer. Math. Monthly* **78** (1971), 748–762.

[20] Mackey, G., *Mathematical Foundations of Quantum Mechanics*, Benjamin, New York, 1963.

[21] Neubrunn, T., 'A Note on Quantum Probability Spaces', Proc. *Amer. Math. Soc.* **25** (1970), 672–675.

[22] Suppes, P., 'The Probabilistic Argument for a Non-Classical Logic of Quantum Mechanics', *Philos. Sci.* **33** (1966), 14–21.

[23] Varadarajan, V., *Geometry of Quantum Theory*, vol. 1, Van Nostrand and Co., Princeton, N.J., 1968.

[24] Watanabe, S., 'Evaluation and Selection of Variables in Pattern Recognition', in J. Tow (ed.), *Computer and Information Sciences*, vol. 2, Academic Press, New York, 1967.

[25] Watanabe, S., 'Modified Concepts of Logic, Probability and Information Based on Generalized Continuous Characteristic Function', *Information and Control* **2** (1969), 1–21.

[26] Watanabe, S., *Pattern Recognition as Information Compression, Frontiers of Pattern Recognition*, Academic Press, New York, 1972.

DISCUSSION

COMMENTATOR: Finch: You state as your motive for not extending an algebra to a sigma algebra that no realistic physical meaning can be given to such extentions. It seems to me that on precisely the same grounds you ought to be willing to do away with points as the basis for integration theory as well.

Gudder: One of my main motivations in retaining points is to stick as closely as I can to classical probability theory in the hope that many of the theorems provable in that theory can be adapted here also (eg. central limit theorem, law of large numbers and so on).

Finch: But if you define your functions over subsets of a set only and if you give enough structure to sets of nested subsets then you can in fact show that you do have point functions and hence re-capture the point functions in this more satisfying way.

Gudder: One other comment is that the points do have physical significance in some circumstances. Roughly speaking, they correspond to the existence of hidden variables. If you have an admissible hidden variable extention of the theory then the resulting logic is isomorphic to the power set algebra of some subset of these points and so the points then come to be interpreted as dispersion-free states.

Finch: I should just like to point out that I commenced from very similar motivations to your own, in respect to doing away with sigma algebras, some years ago, my intention being, however, to also develop the integration theory without basic reference to points. I did publish some initial studies in this in 1962. I had hoped to apply this procedure, which I had carried out for the boolean case directly to quantum logic and indeed it was this which motivated my splitting quantum logics up into families of boolean algebras in order that the integration theory which I had previously worked out could be applied to the individual boolean algebras and, by summing appropriately, to the quantum logic. The complete work was not published, however, essentially because...

Lindley: I have two points concerning the relationship between probability, as the term is used in quantum logic, and its statistical usage. The probabilities used by statisticians are conditional probabilities: that is they are functions of *two* events, that under consideration and the conditioning event. Those considered by quantum logicians appear to be unconditional: that is they are functions of one variable, the event under consideration. My first question is: where does conditional probability enter into the quantum-theoretical treatment of probability?

My second comment is that some probabilists regard Kolmogorov's formulation of probability as too general and would like to restrict it in some way; for example, by introducing a topology into the space. In this way conditional probabilities can always be defined, whereas in the standard treatment they are undefined or not unique. (An excellent reference is *On the Mathematical Foundations of Probability* by Tue Tjur. Institute of Mathematical Statistics, University of Copenhagen, 1972.) My second question is therefore: do these considerations carry across to the quantum theoretical notion of probability? Gudder seeks generalization: Tjur seeks restriction.

Gudder: It is possible that quantum theorists are developing the theory in the wrong direction and that they should be trying to be more specific, rather than more general. But the overwhelming impression one gets upon reflection of the difficulties posed by quantum mechanics is that only by being more general will we be able to achieve deeper insight and more detailed applicability for the theory. As to the development of conditional probabilities, I have just begun to work on this problem. One would hope to obtain some kind of generalized, non-communitive Radom-Nikodym theorem which would provide the foundation for defining conditional probabilities. But to the best of my knowledge these theorems have not been proven, indeed there seems to have been relatively little investigation of the conditional probability structure on quantum logics at all.

Some relevant references to work on conditional probabilities in the context of non-commutative probability theory are the following:

Umegaki, H., *Tohoku Mathematics Journal* 6 (1954), 177.
Umegaki, H., *Kodai Mathematical Sem. Rep.* 14 (1959), 59.
Umegaki, H., *Proceedings of the Japanese Academy* 37 (1961), 459.
Nakamura, M. and Turumaru, T., *Tohoku Mathematics Journal* 6 (1954), 182.
Gudder, S. and Marchand, J,-P., *Journal of Mathematical Physics* 13 (1972), 800.
Recently, J. Wolfe and G. Emch have written a series of articles which are to appear in *Journal of Mathematical Physics.*

ELIHU LUBKIN

QUANTUM LOGIC, CONVEXITY, AND A
NECKER-CUBE EXPERIMENT*

1. Logics

METAPHYSICAL DEFINITIONS. An empirical *domain* is defined by a list of experimental *procedures*. I will require throughout that each procedure be 'factorizable' into a procedure of *preparation*, and the execution of a *test*. The ith procedure of preparation will be said to prepare the ith *state*. A *test* is clearly defined only if it has b specific possible outcomes, or '*bins*', numbered $1, ..., b$. A single *trial* of the test is an association of the procedure for preparing some state with the procedure for effecting the test. Then the bins must be so defined that precisely one of the b possible outcomes is selected as the actual outcome, of that trial. The process by which preparation of the ith state is coupled to execution of the jth test, to give a trial of *type* (i, j), must be empirically defined. Unless a method of coupling is procedurally given, the empirical domain has not been clearly defined.

The experimenter determines p_{ijk}, the probability that a trial of type (i, j) eventuate in bin k, out of the b_j possible bins of test j. This is done by rerunning the whole procedure, performing very many independent trials of type (i, j), taking p_{ijk} as the number of times bin k is selected divided by the total number of trials of type (i, j). Vicissitudes of statistical inaccuracy will be overlooked.

DEFINITIONS. A *logic* is a p_{ijk} function, i.e., a map $p:(i, j, k) \rightarrow p_{ijk}$ from triples of labels, conveniently integers, to non-negative numbers p_{ijk}. There are s state labels, $i = 1, ..., s$, and t test labels, $j = 1, ..., t$. The map p need not be defined for all st values of (i, j). For (i, j) where p is defined, the set of k for which it is defined is $1, ..., b_j$, the map $b: j \rightarrow b_j$ specifying the bin number of test j; formally, an integer-valued function. *Extension and restriction of a logic* are defined by extension and restriction of its p function. Restriction to fixed i yields a state, to fixed j, a test.

The suggestion that empirical domains outside the conventional scope

Harper and Hooker (eds.), Foundations of Probability Theory, Statistical Inference, and Statistical Theories of Science, Vol. III, 143–153. All Rights Reserved. Copyright © 1976 by D. Reidel Publishing Company, Dordrecht-Holland.

of 'physics' be attacked through quantum logics, is here limited to the logics familiar from systems of finite spin in atomic physics:

2. THE MATRIX FORMAT

The object is, given a logic, to associate a square n by n hermitean positive matrix P_i (eigenvalues nonnegative) to each state i and another such matrix A_{jk} to each bin k of each test j. The value of n is unknown. However, in the spirit of fitting with few parameters, one seeks a fit for the least n possible. The format requires $\mathrm{Tr}\, P_i = 1$, and $\sum_{k=1}^{b_j} A_{jk} = I$ (the n by n unit matrix), and $\mathrm{Tr}\, P_i A_{jk} = p_{ijk}$.

Classical logic is achieved by requiring the matrices to be diagonal. Therefore however strained and restrictive the matrix format may seem, it is an extension of classical logic.

3. STRUCTURE OF THE TESTS

Von Neumann's density matrices, the *state matrices* P_i, will have been recognized. The *bin acceptance matrices* A_{jk} are produced by considering mixed tests, parallel to the mixed states of Landau and von Neumann.

DEFINITIONS. A *sharp b-bin test* has associated a list $(P_1, ..., P_b)$ of b mutually orthogonal hermitean projections, which add to I. Let a general list $(A_1, ..., A_b)$ of b positive hermitean matrices which add to I be called a *b-plex*.

Convex combination of b-plexes $(A_1^i, ..., A_b^i)$ with coefficients $p_i \geqq 0$, $\sum p_i = 1$, is defined by $(\sum p_i A_1^i, ..., \sum p_i A_b^i)$. This is obviously also a b-plex.

METAPHYSICAL DEFINITION. This rule of convex combination fits physical *rouletting* of b-bin tests: Let there be several b-bin tests which are interchanged by a sneaky assistant, which register into the same final bins. He selects the test for each trial by, say, spinning a roulette wheel to produce a probability p_i that the ith test is presented.

Nature, e.g. through bin slopover, may frequently provide us with mixed tests rather than sharp tests. In a gross entry into an unexplored empirical domain, it would be folly to seek a fit with a constraint to sharp tests. Professor Finkelstein informs me that Robin Giles has already anticipated this point in the usual discussion of 2-bin tests. An interesting issue arises for b-bin tests, $b \geq 3$:

DEFINITIONS. A convex combination of sharp b-plexes will be said to be *undersharp*. The set of undersharp b-plexes (for fixed n) forms a convex body, the *undersharp body*. A b-plex which is not undersharp will be called *extraneous*. A 2-plex will be called a *question*, a sharp 2-plex a *sharp question*.

THEOREM. There is no extraneous question.

THEOREM. All sharp b-plexes are extreme points of the convex body of all b-plexes.

THEOREM. There exist extraneous b-plexes of n by n matrices, for all (b, n) with $b \geq 3$ and $n = b - 1$.

Should the matrix format be constrained to an *undersharp format* by requiring that only undersharp b-plexes be considered? I think not, for three reasons: First, questions are automatically undersharp. Second, it is difficult to computationally ascertain undersharpness. Third, it is possible that even in ordinary atomic physics, there exist extraneous tests. The issue of undersharp format versus general matrix format is a whole topic in quantum logic inaccessible from a study confined to the lattice of sharp questions, or to questions. In the longer manuscript, there are a series of results showing where undersharpness is a necessary consequence, which delimit search for an extraneous test.

4. A TRIVIAL SOLUTION TO VON NEUMANN'S METAPHYSICAL PROBLEM OWING TO DISCONNECTEDNESS OF HIS TESTS

The lattice of sharp questions $(A, I - A)$, A a projection, is disconnected into $n + 1$ components, associated with the dimension of the image space of A. Von Neumann felt that actual physical tests should not be so formally separated from each other merely by the format of the logic alone; this motivated his search for alternatives to ordinary quantum mechanics, e.g. continuous geometries. The trivial solution here, which applies to analogous disconnectedness of the set of sharp b-plexes even if $b > 2$, is to note that the body of all b-plexes, alternatively the under-sharp b-body, is of course connected. This is a metaphysical solution, because it is impossible a priori to decide whether a test defined by a practical procedure is or is not sharp, or more generally extreme, even though a quality of sharpness or mixity will become imputed to it in an overall fit of many states and tests by matrices.

5. Luxuries

The requirement that a certain state be a tensor product of lower-n states, or modifications of this theme in the manner of Bose or Fermi statistics, are luxuries. The propagation of states in time by Hamiltonians, or with entropy increase, or entropy decrease (friction), are also luxuries. The possible power of the bare $\text{Tr}PA$ format without luxuries is emphasized to the end that experimenters will be eager to gather data for fitting the bare format, without theories of the luxuries. A fit which would reveal familiar luxuries of ordinary quantum mechanics a posteriori would of course be very satisfying.

6. The positive cone and unitarity

Although $(P, A) \to \text{Tr } PA$ is a positive definite inner product in the real n^2-dimensional vector space of hermitean matrices, which suggests that the matrix format is invariant to a high-dimensional orthogonal group, it can be shown that restriction of the matrices to be positive cuts down the ambiguity of a fit to the usual unitary and antiunitary conjugations, provided there are enough states, tests, and empirical probabilities given.

7. Quantum psychology

This investigation started with the attempt to wed quantum logic with economics. The need for easy reproducibility of trials, involving re-fabrication of states, drives one to seek small systems which are already available in many copies, 'atoms'. The economic atom is the person, and so one is squeezed out of conventional economics into psychology. The ready availability of other copies of atoms and molecules may underly the early entry of quantum logic into atomic physics.

The inability to ascertain which slit an electron traversed after a trial of 2-slit diffraction *may* be in broad analogy to the inability of a person to analyze his own motives. There may be Heisenberg-microscope effects to explain the why of a Freudian unconscious mind, and why remembering dreams is so hard.

These are prejudices aimed at stimulating a choice of empirical domain likely to yield an interesting structure of quantum logic, but fortunately powerless to in themselves bias the mechanical fitting of data by matrices.

There is also the authority of Niels Bohr, who observed that complementarity would seem to have a natural place is psychology. David Finkelstein informed me in our first quantum logic conversation of his prior interest in quantum psychology. I know that the authority of Bohr is not enough, I myself having heard Bohr without effect, my suggestions here having developed only through my own reflections on economics, dreams, the matrix format, notions of a classical 'raster' with quantum-logical properties, and subtleties involved in the refutation of super-selection rules which are hard to summarize. If Bohr was not enough for me, the independent interest of Finkelstein, me, and probably Giles, will not likely stimulate the reader; I add one more argument:

It is *likely* that Darwinian evolution of consciousness has produced a system inaccessible to analysis except through quantum logic. The argument is that the stress of evolution lies more in the development of an instrument for control, than for the production of a classically real mental world image. Control involves interaction primarily intended to change or disturb the system interacted with, not the classically ideal measurement in which the system is negligibly disturbed. The images of reality closest to the center of control are therefore likely to have a non-classical structure, better fit by an analysis not itself confined to a classical format. It is therefore hoped that any establishment of quantum psychology may be a first step on a ladder to consciousness.

8. PSYCHOLOGY AND $n=2$

The easiest formal structure has $n=2$, a 'polarization'; the requirement of positivity is especially simple. It is therefore desirable to search among natural flip-flop psychological effects for material: An $n=2$ empirical domain might hopefully be discovered through its property of not having any b-bin sharp test without 0 matrices and with $b > 2$.

An obvious flip-flop phenomenon is a reversing 'optical illusion'. The reversals are perhaps inconveniently rapid, so that timing would be important, yet they indicate a possible near-instability which might accompany a desirable sensitivity.

Any reversing illusion could be used to define a state, by the subject's description of what he sees, or to constitute a test, when applied to a subject whose state is already regarded as having been defined. As a test, it is freely applicable to any subject. The criterion of state-test factorizability is well met.

It is possible that the obvious analogy to a plane-polarizing filter for light may be pushed: The polarizer yields alternative 2-space bases by being rotated; the reversing illusion could conceivably do something similar by merely being rotated in relation to the subject's eyes.

Necker Cubes. The sequence of Necker cubes illustrated suggests a continuous circle of concrete drawings. Each drawing may be seen as a cube

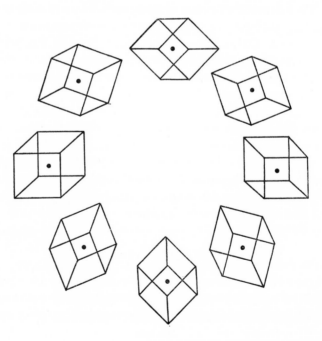

in two distinct ways; the ensemble of ways of seeing has the topology of a Möbius band. A way of seeing may be specified by drawing an arrow from the corner internal to the drawing seen as closest to the viewer, to the internal corner seen as furthest away. Thus, the cube drawn topmost is seen as either → or ←, the cube drawn bottommost as either ↑ or ↓. If a viewer starts topmost with interpretation →, and follows around the circle of drawings always choosing the smaller change from the preceding interpretation ('continuously'), then the viewer will upon returning to the topmost figure be in the state ←. The eight figures drawn provide sixteen states of viewers, represented by an arrow drawn at angle $h\pi/8 = \theta$ clockwise from →, with $h = 0, 1, 2, ..., 15$. Perhaps θ and $\theta + \pi$ (angles are meant mod 2π) are orthogonal. The rotation of the Necker figure through π may be analogous to the rotation of a 2-channel analogue of polaroid, say a Nicol prism, through $\pi/2$. The frequencies of response of a subject prepared in a state θ when presented with the view interpretable as either θ' or $\theta' + \pi$ may be, for the case θ', $(\cos(\theta - \theta'/2))^2$, for $\theta' + \pi$, $(\cos(\theta - \theta' - \pi/2))^2 = (\sin(\theta - \theta'/2))^2$, if the analogy to the polarization of light is perfectly simple.

However, these anticipations of a particular analogy with the quantum logic of the polarization of light, or any other particular anticipations of a structure of quantum logic, are happily not in the end important, *except as guesses for the fruitful selection of an empirical domain.* The program assures that only the state-bin frequencies gathered from the repeated trials of an extended experiment, and not any hypothetical anticipation, determine the final results.

For example, the procedures for preparing states could be more complicated than noting a subject's response to one view. Instead, a whole 'Necker movie' of views at various orientations, interrupted by queries as to which way the current view is seen, or even which way a previously projected view is imagined to have been seen, could be used to define states, different interpretation histories defining different states, different movie exposures or other conditions also defining different states.

A test procedure could be one last view and a query, or more of the more complicated 'movie' procedure. As long as the state selection procedure is readily coupled to the test procedure, and here the coupling is simply to first show the state movie, etc., *then* the test movie, the latter requiring at least one query, and as long as it is clear where the break is, similarity between the state and test procedures is no problem. The front-end state movies and queries and the sequel test movies and queries are clearly permutable.

I anticipate that timing is important, because of the phenomenon of spontaneous reversal of interpretations. How the timing of movie frames should be related to a subject's spontaneous reversal time or times, is something to be empirically decided in terms of a goal of maximal consistency of results.

I feel that, even aside from 'noise' from spontaneous reversal, slow movies will not prove interesting. This is because one can't help come to a definite interpretation of a Necker figure if one looks at it for some time. An interesting coherent superposition of states of mind for seeing the figure in either of the two possible ways can therefore be made unin-terestingly incoherent by a 'thinker' within the mind of the subject, whereas it is the goal of the experimenter to be studying the hopefully simple 'seer' here, without too much extra noise from a competing ob-server, his subject's own 'thinker'.

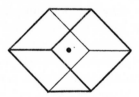

If natural biases, like azimuthal asymmetry of the retina, are not enough, then a biased Necker-cube figure could perhaps introduce a difference in propagation in time of the two competing 'states of mind'. This may be a way to introduce an analogue to the quarter-wave plate of optics, for exploring the full two-dimensional shell of pure states, or rather the three-dimensional ball which is their convex completion, rather than only the boundary and interior of a circle analogous to the linear polarizations.

Cheating. It is possible for human subjects to generate a falsely positive interference, for example, by precalculating a sequence of responses which would yield an interference effect, then reporting this predetermined sequence. Such 'cheating' involves correlation, through the overall guiding plan, of the supposedly independent trials. Other subjective predilections – a tendency to seek to be 'consistent', or to 'alternate' – could have such an effect, if one subject is used repeatedly as an example of the 'same state'. These might come up for an unsophisticated human subject, or even for an animal, so the ready availability of subjects unlearned in quantum logic need not absolutely guarantee a faithful experiment.

Nevertheless, the most obvious program would start without any concern about the matter of cheating, in which case even I could be regarded as an adequate subject. Only if evidence in fact appears in favor of quantum correlations, with such bad subjects, would it be sensible to explore the matter more carefully, in the directions indicated by the preliminary results.

Birds pretrained to peck at an unambiguously closest corner are possible nonhuman subjects.

Fitting Matrices. The proposed fit by matrices, whether for $n=2$ or other n, is through successive trial, to minimize the discrepancies between $\mathrm{Tr}\, P_i A_{jk}$ and the empirical p_{ijk}, e.g., by minimizing the sum of squares of these discrepancies.

For $n=2$, each matrix may be separated into a scalar trace part and a real 3-vector Pauli-matrix part. The matrices commute if and only if their real 3-vectors are collinear. Such would be a classical fit. A nonclassical one is one where the state and acceptance matrices show statistically significant non-collinearity. More interesting is a good nonclassical fit without a good classical fit in the same n (here, $n=2$).

It is difficult to see how a circle's worth of states labeled by θ, the anticipated states of subjects who have just reported the illusion seen in a particular way, could all lie on one line. Of course, a circle can be mapped into a line, but there would be special θ for which the image point on the line reverses its motion as θ increases, or else the whole image is only one point. This one-point image is a conceivable outcome, even though the state of seeing the θ-tipped figure at θ is empirically discriminable from the state of seeing at $\theta+\pi$, since it is not guaranteed that this discrimination can be realized in an $n=2$ format.

The foregoing makes it plausible that any fitting of the Necker-cube domain significantly better than random in an $n = 2$ format, will also be significantly non-classical.

9. SMALLNESS?

If a quantum logic is revealed in psychology by such experiments, it may be possible to argue that the effects follow from great magnification of triggering mechanisms on a very small scale. The form of such argument would rely upon the incoherence demonstrated by measurements which leave an important part of the system out of account. Even though psychological black-box experiments seem gross, what they probe has a fineness which is unknown unless the degree of magnification from thought to grossly observable response is also known. Even a voltage across a single cell membrane seems gross to me. Yet there are arguments to suggest a place for quantum logic on a thoroughly gross level: I have imagined a wave-function behavior of bulk matter vibrations; Finkelstein has written about switching-system models for experiments which disturb states. Exactly what a successful experiment means in terms of grossness or fineness may be secondary to the step on the ladder to consciousness established by the formal relationships between the matrices of a solution. The formal rules of genetics, for example, already gave the broad picture before the days of DNA.

10. SUMMARY

The main goal has been stimulation of experimentation. Incidentally, a Darwinian argument and a comment on dreams have been given to suggest the importance of a quantum approach to psychology.

On the technical side, convex completion of b-bin tests, $b \geq 3$, raises the issue of existence of extraneous experiments, perhaps even in ordinary atomic physics. Connectedness of a convex body provides a simple metaphysical alternative to disconnectedness of the set of *sharp* b-plexes, $b \geq 2$.

Representation of state-forming procedures and of bins of tests by matrices M, M',... with a natural dot product, $M, M' \to \mathrm{Tr}\, M M'$, is a new sort of 'factor analysis'. Very different laboratory procedures could produce nearly equal state matrices, etc.

ACKNOWLEDGMENTS

For my limited interest in economics, numerous conversations, a close reading of my recent manuscript, and the discovery of important mathematical errors, I thank my wife, Thelma Lubkin. David Finkelstein has been unusually kind in encouraging me, even though we disagree about whether reality is one or plural. (I am the pluralist.) Professor Hooker has helped by his policy of making the conference and these proceedings open to an outsider.

The University of Winconsin

NOTE

* This is a report of work done mainly in the fall of 1972, with the mathematical results almost omitted, but with the suggestion for experimental work tying quantum logic to visual perception done more leisurely. In part the following is excerpted from a book done June, July 1973, tentatively entitled *Schrödinger's Cat*.

NOTE ADDED IN PROOF

The existence of extraneous tests in ordinary atomic physics has been established; see E. Lubkin, *J. Math. Phys.* **15**, 663–672 and 673–674 (1974).

P. MITTELSTAEDT

ON THE APPLICABILITY OF THE
PROBABILITY CONCEPT TO QUANTUM THEORY

ABSTRACT. The classical concept of probability can be applied to quantum mechanical properties only if these properties are not objectivized. The objectivation of all, including incommensurable, properties leads to a contradiction with the theory of probability. However, it is shown in this paper that there is still another possibility to interpret quantum theory. The quantum mechanical properties can be objectivized if one takes into account this objectivity already in the foundation of logic and probability. The result is a restricted logical calculus and a generalized probability concept, which is consistent with the quantum mechanical formalism, even if it is interpreted as a theory of objective properties.

1. INTRODUCTION

The question whether the probability concept, which is known from the ordinary probability calculus, can be applied to the quantum theoretical propositions, cannot be answered on empirical grounds only. It depends partially on the interpretation which is used in order to connect the formalism of the quantum theory with the experimental situation. This will be demonstrated here by taking account of two alternative interpretations of the quantum theoretical formalism.

Let us consider a quantum mechanical system S (a nucleus, an atom, etc.) which is in the state $|\varphi\rangle \in H$. We restrict ourselves to observables $a, b, c, \ldots$ which correspond to projection operators $P_a, P_b, P_c \ldots$ which projects onto the closed linear manifold $M_a, M_b, M_c \ldots$ of the Hilbert space H respectively. The quantum theory then allows for the calculation of the so called 'expectation values'

$$p_\varphi(a) = \langle\varphi| \, P_a \, |\varphi\rangle$$

of the observable a in the state $|\varphi\rangle$, which can at least be interpreted in two ways:

(α) $p_\varphi(a)$ is the probability for finding the property a, i.e. the eigenvalue 1 of the operator P_a – after a measuring process for the observable a has been carried out, and a corre-

Harper and Hooker (eds.), Foundations of Probability Theory, Statistical Inference, and Statistical Theories of Science, Vol. III, 155–167. All Rights Reserved. Copyright © 1976 by D. Reidel Publishing Company, Dordrecht-Holland.

sponding transition of the system from the state $|\varphi\rangle$ to a state $|\varphi_a\rangle$, which is eigenstate of P_a, has taken place. (this will be called here the Copenhagen interpretation.)

(β) $p_\varphi(a)$ is the probability for the fact that the system S posesses the property a even before the measurement of P_a has been carried out. Here the objectivity of all possible properties is stated without any recourse to the possibility of observation. (This will be called here the 'objectivizing' interpretation.)

It is well known that the Copenhagen interpretation (α), which does not make any statement about the system before the measuring process has taken place, can be applied to the formalism of Quantum theory without problems. However the less restrictive interpretation (β), which maintains the objectivity of all possible properties of a system even in quantum theory, leads to contradictions with the theory of probability (Section 2). It will be shown (Section 3) that this contradiction can be resolved by means of a generalized probability concept. Similar to the foundation of the ordinary probability concept on the classical logic, this quantum mechanical probability concept can be based on a restrictive logical calculus, which has been called quantum logic. It turns out that the validity of this quantum logic is a consequence of the assumption of objectivity which has been used in the interpretation (β).

2. THE CONTRADICTION BETWEEN OBJECTIVITY AND PROBABILITY – THE COPENHAGEN INTERPRETATION

We consider a physical system S which is in the state $|\varphi\rangle$ and two observables a, b which correspond to the projection operators P_a, P_b respectively. For the sake of simplicity we are dealing here with a state-space of only two dimensions. In this case each of the observables a, b has two eigenstates, which we will denote by $|a\rangle$, $|\neg a\rangle$ and $|b\rangle$, $|\neg b\rangle$ respectively, i.e. we have the equations

$$P_a |a\rangle = |a\rangle \qquad P_b |b\rangle = |b\rangle$$
$$P_a |\neg a\rangle = 0 \qquad P_b |\neg b\rangle = 0$$

If the system S is in the state $|a\rangle$ or $|\neg a\rangle$, the system will be said to have the property a or $\neg a$ (not a) respectively. In general the state $|\varphi\rangle$ is not an eigenstate of P_b and $|b\rangle$ is not an eigenstate of P_a, i.e. $[|\varphi\rangle\langle\varphi|, P_b]_- \neq 0$, $[P_b, P_a]_- \neq 0$. In this case we have the decompositions

$$|\varphi\rangle = |b\rangle\langle b\,|\,\varphi\rangle + |\neg b\rangle\langle\neg b\,|\,\varphi\rangle$$
$$|b\rangle = |a\rangle\langle a\,|\,b\rangle + |\neg a\rangle\langle\neg a\,|\,b\rangle$$

As an experimental situation, for which these equations become relevant, we could think of an idealized two-slit-experiment, in which subsequent measurements of the observable b and a are carried out at a system which was primarily in the state $|\varphi\rangle$ [1, 2].

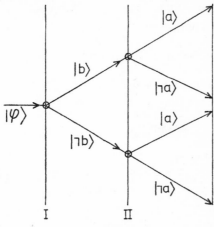

Fig. 1.

In the schematic diagram (Figure 1) it is assumed that in the measuring process I the observable b, and in the process II the observable a, is measured. In the time development of the system each measuring process corresponds to a branching point with two alternative possibilities.

In the framework of this thought-experiment, we can form the expectation values

$$\langle\varphi|\,P_b\,|\varphi\rangle = p_\varphi(b) \qquad\qquad \langle b|\,P_a\,|b\rangle = p_b(a)$$
$$\langle\varphi|\,P_{\neg b}\,|\varphi\rangle = p_\varphi(\neg b) \qquad \langle\neg b|\,P_a\,|\neg b\rangle = p_{\neg b}(a)$$

which can be interpreted as probabilities as follows:

$p_\varphi(b) =$ probability for the system S to have the property b, if previously the system has been in the state $|\varphi\rangle$.

$p_b(a) =$ probability for the system S to have the property a, if previously the property b has been stated.

The expressions $p_\varphi(\neg b)$ and $p_{\neg b}(a)$ can be interpreted in a similar way. Very important for the following discussion are the combined probabilities

$$p_\varphi(a, b) = \quad \langle\varphi|\, P_b P_a P_b\, |\varphi\rangle = p_\varphi(b)p_b(a)$$
$$p_\varphi(a, \neg b) = \langle\varphi|\, P_{\neg b} P_a P_{\neg b}\, |\varphi\rangle = p_\varphi(\neg b)p_{\neg b}(a)$$

whose interpretation is straightforward:

$p_\varphi(a, b) =$ probability for a system to have the property a after the property b has been stated, if previously the system had been in the state $|\varphi\rangle$.

From the formal definitions of these probabilities it follows

(Q) $p_\varphi(a) = p_\varphi(a, b) + p_\varphi(a, \neg b) + p_\varphi^{\text{int}}(a, b)$

where

$$p_\varphi^{\text{int}}(a, b) = \langle\varphi|\, P_b P_a P_{\neg b} + P_{\neg b} P_a P_b\, |\varphi\rangle$$

is the 'interference'-term.

The expression $p_\varphi(a, b)$ must be carefully distinguished from the probability $p_\varphi(a \wedge b)$, that the system has the property a, if it had before the property b and this property is still maintained even after the measuring of the observable a. Obviously for $p_\varphi(a \wedge b)$ somewhat more is demanded than for $p_\varphi(a, b)$. Therefore we have

$p_\varphi(a \wedge b) = p_\varphi(a, b)$ for simultaneously measurable quantities, i.e. for
$$[P_a, P_b]_- = 0$$
and

$p_\varphi(a \wedge b) \leqslant p_\varphi(a, b)$ otherwise.

Formally this result can be obtained if one defines the observable $a \wedge b$ ('a and b') by

$$P_{a \wedge b} = \lim_{n \to \infty} (P_a P_b)^n$$

$P_{a \wedge b}$ projects onto the intersection $M_a \cap M_b$ of the linear manifolds M_a and M_b.

On account of the Equation (Q) we therefore obtain

$$(Q') \qquad p_\varphi(a) \geqslant p_\varphi(a \wedge b) + p_\varphi(a \wedge \neg b) + p_\varphi^{\text{int}}(a, b)$$

In the interpretation (β) one assumes the objectivity of every measurable property. All properties a, b and the connected properties $a \wedge b$, $\neg b$ are considered as properties of the system S even if it is still in the state $|\varphi\rangle$. The properties are objectivized, i.e. it is assumed that a proposition which states the system to possess a certain property is – at least in reality – true or false. For an observer, it is usually not known whether such a proposition is true or not. Therefore we are in a situation in which it is objectively decided whether a certain property exists, but unknown to the observer. Consequently the ordinary theory of probability can be applied. Since the properties $a \wedge b$ and $a \wedge \neg b$ cannot simultaneously exist, it results that

$$(P') \qquad p_\varphi(a) = p_\varphi(a \wedge b) + p_\varphi(a \wedge \neg b)$$

If $p_\varphi^{\text{int}}(a, b) > 0$ the formulas (Q') and (P') are in contradiction.

It is well known how this contradiction can be avoided in the framework of the Copenhagen interpretation (α): Since (Q') and (P') are in contradiction and (Q') is true (supposed quantum theory is true), it follows that (P') must be false. The Equation (P') is a consequence of the requirement of simultaneous objectivity of all measurable properties. Therefore the assumption of objectivity was wrong. The objectivity of an observable can only be stated if the measuring process of this quantity has been carried out, and the observer has not yet taken note of the result of this measurement. Consequently, $p_\varphi(a)$ is the probability for finding the property a after the measuring process, when the transition from state $|\varphi\rangle$ to a state which is eigenstate of P_a has taken place. Before the measurement one cannot state the objectivity of an arbitrary property. The concept of probability is related to a situation after the measuring process.

3. The Resolution of the Contradiction by Means of the Quantum Mechanical Probability Theory

3.1. The Relation between Logic and Probability

Let $\{a\}$ be a set of propositions $a, b, c \ldots$. On this set one can define the *operations* $a \wedge b$ (a and b), $a \vee b$ (a or b). $a \rightarrow b$ (a then b), $\neg a$ (not a) by formal procedures which decide whether these propositions are true or false. Furthermore we define a *relation* $a \leqslant b$ by the statement, that the relation $a \leqslant b$ holds if and only if $a \rightarrow b$ is true. The propositions $\{a\}$ then form in respect to the operations $\wedge$, $\vee$, $\rightarrow$ and $\neg$ a Boolean lattice L_B with $\leqslant$ as the partly ordering relation. In this lattice one can derive the formula

(L) $a = (a \wedge b) \vee (a \wedge \neg b)$

which is very important for the following considerations.

Starting from this lattice L_B of propositions, the classical (or ordinary) probability can be defined as a real function $p(x)$, which is defined for all elements $x \in L_B$ and which satisfies the following axioms [3, 4].

(A1) $0 \leqslant p(x) \leqslant 1$ for all elements $x \in L_B$

(A2) $p(0) = 0$, $p(I) = 1$, where 0 and I are the null and unit elements of the lattice

(A3)   If $\{x_i\}$ is a (finite or infinite) series with $x_i \leqslant \neg x_k$ for $i \neq k$ then $p(x_1) + p(x_2) + \cdots = p(x_1 \vee x_2 \vee \cdots)$

From these axioms the formula

$$p(x) = p(x \wedge y) + p(x \wedge \neg y)$$

which is equivalent to the Equation (P′) mentioned above can be derived. The proof is easy:

If for two elements x, y we have $x \leqslant y$ it follows $x \leqslant \neg(\neg y)$ and on account of (A3)

$$p(x \vee \neg y) = p(x) + p(\neg y)$$

From $y \vee \neg y = I$ and $y \wedge \neg y = 0$ it follows

$$p(\neg y) = 1 - p(y)$$

and therefore

$$p(x \vee \neg y) = 1 + p(x) - p(y)$$

from which we finally obtain $p(x) \leqslant p(y)$. Thus we arrive at the conclusion that for any two elements x, y for which the relation $x \leqslant y$ holds, we have the inequality $p(x) \leqslant p(y)$. If we apply this result to the relation (L) which is always true in L_B, we obtain the equation

$$p(x) = p(x \wedge y) + p(x \wedge \neg y)$$

As a result of this discussion we find that the Equation (P'), which in the interpretation (β) contradicts the formula (Q'), is a consequence of the axioms (A1), (A2), (A3). These axioms, on the other hand, are based on the Boolean lattice which is formed by the propositions about the physical system S.

3.2. *The Relation between Logic and Objectivity*

Propositions about a physical system form a Boolean lattice L_B, if one considers the properties of a classical system. If the propositions are related to the properties of a quantum mechanical system, and if the simultaneous objectivity of all, including incommensurable, properties is demanded (interpretation β) – then these propositions do not form a Boolean lattice L_B. Instead of a Boolean lattice, the propositions constitute with regard to the operations $\wedge$, $\vee$, $\rightarrow$, $\neg$ and the relation $\leqslant$ an ortho-complemented, quasimodular lattice L_Q.

The reason that for quantum mechanical propositions not the well established classical logic, but only the restrictive quantum logic can be justified, is the requirement of the simultaneous objectivity of all, including incommensurable, propositions. This can be demonstrated on the basis of the operational foundation of logic [5, 6], if one takes into account the mutual incommensurability of quantum mechanical propositions. Some obvious modifications of the operational method, which come from the incommensurability of the quantum mechanical propositions, lead to a restrictive propositional calculus, the so called quantum logic, which in terms of lattice theory, is an orthocomplemented quasimodular lattice L_Q.

It is not possible to present here a detailed analysis of this operational foundation of quantum logic. This has been done elsewhere and should therefore not be repeated here [7, 8]. For the purpose of this paper, it is sufficient to mention the fact that the requirement of objectivity together with the incommensurability of quantum mechanical propositions has the consequence that the operational technique to justify a logical law – by means of dialogs whose rules have to be formulated very carefully

[6] – must be reduced in some way, so that only the laws of quantum logic can be established.

The decisive difference between the lattice L_B of the classical logic and the lattice L_Q of the quantum logic is that in this lattice L_Q the distributive law $(a \vee b) \wedge (a \vee c) = a \vee (b \wedge c)$ which is known to be valid in a Boolean lattice, can no longer generally be proved, but only under the additional assumption that the relations $a \leqslant b$ and $c \leqslant \neg b$ are fulfilled [9]. However, the elements of a subset $\{a\}_B \subseteq \{a\}$ of propositions with the property that for any two elements $x, y \in \{a\}_B$ the corresponding properties are commensurable, form a Boolean sublattice of L_Q. In the framework of the propositional lattice L_Q two propositions x and y are called commensurable, if the relation $C(x, y)$, defined by

$$C(x, y) \Leftrightarrow x = (x \wedge y) \vee (x \wedge \neg y)$$

is fulfilled. It can be shown that within the lattice L_Q this relation is symmetric [10], i.e. $C(x, y) \Leftrightarrow C(y, x)$. For two arbitrary propositions a and b of L_Q one can – instead of (L) – prove only the weaker relation

$$(\tilde{\text{L}}) \qquad (a \wedge b) \vee (a \wedge \neg b) \leqslant a$$

which is valid for any lattice.

3.3. *The Resolution of the Contradiction*

In summarizing the results of the preceding section we find that under the assumption of objectivity the totality of quantum mechanical propositions constitutes a lattice L_Q. In order to be able to introduce a probability for the propositions summarized in this lattice, we define as a generalized (quantum mechanical) probability a real function $p^{(q)}(x)$, which is defined for all elements $x \in L_Q$ and which satisfies the following axioms: [11, 12]

$(A^{(q)}1)$ $0 \leqslant p^{(q)}(x) \leqslant 1$ for all elements $x \in L_Q$

$(A^{(q)}2)$ $p^{(q)}(\underline{0}) = 0, p^{(q)}(I) = 1$ where $\underline{0}$ and I are the null and unit elements of the lattice

$(A^{(q)}3)$ If $\{x_i\}$ is a (finite or infinite) series with $x_i \leqslant \neg x_k$ for $i \neq k$ then $p^{(q)}(x_1) + p^{(q)}(x_2) + \cdots = p^{(q)}(x_1 \vee x_2 \vee \cdots)$

$(A^{(q)}4)$ For every finite series $\{x_i\}$ it follows from $p^{(q)}(x_i) = 1$ for all $x_i \in \{x_k\}$ that $p^{(q)}(x_1 \wedge x_2 \wedge \cdots) = 1$

It can easily be seen that the quantum mechanical probability $p^{(q)}(x)$ determined by $(A^{(q)}1)$–$(A^{(q)}4)$ is in fact a nontrivial generalization of the classical probability concept $p(x)$. Since the axiom $(A^{(q)}3)$ is equivalent to the axiom

$(A^{(q)}3')$ $p^{(q)}(x \wedge y) + p^{(q)}(x \vee y) = p^{(q)}(x) + p^{(q)}(y)$ if $C(x, y)$ and if
$p^{(q)}(0) = 0$

the formula $p^{(q)}(a \wedge b) + p^{(q)}(a \vee b) = p^{(q)}(a) + p^{(q)}(b)$ is valid for $p^{(q)}(x)$ only under the condition that the relation $C(a, b)$ holds, whereas for the classical probability $p(x)$ this equation is generally true. On the other hand for a Boolean sublattice the probabilities $p^{(q)}(x)$ are in agreement with the classical probability concept defined by $(A1)$–$(A3)$, since for Boolean lattices the axiom $(A^{(q)}4)$ is a consequence of the remaining axioms $(A^{(q)}1)$, $(A^{(q)}2)$ and $(A^{(q)}3)$ [12].

In the framework of the quantum mechanical probability theory represented by $(A^{(q)}1)$–$(A^{(q)}4)$, it follows from these axioms that [4]

$$a \leqslant b \Rightarrow p^{(q)}(a) \leqslant p^{(q)}(b)$$

as well as in the classical theory of probability. Therefore one obtains on account of $(\tilde{L})$

$(\tilde{P})$ $p^{(q)}(a \wedge b) + p^{(q)}(a \vee b) \leqslant p^{(q)}(a)$

This inequality $(\tilde{P})$, which is valid for objectivized quantum mechanical propositions, does not contradict the relation (Q'). In fact, if we distinguish the three cases $p_\varphi^{int}(a, b) \gtrless 0$ we find that in none of these cases we are led to a contradiction if we use the lattice L_Q-whereas the application of a Boolean lattice L_B leads for $p_\varphi^{int}(a, b)$ to a contradiction. The three cases are shown in Table I:

If one uses the lattice L_Q as propositional calculus and the axioms

TABLE I

$P_\varphi^{int}(a, b)$	L_B	L_Q
$P_\varphi^{int} = 0$	$Q \Leftrightarrow P'$	$Q' \Leftrightarrow \tilde{P}$
$P_\varphi^{int} > 0$	Q' contradicts P'	$Q' \Rightarrow \tilde{P}$
$P_\varphi^{int} < 0$		$\tilde{P} \Rightarrow Q'$

$(A^{(q)}1)-(A^{(q)}4)$ for the definition of the probability concept, then there are in any one of the three cases functions $p^{(q)}(x)$ which satisfy simultaneously the relations Q' and $\tilde{P}$. Therefore the contradiction between the quantum mechanical formula Q' and the theory of probability can be completely removed, if instead of the classical probability $p(x)$ the quantum mechanical probability $p^{(q)}(x)$ is used.

4. CONCLUSION

It has been shown that there are at least two consistent interpretations of the quantum mechanical formalism which have been called here the interpretations (α) and (β). In the Copenhagen interpretation (α) the properties of a quantum mechanical system are in general not objectivized. Therefore the classical logic is valid without any restrictions for quantum mechanical propositions, and the classical theory of probability, which is based on the lattice of propositions, can be consistently applied to the quantum mechanical expectation values. In the Copenhagen interpretation there is no contradiction between the quantum mechanical formula Q' and the theory of probability.

In the interpretation (β) the totality of all, including incommen-

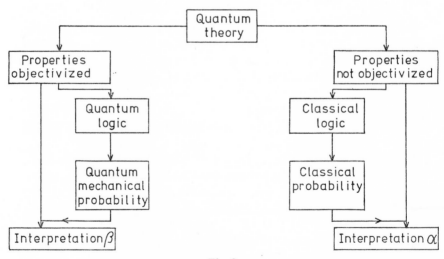

Fig. 2.

surable, properties of a quantum mechanical system are objectivized. As a consequence of this assumption, only a restricted propositional calculus can be proved to be valid for quantum mechanical propositions as it can be shown in the framework of the operational foundation of logic. On the basis of this propositional calculus – called quantum logic – a generalized quantum mechanical theory of probability can be established. This generalized probability theory can be consistently applied to the quantum mechanical expectation values, even if they are interpreted in the sense of interpretation (β). The quantum mechanical formula Q' is compatible with the relation $\tilde{P}$, which follows from the quantum mechanical probability calculus.

The two possibilities of a consistent interpretation of the quantum mechanical formalism are schematically represented in Figure 2. On the left hand side the objectivizing interpretation is shown, whereas the right hand side represents the well-known Copenhagen interpretation.

University of Cologne

BIBLIOGRAPHY

[1] Mittelstaedt, P., *Philosophical Problems of Modern Physics*, D. Reidel Publishing Company, Dordrecht, 1976.
[2] Feynman, R. P. *et al.*, *The Feynman Lectures of Physics*, vol. III, Addison-Wesley, Reading, Mass, 1965, pp. 1–4.
[3] Birkhoff, G., 'Lattice Theory', *Ann. Math. Soc. Coll. Publ.* **25** [Rev. ed.] (1961), 197.
[4] Ref. [1], Ch. VI.
[5] Lorenzen, P., *Metamathematik*, Bibliographisches Institut, Mannheim, 1962.
[6] Lorenz, K., *Archiv. f. Math. Logik und Grundlagenforschung*, 1968.
[7] Ref. [1], Ch. VI.
[8] Mittelstaedt, P. and Stachow, E. W., *Foundations of Physics*, 4 (1974), 355.
[9] Jauch, J. M., *Foundations of Quantum Mechanics*, Addison-Wesley, Reading, Mass., 1968.
[10] Kamber, F., *Math. Ann.* **158** (1965), 158.
[11] Mittelstaedt, P., in *Einheit u. Vielheit* (ed. by E. Scheibe and G. Süssmann), Vandenhock u. Ruprecht, Göttingen, 1972; and Ref. [1], Ch. Vl.
[12] Ref. [9]– p. 94, 95.

DISCUSSION

Commentator: van Fraassen: The new and important part of your paper is the development of the dialogue logic. I have an objection which concerns the relationship of the dialogue logic to the lattice of subspaces of a Hilbert space, which provides the logical structure in the traditional approach to the logic of quantum mechanics. This objection has to do with the interpretations of the propositions a, b, c and so on. If you interpret a as being true if and only if the system vector is in a subspace s_a, then it is true that the lattice of propositions will be isomorphic to the lattice of subspaces. But in this case all the propositions must refer to exactly the same time. Now in the dialogue logic you have a special rule which says that if O, say, introduces a proposition a then it cannot be imported lower down in the dialogue and the justification of this rule is that the information represented by a at the *time* O introduced it may be destroyed by the introduction of b in a succeeding step of the dialogue, at the *time* it was introduced, because a and b represent incompatible partial determinations of the quantum system in question. But now in this case you divorce the interpretations of the propositions a, b, c etc. from that interpretation which permitted you to show that the lattice of propositions was the lattice of subspaces of a hilbert space.

Mittelstaedt: In the dialogue logic the notion of time is not really crucial, since we could always switch from the Schroedinger picture to the Heisenberg picture. What is important is the order in which measurements are made.

van Fraassen: Yes, but that does not affect my point. The justification of the rule for not importing earlier propositions to the later dialogue, *whether* the justification mentions the order of incompatible measurements or the times at which those measurements were made, rules out the interpretation which showed that the lattice of propositions was indeed the lattice of subspaces of a Hilbert space. For in the latter interpretation, all propositions are evaluated jointly with reference to a single state. In the case of the law of distribution, for example, we say that the law does not hold because there is a state which belongs to the proposition (sub-space) or the right hand side of the equation sign, but not to the one on the left hand side. So that, in your account, two *distinct* interpretations of the propositions are offered.

Mittelstaedt: I start with elementary propositions, the demonstration of which is given by a measurement. Connected propositions are defined by dialogs. The quantum logic discussed here deals with arbitrarily connected propositions of this kind. It is a result of the investigations mentioned here, that the calculus of these propositions forms an ortho-modular lattice – just like the subspaces of Hilbert space.

C. H. RANDALL AND D. J. FOULIS

A MATHEMATICAL SETTING FOR
INDUCTIVE REASONING

1. INTRODUCTION

The aim of this paper is to develop and describe a mathematical structure rich enough to provide an adequate setting for inductive reasoning. It is not our purpose here to advocate any particular inference procedure – rather, we propose a mathematical framework within which the possibilities can be studied formally with a minimum of prejudice. In particular, we shall have a look at a generalization of the Bayesian inference procedure in this framework. In the process of constructing this system, four of the principal kinds of probability arise quite naturally and in harmony. As a consequence, the customary mathematical representation of the notion of conditioning is resolved into a number of conditioning concepts. Although this excess of conditioning operations creates many mathematical problems, it also provides the machinery to unravel many of the confusing issues that are associated with inference.

The subject-predicate (object-property) structure and the connectives of classical logic are not employed here in an essential way. The primitive concept upon which our mathematical structure is based is the notion of a physical operation or experiment. In most well-conceived statistical projects one must analyze data secured not from a single physical operation, but rather from a coherent collection of such operations. Thus, we shall be concerned with a class – or *manual* – of admissible physical operations.

It is customary to assume (often implicitly) that there exists – at least in principle – a 'grand canonical' physical operation that can be regarded as a common refinement of all the admissible physical operations in the manual under consideration. A well known example of such an operation in statistical physics is the grand canonical measurement of classical mechanics – the operation that was assumed to determine the location and momentum of every particle of a physical system. The tenets of quantum physics rule out such a grand canonical operation. Con-

Harper and Hooker (eds.), Foundations of Probability Theory, Statistical Inference, and Statistical Theories of Science, Vol. III, 169–205. *All Rights Reserved. Copyright* © 1976 *by D. Reidel Publishing Company, Dordrecht-Holland.*

sequently, in setting up our mathematical formalism, we do not feel entitled to assume, a priori, the existence of a common refinement for all of the admissible physical operations under consideration.

2. MANUALS OF OPERATIONS

By a *physical operation* we shall mean instructions that describe a well-defined, physically realizable, reproducible procedure and furthermore that specify what must be observed and what can be recorded as a consequence of an execution of this procedure. In particular, a physical operation must require that, as a consequence of each execution of the instructions, one and only one symbol from a specified set E be recorded as the *outcome* of this realization of the physical operation. We refer to the set E as the *outcome set* for the physical operation.

It must be emphasized at this point that the outcome of a realization of a physical operation is merely a *symbol*; it is not any real or imagined occurrence in the 'real world out there'. Also, note that if we delete or add details to the instructions for any physical operation, especially if we modify the outcome set in any way, we thereby define a new physical operation.

This definition appears to us to be the only tractable one, since the only means of settling the question of whether two individuals performed the 'same operation' is with a description. Since no description can be complete, then no two executions of a set of instructions can be identical in all particulars; hence, statistics must ultimately enter the picture. This point of view regarding physical operations must be adopted in some sense if experimental results are to be used to predict future events. It is, of course, implicit in any objective statistical analysis; here, we simply recognize the fact formally.

Our definition by no means restricts us to operations involving only traditional laboratory procedures. In fact, test procedures on an assembly line, data gathering procedures in general (such as opinion polling), pencil-and-paper procedures (such as executing computational algorithms), and even procedures involving subjective approvals or disapprovals are all admissible provided that they satisfy the criteria of the definition.

Evidently, the subjective judgment of the observer is implicit in every realization of a physical operation, not only in regard to the interpretation of the instructions, but also in connection with the decision as to which symbol to record as the outcome. In our view, if a competent observer believes that he has executed a particular physical operation and obtained a particular outcome, then, in fact, the operation has been realized and the outcome in question has indeed been secured. Each realization of a physical operation is to be understood here as a 'Ding an sich', isolated, with no 'before' and no 'after'. Physical history, as it were, begins and ends with each execution of a physical operation. To put the matter in more traditional terms, the various realizations of the admissible physical operations in a manual are always to be regarded as 'independent trials'.

If physical procedures are to be carried out in a 'connected sequence', then the instructions for such a *compound operation* must say so. When a compound physical operation is built up from more primitive physical operations by concatination, it is understood that each constituent operation thereby loses its identity, since it may have temporal antecedents and consequences. Notice in regard to this that the recording of the passage of time is often an important constituent operation of a compound operation.

Once we have assembled those physical operations of concern to us in a particular discourse, we are almost inevitably moved, either by custom or by a particular intent, to identify certain outcomes of different operations. For instance, we often prefer to regard a number of outcomes of distinct physical operations as registering the same 'property', or, if you prefer, as representing the same 'measurement'. If a voltage is measured using different instruments – or even different methods – identical numerical results are ordinarily taken to be equivalent. Similarly, the instructions for carrying out the admissible procedures may all but dictate the identification of certain outcomes on purely syntactic grounds. We surely wish to avoid the necessity of taking a stand on the 'acceptability' of any such identifications since we hope to keep our formal language as free as possible from ad hoc decisions. On the other hand, we wish our language to be able to handle this common practice of outcome identification and if we permit unrestricted identification of outcomes, grammatical chaos could result. Accordingly, we shall subject the outcome identification process to certain mild constraints.

In order to make the nature of these constraints precise, let us suppose that we are considering a particular manual of admissible physical operations and that we have already made what we consider to be the appropriate outcome identifications. (Naturally, these identifications will often be motivated by some 'picture of the real world'.) As our first condition, which we shall refer to as the *determination condition*, we require that each outcome is so constituted that the set of all admissible physical operations capable of yielding this outcome can be discerned from the symbolic pattern of the outcome itself. Thus, when we assert that such an outcome has been obtained, we understand that what we are really asserting is that it was obtained as a consequence of an execution of one of these admissible physical operations – although it is not necessary to specify which one.

The second condition on such an identification process, which we shall call the *irredundancy condition*, requires that for each admissible physical operation $\mathscr{P}$, say with outcome set E, there is only one admissible physical operation – namely $\mathscr{P}$ itself – capable of yielding each and every outcome in E. An immediate consequence of this condition is that each physical operation in our manual not only determines, but is uniquely determined by the set of all of its outcomes. As a result, we can and shall identify each physical operation with its outcome set.

In view of the above, we propose to introduce as a formal mathematical representation for a manual of admissible physical operations a non-empty set $\mathscr{A}$ of non-empty sets. Each set $E \in \mathscr{A}$ is supposed to correspond uniquely to the set of all outcomes of one of the admissible physical operations and each admissible physical operation is supposed to be so represented. The condition of irredundancy now translates into the assertion that if $E, F \in \mathscr{A}$ with $E \subseteq F$, then $E = F$. The elements of $\mathscr{A}$ will henceforth be referred to simply as $\mathscr{A}$-*operations*, while the set theoretic union $X = \cup \mathscr{A}$ of all of the $\mathscr{A}$-operations will be referred to as the set of all $\mathscr{A}$-*outcomes*.

If x and y are two $\mathscr{A}$-outcomes with $x \neq y$, and if there exists an $\mathscr{A}$-operation E with $x, y \in E$, then we shall say that x is *orthogonal* to y and we shall write $x \perp y$. Notice that when $x \perp y$ as above, then x and y reject each other operationally in the sense that an execution of E that yields the outcome x cannot yield the outcome y and vice versa. A set D of $\mathscr{A}$-outcomes will be called an *orthogonal* set provided that $x \perp y$ holds for all pairs x, y of distinct elements of D. Obviously, every $\mathscr{A}$-operation is an orthogonal set and every subset of an orthogonal set is again an orthogonal set.

If E is an $\mathscr{A}$-operation, then a subset D of E will be called an *event for* E. As usual, if the physical operation corresponding to E is executed and an outcome $d \in D$ is obtained as a consequence, then we shall say that the event D has *occurred*. Naturally, an $\mathscr{A}$-*event* is defined to be a set of $\mathscr{A}$-outcomes that is an event for at least one $\mathscr{A}$-operation. When we assert that an $\mathscr{A}$-event D has occurred, we of course are asserting that it has occurred as a consequence of an execution of a physical operation corresponding to *some* $E \in \mathscr{A}$ for which $D \subseteq E$.

If A and B are two $\mathscr{A}$-events, then we shall say that A is *orthogonal* to B and write $A \perp B$ provided that $a \perp b$ holds for all $a \in A$ and all $b \in B$. Our third condition, named the *coherence condition*, in effect permits us to extend the interpretation for the orthogonality relation $\perp$ (as operational rejection) from $\mathscr{A}$-outcomes to $\mathscr{A}$-events. Specifically, the coherence condition requires that if A and B are $\mathscr{A}$-events with $A \perp B$, then there must exist an $\mathscr{A}$-operation E such that both A and B are events for E. In particular, the coherence condition requires that the union of two orthogonal $\mathscr{A}$-events is again an $\mathscr{A}$-event.

Let us summarize by making the following formal definitions: A *premanual* is defined to be a non-empty set $\mathscr{A}$ of non-empty sets. An element $E \in \mathscr{A}$ is called an $\mathscr{A}$-*operation* and the set theoretic union $X = \cup \mathscr{A}$ is called the set of $\mathscr{A}$-*outcomes*. We shall call $\mathscr{A}$ an *irredundant* premanual provided that $E, F \in \mathscr{A}$ and $E \subseteq F$ implies that $E = F$. Two $\mathscr{A}$-outcomes $x, y \in X$ are said to be *orthogonal*, in symbols, $x \perp y$, provided that $x \neq y$ and there exists an $E \in \mathscr{A}$ with $x, y \in E$. A subset D of X is called an *orthogonal* set if $x \perp y$ holds for all $x, y \in D$ with $x \neq y$, while a subset D of X is called an $\mathscr{A}$-*event* if there exists an $E \in \mathscr{A}$ with $D \subseteq E$. If A and B are subsets of X, we say that A and B are *orthogonal* and we write $A \perp B$ provided that $a \perp b$ holds for all $a \in A$ and all $b \in B$. We call the premanual $\mathscr{A}$ *coherent* provided that the union of any two orthogonal $\mathscr{A}$-events is again an $\mathscr{A}$-event. A *manual* is defined to be an irredundant and coherent premanual.

3. THE OPERATIONAL LOGIC OF A MANUAL

Let $\mathscr{A}$ be a manual corresponding, as above, to some collection of admissible physical operations. Let us consider, for the time being, only those propositions that are operationally well-defined in the sense that they are confirmed or refuted strictly in terms of evidence secured as a consequence of the execution of $\mathscr{A}$-operations. Specifically, we define an *operational proposition* (for $\mathscr{A}$) to be an ordered pair (A, B) of subsets A, B of $X = \cup \mathscr{A}$. If an operation $E \in \mathscr{A}$ is executed and the outcome $e \in E$ is obtained as a consequence, we shall say that the operational proposition (A, B) is *confirmed* precisely when $e \in A$ and that it is *refuted* precisely when $e \in B$. Thus, A will be called the *confirmation set* and B the *refutation set* for this operational proposition. Since there is no requirement that $A \cup B = X$, the operational proposition (A, B) can fail to be either confirmed or refuted as a consequence of an execution of a given $\mathscr{A}$-operation.

Notice that an operational proposition is completely described by specifying its confirmation and refutation sets and, as promised, does not involve a subject predicate (object-property) formalism in any essential way. Also, an operational proposition is 'sharp' in the sense that it will definitely be confirmed, refuted or neither confirmed nor refuted as a consequence of a given single realization of a given $\mathscr{A}$-operation. Although an operational proposition admits three possible 'truth values' – confirmed, refuted, neither confirmed nor refuted – its 'truth values' are generally instable in the sense that they will change from one realization of an admissible operation to another.

If A is any subset of X, we define $A^{\perp} = \{x \in X \mid x \perp a, \forall a \in A\}$, and we define $A^{\perp\perp} = (A^{\perp})^{\perp}$, $A^{\perp\perp\perp} = (A^{\perp\perp})^{\perp}$. Evidently, $A \subseteq A^{\perp\perp}$, $A^{\perp\perp\perp} = A^{\perp}$, $A \cap A^{\perp} = \emptyset$ and if $A \subseteq B \subseteq X$, then $B^{\perp} \subseteq A^{\perp}$. Notice that for $A, B \subseteq X$, $A \perp B$ holds if and only if $A \subseteq B^{\perp}$. Now, consider an operational proposition (A, B). If $A \perp B$, that is, if every outcome that could confirm (A, B) operationally rejects every outcome that could refute (A, B), then we shall say that the operational proposition (A, B) is *orthoconsistent*. One pleasant feature of an orthoconsistent operational proposition is that it can never be simultaneously confirmed and refuted by a single execution of an admissible operation $E \in \mathscr{A}$. Notice that any outcome $x \in A^{\perp}$ will operationally reject every outcome which could confirm (A, B); hence, an outcome $x \in A^{\perp}$ will be said to *virtually refute* (A, B). Similarly, an outcome $y \in B^{\perp}$ will be said to *virtually confirm* (A, B).

An operational proposition (A, B) is said to be *closed* if it is orthoconsistent, $B^{\perp} \subseteq A$ and $A^{\perp} \subseteq B$. Notice, for instance, that the condition

$B^{\perp} \subseteq A$ simply requires that any outcome that virtually confirms (A, B) does, in fact, confirm (A, B), while orthoconsistency simply requires that any outcome that confirms (A, B) will also virtually confirm (A, B). It is easy to see that an operational proposition is closed if and only if it is of the form $(C^{\perp\perp}, C^{\perp})$ for some subset C of X.

An $\mathscr{A}$-operation E is said to *test* the operational proposition (A, B) in case $E \subseteq A \cup B$; that is, in case every outcome of E must confirm or refute (A, B). A collection of operational propositions is said to be *simultaneously testable* if there exists a single $\mathscr{A}$-operation that is a test operation for every operational proposition in the collection.

It is natural to associate with every $\mathscr{A}$-event D the operational proposition $(D, D^{\perp})$, since its test operations are precisely those $\mathscr{A}$-operations E for which $D \subseteq E$. Furthermore, if such a test operation for $(D, D^{\perp})$ is executed, then $(D, D^{\perp})$ is confirmed precisely when the event D occurs and refuted precisely when the event D does not occur. However, there may be operations E with $D \nsubseteq E$ whose execution could confirm or refute $(D, D^{\perp})$. Thus, the assertion that the $\mathscr{A}$-event D occurred is not quite the same as the assertion that the proposition $(D, D^{\perp})$ was confirmed. Also, in general, although $(D, D^{\perp})$ is orthoconsistent, it need not be closed. However, there is a unique closed operational proposition $p(D)$ which is confirmed if $(D, D^{\perp})$ is confirmed and refuted if $(D, D^{\perp})$ is refuted, namely $p(D) = (D^{\perp\perp}, D^{\perp})$. In this paper, we shall concern ourselves only with operational propositions having the form $p(D) = (D^{\perp\perp}, D^{\perp})$ for some $\mathscr{A}$-event D and we shall define $\pi(\mathscr{A}) = \pi$ to be the set of all such operational propositions.

If C and D are $\mathscr{A}$-events, we shall say that the operational proposition $p(C)$ *implies* the operational proposition $p(D)$ and write $p(C) \leqslant p(D)$ in case every $\mathscr{A}$-outcome that confirms $p(C)$ also confirms $p(D)$, that is $C^{\perp\perp} \subseteq D^{\perp\perp}$. Notice that $p(C) \leqslant p(D)$ if and only if $D^{\perp} \subseteq C^{\perp}$, that is, if and only if every $\mathscr{A}$-outcome that refutes $p(D)$ also refutes $p(C)$. Evidently, the relation $\leqslant$ is a partial order on $\pi(\mathscr{A})$ and we have $p(\emptyset) \leqslant p(D) \leqslant p(E)$ for any $\mathscr{A}$-event D and any $\mathscr{A}$-operation E. We shall say that $p(C)$ is *orthogonal* to $p(D)$ and write $p(C) \perp p(D)$ provided that every $\mathscr{A}$-outcome that confirms $p(C)$ also refutes $p(D)$, that is $C^{\perp\perp} \subseteq D^{\perp}$. Observe that $p(C) \perp p(D)$ holds if and only if $C \perp D$. Thus, $\perp$ is a symmetric binary relation defined on $\pi(\mathscr{A})$. The system $(\pi(\mathscr{A}), \leqslant, \perp)$ is called the *operational logic* of the manual $\mathscr{A}$.

Most of the manuals that arise naturally in practical considerations have the following property: For every $\mathscr{A}$-event D there exists at least one other $\mathscr{A}$-event B such that $B^{\perp\perp} = D^{\perp}$. When such an event B exists, then $E = B \cup D$ is an $\mathscr{A}$-operation with respect to which B and D are relative complements of one another and the confirmation set for $p(D)$ is the refutation set for $p(B)$ and vice-versa. Given the existence of at least one such B for each D, we can define a mapping $'$ on the operational logic $\pi(\mathscr{A})$ by $p(D)' = p(B) = p(E \setminus D) = (D^{\perp}, D^{\perp\perp})$. This mapping is then seen to be an orthocomplementation [9, p. 113] for the logic $\pi(\mathscr{A})$ and naturally the proposition $p(D)'$ is regarded as the negation of the proposition $p(D)$. In most of the interesting manuals, the operational logic is not only orthocomplemented in this way, but actually forms an orthomodular poset [6]. The latter condition turns out to be equivalent to the requirement that if E and F are two operations both containing an $\mathscr{A}$-event D, then $p(E \setminus D) = p(F \setminus D)$. In brief, in the orthomodular case, $p(D)'$ corresponds to *all* of the relative complements of D.

The operational logic $\pi(\mathscr{A})$ of the manual $\mathscr{A}$ will be an orthomodular poset, as above, if and only if $\mathscr{A}$ satisfies the so-called *Dacey condition* [7]: If x and y are $\mathscr{A}$-outcomes and if there exists an $\mathscr{A}$-operation E such that every outcome $e \in E$ that is not orthogonal to x is orthogonal to y, then x is orthogonal to y. The Dacey condition is similar to the ir-redundancy and coherence conditions and could be given a similar heur-istic motivation. As we have observed, this condition is equivalent to the stipulation that all of the relative complements of an event (with respect to the operations that contain it) correspond to the same operational proposition.

Since any $\mathscr{A}$-operation for which D is an event is a test operation for $p(D)$, then every operational proposition in $\pi(\mathscr{A})$ is testable. For a Dacey manual (that is, a manual satisfying the Dacey condition) the converse is true in the sense that the operational logic $\pi(\mathscr{A})$ consists precisely of the closed and testable operational propositions for $\mathscr{A}$ [23]. In a Dacey manual, an operation E tests the operational proposition $p(D)$ if and only if there exists an event $C \subseteq E$ such that $p(C) = p(D)$ [23].

If $\mathscr{A}$ is any manual and if A and B are $\mathscr{A}$-events, we say that $p(A)$ *commutes* with $p(B)$ if there exist pairwise orthogonal $\mathscr{A}$-events A_1, B_1, D such that $p(A) = p(A_1 \cup D)$ and $p(B) = p(B_1 \cup D)$. If $\mathscr{A}$ is a Dacey manual, this definition coincides with the customary notion of commutativity in the orthomodular poset $\pi(\mathscr{A})$ and here it can be shown that $p(A)$ commutes with $p(B)$ if and only if $p(A)$ and $p(B)$ are simultaneously testable [23]. In any case, we shall say that an operational proposition belongs to the *center* of the logic $\pi(\mathscr{A})$ if it commutes with every other operational proposition in this logic. B. Jeffcott [15] has shown that the center of an operational logic is always a Boolean algebra. We shall say that $\mathscr{A}$ is a *Boolean* manual if and only if $\pi(\mathscr{A})$ is its own center. Evidently, if $\mathscr{A}$ is a Boolean manual, it is automatically a Dacey manual and any *finite* collection of operational propositions in $\pi(\mathscr{A})$ is simultaneously testable. Thus, we are inclined to regard the experimental situations described by Boolean manuals as being 'classical'.

Let $(D_j \mid j \in J)$ be any family of pairwise orthogonal $\mathscr{A}$-events indexed by the set J. Let $D = \bigcup_{j \in J} D_j$, noting that D is an orthogonal set of $\mathscr{A}$-outcomes. If J is a finite set, then, by coherence, D will also be an $\mathscr{A}$-event. In any case, if D is an $\mathscr{A}$-event, then $p(D)$ is effective as the supremum (least upper bound) of the operational propositions $(p(D_j) \mid j \in J)$, and we shall write $p(D) = \oplus_{j \in J} p(D_j)$ to denote such an orthogonal supremum when it exists. More general suprema and infima, together with their interpretations, are discussed in [23].

4. COARSENING OF PHYSICAL OPERATIONS

Let $\mathscr{P}$ be a physical operation with outcome set E and let $(D_j \mid j \in J)$ be a family of pairwise disjoint non-empty subsets of E indexed by the set J such that $\bigcup_{j \in J} D_j = E$. Such a partition of E determines a 'coarsened version' $\mathscr{P}^*$ of the physical operation $\mathscr{P}$ as follows: To execute $\mathscr{P}^*$, we carry out the instructions for $\mathscr{P}$ to obtain (say) the outcome $e \in E$, and we record the outcome of this execution of $\mathscr{P}^*$ as the unique event D_j for which $e \in D_j$.

Given a manual $\mathscr{A}$, it is now clear how to form the manual $\mathscr{A}^*$ representing all possible coarsenings (in the above sense) of all of the physical operations represented by $\mathscr{A}$. We simply define $\mathscr{A}^*$, called the *event saturation* of $\mathscr{A}$, to be the set of all partitions of all $\mathscr{A}$-operations. It is not difficult to verify that $\mathscr{A}^*$ is a manual, that the set of $\mathscr{A}^*$-outcomes is precisely the set of all non-empty $\mathscr{A}$-events, that two such $\mathscr{A}^*$-outcomes A and B are orthogonal with respect to the manual $\mathscr{A}^*$ if and only if the $\mathscr{A}$-events A and B are orthogonal, and that the logic $\pi(\mathscr{A}^*)$

is canonically isomorphic to the logic $\pi(\mathscr{A})$. To put the matter succinctly, $\mathscr{A}^*$ is obtained from $\mathscr{A}$ by promoting the (non-empty) $\mathscr{A}$-events to the status of outcomes. Notice that each $\mathscr{A}$-operation E has a natural representative in $\mathscr{A}^*$, namely, the partition of E into one element subsets. Clearly, in the passage from $\mathscr{A}$ to $\mathscr{A}^*$ we have lost very little – if anything at all – that is of physical significance.

If we are concerned only with the finite (respectively, countable) coarsenings of the operations in the manual $\mathscr{A}$, we can look at the manual $\mathscr{A}_0^*$ (respectively, $\mathscr{A}_\infty^*$) consisting only of the finite (respectively countable) operations in $\mathscr{A}^*$. Again, it is easy to verify that both $\mathscr{A}_0^*$ and $\mathscr{A}_\infty^*$ are manuals and that their respective operational logics remain canonically isomorphic to $\pi(\mathscr{A})$. Furthermore, the $\mathscr{A}_0^*$-outcomes, as well as the $\mathscr{A}_\infty^*$-outcomes, consist precisely of all non-empty $\mathscr{A}$-events.

A manual $\mathscr{A}$ is said to be *locally finite* (respectively, locally countable) provided that every $\mathscr{A}$-operation is a finite (respectively, countable) set. The mathematical arguments required in certain convergence considerations often require local countability or local finiteness of the manual in question. Notice, however, that for any manual $\mathscr{A}$, $\mathscr{A}_0^*$ is locally finite, while $\mathscr{A}_\infty^*$ is locally countable. Hence, when we are hard-pressed for local countability, or even local finiteness, we can always replace our manual $\mathscr{A}$ by $\mathscr{A}_\infty^*$ or by $\mathscr{A}_0^*$ with very little – if any – real loss of physical content.

Although one might wish to consider non-locally countable manuals for certain purposes (such as the mathematical modeling of idealized or in-principle physical operations, e.g., the 'grand canonical measurement of statistical physics') it is our feeling that a strict interpretation of our definition of a physical operation would enforce local countability – and perhaps even local finiteness – on any manual of bona fide physical operations.

Consider, for example, the operation of measuring the temperature of a bucket of water with a mercury thermometer and recording the outcome in degrees Centigrade. Here, the outcome set E would ordinarily be presumed to be the closed interval $[0, 100]$ of all real numbers between 0 and 100. It is difficult to believe that all of the real numbers in the uncountable interval $[0, 100]$ could be represented by distinguishable recordable symbols; hence, it would seem that the operation just described would not conform in a strict sense to our definition of a physical operation. Here, it would perhaps be more realistic to consider a subdivision of the interval $[0, 100]$ into (say) 1000 subintervals and to record the outcome of our temperature measurement as the appropriate subinterval. This would result in a bona fide physical operation according to our definition and this physical operation would formally represent a coarsening of the idealized temperature measuring operation originally described.

5. THE COMPOUNDING OF MANUALS

In this section, let $\mathscr{A}$ be a manual with outcome set X. We shall refer to $\mathscr{A}$ as the *base manual* and we shall regard $\mathscr{A}$ as a reservoir of primitive physical operations from which we intend to synthesize compound operations requiring the execution of the primitive operations in 'connected sequences'. Suppose, for instance, that $E_1, E_2, \ldots, E_n$ are $\mathscr{A}$-operations and that these are executed in a connected sequence (first E_1, then E_2, ..., and finally E_n) so as to obtain the sequence $x_1, x_2, \ldots, x_n$ of respective outcomes. Let us agree to record the formal product $x_1 x_2 \ldots x_n$ to denote the acquisition of such a sequence as a consequence of the execution of the compound operation just described. In order to be able to give such a representation to all of the outcomes of all of the possible compound operations that could be synthesized from $\mathscr{A}$, we are obliged to consider the free semigroup S over X.

The free semigroup S over X consists of all formal products $x_1 x_2 \ldots x_n$ with $x_1, x_2, \ldots, x_n \in X$, n running through the positive integers. The product in S of the 'word' $a = x_1 x_2 \ldots x_n$ and the 'word' $b = y_1 y_2 \ldots y_m$ is, of course, the 'word' $ab = x_1 x_2 \ldots x_n y_1 y_2 \ldots y_m$. In the following, it will be convenient to adjoin a formal identity 1 to the semigroup S so as to obtain a semigroup $X^c = S \cup \{1\}$ with identity 1, which we shall refer to as the *free monoid* over X. One can regard the symbol 1 as representing an 'empty word'. If $b \in X^c$ with $b \neq 1$, then b is uniquely expressible in the form $b = x_1 x_2 \ldots x_n$ with $x_1, x_2, \ldots, x_n \in X$; hence, we define the *length* of the word b to be $|b| = n$. Naturally, we define $|1| = 0$. The elements of X^c of length one are naturally identified with the corresponding elements of X, so that $X \subseteq X^c$.

A subset A of X^c is said to be *bounded* if there is a non-negative integer n such that $|a| \leq n$ holds for all $a \in A$. If A is non-empty and bounded, we define $|A|$ to be the minimum of all such non-negative integers n, and we define $|\phi| = -1$. If $A, B \subseteq X^c$, we naturally define the product AB to be the set of all elements of X^c of the form ab with $a \in A$ and $b \in B$. If $a \in X^c$ and $B \subseteq X^c$, we define $aB = \{a\}B$.

In the following, $\{1\}$ will be regarded as representing a trivial physical operation requiring that we do nothing (other than to record the symbol 1 as the outcome). Of course, each basic operation $E \in \mathscr{A}$ can be regarded as a one-stage compound operation. A two-stage compound operation is formed as follows: First, select a basic operation $E \in \mathscr{A}$, an $\mathscr{A}$-event $D \neq \phi$ with $D \subseteq E$, and a basic operation $F_d \in \mathscr{A}$ for each $d \in D$. The two-stage compound operation in question – let us call it G – is executed by first executing E to obtain (say) the outcome e; if $e \notin D$, we are done and we record the outcome of G as e, but if $e \in D$, we are obliged to execute F_e to obtain (say) the outcome $x \in F_e$ and to record the outcome of this execution of G as $ex \in X^c$. Evidently, the outcome set for G is $(E \setminus D) \cup \cup (\bigcup_{d \in D} dF_d)$. If we set $F_e = \{1\}$ for $e \in E \setminus D$, then the outcome set for G is simply the set $\bigcup_{e \in E} eF_e$. Multistage compound operations can now be built up inductively by iteration of the above procedure. As usual, we propose to identify such compound operations with their outcome sets. The interested reader should convince himself that the resulting outcome identifications should be harmless so long as 'nature' is oblivious to our intentions and responsive only to our actions.

The above construction of compound operations over $\mathscr{A}$ can be formalized as follows: If $E, G \subseteq X^c$ with $E \neq G$, and if there exists for each $e \in E$ a set F_e such that either $F_e \in \mathscr{A}$ or else $F_e = \{1\}$, and if $G = \bigcup_{e \in E} eF_e$, then we shall call G a *direct successor* of E. If there exists a finite sequence $G_1, G_2, ..., G_n$ such that $E = G_1$ and G_{i+1} is a direct successor of G_i for $i = 1, 2, ..., n-1$, then we shall say that G_n is a *successor* of E. We define $\mathscr{A}^c$ to be the collection of subsets of X^c consisting of $\{1\}$ together with all of the successors of $\{1\}$.

It should be clear that if E is a non-empty bounded subset of X^c and G is a direct successor of E, then G is bounded and $|G| = |E| + 1$. It follows that every $G \in \mathscr{A}^c$ is a non-empty bounded subset of X^c. A set $G \in \mathscr{A}^c$ will be called a *compound operation* over $\mathscr{A}$. If G is such a compound operation, then $|G|$ represents the maximal number of sequential executions of basic operations that could be required to complete an execution of G. Clearly, $\mathscr{A} \subseteq \mathscr{A}^c$; in fact, $\mathscr{A}$ is exactly the subset of $\mathscr{A}^c$ consisting of the compound operations G with $|G| = 1$.

It can be shown without great difficulty that $\mathscr{A}^c$ is always a manual. Moreover, for $a, b \in \cup \mathscr{A}^c = X^c$, we have $a \perp b$ if and only if there exist $c, d, e \in X^c$ and there exist $x, y \in X$ with $a = cxd$, $b = cye$ and $x \perp y$. Also, $\mathscr{A}$ is a Dacey manual if and only if $\mathscr{A}^c$ is a Dacey manual and if $\pi(\mathscr{A})$ is an orthomodular lattice, then so is $\pi(\mathscr{A}^c)$. If $\mathscr{A}$ is locally finite (respectively, locally countable) then so is $\mathscr{A}^c$. The logic $\pi(\mathscr{A})$ is always totally non-atomic provided that there is an $\mathscr{A}$-operation E consisting of at least two distinct outcomes. If $\mathscr{A}$ consists of a single operation, then both $\mathscr{A}$ and $\mathscr{A}^c$ are Boolean manuals; however, if $\mathscr{A}$ is a Boolean manual, it need not follow that $\mathscr{A}^c$ is a Boolean manual. If $\mathscr{A} = \{E\}$, where $E = \{x, y\}$, then $\pi(\mathscr{A}^c)$ is the free Boolean algebra on countably many generators.

6. Complete stochastic models (weights and states)

By a *weight function* for a manual $\mathscr{A}$ with outcome set $X = \cup \mathscr{A}$, we mean a real valued function ω defined on X, taking on its values in the closed unit interval, and such that the unordered sum $\sum_{e \in E} \omega(e)$ converges to 1 for every $\mathscr{A}$-operation E. The set of all such weight functions for $\mathscr{A}$ is denoted by $\Omega = \Omega(\mathscr{A})$. It is natural to extend an $\omega \in \Omega$ to the $\mathscr{A}$-events by defining $\omega(D) = \sum_{d \in D} \omega(d)$ for any $\mathscr{A}$-event D. It then follows that $0 \leqslant \omega(D) \leqslant 1$ for all $\mathscr{A}$-events D and that ω is *finitely additive* in the sense that $\omega(\bigcup_{i=1}^{n} D_i) = \sum_{i=1}^{n} \omega(D_i)$ for any finite family $(D_i \mid 1 \leqslant i \leqslant n)$ of pairwise orthogonal $\mathscr{A}$-events. In general, an $\omega \in \Omega$ need not be countably additive – such additional features as countable additivity will depend on the detailed structure of the manual $\mathscr{A}$.

A weight function $\omega \in \Omega(\mathscr{A})$ can be regarded as a possible complete stochastic model in the frequency sense for the empirical situation described by the manual $\mathscr{A}$. This is to be understood as follows: For every $\mathscr{A}$-outcome $x \in X = \cup \mathscr{A}$, $\omega(x)$ is interpreted as the 'long run relative frequency' with which the outcome x is secured as a consequence of the execution of operations for which x is a possible outcome. Notice that the implicit decision to ignore the actual operations that are executed is already present in the outcome identification process used to form the manual $\mathscr{A}$.

An $\omega \in \Omega(\mathscr{A})$ can also be regarded as a consistent assignment of betting rates to the $\mathscr{A}$-outcomes in the following sense: $\omega(x)$ is interpreted as the appropriate betting rate for the outcome x versus the event $E\backslash\{x\}$ for any execution of the $\mathscr{A}$-operation E, provided that $x \in E$. Again, for this interpretation, because of the decisions made in connection with the outcome identification procedure, the betting rate for x is independent of the operation E, just so x is a possible outcome of E.

Suppose now that C and D are $\mathscr{A}$-events and that $p(C) \leqslant p(D)$; that is, $D^{\perp} \subseteq C^{\perp}$. Let $\omega \in \Omega(\mathscr{A})$ and select any $\mathscr{A}$-operation E for which $D \subseteq E$. Define $B = E\backslash D$, noting that $B \subseteq D^{\perp} \subseteq C^{\perp}$. It follows from coherence that $B \cup C$ is an $\mathscr{A}$-event and by the finite additivity of ω that $\omega(B) + \omega(C) = \omega(B \cup C) \leqslant 1 = \omega(E) = \omega(B \cup D) = \omega(B) + \omega(D)$; hence, $\omega(C) \leqslant \omega(D)$. In particular, if $p(C) = p(D)$, then $\omega(C) = \omega(D)$. This fact permits us lift ω to a function (still denoted by ω) defined on the operational logic $\pi(\mathscr{A})$ simply by setting $\omega(p(D)) = \omega(D)$ for each $\mathscr{A}$-event D. This ω, defined on $\pi(\mathscr{A})$, will be referred to as the *regular state* induced on $\pi(\mathscr{A})$ be the original weight function $\omega \in \Omega(\mathscr{A})$. Notice that, for any $\mathscr{A}$-outcome x, $\omega(x) = \omega(p(\{x\}))$; hence, the original weight function ω can be recaptured from the regular state that it induces.

As usual, a *state* is a function defined on a logic – in this case, $\pi(\mathscr{A})$ – taking on its values in the closed unit interval, finitely additive over orthogonal propositions and assuming the value 1 on the order unit in the logic – which in this case is $p(E)$, where E is any $\mathscr{A}$-operation. Clearly, every regular state on $\pi(\mathscr{A})$ is a bona fide state; however, there may exist states on $\pi(\mathscr{A})$ that are not regular. If $\mathscr{A}$ is a locally finite manual, then every state on $\pi(\mathscr{A})$ is indeed regular. In particular, the states on $\pi(\mathscr{A})$ are precisely the regular states on $\pi(\mathscr{A}_0^*)$.

If ω is a regular state, it can be shown that if $E \in \mathscr{A}$ is a test operation for a proposition $p(D) \in \pi(\mathscr{A})$, then $\omega(p(D)) = \omega(E \cap D^{\perp\perp})$. Thus, if ω is interpreted as a complete stochastic model in the frequency sense, then we can interpret $\omega(p(D))$ as the 'long run relative frequency' with which $p(D)$ will be confirmed as a consequence of the execution of test operations for $p(D)$. Similarly, if ω is interpreted as a consistent assignment of betting rates, then $\omega(p(D))$ can be interpreted as the appropriate betting rate for a bet on the confirmation of the proposition $p(D)$ as a consequence of a given execution of a test operation E for $p(D)$.

A weight (or a state) that assumes only the values 0 and 1 is said to be *dispersion free.* Such a weight (or state) ω, interpreted as a complete stochastic model in the frequency sense, clearly represents a deterministic situation; for instance, if $\omega(p(D)) = 1$ then (according to this stochastic model) the proposition $p(D)$ is virtually certain to be confirmed as a consequence of the execution of any test operation for it. In this sense, such a dispersion free stochastic model implies virtual stability of the 'truth values' of the operational propositions in $\pi(\mathscr{A})$, at least insofar as test operations for these propositions are concerned.

Two $\mathscr{A}$-events A and B are said to be *compatible* if there exists an $\mathscr{A}$-operation E with $A, B \subseteq E$. If $\omega \in \Omega(\mathscr{A})$ and $\omega(B) \neq 0$, where $A, B \subseteq E$ as above, we can define the *conditional weight of A given B* by $\omega(A/B) = = \omega(A \cap B)/\omega(B)$. If ω is interpreted as a complete stochastic model in the frequency sense, then $\omega(A/B)$ can be interpreted as usual as the 'long run relative frequency' with which the event A will occur in the sub-ensemble of all realizations of E in which B occurs. On the other hand, if ω is interpreted as a complete assignment of betting rates, then $\omega(A/B)$ can be interpreted as the betting rate for a conditional bet on A given B for a single realization of the operation E. In either case, note the 'local' nature of the weight $\omega(B/A)$ as a function of the $\mathscr{A}$-event B – it only makes sense for events B that are compatible with A.

A second conditioning notion is available for a compound manual $\mathscr{A}^c$. Indeed, suppose that $\omega \in \Omega(\mathscr{A}^c)$ and that $a \in X^c$ with $\omega(a) \neq 0$. Define $\omega_a : X^c \to [0, 1]$ by $\omega_a(b) = \omega(ab)/\omega(a)$ for all $b \in X^c$. It can be shown [8] that ω_a is again a weight function for the compound manual $\mathscr{A}^c$, and we shall refer to ω_a as the weight function obtained by *operationally conditioning* ω by the outcome a. Similarly, if D is an $\mathscr{A}^c$-event with $\omega(D) \neq 0$, we can define $\omega_D \in \Omega(\mathscr{A}^c)$ by $\omega_D(b) = \omega(Db)/\omega(D)$ for all $b \in X^c$. If we put $A = \{d \in D \mid \omega(d) \neq 0\}$, then A is a non-empty $\mathscr{A}^c$-event and the weight function ω_D can be written as a convex combination $\omega_D = \sum_{d \in A} t_d \omega_d$ where $t_d = \omega(d)/\omega(D)$ for each $d \in A$. If ω is an extreme point of the convex set $\Omega(\mathscr{A})$ – a so-called *pure weight* – then it can be shown [8] that ω_a will again be an extreme point of $\Omega(\mathscr{A}^c)$ whenever $\omega(a) \neq 0$. Thus, operational conditioning by $\mathscr{A}^c$-outcomes preserves extreme points of $\Omega(\mathscr{A}^c)$, whereas, operational conditioning by $\mathscr{A}^c$-events in general will not. Furthermore, it should be noted that in general it will not be possible to condition in this operational sense by operational propositions in any naive way, since there are easy examples of $\mathscr{A}^c$-events A, B for which $p(A)=p(B)$, but $\omega_A \neq \omega_B$. In particular, even if E is an $\mathscr{A}^c$-operation, ω_E need not coincide with ω.

If $\omega \in \Omega(\mathscr{A}^c)$ is interpreted as a complete stochastic model in the frequency sense, then clearly $\omega_a(b)$ can be regarded as the 'long run relative frequency' with which the outcome b will be secured (as a consequence of compound operations for which it could be secured) immediately after the execution of a compound operation for which the outcome a was secured. Here, there is a definite temporal order involved – a occurs *first*, then b. Moreover, in general, there is no temporal symmetry, as can be seen by the failure of the classical multiplication rule: $\omega_a(b)\omega(a)$ need not coincide with $\omega_b(a)\omega(b)$. The reader should have no difficulty in giving an interpretation of $\omega_a(b)$ as a betting rate on the outcome b, given that the outcome a was previously obtained, when ω is interpreted as a complete assignment of betting rates.

It is surely desirable to have a lavish supply of weight functions for a manual $\mathscr{A}$ and the physical circumstances which it describes. Any ad hoc assumption assuring such a supply of weights would necessarily be a non-trivial constraint on the manual, since there are large classes of orthomodular lattices that admit only one state, or no states at all [12]. Nevertheless, in any realistic situation there always appears to be a generous supply of weight functions in one of the following senses: Let Δ be a set of states defined on the operational logic $\pi(\mathscr{A})$. We say that Δ is a *full* set of states for $\pi(\mathscr{A})$ provided that the condition $\alpha(p(C))\leqslant$ $\leqslant\alpha(p(D))$ for all $\alpha\in\Delta$ implies the condition $p(C)\leqslant p(D)$, where $p(C)$ and $p(D)$ are any two propositions in $\pi(\mathscr{A})$. Similarly, Δ is said to be a *strong* set of states for $\pi(\mathscr{A})$ provided that whenever $\alpha(p(C))=1$ implies $\alpha(p(D))=1$ for all $\alpha\in\Delta$, then $p(C)\leqslant p(D)$, where again $p(C)$ and $p(D)$ are any two propositions in $\pi(\mathscr{A})$. A set of weights $\Delta\subseteq\Omega(\mathscr{A})$ is said to be *full* (respectively, *strong*) provided that the corresponding set Δ of regular states if full (respectively, strong) for the logic $\pi(\mathscr{A})$.

It can be shown [7] that a set of weights $\Delta\subseteq\Omega(\mathscr{A})$ is full (respectively, strong) if and only if, given any non-orthogonal pair of $\mathscr{A}$-outcomes x and y, there exists an $\omega\in\Delta$ such that $1<\omega(x)+\omega(y)$ (respectively, $\omega(x)=1$ and $\omega(y)\neq0$). Evidently, any strong set of weights or states is necessarily full. Moreover, any full set of states will separate the propositions in $\pi(\mathscr{A})$, and the existence of a separating set of states for $\pi(\mathscr{A})$ implies that $\pi(\mathscr{A})$ is an orthomodular poset and hence that $\mathscr{A}$ is a Dacey manual.

If $\mathscr{A}$ is a manual with a strong set of weights $\Omega(\mathscr{A})$, it can be shown that $\Omega(\mathscr{A}^c)$ is again a strong set of weights for the compound manual $\mathscr{A}^c$. Any full set of dispersion free weights (or states) is necessarily strong. The existence of a full set of dispersion free weights (or states) is often construed as implying the existence of so-called 'hidden classical variables' [20]. It can be shown that if the manual $\mathscr{A}$ admits a full set of dispersion free weights, then so does the compound manual $\mathscr{A}^c$ [22].

7. EXAMPLES OF MANUALS

In the present section, we shall consider three particular manuals, their logics and their associated sets of weights. Of course, additional examples can be constructed from these, say by compounding or saturating.

Example I. Let E by any non-empty set and let $\mathscr{A} = \{E\}$ be the manual consisting just of the single set E. In this case, the logic $\pi(\mathscr{A})$ is isomorphic to the complete atomic field of all subsets D of E under the correspondence $D \leftrightarrow p(D)$. Here, if $x \in E$, then the function $\delta_x : E \to [0, 1]$ defined by $\delta_x(y) = 1$ or 0 according to whether $y = x$ or $y \neq x$ is a dispersion free weight function for $\mathscr{A}$; hence, the set of all dispersion free weights is strong in this case. If E is a countable set, then every weight function on E is a unique countable convex combination of these dispersion free weights; however, if E is infinite there will always exist non-regular states on the logic $\pi(\mathscr{A})$.

Example II. Let $(S, \mathscr{F})$ be a measurable space – that is, S is a non-empty set and $\mathscr{F}$ is a σ-field of subsets of S. Let $\mathscr{A}$ consist of all countable partitions of S into non-empty sets in $\mathscr{F}$. In this case, the logic $\pi(\mathscr{A})$ is isomorphic to the σ-field $\mathscr{F}$ (a countably complete Boolean algebra) under the correspondence that associates $p(\{A\})$ with the non-empty set $A \in \mathscr{F}$ and associates $p(\phi)$ with $\phi \in \mathscr{F}$. It follows from this isomorphism that the weights for $\mathscr{A}$, that is, the regular states for $\pi(\mathscr{A})$, are in natural one-to-one correspondence with the countably additive probability measures on the measurable space $(S, \mathscr{F})$. Again, we have a full set of dispersion free regular states. Here, a measurable space is in effect regarded as representing, not a single operation as in Example I, but many operations, all of which can be viewed as coarsenings of a single idealized operation with outcome set S.

The manual $\mathscr{A}$ of Example I is locally finite (respectively, locally countable) if and only if E is a finite (respectively, countable) set, while the manual $\mathscr{A}$ of Example II is always (at least) locally countable. It is worthwhile noting that in Example II, we can always form the submanual $\mathscr{A}_0$ of $\mathscr{A}$ consisting of all the *finite* $\mathscr{F}$-measurable partitions of S. The logic $\pi(\mathscr{A}_0)$ remains naturally isomorphic to $\mathscr{F}$; however, the regular states for $\pi(\mathscr{A}_0)$ are now all of the *finitely* additive probability measures on the measurable space $(S, \mathscr{F})$. Examples I and II indicate how we can subsume conventional probability theory under our more general formalism.

Example III. All proposed 'quantum logics' [1], [19], [13], seem to be (at least) orthomodular posets. Given such an orthomodular poset L, we can define $\mathscr{A}_0$ to be the set of all finite maximal pairwise orthogonal subsets of $L \setminus \{0\}$. Then $\mathscr{A}_0$ is a locally finite manual whose logic $\pi(\mathscr{A}_0)$ is naturally isomorphic to L, while the regular states on $\pi(\mathscr{A}_0)$ correspond to the finitely orthoadditive generalized probability measures (states) on L. If L is countably orthocomplete (as a respectable 'quantum logic' is usually assumed to be) then we can form the manual $\mathscr{A}$ consisting of all countable maximal pairwise orthogonal subsets of $L \setminus \{0\}$. Again, $\pi(\mathscr{A})$ is canonically isomorphic to L, but now the regular states on $\pi(\mathscr{A})$ correspond to the countably orthoadditive states on L. Of course, a particularly important example of such an L is obtained by taking L to be the lattice of all self-adjoint projection operators on a separable, infinite dimensional Hilbert space $\mathscr{H}$. In this case, the countably ortho-additive states on L are in natural one-to-one correspondence with the von Neumann density operators on $\mathscr{H}$ [10].

8. INDUCTIVE LOGIC AND CREDIBILITIES

A great deal of confusion can be avoided in the ensuing discussion of inference procedures if a careful distinction is made between an *event* that might occur as a consequence of the execution of one of the admissible reproducible physical operations $E \in \mathscr{A}$, a *prediction* that in fact one such event will occur in a particular single realization of such an $E \in \mathscr{A}$, and a *statistical hypothesis* that makes some claim regarding the frequency with which such an event occurs in very many realizations of such operations. For example, the occurrence of 'heads' in the toss of a penny is an event; it refers to a possible consequence of a reproducible physical operation (the toss of the penny). On the other hand, an assertion that the penny will fall 'heads' on the very next toss is a prediction in that it makes an immediately verifiable claim regarding a particular realization of the operation. Finally, an assertion that the penny is a 'fair coin' is a statistical hypothesis, since it declares that, in the long run, the penny will fall 'heads' approximately half the time.

As we have mentioned, it is perhaps not unreasonable to entertain the notion that $\omega(D)$, for an $\omega \in \Omega(\mathscr{A})$, represents the 'long run relative frequency' with which the $\mathscr{A}$-event D occurs as a consequence of executing an operation $E \in \mathscr{A}$ for which D is an event. One might be willing to bet on predictions; consequently, they should admit the assignment of odds or betting rates. In fact, we shall have occasion to interpret certain elements of $\Omega(\mathscr{A})$ as representing consistent assignments of betting rates for predictions of the occurrence of events. Statistical hypotheses, on the contrary, are very poor subjects for betting since, in general, it would be very difficult – if not impossible – to settle on their veracity. Moreover, it makes little sense to consider the relative frequency with which a particular statistical hypothesis is 'true'. Nevertheless, it is possible to harbor various degrees of confidence (that is, *credibilities*) concerning the veracity of statistical hypotheses.

In this section, we shall formalize the notion of a statistical hypothesis and introduce the credibilities that might be defined on them. In this connection, we have already regarded the weights $\omega \in \Omega(\mathscr{A})$ as possible stochastic models in the frequency sense. From this point of view, an $\omega \in \Omega(\mathscr{A})$ is regarded as a complete or elementary statistical hypothesis for the manual $\mathscr{A}$. An obvious extension of this point of view would regard a subset of $\Omega(\mathscr{A})$ as a (partial) statistical hypothesis concerning $\mathscr{A}$ – one that may or may not be 'supported' by data collected during the course of many executions of the admissible operations in $\mathscr{A}$. In other words, a subset $\Lambda \subseteq \Omega(\mathscr{A})$ could be interpreted as the hypothesis that the 'true' complete stochastic model ω for $\mathscr{A}$ (in the frequency sense) belongs to Λ. Conversely, any well-formed statistical assertion concerning the 'long run relative frequencies' with which $\mathscr{A}$-events occur could reasonably be represented by the subset Λ of $\Omega(\mathscr{A})$ consisting of the stochastic models $\omega \in \Omega(\mathscr{A})$ that satisfy its claims.

For example, the set $\{\omega \in \Omega \mid \omega(x) = p\}$ can be interpreted as the statistical hypothesis asserting that the 'long run relative frequency' with which the $\mathscr{A}$-outcome x will be secured (as a consequence of the execution of $\mathscr{A}$-operations E with $x \in E$) is p. If we define, for each $\mathscr{A}$-outcome x, the function $f_x: \Omega \to [0, 1]$ by $f_x(\omega) = \omega(x)$ for all $\omega \in \Omega$, then the latter set can conveniently be written as $f_x^{-1}(p)$. Likewise, if T is a subset of the unit interval $[0, 1]$, then $f_x^{-1}(T)$ can be viewed as asserting that the $\mathscr{A}$-outcome x will be secured with a 'long run relative frequency' corresponding to some number in the set T.

In view of the above, we propose to interpret the subsets of $\Omega(\mathscr{A})$ as representing statistical hypotheses concerning the experimental universe of discourse represented by the manual $\mathscr{A}$. Notice that the subsets of $\Omega(\mathscr{A})$, thus interpreted, make assertions concerning infinite ensembles of realizations of the admissible operations $E \in \mathscr{A}$; consequently their veracity cannot be settled on the basis of finitely many realizations of these operations. On the other hand, we have seen that, as a consequence of their very definition, operational propositions can be confirmed or refuted by the execution of individual test operations. In some sense, we should be prepared to regard the 'truth value' of a statistical hypothesis as being stable (in spite of its direct operational inaccessibility) while the 'truth value' of a given operational proposition (although directly accessible operationally) does not necessarily display this stability. However, a prediction that a given event D will occur as a consequence of a particular execution of an admissible operation E with $D \subseteq E$ is both directly accessible in an operational sense (perform the intended realization of E and see what happens) and stable (since it refers only to a particular single execution of E).

Although statistical hypotheses will generally not be directly verifiable in the same sense as the operational propositions, nevertheless, the laws of empirical science are of this form. How, then, are these laws supported? The answer, of course, is by means of scientific induction or statistical inference. If this inference machinery were well defined, we could identify those particular subsets of Ω that might be inductively supported. Unfortunately, this is not the case. However, it might be feasible to identify certain statistical hypotheses that ought to be supportable under any plausible inference procedure. At the very least, we feel that sets of the form $\{\omega \in \Omega \mid a \leqslant \omega(D) \leqslant b\}$, where D is any $\mathscr{A}$-event and a, b are rational numbers with $0 \leqslant a \leqslant b \leqslant 1$, should be so supportable. Moreover, it seems reasonable to suppose that finite unions, finite intersections, and complements of inductively supportable sets should again be inductively supportable. Thus, the field $\mathscr{I}_0$ of subsets of Ω generated by all sets of the form $\{\omega \in \Omega \mid a \leqslant \omega(D) \leqslant b\}$, D running through all $\mathscr{A}$-events and a, b running through all rational numbers with $0 \leqslant a \leqslant b \leqslant 1$, ought to be included in the 'inductive logic' of all potentially supportable statistical hypotheses.

The computational attractions of mathematical analysis suggest that we require that the potentially supportable statistical hypotheses form not only a field, but a σ-field of subsets of Ω. Thus, for our present purposes, we shall define the *inductive logic* for $\mathscr{A}$ to be the σ-field of subsets of Ω generated by $\mathscr{I}_0$ and we shall denote this σ-field by $\mathscr{I} = \mathscr{I}(\mathscr{A})$. Note that if D is any $\mathscr{A}$-event and if a, b are real numbers with $0 \leqslant a \leqslant b \leqslant 1$, then $\{\omega \in \Omega \mid a \leqslant \omega(D) \leqslant b\}$ belongs to $\mathscr{I}$.

We define a *credibility* for $\mathscr{A}$ to be a normed measure on the σ-field $\mathscr{I}$, that is, a probability measure on $\mathscr{I}$. The set of all such credibilities will be denoted by $M = M(\mathscr{A})$. Given a $\mu \in M$ and a $\Lambda \in \mathscr{I}$, $\mu(\Lambda)$ will be interpreted as the degree of belief, measure of confidence, or amount of credibility that we are willing to assign to the statistical hypothesis Λ according to μ. Thus, a $\mu \in M$ can be viewed as a consistent model of beliefs concerning the manual $\mathscr{A}$. As we shall see when we consider the question of inference, the $\mu \in M$ can also be looked upon as encodings of information. Thus, these credibilities roughly correspond to the subjective probabilities of Jaynes [14] and Cox [4].

An additional conditioning notion is now available for the credibility measures: Indeed, given a $\mu \in M$ and a $\Delta \in \mathscr{I}$ for which $\mu(\Delta) \neq 0$, we can form the classical conditional measure μ_Δ, $\mu_\Delta(\Lambda) = \mu(\Delta \cap \Lambda)/\mu(\Delta) = \mu(\Lambda/\Delta)$ for all $\Lambda \in \mathscr{I}$. Note that μ_Δ is again a credibility. We regard $\mu(\Lambda/\Delta)$ as the credibility of Λ on the hypothesis Δ.

Notice that these credibility conditionings behave like inference procedures in that they appear to alter beliefs. The $\mu \in M$ have been interpreted as consistent models of beliefs held regarding $\mathscr{A}$ and the conditionings $\mu \rightsquigarrow \mu_\Delta$ do modify them, essentially by discarding those weights that do not satisfy the statistical hypothesis $\Delta \in \mathscr{I}$. However, there is a serious impediment to such an inference interpretation, since the $\Delta \in \mathscr{I}$ make assertions concerning statistical laws that can rarely be verified with certainty solely by hard experimental data. Technically, a $\Delta \in \mathscr{I}$ can be postulated in this fashion only to study its consequences; yet such statistical hypotheses are frequently postulated in practice as a result of (perhaps ill-defined) previous experience. Thus, in some instances, we might unofficially look upon these credibility conditionings as inference based on 'soft data'. Of course, such conditionings satisfy all of the usual laws, including the multiplication law, the law of total probability, and Bayes' law. Moreover, such conditionings commute when they are defined, that is, the order in which 'soft data' is processed is irrelevant.

9. BETTING RATES

A predictive apparatus that provides an assignment of rational betting rates for simple bets concerning the occurrence of $\mathscr{A}$-events is already implicit in the present formalism. Furthermore, given the inference procedures discussed in the subsequent sections, we can also make such betting rate assignments for more complex conditional bets.

By a *simple bet* or wager concerning an $\mathscr{A}$-event D, we mean a contract of the following form: The first party will place \$$a$ in a pool and the second party will place \$$b$ in the pool for a total *stake* of \$$s = \$(a+b)$. The total stake \$$s$ goes to the first party if the event D occurs as a consequence of a specified realization of an operation $E \in \mathscr{A}$ for which $D \subseteq E$; while it goes to the second party if the event D does not occur as a consequence of this realization. The *betting rate* or quotient for this bet concerning the event D is by definition $\sigma(D) = a/s$. The first party is said to have bet *on* the event D giving the odds $a:b$, while the second party is said to have bet *against* the event D giving the odds $b:a$. An individual is said to *make* this simple bet with positive stake s (respectively, with negative stake $-s$) against another individual if he agrees to the contract as the first party (respectively, as the second party).

A mapping σ that assigns a betting rate $\sigma(D) \in [0, 1]$ to each $\mathscr{A}$-event D is called a *simple betting rate assignment*. Note that any finite sequence $D_1, D_2, ..., D_n \subseteq E \in \mathscr{A}$ of compatible events determines a partition $\{E_1, E_2, ..., E_N\}$, $N \leqslant 2^n$, of E in the usual way. Define $\chi(D_i, E_k) = 0$ or 1 according to whether $D_i \cap E_k = \phi$ or $E_k \subseteq D_i$ respectively, for $1 \leqslant i \leqslant n$, $1 \leqslant k \leqslant N$. Given a combination of simple bets concerning $D_1, D_2, ..., D_n$ with the respective stakes (positive or negative) $s_1, s_2, ..., s_n$ on a single execution of E, the *profit* or net gain to an individual making the bets at the rates given by σ, for an outcome $x \in E_k$ is

$$P(E_k) = \sum_{i=1}^{n} s_i [\chi(D_i, E_k) - \sigma(D_i)].$$

Such a simple betting rate assignment is said to *admit dutch book* if there exists a combination of bets as above for which $P(E_k) > 0$ for all $k = 1, 2, ..., N$. It is said to *admit weak dutch book* if there exists a combination of bets as above for which $P(E_k) \geqslant 0$ for all $k = 1, 2, ..., N$ and there exists at least one such k for which $P(E_k) > 0$. The simple betting rate assignment σ is said to be *consistent* (or coherent or fair) if it does not admit dutch book and *strictly consistent* if it does not admit weak dutch book.

By the same argument as in [21], [5], [18], [16], [25], we see that a simple betting rate assignment σ is consistent if and only if it is normalized ($\sigma(E) = 1$ for all $E \in \mathscr{A}$) and finitely additive ($\sigma(A \cup B) = \sigma(A) + \sigma(B)$ for all orthogonal $\mathscr{A}$-events A and B). There is a one-to-one correspondence $\sigma \leftrightarrow \alpha$ between consistent simple betting rate assignments σ and states α on $\pi(\mathscr{A})$ given by $\alpha(p(D)) = \sigma(D)$ for all $\mathscr{A}$-events D. Henceforth, we shall simply identify such a σ with the corresponding α. Notice that σ is strictly consistent if and only if it is a strictly positive state (that is, if D is an $\mathscr{A}$-event with $\sigma(D) = \sigma(p(D)) = 0$, then $D = \emptyset$).

Each credibility $\mu \in M(\mathscr{A})$ gives rise in a natural way to an assignment σ_μ of consistent simple betting rates in the following way: Given an $\mathscr{I}$-measurable function f on Ω (that is, a random variable) we define, as usual, the *expected value of f for* μ, when it exists, by $E_\mu(f) = \int_\Omega f \, d\mu$. In case f is not defined on all of Ω, but only on some $\mathscr{I}$-measurable subset Λ of Ω, we define $E_\mu(f) = \int_\Lambda f \, d\mu$. In particular, any $\mathscr{A}$-event D defines an $\mathscr{I}$-measurable function f_D on Ω by $f_D(\omega) = \omega(D)$ for all $\omega \in \Omega$. Thus, we obtain the promised state σ_μ by defining $\sigma_\mu(D) = E_\mu(f_D)$ for every $\mathscr{A}$-event D.

If $\mathscr{A}$ is locally countable, then σ_μ is actually a regular state and therefore corresponds to a unique weight function σ_μ. Consequently, in this case, we might be inclined to interpret σ_μ as a bona fide stochastic model in the frequency sense; but this would be unreasonable. Indeed, suppose our current credibility μ is such that $\mu(\{\omega_1\}) = t$, $\mu(\{\omega_2\}) = 1 - t$, where $0 < t < 1$ and ω_1, ω_2 are distinct weight functions. Thus, we are certain that the 'true' frequency model for $\mathscr{A}$ is either ω_1 or ω_2. Notice, however, that $\sigma_\mu = t\omega_1 + (1-t)\omega_2 \neq \omega_1, \omega_2$; hence, we cannot regard σ_μ as the 'true' frequency model for $\mathscr{A}$. This example also shows that σ_μ is generally not even a good approximation for the 'true' frequency model. Indeed, suppose that $t = 1/2$, $\omega_1(x) = 1$ and $\omega_2(x) = 0$, where x is some $\mathscr{A}$-outcome. Then, $\sigma_\mu(x) = 1/2$ – nowhere near the 'true' value, which is either 1 or 0.

Thus, we are forced to look elsewhere for an interpretation of σ_μ; in brief, this has been accomplished by interpreting σ_μ to be a rational betting rate assignment in the sense, for example, of Savage [24], de Finetti [5], and Good [11]. Notice that σ_μ is a subjectively weighted mixture of possible frequency models for $\mathscr{A}$ and the map $\mu \to \sigma_\mu$ carries the degree of belief μ from the level of statistical hypotheses to the level of outcomes and events. In a sense, $\sigma_\mu(D)$ can also be interpreted as a measure of confidence in a prediction – that is, in an assertion that the event D will occur in a particular realization of an admissible operation $E \in \mathscr{A}$ for which $D \subseteq E$.

In addition to the simple bets described above, there are at least two possible types of conditional bets, compatible conditional bets and independent conditional bets. Their descriptions are as follows:

Let A, B be a compatible pair of $\mathscr{A}$-events, so that A, $B \subseteq E$ holds for some $E \in \mathscr{A}$. A *compatible conditional bet* concerning the ordered pair (A, B) is a contract of the following form: The first party will place \$$a$ in a pool and the second party will place \$$b$ in the pool for a total *stake* of \$$s = \$(a+b)$. The $\mathscr{A}$-operation E is to be executed, where A, $B \subseteq E$. If the event B does not occur as a consequence of this execution, the bet is off and each party is returned his own contribution to the pool. If the event $A \cap B$ occurs for this realization of E, then the total stake \$$s$ goes to the first party, while if the event $B \setminus A$ occurs for this realization of E, then the total stake \$$s$ goes to the second party. The *betting rate* for this wager is by definition $\sigma(A/B) = a/s$.

An *independent conditional bet* concerning an ordered pair (C, D) of any two $\mathscr{A}$-events is a contract of the following form: The first party will place \$$a$ in a pool and the second party will place \$$b$ in the pool for a total *stake* of \$$s = \$(a+b)$. An $\mathscr{A}$-operation $E \in \mathscr{A}$ with $C \subseteq E$ is to be executed and, independently, an $\mathscr{A}$-operation $F \in \mathscr{A}$ with $D \subseteq F$ is to be executed. If the event D does not occur as a consequence of this execution of F, the bet is off and each party is returned his own contribution to the pool. If the event D does occur as a consequence of this execution of F, then the total stake \$$s$ goes to the first or to the second party according to whether or not the event C occurs as a consequence of the specified execution of E. The betting rate for this wager is by definition $\sigma(C//D) = a/s$.

Given compatible $\mathscr{A}$-events $A, B \subseteq E \in \mathscr{A}$ and an $\mathscr{A}$-event $G \subseteq F \in \mathscr{A}$, we can define a *mixed conditional bet* concerning (A given B) and independently given G, in an obvious way. The betting rate for this mixed conditional bet will be denoted by $\sigma(A/B//G)$.

Now let σ be an assignment of betting rates to all of the above types of bets – simple, compatible conditional, independent conditional, and mixed conditional. We define σ to be *consistent* (*strictly consistent*) if it does not admit dutch book (weak dutch book) as described above. It can be shown that σ is consistent if and only if it satisfies the following conditions:

(1) $\sigma(D//E) = \sigma(D)$,

(2) $\sigma(E//F) = 1$,   when $\sigma(F) \neq 0$,

(3) $\sigma(A \cup B//F) = \sigma(A//F) + \sigma(B//F)$ if $A \cap B = \emptyset, \sigma(F) \neq 0$,

(4) $\sigma(G//F)\,\sigma(F) = \sigma(F//G)\,\sigma(G)$,

(5)   If $\sigma(F) \neq 0$,   then $\sigma(A/B//F)\,\sigma(B//F) = \sigma(A \cap B//F)$,

where D is any $\mathscr{A}$-event, A and B are any compatible $\mathscr{A}$-events, E is any $\mathscr{A}$-operation and F, G are any non-empty $\mathscr{A}$-events. Moreover, σ is strictly consistent if and only if it satisfies (1)–(5) and also

(6) $\sigma(D//F) = 0$ implies $D = \emptyset$.

We have seen that, given a credibility $\mu \in M(\mathscr{A})$, σ_μ provides a consistent assignment of betting rates for simple bets. In order to obtain, in addition, an assignment of betting rates for conditional bets, we shall require the inference procedures discussed in the subsequent sections.

10. INFERENCE PROCEDURES

The role of an inference process is to establish and reappraise beliefs on the strength of data. In this connection, the only experimental data that ought to be admitted in the universe of discourse described by a manual $\mathscr{A}$ are those events that occur as a consequence of the execution of $\mathscr{A}$-

operations. Since we have represented consistent sets of beliefs held in regard to the manual $\mathscr{A}$ by credibilities $\mu \in M(\mathscr{A})$, we define an *inference strategy* to be a function $S:(\mu, D) \rightsquigarrow v = S(\mu, D)$ mapping each pair (μ, D) consisting of a credibility μ and a non-empty $\mathscr{A}$-event D to a credibility $v = S(\mu, D)$. Here, we shall refer to μ as the *prior credibility* and to v as the *posterior credibility on the data D*. An *inference procedure* is defined to be an ordered pair (S, μ_0) consisting of an inference strategy S and a $\mu_0 \in M$ called a *primitive prior* credibility.

The primitive $\mu_0 \in M$ is regarded as a classical probability in the sense of Laplace [17] and Carnap [2], [3]. It is understood to be assigned without the support of explicit experimental data and, as a consequence, it can only depend of the formal structure of $\mathscr{A}$ and imposed hypotheses. As Carnap [3] suggested, μ_0 represents the pristine character of an inference procedure. One advantage of the representation (S, μ_0) of an inference procedure is that it factors such a procedure into a generally acceptable part and a relatively controversial part. There are many statisticians and philosophers who would object to the notion of a primitive prior credibility, and even more who could not agree on an acceptable method of choosing one, but who could agree on a strategy S – or at least on many of the conditions that such a strategy should satisfy.

Now that we have inference procedures available, we can produce the conditional betting rates promised in the previous section. Thus suppose A and D are $\mathscr{A}$-events, $D \neq \emptyset$, and μ is our prior credibility. Let $v = S(\mu, D)$. We compute the corresponding conditional betting rates as follows:

(i) $\sigma_\mu(A//D) = \sigma_v(A)$.

(ii)   If A and D are compatible, $\sigma_\mu(A/D) = E_v(f_{A/D})$, where $f_{A/D}$ is the $\mathscr{I}$-measurable function defined by $f_{A/D}(\omega) = \omega(A \cap D)/\omega(D) = \omega(A/D)$ for all $\omega \in \Omega$ with $\omega(D) \neq 0$.

If A and B are compatible $\mathscr{A}$-events, we combine (i) and (ii) to produce

(iii) $\sigma_\mu(A/B//D) = \sigma_v(A/B)$.

The above assignment of betting rates for conditional bets suggests the following notational conventions, which we shall use whenever they are convenient: Let μ be our prior credibility, let D be a non-empty $\mathscr{A}$-event and let $v = S(\mu, D)$ be our posterior credibility. For $A \in \mathscr{I}$ we write by definition $\mu(\Lambda//D)=\nu(\Lambda)$. Thus, $\mu(\Lambda//D)$ is interpreted as the degree of belief that we are willing to assign to the statistical hypothesis Λ given the prior μ and given that we are in receipt of the experimental data represented by the assertion that the event D occurred as a consequence of the execution of an $\mathscr{A}$-operation E with $D\subseteq E$. If C is another non-empty $\mathscr{A}$-event, we shall write, by definition, $\mu(\Lambda//D, C)=\nu(\Lambda//C)$.

In our discussion of 'soft inference', we have already introduced the notation $\mu(\Lambda/\Delta)=\mu_\Delta(\Lambda)$ for the conditional credibility of Λ on the hypothesis Δ, provided $\mu(\Delta)\neq0$. Thus, if $\mu(\Delta)\neq0$, we define $\mu(\Lambda/\Delta//D)=$ $=\mu_\Delta(\Lambda//D)$ and if $\nu(\Delta)\neq0$, we define $\mu(\Lambda//D/\Delta)=\nu_\Delta(\Lambda)$.

We shall now enumerate and then discuss some of the generally acceptable conditions that could be imposed on an inference strategy S:

(1) $\mu(\Lambda//E)=\mu(\Lambda)$ for any $\Lambda\in\mathscr{I}$ and any $E\in\mathscr{A}$.

(2) $\mu(\Lambda//C, D)=\mu(\Lambda//D, C)$ for any $\Lambda\in\mathscr{I}$ and any non-empty $\mathscr{A}$-events D, C.

(3) $\mu(\Lambda/\Delta//D)=\mu(\Lambda//D/\Delta)$ for any $\Lambda\in\mathscr{I}$, any non-empty $\mathscr{A}$-event D and any $\Delta\in\mathscr{I}$ for which $\mu(\Delta)\neq0$ and $\mu(\Delta//D)\neq0$.

(4) $\sigma_\mu(D//C)\,\sigma_\mu(C)=\sigma_\mu(C//D)\,\sigma_\mu(D)$ for any two non-empty $\mathscr{A}$-events C, D.

(5) $\sigma_\mu(A\cap B//D)=\sigma_\mu(B//D)\,\sigma_\mu(A/B//D)$, where A and B are compatible $\mathscr{A}$-events and D is an $\mathscr{A}$-event with $\sigma_\mu(D)\neq0$.

(6)   If D is a non-empty $\mathscr{A}$-event and if $\Lambda\in\mathscr{I}$ is such that $\omega(D)=0$ for all $\omega\in\Lambda$, then $\mu(\Lambda//D)=0$ if $\sigma_\mu(D)\neq0$.

(7)   If D is a non-empty $\mathscr{A}$-event and if $\Lambda\in\mathscr{I}$ is such that $\omega(D)=1$ for all $\omega\in\Lambda$, then $\mu(\Lambda)\leqslant\mu(\Lambda//D)$.
       If, in addition, $0<\sigma_\mu(D)<1$, then $\mu(\Lambda)<\mu(\Lambda//D)$.

(8)   If D is an $\mathscr{A}$-event, $\Lambda\in\mathscr{I}$, $\sigma_\mu(D)\neq0$, $\mu(\Lambda)\neq0$ and $\sigma_\mu(D)=$ $\sigma_\nu(D)$ where $\nu=\mu_\Lambda$, then $\mu(\Lambda//D)=\mu(\Lambda)$.

(9)   If A and B are non-empty $\mathscr{A}$-events with $p(A)=p(B)$, then $\mu(\Lambda//A)=\mu(\Lambda//B)$ for any $\Lambda\in\mathscr{I}$.

(10)   If D_1 and D_2 are orthogonal non-empty $\mathscr{A}$-events and $D=D_1\cup D_2$ with $\sigma_\mu(D)\neq0$, then $\mu(\Lambda//D)=t\mu(\Lambda//D_1)+$ $+(1-t)\mu(\Lambda//D_2)$ for any $\Lambda\in\mathscr{I}$, where $t=\sigma_\mu(D_1)/\sigma_\mu(D)$ and of course $1-t=\sigma_\mu(D_2)/\sigma_\mu(D)$.

(11)   If $\mu=t\mu_1+(1-t)\mu_2$ with $0\leqslant t\leqslant1$ and if D is an $\mathscr{A}$-event with $\sigma_\mu(D)\neq0$, then, for any $\Lambda\in\mathscr{I}$, $\mu(\Lambda//D)=s\mu_1(\Lambda//D)+$

$+(1-s)\mu_2(\Lambda//D)$, where $s=t\sigma_{\mu_1}(D)/\sigma_\mu(D)$ and of course $1-s=(1-t)\sigma_{\mu_2}(D)/\sigma_\mu(D)$.

(12)   If D is a non-empty $\mathscr{A}$-event and $v=S(\mu, D)$, then v is absolutely continuous with respect to μ (that is, if $\Lambda \in \mathscr{I}$ and $\mu(\Lambda)=0$, then $v(\Lambda)=0$).

Condition (1) simply says that one should not modify ones beliefs merely on the information that an $\mathscr{A}$-operation was executed. Conditions (2) and (3) just require that the order in which information is processed is irrelevant. In this connection, notice that condition (2) is consistent with our views concerning the independence of the execution of $\mathscr{A}$-operations.

If we wish our betting rate assignments to be consistent, then every σ_μ must satisfy conditions (1)–(5) of Section 9. Because of the agreements already made concerning such assignments in (i), (ii) and (iii) of the present section and because of condition (1) above, each σ_μ already satisfies conditions (1), (2) and (3) of Section 9. In order to secure conditions (4) and (5) of Section 9, they must be imposed as conditions (4) and (5) above.

Conditions (6), (7) and (8) are, in our view, the sine qua non of scientific inference. Condition (6) asserts that when a statistical hypothesis Λ implies that the $\mathscr{A}$-event D will not occur, then our degree of belief in Λ, given that D did occur, should be zero. Condition (7) asserts that if a statistical hypothesis Λ implies that an $\mathscr{A}$-event D must occur, then our degree of belief in Λ, given that D did occur, should not decrease. Condition (8) asserts, in effect, that when the statistical hypothesis Λ is irrelevant to the betting rate for D, then the data D is irrelevant to the credibility of Λ.

Conditions (9), (10) and (11) are mathematically attractive, but nowhere near as compelling as the previous conditions. Condition (9) says that two $\mathscr{A}$-events which are equivalent in the sense that they correspond to the same operational proposition should cause us to reappraise our beliefs in the same way. As for condition (10), to assert that D occurred is equivalent to asserting that either D_1 or D_2 occurred; hence, our belief in Λ given that D occurred ought to be a weighted average of our belief in Λ given that D_1 occurred and our belief in Λ given that D_2 occurred. Moreover, the coefficients involved in forming this average ought to be proportional to the respective betting rates for D_1 and D_2.

As to condition (11), it is reasonable to suppose that if a credibility μ is a weighted average of credibilities μ_1 and μ_2, then $S(\mu, D)$ is a weighted average of $S(\mu_1, D)$ and $S(\mu_2, D)$. Some computation with credibilities supported on finite subsets of Ω, employing the remaining eleven conditions, quickly suggests the chosen coefficients s and $1-s$ in (11).

Condition (12) is an all but universally applied 'obstinacy' condition; it asserts that if we are absolutely certain that a given statistical hypothesis is false, then no finite amount of data can change our minds.

We now turn briefly to the more controversial matter of the primitive a priori μ_0. Starting with Laplace [17], many attempts to establish μ_0 have required the imposition of symmetry constraints. Here, we shall abstract and generalize this approach to fit our present formalism.

An *automorphism* of the manual $\mathscr{A}$ with outcome set $X = \bigcup \mathscr{A}$ is defined to be a bijection $\Phi: X \to X$ such that for every $A \subseteq X$, $\Phi(A) = = \{\Phi(a) \mid a \in A\}$ is an $\mathscr{A}$-operation if and only if A is an $\mathscr{A}$-operation. The set of all such automorphisms, $\mathrm{Aut}(\mathscr{A})$, forms a group under ordinary function composition. Furthermore, if Φ is such an automorphism, then it induces an automorphism Φ^* of the Boolean σ-algebra $\mathscr{I}$ by $\Phi^*(\Lambda) = \{\omega \circ \Phi \mid \omega \in \Lambda\}$ for all $\Lambda \in \mathscr{I}$.

It is sometimes convenient to represent the 'physical symmetries' of the experimental universe of discourse represented by the manual $\mathscr{A}$ as a subgroup G of $\mathrm{Aut}(\mathscr{A})$. Supposing that this has been done, it is then reasonable to assume that the primitive a priori μ_0 will satisfy the following condition:

(13)   For any $\Phi \in G$, for any $\Lambda \in \mathscr{I}$ and for any non-empty $\mathscr{A}$-events $D_1, D_2 \ldots, D_n$,
$$\mu_0(\Lambda // D_1, D_2 \ldots, D_n) = \mu_0(\Phi^*(\Lambda) // \Phi(D_1), \Phi(D_2) \ldots, \Phi(D_n)).$$

In particular, if we take $G = \mathrm{Aut}(\mathscr{A})$ in (13), we are requiring the invariance of the primitive a priori under all formal 'changes of variable'.

11. A GENERALIZED BAYESIAN STRATEGY

The customary formulation of the Bayes' rule of inference is

$$P(H/D) = P(H) \frac{P(D/H)}{P(D)},$$

where $P(H/D)$ is the probability of the hypothesis H given the data D (the posterior probability of H), $P(H)$ is the prior probability of H, $P(D/H)$ is the probability of the data D given that the hypothesis H is true, and $P(D)$ is the probability of observing the data D. The ratio $P(D/H)/P(D)$ is frequently referred to as the likelihood ratio. This rule, of course, is suggested by the trivial Bayes' theorem of elementary probability; however, this rule of inference is by no means a triviality.

In most accounts of this Bayesian rule, there is a systematic obfuscation of the distinctions among statistical hypotheses, events, and predictions – not to mention a complete failure to distinguish among what we have called credibilities, weights (as frequency models), and betting rates. Given our present formalism, the Bayes' rule can be written with precision as follows:

$$\mu(\Lambda//D) = \begin{cases} \mu(\Lambda)\dfrac{\sigma_\mu(D/\Lambda)}{\sigma_\mu(D)} & \text{if } \sigma_\mu(D) \neq 0 \\ \mu(\Lambda) & \text{if } \sigma_\mu(D) = 0, \end{cases}$$

where $\sigma_\mu(D/\Lambda)$ is understood to be $\sigma_{\mu_\Lambda}(D)$, for any statistical hypothesis $\Lambda \in \mathscr{I}$, any credibility $\mu \in M$, and any non-empty $\mathscr{A}$-event D.

If we put $v(\Lambda) = \mu(\Lambda//D)$ for all $\Lambda \in \mathscr{I}$, as above, then, for $\sigma_\mu(D) \neq 0$, the Radon-Nikodym derivative $dv/d\mu$ is simply $f_D/\sigma_\mu(D)$ and we have $\mu(\Lambda//D) = (\int_\Lambda f_D \, d\mu)/(\int_\Omega f_D \, d\mu)$. Also notice, if C and D are $\mathscr{A}$-events with $\sigma_\mu(D) \neq 0$, then we have $\sigma_\mu(C//D) = (\int_\Omega f_D f_C \, d\mu)/\sigma_\mu(D)$. It is now easy to verify that this Bayes' strategy satisfies conditions (1)–(12) of Section 10.

The following simple, but non-classical, example illustrates how data from one operation can influence the betting rates for other operations: In the city of Bayesville, a controversy is currently raging over the adequacy of the municipal school system and the school tax rate. The Citizen's Action Committee is interested in determining the real opinions of concerned citizens on these matters. They propose to determine these opinions by conducting a poll. It is clear to the committee from the outset that questions concerning the school tax rate and questions concerning the adequacy of the school system could interfere with each other when posed to a particular individual. Thus, they plan to divide their pollsters into two groups. The first group will execute operation E and the second group will execute operation F.

E: First ask individual to be polled if he is concerned with the current school issues. If the answer is 'no', the symbol *n* is recorded. If the answer is 'yes', the pollster then asks whether the individual believes the municipal school facilities to be adequate. If the answer is 'yes', then the symbol *a* is recorded, while, if the answer is 'no', then the symbol *b* is recorded and the operation is completed. Thus, according to our conventions, $E = \{n, a, b\}$

F: First ask individual to be polled if he is concerned with the current school issues. If the answer is 'no', the symbol *n* is recorded. If the answer is 'yes', the pollster then asks whether the individual believes the school tax rate to be too high. If the answer is 'yes', then the symbol *h* is recorded, while, if the answer is 'no', then the symbol *g* is recorded and the operation is completed. Thus, according to our conventions, $F = \{n, h, g\}$.

Notice that we have identified the outcome *n* of *E* with the outcome *n* of *F*. The reason for this identification, in this instance, is self evident; indeed, the physical procedures carried out in the two operations to secure the outcome *n* are identical. The set of operations $\mathscr{A} = \{E, F\}$ pertinent to the present discourse is easily seen to be a Dacey manual. The logic $\pi(\mathscr{A})$ is a twelve element orthomodular lattice which is not a Boolean algebra. For instance, $p(\{a\})$ does not commute with $p(\{h\})$, and this is not surprising since we have allowed for the possibility of interference between the associated questions. It is also interesting to note that $p(\{n\})$ belongs to the center of $\pi(\mathscr{A})$, that is, it commutes with all other propositions in the logic. This is a consequence of the fact that the question associated with n initiates both *E* and *F*.

Evidently, an $\omega \in \Omega(\mathscr{A})$ is completely determined by the three parameters $x = \omega(a)$, $y = \omega(h)$, and $z = \omega(n)$. These parameters must satisfy the following five constraints: $0 \leqslant x$, $0 \leqslant y$, $0 \leqslant z$, $x + z \leqslant 1$, and $y + z \leqslant 1$. Thus, Ω will be represented by a pyramid in *xyz*-space with a square base in the *xy*-plane and an apex at $(0, 0, 1)$. The five vertices of this pyramid represent the five pure weights in Ω, which in this case happen all to be dispersion free. In this example, these dispersion free weights are in fact a strong set of weights.

Notice that the pyramid representing Ω is compact and that the inductive logic $\mathscr{I}$ corresponds to the σ-field of Borel subsets of this pyramid. Consequently, the credibilities $\mu \in M(\mathscr{A})$ are represented by the Borel probability measures on the pyramid. There are many such credibilities that satisfy Condition (13) of Section 10, and we have no particular justification for selecting any one of them as our primitive a priori μ; hence, in the interest of computational simplicity, we might as well take μ to be normalized Lebesgue measure on the pyramid.

Now, suppose that the poll has been taken and the following data reported: Outcomes a, b, n, g, h were secured A, B, N, G, H times respectively. We wish to compute the betting rates on the various outcomes for a query of 'Mr. John Q. Public' – that is, we want to calculate $\sigma_\mu(w//\text{data})$ for $w = a, b, n, g, h$. For this purpose, we notice that if $v = S(\mu, \text{data})$, then the Radon-Nikodym derivative $dv/d\mu$ is $f_a^A f_b^B f_n^N f_g^G f_h^H / \int_\Omega f_a^A f_b^B f_n^N f_g^G f_h^H \, d\mu$; hence, for example, $\sigma_\mu(a//\text{data})$ is the ratio of $\int_0^1 dz \int_0^{1-z} dy \int_0^{1-z} dx \, x^{A+1} (1-x-z)^B z^N y^H (1-y-z)^G$ to the same integral with x^{A+1} replaced by x^A. The result is

$$\sigma_\mu(a//\text{data}) = \frac{(A+1)(3+A+B+G+H)}{(A+B+2)(4+A+B+G+H+N)}.$$

Similarly, one can compute

$$\sigma_\mu(n//\text{data}) = \frac{(N+1)}{(4+A+B+G+H+N)},$$

and the remaining betting rates can now be obtained by using the obvious symmetries.

Observe that the outcome n, which corresponds to a central proposition $p(\{n\})$ in $\pi(\mathscr{A})$, has a betting rate $\sigma_\mu(n//\text{data})$ which asymptotically approaches the relative frequency with which n occurs in all trials of E and F as the data accumulates. Such an analogous asymptotic result does not obtain for the outcome a corresponding to the non-central proposition $p(\{a\})$ in $\pi(\mathscr{A})$.

The following table illustrates the manner in which the computed betting rates will change as data is processed:

For example, in the second row, a single piece of data secured as a consequence of the execution of operation E modified the betting rates on all of the outcomes for the operation F (in spite of the fact that the operation F had not yet been executed). In more complex manuals, such modifications will generally propagate from operation to operation along orthogonality chains.

A	B	N	G	H	a	b	n	g	h
0	0	0	0	0	3/8	3/8	1/4	3/8	3/8
1	0	0	0	0	8/15	4/15	1/5	2/5	2/5
0	0	1	0	0	3/10	3/10	2/5	3/10	3/10
1	0	1	0	0	4/9	2/9	1/3	1/3	1/3
0	0	2	0	0	1/4	1/4	1/2	1/4	1/4
2	0	0	0	0	5/8	5/24	1/6	5/12	5/12
10	30	15	5	20	.212	.598	.190	.180	.630
100	300	150	50	200	.204	.608	.188	.164	.648

The data and the resulting betting rates in the last two rows of the above table are realistic insofar as they reflect the well known and irrational preferences of 'John Q. Public' for decreased taxes on the one hand and increased services to himself on the other. A traditional poll, posing all questions to each individual, would undoubtedly imply a more rational attitude toward taxes and services than that which 'John Q. Public' actually holds – even an irrational individual will ordinarily seek to avoid the appearaence of irrationality and self-contradiction.

University of Massachusetts

BIBLIOGRAPHY

[1] Birkhoff, Garrett and von Neumann, John, 'The Logic of Quantum Mechanics', *Annals of Math.* **37** (1936), 823–843.
[2] Carnap, R., *Logical Foundations of Probability*, Univ. of Chicago Press, Chicago, Ill., 1950.
[3] Carnap, R., 'The Aim of Inductive Logic', *Logic, Methodology and Philosophy of Science* (Proceedings of 1960 International Congress) (ed. by E. Nagel, P. Suppes and A. Tarski), Stanford Univ. Press, Stanford, Calif., 1962, pp. 303–318.
[4] Cox, R. T., *An Algebra of Probable Inference*, The Johns Hopkins Press, Baltimore, Md., 1961.
[5] de Finetti, B., 'Foresight: Its Logical Laws, Its Subjective Sources', *Studies in Subjective Probability* (ed. by H. E. Kyburg, Jr. and H. E. Smokler), Wiley Press, New York, N.Y., 1964, pp. 93–158.
[6] Foulis, D. J., 'A Note on Orthomodular Lattices', *Portugalia Math.* **21** (1962), 65–72.
[7] Foulis, D. J. and Randall, C. H., 'Operational Statistics I. Basic Concepts', *J. Math. Physics* **13** (1972), 1667–1675.
[8] Foulis, D. J. and Randall, C. H., 'The Stability of Pure Weights under Conditioning' *Glasgow Math. J.* **15** (1974), 5–12.

[9] Gericke, H., *Lattice Theory*, Frederick Ungar Publishing Co., New York, N.Y., 1966.

[10] Gleason, A. N., 'Measures on the Closed Subspaces of a Hilbert Space', *J. Math. Mechanics* **6** (1957), 885–893.

[11] Good, I. J., *The Estimation of Probabilities*, Research Monograph No. 30, M.I.T. Press, Cambridge, Mass., 1965.

[12] Greechie, R. J., 'Orthomodular Lattices Admitting no States', *J. Combinatorial Theory* **10** (1971), 119–132.

[13] Jauch, J., *Foundations of Quantum Mechanics*, Addison-Wesley, Reading, Mass., 1968.

[14] Jaynes, E. T., *Probability Theory in Science and Engineering*, Colloquium Lectures in Pure and Applied Science No. 4, Field Research Laboratory, Socony Mobil Oil Co., Inc., Dallas, Texas, 1958.

[15] Jeffcott, B., 'The Center of an Orthologic', *J. Symbolic Logic* **37** (1972), 641–645.

[16] Kemeny, J. G., 'Fair Bets and Inductive Probabilities', *J. Symbolic Logic* **20** (1955), 263–273.

[17] de Laplace, Pierré Simon, *A Philosophical Essay on Probabilities*, Dover Press, New York, N.Y., 1951 (Original French Edition 1814).

[18] Lehman, R. S., 'On Confirmation and Rational Betting', *J. Symbolic Logic* **20** (1955), 251–262.

[19] Mackey, G. W., *Mathematical Foundations of Quantum Mechanics*, Benjamin, New York, N.Y., 1963.

[20] von Neumann, J., *Mathematical Foundations of Quantum Mechanics*, Princeton Univ. Press, Princeton, N.J., 1955.

[21] Ramsey, Frank, 'Truth and Probability', *Studies in Subjective Probability* (ed. by H. E. Keyburg, Jr. and H. E. Smokler), Wiley Press, New York, N.Y., 1964, pp. 61–92.

[22] Randall, C. H. and Foulis, D. J., 'States and the Free Orthogonality Monoid', Math. Systems Theory **6** (1972), 268–276.

[23] Randall, C. H. and Foulis, D. J., 'Operational Statistics II. Manuals of Operations and Their Logics', *J. Math. Physics* **14** (1972), 1472–1480.

[24] Savage, L. J., *The Foundations of Statistics*, Wiley Press, New York, N.Y., 1961.

[25] Shimony, A., 'Coherence and the Axioms of Confirmation', *J. Symbolic Logic* **20** (1955), 1–28.

DISCUSSION

Commentator: Garner: In most situations of statistical testing it is not the case that the available evidence completely confirms or refutes the statements being tested, rather the evidence only partially confirms or refutes the statements being tested. How does this square with your account?

Foulis: I completely agree that there are very many physically meaningful statements which cannot be conclusively confirmed or refuted on the basis of simple observational evidence, more particularly, on the basis of any simple observational evidence available in any one set of experiments. But the propositions here which I refer to as operational propositions are by definition the ones which can be confirmed or refuted by the evidence available from the sequence of experiments being considered. Of course there are many, many other physically interesting propositions which are not, therefore, operational propositions in this sense. Indeed, I can show that you can construct an entire hierarchy of logics containing propositions of different types, amongst which are included statistical hypotheses and other physically interesting propositions which will not be directly confirmed or refuted by direct experimental evidence from some, and in some cases any, sequence of experiments.

I should add that the operational propositions may not be those which are normally considered by an operating physicist when he carries out an experiment, though I believe that the questions a physicists typically considers (e.g. what is the momentum of the particles in the beam?) can be reduced to a logical combination of operational propositions (e.g. the momentum of particles in the beam is between one and two units, the momentum is between two and three units, etc. etc.). Moreover, one can only offer an informal definition of these operations – I offered mine in the English language as metalanguage – for I do not see that it is possible to ever construct an axiomatized mathematical system which will include all of the factors which go into the assertion that the operation has been properly carried out and that the answer is really thus and so, for these factors would have to include the proper setting up of the equipment, the checking of its operation, the certification of a truth-telling scientist who reports the results (as well as checks the equipment etc.) and so on and these things surely cannot be built into a mathematical theory.

Finch: Why do you always insist upon a formulation in terms of a complete stochastic model for the entire set of experimental outcomes?

Foulis: It does seem to me that it ought to be possible to work with only local stochastic models and to piece these together in an appropriate way so as to extend the network over the entire set of possible outcomes. We have not attempted to complete this approach but I intuitively feel that it can be successfully carried out.

Giere: I think you ought to concede that no actual experiments in real science ever concern themselves with, or ever involve, your idealized operational propositions. I believe that the point of introducing such propositions is to specify a semantics for a precise scientific language within which realistic propositions would be analyzed. But this task is only thoroughly confused by the attempt to justify the introduction of operational propositions using so doubtful epistemological arguments.

Foulis: I don't agree that operational propositions are not those which appear in the actual accounts that are offered of real physical experiments. We are specifying the syntax of a precise scientific language within which the concepts such as evidence and hypothesis can be formulated exactly and therefore within which scientific procedure and the evaluation of scientific evidence can be treated exactly. I don't think that we expect that this model will capture realistic physical theory – Eddington might have hoped this, but I don't think we expect it. But we do nevertheless insist that it must be in a language of this sort that we discuss precisely the status and support for physical laws, statistical hypotheses and so on. We don't seriously suggest that before you begin an experiment on a theory you write down the complete experimental manual, specify the operational logic and so on. This would be rather like demanding that before you begin to use the propositional calculus you write down a list of all conceivable atomic formula which you might have occasion to use and then explicitly show how to construct all the other formula recursively from these using the usual truth functional operations. We don't expect, in this sense, that actual physical experiments need to be recaptured in the language. But we do insist that this precise language provides the necessary structure within which experimental procedures and the evaluation of physical theories in the light of evidence is to be carried out – in just the same way that it is the formal properties of valid reasoning in the propositional calculus which determines the precise evaluation of ordinary, complex arguments carried out in the English language.

Hooker: Have you investigated whether it is possible to also place a non-Boolean structure on the higher order space which you use as the basis for statistical inference in order to obtain a non-standard structure for statistical inference? Some people believe that only by carrying through the introduction of the non-Boolean logical structure of quantum mechanics to every level in this way can a coherent quantum logical approach be taken. For example take your second level space Ω and place on it probability measures defined on the subspaces of it (I assume it to be some kind of linear space) rather than the standard set theoretic measures.

Foulis: No, we have not explored this possibility at all at least in connection with inference. There are enough theorems which we would like to prove within the existing formulism, and can not – e.g. theorems concerning the convexity structure of Ω and its relation to the operational logic – that we are content to work with this for the time being. In any case, we believe that the project you mention might be both more difficult and less rewarding.

LASZLO TISZA

CLASSICAL STATISTICAL MECHANICS VERSUS QUANTAL STATISTICAL THERMODYNAMICS: A STUDY IN CONTRASTS*

1. INTRODUCTION

This meeting seems to have two important leitmotifs which are in a certain disharmony with each other. First the tendency to establish mathematical probability theory and statistics as a universal scheme covering all aspects of rational inference, and second, the insistence that the laws of quantum mechanics (QM) are outside our traditional methods of reasoning to the extent that they require the adoption of a new 'quantum logic'.

One might easily gain the impression that the integration of statistics into classical physics was a very happy one, and the difficulties were brought about only by the quantum revolution. Yet nothing could be farther from the truth. My thesis is that the integration of statistics with classical mechanics is beset by fundamental difficulties, and only QM opened up the possibility for the joint use of statistical and dynamic concepts. Not all major problems arising out of this program have been solved as yet, but many of them have been, to a large extent, clarified. I believe the solution of the outstanding problems could be furthered by clearly putting in focus what has been achieved.

I am inclined to interpret the situation outlined as a bias against QM, and indeed, there is a great deal of evidence that there is a widespread tendency to overemphazise the alleged paradoxical aspects of QM. This is particularly evident if we look at the exceptions. Thus Weisskopf [1] has been particularly persuasive in stressing the power of QM to account for the structural stability and reactivity of chemical substances, in stark contrast with the breakdown of classical mechanics in the face of these 'morphic' aspects of the properties of matter. I have been concerned with these problems myself, particularly with the emerging new ontology that shapes up from the synthesis of thermodynamics, chemistry and quantum mechanics [2]. Indeed, if QM has not been very generously credited for the above mentioned achievements, this seems to stem from a disappoint-

Harper and Hooker (eds.), Foundations of Probability Theory, Statistical Inference, and Statistical Theories of Science, Vol. III, 207–219. *All Rights Reserved. Copyright © 1976 by D. Reidel Publishing Company, Dordrecht-Holland.*

ment that although, the structural, 'morphic' aspects of chemistry are accounted for by QM, this is on terms that do not conform to the ontology of classical physics.

I realize, of course that this statement might be considered shocking. Is it not true that physicists have shown the way, how to avoid metaphysical entanglements? Yet I claim that physicists do, in fact, acknowledge ontological committments in the following sense: some theories are deemed 'fundamental', and others are accepted as 'real' only to the extent that they are reducible to the former. To physicists of the last century the *par excellence* fundamental theory was the classical mechanics of point masses interacting with conservative forces. I refer to this theory as CMP. The well known program of reducing classical thermodynamics (CTD) to CMP is a manifestation of this ontological committment. This is by no means the only program of this sort, the search for mechanical models to account for the theory of the electromagnetic field is another. However, I shall consider only the case of CTD and the term 'reduction' is always to be taken in the sense of reducing CTD to a basic particle dynamics.

The next section contains a very selective survey of some of the attempts of reducing CTD to CMP.

2. THE CLASSICAL REDUCTION PROBLEM

The reduction of CTD is so closely associated in our minds with statistical mechanics (SM) that it may come as a surprise that in his first paper on the subject, Boltzmann attempted to derive the second law of CTD as a purely mechanical theorem [3, 4]. At this stage neither CMP nor CTD seemed to have anything to do with statistics, both theories operate with differential equations, and are deterministic in their own different ways. The relaxation of an internal constraint in an isolated thermodynamic system triggers a monotonic approach to a well defined final equilibrium state, and the 'memory' of the initial state is abolished. This is to be compared with the determinism of CMP based on 'remembering' the initial state. The reconciliation of this fundamental contrast was hopeless unless statistical descriptions were admitted into the theory. Although this was recognized almost immediately after the quoted paper of Boltzmann, it took about forty years before Ehrenfest demonstrated in terms of his urn model, that purely stochastic systems do display, in the limit of large number of degrees of freedom, a behavior that can be considered as a description of the trend toward thermodynamic equilibrium [5, 4]. The reason for this delay may well be that statistical method cannot be injected into the continuum mathematics of classical physics without causing serious disruption. Thus the uses of statistics within CMP are very restricted. We may assume an ensemble of systems the initial phases of which are given by a probability distribution function (d.f.), but we cannot assume that the temporal unfolding of the phase curve in the many-dimensional Γ-phase space has a random character without getting into conflict with the fundamental dynamic law of CMP.

Yet the Boltzmann kinetic equation is an example that, at least pragmatically, the stochastic and dynamic methods can be successfully blended, although the justification for some of the assumptions (stosszahlansatz) was far from clear. Boltzmann himself was groping for a more satisfactory solution. He formulates his famous ergodic hypothesis aiming at a theory in which randomization occurs as the natural long time behavior of the dynamics of systems of many degrees of freedom. The success of this approach would obviate the need for genuine stochastic assumptions.

It is well known that the original ergodic hypothesis was demonstrated to be impossible. Although weaker substitutes were more successful [1], the results are inconclusive. There is little doubt that the mixing effect in phase space is real, dynamics does lead to an apparent randomization under proper conditions, but there is no justification for the contention that all the random effects evident in thermodynamic phenomena can be explained in such a fashion.

In view of these difficulties there could have been no question of integrating sophisticated results of modern statistics into a theoretical framework centered around CMP. To be sure, Gibbs' statistical mechanics [7] involves subtle statistical elements, but Gibbs made only a token attempt to derive his results from fundamental dynamics. His formalism came to fruition only within the modern theory that he anticipated to a remarkable extent.

3. THE MODERN REDUCTION PROBLEM

As we have seen in the last section, the reduction problem can be interpreted in two alternative ways:

(i) Establish a theory in which dynamic and stochastic elements are used in a consistent fashion.

(ii) Show that behind apparently stochastic phenomena there is a hidden purely dynamic theory.

If one takes the second point of view, the effect of replacing CMP with QM does not change the problem in a fundamental fashion. Only relatively few authors take this deeper point of view. I would note J. von Neumann [8] and Pauli and Fierz [8a] as outstanding examples. See also reference [6]. Basically the situation is nearly as inconclusive as it was in the classical era.

The picture is altogether different, however, if one takes the point of view view (i). I believe that one of the great methodological achievements of QM is that it enables us to handle consistently both the stochastic and dynamics aspects of phenomena.

In fact, whereas joining stochastic assumptions is disruptive in CMP, this is not at all the case in QM. It was among the first insights of the old quantum theory, that one cannot deal with stationary states without admitting also the probabilistic nature of the transitions between these.

The same situation appears even clearer from the point of view of the time independent Schrödinger equation. Setting up this equation involves, of course, the Hamiltonian, i.e., the dynamics of the system. Again the set of eigenstates are connected by random transitions.

However, one of the aspects of QM is the use of probability amplitudes. If this appears disturbing to the mathematical statistician, he must keep in mind that this is the price to be paid for integrating statistics with dynamics.

This problem of integration arises of course, also in many more subtle situations, but I wish to confine myself to the simplest case, in order to bring out another point which is not generally appreciated.

The replacement of CMP by QM is by no means the only difference between the classical and the modern version of the reduction problem, as there is ample reason to modernize CTD itself, although this theory has often been considered as a case of ossified perfection.

I believe the point of departure of the new development is a paper by Einstein [9] in which he established a theory of fluctuations by considering the thermodynamic quantities rather than the phase space coordinates of the particles as random variables. Einstein's motivation was to avoid the equipartition catastrophe without invoking explicit quantal assumptions. His departure triggered a slow moving but extensive development, including well known theories of Onsager and Landau. Personally, I have been concerned for many years with the task of casting these theories into a systematic form [2]. The basic idea is that thermodynamics is phenomenological, a theory in close contact with measurement. During the last century this meant automatically: macroscopic. Yet the dominating fact of twentieth century physics is the opening up of the atomic domain to experimental study. The purpose of generalized thermodynamics (GTD) is to keep up with these advances. GTD is a too wide ranging theory to be subsumed to a close-knit deductive system, but certain well defined subfields can be so organized. Reference [2] contains two of these systems. The first is refinement of CTD. The second goes beyond the classical theory, since it has a statistical character. It is briefly outlined in the next section.

4. THE STATISTICAL THERMODYNAMICS OF EQUILIBRIUM: STE[2]

The theory STE as defined in reference [10] is centered around the discussion of a basic situation: the systems under consideration may be either isolated, or coupled to other systems by the exchange of energy and matter. (For simplicity, I shall confine myself to the discussion of the exchange of energy.) The internal dynamics of a system determines the set of stationary states, the energy spectrum, but the probability of finding a system in a given state is influenced by the nature of the coupling with other systems.

Whereas in the strict interpretation of SM one considers only the dynamic evolution in isolated systems and statistics is an expression of our ignorance of the complete state, in STE the coupling and decoupling of systems is part of the theory, and is an objective source of statistical uncertainty.

The definition of equilibrium is given at first in broad generality by the assumption, that under constant coupling conditions the probability distribution functions (d.f.) of the system are constant in time. More specifically we formulate two d.f.'s corresponding to two standard situations out of which others can be built up.

First of all we follow the practice of CTD by introducing classes of environment systems called reservoirs $R(\vartheta)$ characterized by a single parameter ϑ, a qualitative measure of temperature.

We consider now the situation depicted in Figure 1. Suppose the thermal switches A'' and B are open, whereas the switch A' is alternately closed and opened. The energy values u' of the first system form a random

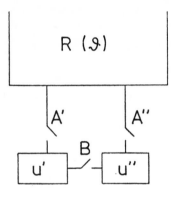

Fig. 1.

series with the d.f. $dF'(u' \mid \vartheta, x)$ that we call *canonical*. The vertical bar indicates that the d.f. is conditioned by the reservoir temperature and also by the parameter x that symbolizes all the non-random parameters that specify the system, such as its volume, and its chemical composition. A similar d.f. dF'' is valid for the second system, and also for the composite system obtained by permanently closing the switch B: $dF(u \mid \vartheta, x', x'')$, with $u = u' + u''$.

Consider now the situation in which A', A'' have been kept open and B closed long enough for the composite system to reach equilibrium. Subsequently the switch B is opened yielding two isolated subsystems, and we define the microcanonical d.f. $d\mathscr{F}(u' \mid u, x', x'')$ as the probability of producing the energy partition $u' + u'' = u$.

The two d.f.'s are connected by a remarkable functional equation first derived by Szilard [11]:

$$dF'(u' \mid \vartheta, x') \, dF''(u'' \mid \vartheta, x'') =$$
$$= d\mathscr{F}(u' \mid u, x', x'') \, dF(u \mid \vartheta, x', x''). \quad (1)$$

The left hand side of this equation corresponds to a situation in which B is permanently open, whereas for the right hand side B is at first closed and opened later. One may look at Equation (1) as expressing the fact that a state of thermodynamic equilibrium (including fluctuations!) is independent of the history, that is the method of preparation of the system[3].

The functional Equation (1) can be solved and yields the following expressions for the d.f.'s

$$dF(u \mid \vartheta, x) = dG(u, x) e^{-\Phi(\vartheta, x) - B(\vartheta) u} \tag{2}$$

$$d\mathscr{F}(u' \mid u) = \frac{dG'(u') \, dG''(u'')}{dG(u)} \tag{3}$$

Here $B(\vartheta)$ is a function only of the reservoir temperature, whereas $G(u, x)$ depends only on the system; finally Φ depends on the temperature and the nature of the system, but not on its random state, in common parlance, it is an ensemble function.

We have moreover

$$\Phi(\vartheta, x) = \Phi'(\vartheta, x') + \Phi''(\vartheta, x''). \tag{4}$$

The normalization of probabilities $\int d\mathscr{F} = 1$ and $\int dF = 1$ yields the convolution relation

$$dG(u) = \int_{u'} dG'(u') \, dG''(u - u') \tag{5}$$

and

$$e^{\Phi(\vartheta, x)} = \int_{u} e^{-B(\vartheta) u} \, dG(u, x) \tag{6}$$

Since the integral depends on ϑ only through $B(\vartheta)$, we can introduce $\beta = B(\vartheta)$ as a measure of the temperature that is 'absolute' in the sense of being independent of any thermometric substance. Thus it must be basically identical to the Kelvin-Carathéodory temperature. Moreover with such a choice Equation (6) takes the form of a Laplace transform

$$e^{\Phi(\beta, x)} = \int e^{-\beta u} \, dG(u, x) \tag{6a}$$

and the canonical d.f. becomes

$$dF(u \mid \beta, x) = dG(u, x) \, e^{-\Phi(\beta) - \beta u} \tag{2a}$$

By differentiating (6a) we obtain

$$\frac{\partial \Phi}{\partial \beta} = - \langle u \rangle \equiv - \bar{u} \tag{7}$$

$$\frac{\partial^2 \Phi}{\partial \beta^2} = \langle (u - \bar{u})^2 \rangle, \tag{8}$$

where the averages are taken with the canonical d.f. (2a)

Up to this point the developments are straightforward mathematical implications from the initial assumptions. Although these developments are rather unconventional, the results are familiar, and there is no difficulty in spelling out the physical meaning of the heretofore undetermined functions.

The function $G(u, x)$ can be interpreted as the number of linearly independent solutions of the time-independent Schrödinger equation associated with eigenvalues $E \leq u$ whereby the x (volume, number of particles, etc.) are kept constant. In particular, for discrete nondegenerate eigenvalues the canonical d.f. becomes

$$f_i = e^{-\Phi(\beta) - \beta E_i}. \tag{2b}$$

The parameter $\beta = 1/kT$, where T is the absolute temperature and k is Boltzmann's constant.

The interpretation of $\Phi(\beta, x)$ is subtle because is has several facets. We see from (7) and (8) that Φ is the moment generating function. It is also a Laplace transform, it is infinitely often differentiable and convex.

It is an interesting point that all these results are the direct consequences of the replacement of the qualitative temperature ϑ with the thermodynamic temperature k/β.

Although we have started from a statistical theory we have arrived at a formalism in which the interesting results, (the moments of all orders) can be derived from a fundamental function $\Phi = \Phi(\beta, x)$ by means of analytic operations. This is, however, just what CTD is all about. Indeed Equation (7) becomes a relation of CTD if we consider $\langle u \rangle$ as the thermodynamic energy, and $\Phi = \Phi(\beta, x)$ the Massieu function. The definition of the entropy follows hence without ambiguity by Legendre transformation:

$$S/k = \Phi + \beta \langle u \rangle$$
$$= \langle \Phi + \beta u \rangle \tag{9}$$

By taking the average with the canonical d.f. in the form (2b) we obtain

$$S/k = - \sum_i f_i \ln f_i \tag{9a}$$

the well known statistical expression for the entropy.[4] It is apparent already, and it is borne out by the more detailed developments, that STE is a synthesis of Gibbsian phenomenological thermodynamics (CTD) and much of his statistical mechanics: including the entire theory of ensembles. but excluding the connection with CMP.

Whereas in CTD a system is described in terms of a set of conjugate pairs of parameters, such as energy U and $1/T$, in STE we recognize that a system in contact with a reservoir has a fluctuating energy and no definite temperature. Yet by using the average energy of the system and the temperature of the reservoir as conjugate pairs, the classical Gibbsian formalism can be upheld in full rigor.

The situation is reminiscent of the transition of CMP to QM. In the former, we attribute coordinates and conjugate momenta to each particle. In QM the use of the classical pair of conjugates is limited by Planck's constant, in STE by Boltzmann's constant.

Up to this point, however, there is an asymmetry in the theory since we use only sharp temperatures and unsharp energies. The quantum analogy suggests the possibility of a sharp energy, and uncertain temperature It is, indeed, possible to reinterpret CTD in this fashion. The basis is the interesting, and most original idea of Mandelbrot [12], according to which thermometry can be considered as an instance of parameter estimation. We measure the energy u_0 of a system (the thermometer), and estimate the temperature of the reservoir with which the system might have been in contact to acquire this energy. This can be carried out in detail by the maximum likelihood estimate, provided one quantifies the temperature in terms of the parameter β introduced above.

It is shown in reference [10] that this idea can be made the basis for a formalism in which CTD is interpreted in terms of a *sharp energy* and an *estimated temperature.* One obtains in addition a most useful formal expression of the entropy maximum principle.

It may be of interest to point out that this part of STE is based on the *subjective* interpretation of probability, whereas the formulation given earlier deals with *objective* probabilities.

5. DISCUSSION

The role assigned to mathematical probability theory and statistics in theoretical physics depends greatly on the ontological committment implicit in the formulation of the physical theories. If classical point mechanics is considered absolutely fundamental, the role that can be assigned to statistics is most precarious. This is the origin of the well known difficulties in the foundations of statistical mechanics.

My purpose was to show that the situation is more favorable from the point of view of a new ontology that is shaping up at present, at least in outlines, from the harmonization of quantum mechanics with a generalized form of Gibbsian thermodynamics and statistics. The situation is entirely stisfactory within a rather wide range of phenomena. There is an additional huge twilight region that I have not discussed in this paper. However, the difficulties of the theory of elementary particles indicates that there are still fundamentally new ideas required before we can consider the new ontology satisfactory.

Massachusetts Institute of Technology

NOTES

* Center for Theoretical Physics Publication #380.
[1] For a recent review article see reference [6].
[2] The material of this section is based on the work of Tisza and Quay [10], reprinted in reference [2]. I refer to this paper both for the rigorous development of detail, and also for the historical background with credit to earlier workers.
[3] From the point of view of mathematical statistics, Eq. (1) is the expression of the proposition that the energy is a sufficient statistic for the estimation of the temperature. This interesting insight was advanced by Mandelbrot [12] who practically 'discovered' Szilard's all but forgotten paper. I am personally most grateful to Dr. Mandelbrot for introducing me to this fruitful and still little known connection of mathematical statistics and statistical thermodynamics.
[4] This is the expression that Jaynes [13] took as a point of departure for his well known derivation of the formalism of statistical thermodynamics.

BIBLIOGRAPHY

[1] Weisskopf, V. F., *Physics in the Twentieth Century*, M.I.T. Press, Cambridge, Mass., 1972, Part 1. Fundamental Questions.

[2] Tisza, L., *Generalized Thermodynamics*, M.I.T. Press, Cambridge, Mass., 1966, Part C. On Method.

[3] Boltzmann, L., *Wien, Ber.* **53** (1866), 195.

[4] Klein, M. J., *Paul Ehrenfest*, vol. 1, North-Holland Publ. Co., Amsterdam, 1970, Chapter 6.

[5] Ehrenfest, P. and T., *Phys. Z.* **8** (1907), 311.

[6] Lebowitz, J. L. and Penrose, O., *Phys. Today* (February 1973), p. 23.

[7] Gibbs, J. W., *Elementary Principles in Statistical Mechanics*, Yale University Press, 1902.

[8] von Neumann, J., *Z. f. Physik* **57** (1929) 30.

[8a] Pauli, W. and Fierz, M., *Helv. Phys. Acta* **106**, (1937), 572.

[9] Einstein, A., *Ann. Physik* **33** (1910), 1275.

[10] Tisza, L. and Quay, P. M., *Ann. Phys. (N.Y.)* **25** (1963), 48;
Quay, P. M., Thesis, M.I.T., 1958.

[11] Szilard, L., *Z. f. Physik* **53** (1925), 840.

[12] Mandelbrot, B., *Inst. Radio Eng. IRE Trans. Information Theory* IT-2 (1956), 190. *Ann. Math. Stat.* **33** (1962), 1021; *J. Math. Phys.* **5** (1964), 164.

[13] Jaynes, E. T., *Phys. Rev.* **106** (1957), 620; and *Phys. Rev.* **108**, (1957), 171.

Commentator: Mario Bunge. You have rightly emphasized the contrast between thermodynamics and the mechanics of particles. But there is no contrast between thermodynamics and continuum mechanics: both are theories of continua. Therefore my first question: Would it be possible to get thermodynamics out of statistical continuum mechanics, particularly since continuum mechanics is basically irreversible? I know that statistical continuum mechanics hardly exists, but Kampé de Fériet made a promising start twenty years ago when he studied the statistical mechanics of the continuous vibrating string. Besides, since then progress has been made in understanding the integrals in phase space that arise in continuum statistical mechanics: they are the same that occur in Feynman's integral path formulation of quantum mechanics. My second question is this: your theory seems to rest on the assumption that the system has no memory. Would it be possible to expand it to cover materials with memory, such as a razor blade?

Tisza: The statement that 'thermodynamics is a theory of the continuum' is ambiguous. What is evidently continuous is the mathematical formalism, but this circumstance admits two physical interpretations. Traditionally the mathematical continuity is attributed to the continuous distribution of matter. Since this continuity is only a macroscopic approximation, according to this point of view thermodynamics cannot be considered a truly fundamental discipline.

In contrast, the underlying philosophy of my Generalized Thermodynamics is that thermodynamics is phenomenological, but not necessarily macroscopic.

(i) Experimentation is no longer confined to the macroscopic domain as it has been until the turn of the century.

(ii) The continuity of the formalism can be interpreted as a mathematical description of a discontinuous situation. The key is Equation (6) of my paper. The structure function $G(u, x)$ on the r.h.s. describes the spectrum of a system of *particles* that will have, in general, also *quantal discontinuities.* The l.h.s. of the relation is nevertheless absolutely continuous and differentiable. This is a well known property of the Laplace transformation. In other words, a probability distribution can be described in terms of a continuous differentiable moment generating function.

As to the second question, there are many theories that deal with one aspect of memory, or another, e.g. theories involving relaxation times. However, I doubt that a unified theory could deal with memory in all generality.

B. C. VAN FRAASSEN AND C. A. HOOKER

A SEMANTIC ANALYSIS OF NIELS BOHR'S
PHILOSOPHY OF QUANTUM THEORY

ABSTRACT. Niels Bohr is justly famed for his contributions to the understanding of physics in general and quantum theory in particular and almost equally notorious for the alleged obscurity of his doctrines. In this paper we develop an essentially semantical interpretation of Bohr's central doctrines and offer a precise logical characterization of the doctrines we attribute to Bohr. Our characterization revolves essentially around the representation of a class of non-standard conditional sentences. The technical core of the paper is concerned with the development of an extended theory of conditional probabilities to deal with the representation of these conditionals in the context of quantum theory. In the end, we are not only able to offer a precise characterization of our Bohrian position but show how quantum logic is in one sense an answer to the question of the logic of these conditional sentences.

I. INTRODUCTION

Niels Bohr is perhaps the most important figure in the discussion of the foundations of quantum theory to this date. Unfortunately, he is also regarded as one of the more obscure writers and this despite his own strenuous efforts to be clear. There is a tradition in philosophy which does not accept a position pertaining to conceptual structures as clarified until a rather precise formal analysis has been presented in which we can grasp the theses advanced in a sharp formulation. Recently one of us has studied Bohr's writings carefully and advanced a certain view of what his doctrines were [2]. This view fortunately lends itself to further development and in this paper we extend this version of Bohr's position in a rather more formal direction.

We do not here aim at providing an exhaustive analysis of every feature of Bohr's multi-faceted position. Rather we aim to characterize only that dimension of his philosophy which is directly amenable to analysis in terms of logical structure. We do not here enter upon the discussion of substantive issues concerning the nature of, and criteria for, acceptable physical theories. Even so, structural clarification is a necessary prerequisite for this latter.

First we shall examine Bohr's own account and attempt a more formal presentation of it (Sections II and III), then we shall develop the resulting

Harper and Hooker (eds.), Foundations of Probability Theory, Statistical Inference, and Statistical Theories of Science, Vol. III, 221–241. *All Rights Reserved. Copyright* © 1976 *by D. Reidel Publishing Company, Dordrecht-Holland*

logical structure in some detail (Sections IV to VI) and show how this approach recaptures, in its own fashion, another well-known approach, that of 'quantum logic', as a special case (Section VII). In no sense do we believe that Bohr has uttered the last word on this subject; our interest here, however, is not on the correctness, or even the plausibility, of his position, but solely its formal presentation.

II. THE NATURE OF BOHR'S POSITION

It is appropriate to commence with the fundamentals of Bohr's doctrine as they were set out in a previous investigation [2]. There the conclusion was reached that Bohr's doctrine was to be understood *primarily* as pertaining to an analysis of what it was to use concepts and a conceptual scheme in physical science (though he clearly thought, we should say very plausibly, that his doctrines applied to all concepts and conceptual schemes). The core of Bohr's views concerning the use of concepts is captured in the following four doctrines:

(B1)   All experimental outcomes are described from within the classical conceptual framework.

(B2)   The applicability of classical (and all other) concepts to a particular situation is dependent upon the relevant (physical) conditions obtaining in that situation.

(B3)   There exists a finite quantum of action associated with all micro processes in consequence of which the microsystem under investigation and the macro measuring instruments are indivisibly connected (in definite ways characteristic of the quantum theory, eg., $E = h\nu$, $p = h/\lambda$ etc.).

(B4)   Because of (B2) and (B3), there is an inherent limitation on the simultaneous applicability of classical concepts, and of classical descriptions containing these concepts, to the same physical system under the same physical conditions. Which concepts are applicable to a given system depends upon the entire physical situation in which the system is located, including, in particular, the measuring apparatus involved.

The doctrine (B1) is the doctrine that only classical concepts (regarded by Bohr as being refined versions of our ordinary, everyday concepts together with some harmless additions, e.g., moment of inertia) can be used in the description of experimental results.

(B2) claims that our concepts are always applied in a certain implicit or presupposed context, which is of crucial importance for understanding how they function. It is not easy to define exactly what is intended by this notion of tacit presupposition and relevance. Perhaps a faithful example is obtained by considering the definition of hardness on the Mohs scale by (relative) scratchability: A is harder than $B =_{df} A$ scratches B and it is not the case that B scratches A. This definition applies to two substances A and B only on condition that they are both in solid form. We might say that "A is harder than B" tacitly assumes, or presupposes, that both A and B are solids. At any rate this example offers something like the correct idea: A concept C presupposes conditions R in Bohr's sense if part of the physical circumstances that must obtain for C to be definable at all in a given physical situation includes R. They show that the relation of presupposition which we want here is probably a subset of an entailment relation. The assumption that two complementary concepts applied to, or were relevant to, a given situation S, would then entail incompatible statements concerning the conditions prevailing in S.

According to (B2), the classical concepts of position, time velocity, momentum, energy, and so on all presuppose the obtaining of certain physical conditions for their applicability – roughly, it must be physically possible to determine unambiguously the position of the relevant system in a context to which the concept of position is to be applicable, to determine unambiguously the momentum in a context to which the concept of momentum is to apply, and so on.

Bohr believed that while it has seemed to us at the macro level of classical physics that the conditions were in general satisfied for the joint applicability of all classical concepts, we have discovered this century that this is not accurate and that the conditions required for the applicability of some classical concepts are actually incompatible with those required for the applicability of other classical concepts. This is the burden of the doctrine (B4).

This conclusion is necessitated by the discovery of the quantum of action and only because of its existence. It is not therefore a purely conceptual discovery that could have been made a priori merely through a more critical analysis of classical concepts. It is a discovery of the *factual absence* of the conditions required for the joint applicability of certain classical concepts. The discovery of which conditions classical concepts presupposed and, hence, of the possibility of a clash arising, might, however, have been made by a careful analysis of those concepts – though this is not to say that quantum theory, or even the existence of h, could have been discovered in this fashion since these depend on the particular relations which apply in the quantum domain among the myriad that might have obtained. It is the business of the quantal formalism to deal systematically with the new connections which have been discovered – thus (B3).

III. FORMAL DEVELOPMENT OF BOHR'S DOCTRINE

The foregoing presentation of Bohr's view suggests, on further reflection, a certain point of view as to the nature and significance of his approach. It suggests that *what Bohr was proposing was a set of meta-linguistic semantical rules for the use of object (descriptive) language concepts.* The function of the metalinguistic rules Bohr proposed was to regulate the occurrence of descriptive object language sentences in the various physical contexts. Roughly speaking, Bohr's rules select the range of descriptive sentences which are physically meaningful or significant in a given context. We are led then to a metalinguistic formulation of a *language of contexts*; to each physical situation or context is assigned the set of descriptive sentences in the object language that are physically significant in that context.

More formally, let the object language for physical description $\mathscr{L}$ be comprised of a collection of sentences $\mathscr{P}$, together with the usual connectives. In the usual analysis of the logical structure of physical theories, only sentences of the following form are considered: "The value of observable m lies in the (Borel) set $E \subseteq R$ of numbers" (R is the real line). For fixed m, these sentences form a boolean algebra; for exposition, see part II of [4]. We note that there will in general be many syntactically well-formed sentences in $\mathscr{L}$ that are not physically significant in Bohr's sense in some, or all, physical situations. For example, the conjunction "The value of the observable momentum lies in the interval E_1 and the value of the observable position lies in the interval E_2", though faultless as a syntactical structure, will be without physical significance according to Bohr if length E_1 × length $E_2 \lesssim h$, since quantum theory precludes the occurrence of such situations. Recalling our presentation of Bohr's doctrine as a formal, semantical doctrine, we call these sentences *physically ill formed*. According to Bohr, the great quantum revolution is the discovery that syntactical properness (more intuitively, grammatical correctness) and semantic physical-properness do not coincide. Let $\mathscr{C} = \{C_i\}$ be the collection of all physical contexts. (Note: what these latter are will, of course, be ultimately determined by theory.) Then Bohr is to be understood as offering a set of rules which provide a map F from the C_i into sub-sets of the $\mathscr{P}$:

$$F : \mathscr{C} \to \mathbf{P}(\mathscr{P})$$

where $\mathbf{P}(X)$ is the power set of X. Intuitively, $F(C_i)$ is the set of physically well formed, or physically meaningful, sentences in the situation C_i. We shall interpret this to mean that $F(C_i)$ is the set of sentences *having a truth value* in C_i. S is physically meaningful $= S$ has a truth value.

There are now several ways to proceed to characterize the structure thus imposed upon L. One way would be to concentrate on the syntactic structure of the resulting $F(C_i)$, all i. To pursue this it would be necessary to first examine the structure of C (pretty clearly a lattice, though doubtfully a complemented one), then characterize the relations between the C_i and $F(C_i)$ according to Bohr and so finally deduce some structure to the $\{F(C_i)\}$.

But rather than pursue this route we shall take our departure from our characterization of Bohr's position in semantical terms and opt for a semantical approach. We begin by recalling that, according to Bohr, every propositional claim made tacit reference to a physical situation in which the claim was advanced and that this situation served to define the meaningfully applicable concepts. Such situations are properly characterized by the measurements which can be made in them. In keeping with this we now reconstrue "The observable M' takes a value in E" as "If an m-measurement situation obtains then an M'-measurement would yield a value in E".

Obviously only those M'-measurements can be made which are physically compatible with the m-measurement in question. Quantum mechanics permits us to express these in terms of m-measurements when the m-measurement situation is one in which m is a maximal observable and the situation permits a precise determination of the value of m. Without loss of generality these are the only situations we shall consider, hence we need only consider m-measurements in m-measuring situations. Finally, Bohr construes measurement descriptions classically within a context and so there is no essential difference between an m-measurement situation and an actual m-measurement. We thus arrive at an examination of sentences of the form "If an m-measurement is made, the outcome will be in E", and these are the only sentences we shall study. We write these sentences in the form "$M \rightarrow E$". We must now characterize the conditional appearing in them.

Surely the following is uncontroversial. In a particular situation, the conditional $M \rightarrow E$ is true if an m-measurement is made (M true) and the outcome is in E (E true); it is false if M is true and E is false (the outcome lies outside of E). Thus we have, for example:

$$X, Y \Vdash X \rightarrow Y$$
$$X, \neg Y \Vdash \neg (X \rightarrow Y)$$
$$X, X \rightarrow Y \Vdash Y$$

Where $\neg X$ is true if and only if X is false.

Now we must consider conjunctions of sentences of the form '$(M \rightarrow E)$ and $(M' \rightarrow E')$', for in many of these cases Bohr will rule the conjunction physically meaningless. We propose the following reading of Bohr's views (see again Section II above):

(a) sentences can be jointly satisfied (be true in some situation) if and only if they can all jointly be predictively certain (i.e. have probability one);

(b) a conjunction is true in a given situation if and only if all its conjuncts are;

(c) distinct situations are mutually incompatible: if all the sentences true in one situation are also true in another, then all the same sentences are true in both.

(These clauses may be compared with 12 (a)–(d) on page 101 of [4]. There a physical situation is represented by *two* states α and λ, in response to certain problems about the interpretation of mixture. This may be ignored in the present paper.)

What this reading does is to rule out as physically meaningless just those conjunctions of propositions whose truth would violate the Heisenberg Uncertainty Relations (construed as to apply to the individual case). This seems to us to faithfully capture part of the intention behind Bohr's doctrine B4. Notice that we say "... can all have probability 1 ...", i.e. for some possible element of the relevant Hilbert Space will have probability 1; we do not claim that it is probability 1 for more than 1 such element, much less for all elements. An alternative equivalent reading would be: In any given situation, all conjunctions of sentences which have probability 0 for all elements of the relevant Hilbert Space are physically meaningless.

In particular, if $E = R$ then $M \to E$ (i.e. $M \to R$) is always true. In general we have:

If $\square(X \supset Y)$ then $X \to Y$.

This means that M, M' may be physically incompatible propositions, i.e. M and $M' \Vdash$ everything, and yet $(M \to E)$ and $(M' \to E')$ be true. Bohr faced just such a situation in Einstein's ingenious *gedankenexperiment* (known now as the Einstein-Podolsky-Rosen paradox, see [2] for a detailed treatment), where two sentences $M \to E$, $M' \to E'$ each had probability 1, with physically incompatible M, M'. Einstein concluded that a physical state corresponding to the joint realization of both the outcomes (i.e. corresponding to EE') actually occurred and that this state violated the Uncertainty Relations. Bohr's answer was quite clear: both sentences are true, and so their conjunction can be taken as true, but since M, M' refer to physically incompatible situations a joint state corresponding to EE' cannot be realized, indeed the descriptions of E, E' are conceptually mutually excluding (B4), hence no violation of quantum theory results.

IV. CONDITIONAL PROBABILITY

Having arrived at the conclusion that we need only consider as relevant situations those in which a system is subjected to the measurement of a specific maximal observable, we can now turn to formal representation. A situation such as this is characterized by two formal objects, the *observable* that is to be measured, m_0, and a quantum-mechanical *state*, α, for the system. We shall refer to this situation as $S(\alpha, m_0)$; since both α and m_0 will be kept fixed for the time being, we abbreviate it to S.

Quantum mechanics gives us the set Q of maximal observables from which m_0 is taken, and the set H of states from which α comes. In addition it gives, by the Born rules, probabilities $P(\alpha, m_0, E)$ for each Borel set E, which may be read informally as "the probability that, if a system in state α be subjected to a measurement of m_0, the outcome will/would be in E". With reference to situation S we must now deal with three sorts of propositions:

M: "the measurement (on this system) is of observable m". In situation S, the probability that M is true is one if $m = m_0$ and is zero otherwise.

E: "the measurement (on this system) has an outcome in (Borel set) E". In situation S, where we know that it is m_0 which is/will be measured, the probability of E is $P(\alpha, m_0, E)$. However, the *conditional* probability of E given M equals $P(\alpha, m, E)$ whether or not $m = m_0$.

$M \rightarrow E$ "the measurement (on this system), if it be an m-measurement, has an outcome in E". The probability in S of $M \rightarrow E$ is fixed entirely by state α, and is indeed the conditional probability of E given M.

To achieve a formal representation of situations and of propositions, we shall proceed in several steps. First, in this section, we shall give a representation of S in which only the first two kinds of propositions are dealt with. We do this by adding as a "hidden variable" the real number which is the *actual* outcome of the measurement (whatever that turns out to be). This is not acceptable as an "explication" of course, and we shall make this clear by giving distinct names to the objects, M^* and E^* which represent propositions M and E. Then, in the next section, we shall add still more "hidden variables" to accommodate conditionals. In the section after that it will be shown how the effect of these hidden variables can be eliminated, and how quantum logic, from our point of view, is an answer to a question about the logic of these conditionals.

The first question that our exposition must face is: does there exist a conditional probability function P such that $P_\alpha(E^*/M^*) = p(\alpha, m, E)$ for all maximal observables m and Borel sets E? Such a function is a mathematical entity, and describing it does not guarantee its existence – may indeed lead to contradiction.

This is not a trivial problem, for on the most obvious construal, the assertion does indeed lead to inconsistency. Kolmogorov's axiomatic theory of probability has become the standard theory, and there we see conditional probability characterized by:

1. $P(A/B)=P(A \cap B)/P(B)$, provided $P(B) \neq 0$
            and undefined otherwise.

There are uncountably many maximal observables in quantum theory (even for the trivial Hilbert space of dimension two). No two of these are simultaneously measurable. Hence there are uncountably many mutually incompatible propositions of form M^*. Since $P_\alpha(E^*/M^*)$ must be defined for each M^*, the Kolmogorov account requires that $P_\alpha(M^*)$ be non-zero for each of these. But that is impossible for more than countably many incompatible propositions. So there is no such function as P_α, contrary to the intuition that led us to talk as if there were.

This conclusion would have astonished the workers on probability who preceded the influence of Kolmogorov. Indeed, it was considered quite an advance at one point that probability should be conceived as essentially conditional, with absolute probability defined by

2. $P(A)=P(A/\text{a tautology})$.

After Kolmogorov, the main proponent of irreducibly conditional probability, was Karl Popper. He gave an axiomatic treatment, but did not show how to construct such functions, except in trivial cases. Recently his conditional probabilities, referred to as "Popper functions", have played an important role in discussions of counterfactual conditionals.

Briefly, the details about the *relevant* part of Kolmogorov's and Popper's probability functions are these. A *sample space* is a couple $\langle W, F \rangle$ where W is a non-empty set and F a Borel field of subsets of W. A *probability measure P* on this sample space is a map of F into the interval $[0, 1]$ such that

3. (a) $P(W)=1$
   (b) $P(\cup G)=\sum\{P(A): A \in G\}$ for any countable disjoint sub-
            family of F.

Finally, a *Popper measure P* on the sample space is a map of $F \times F$ into $[0, 1]$ such that

4. (a)   The relativization $P_A:P_A(B)=P(B/A)$ is either a probability measure or the constant function I mapping F into $\{1\}$

(b)   If $P(A/B)=P(B/A)=1$ then $P_A=P_B$

(c) $P(A\cap B/C)=P(A/C)P(B/A\cap C)$ for all A, B, C in F.

The word 'function' usually replaces 'measure' in the above terms when clause 3(b) is asserted for finite disjoint families only.

The remainder of this section will be devoted to showing that there does exist a function P_α, constructible by means of Kolmogorov's tools. This function will not be a probability measure in Kolmogorov's sense, but it will be a Popper function. Hence we shall be justified in talking of it as a conditional probability.

We must first delimit the set of events or situations that will form the probability space. Continuing our previous idealization, these will be events in which a particular maximal observable m is measured, and a specific outcome r is obtained. Since no two maximal observables can be simultaneously measured, any two such situations are distinct. Therefore we can represent each by a corresponding ordered couple:

$$K=\{\langle m,r\rangle: m \text{ is in } Q \text{ and } r \text{ is in } R\}$$

where Q is the set of maximal observables and R the set of real numbers. We identify, as is usual, a proposition with the set of situations in which it is true. Let us single out for special consideration the following propositions and families thereof:

$m^*=\{\langle m,r\rangle:r \text{ is in } R\}$: "$m$ is measured"
$E^*=\{\langle m,r\rangle:m \text{ is in } Q \text{ and } r \text{ is in } E\}$: "the outcome is in E"
$m^*\cap E^*:m$ is measured and the outcome is in E
$[m^*]=\{m^*\cap E^*:E \text{ is a Borel set}\}$
F = the least Borel field containing each family $[m^*]$

The family F will be, for now, the largest family of propositions which we shall discuss.

Consider now state α. The function $P(\alpha, m, E)$ yields for each α and m a probability measure (in the standard or Kolmogorov sense) on R. A fortiori it yields a probability measure on the Borel field $[m^*]$:

$$P_\alpha^m(m^*\cap E^*)=P(\alpha, m, E)$$

which can be trivially extended to a probability measure on F. Furthermore consider Q as well-ordered, so that we may always speak of "the first m in Q such that" with M_0 as the very first. Then define

$$P_\alpha(A/B) = P_\alpha^m(A/B) \text{ for the first } m \text{ in } Q \text{ such that } P_\alpha^m(B) \neq 0;$$
$$\text{and} = 1 \text{ if there is no such } m.$$

(The conditional probability $P_\alpha^m(A/B)$ on the right hand side is to be understood in the sense of Kolmogorov of course.)

That P_α so defined is a Popper measure is easily verified. The question is whether 4(b) and 4(c) hold. Note for 4(b) that $P_A = I$ only if $P(A/m^*) = 0$ for all, and that $P_\alpha^m(A/B) = 1$ and $P_\alpha^m(B) \neq 0$ imply $P_\alpha^m(A) \neq 0$. Hence if P_A or P_B is I then both are. Secondly, if $P_\alpha^m(A/B) = 1$ and m is the first observable such that $P_\alpha^m(B) = 1$, then m comes no earlier than the first observable m' such that $P_\alpha^{m'}(A) = 1$. So we see that $P_A = P_B$ also if neither is I. Note for 4(c) that if $P_{A \cap C}$ is not I, neither is P_C. If $P_{A \cap C}$ is I, and P_C is not, then $P(A \cap B/C) \leqslant P(A/C) = P(A \cap C/C) = 0$, so both sides of 4(c) are zero. Finally if neither relativization is I, note that $P_{A \cap C} = P_\alpha^m$ and $P_\alpha^{m'}$ where m' comes no later than m. If $m = m'$ then clause 4(c) holds by the Kolmogorov definition of conditional probability. If $m \neq m'$, then again, $P(A \cap B/C) = P_\alpha^{m'}(A \cap B/C) \leqslant P^{m'}(A/C) = P^{m'}(A \cap C/C) = 0$ because $P_\alpha^{m'}(A \cap C) = 0$. So both sides are zero. This finishes the verification; and it establishes, along the way, a simple and general way to construct Popper functions out of probability functions.

The function P_α we have now constructed is exactly as required:

$$P_\alpha(E^*/m^*) = P_\alpha^m(E^*/m^*) = P_\alpha^m(m^* \cap E^*)/P_\alpha^m(m^*)$$
$$= P_\alpha^m(m^* \cap E^*) = P(\alpha, m, E).$$

Also, $P_\alpha(X/m^*)$ is the same as $P_\alpha(X/K) = P_\alpha(X)$, just because we stipulated that m_0 should be the first observable in the ordering of Q. In conclusion, then, it is indeed justifiable to say that quantum theory provides us, for each state, with a conditional probability measure for outcomes of measurements.

V. CONDITIONALS ABOUT MEASUREMENTS

We have just found that, if we widen the notion of probability to include Popper functions, then we can explicate the Bohrian view that the empirical content of quantum theory lies in the conditional probabilities of measurements it gives us. But in earlier sections we had already indicated an alternative, namely, that we can read Bohr as saying the following:quantum theory is concerned with empirical assertions which are themselves conditional, and to which it assigns (absolute) probabilities (Numerically, these probabilities are exactly the conditional probabilities discussed in the preceding section of course.) Recent work on conditionals has been much occupied with the idea of equating probabilities of conditionals with conditional probabilities. We shall now adapt this recent work to the present case, the complications needed again being due to the fact that there are uncountably many maximal observables.

Our starting point is again the situation space K, the state α will be considered fixed, and we shall now omit the letter 'α' for convenience. We have then a whole lot of probability measures P^m on K, such that P^m $(m^* \cap E^*) = P^m(E^*)$ is the probability that the outcome is in E if m is measured. The domain of definition of each of these measures is the Borel field F.

To define the conditional propositions $m^* \to E^*$ ("if an m-measurement be (were) made, the outcome will (would) be in E") we shall follow the procedure introduced by Stalnaker(for exposition, see [3]). According to Stalnaker, to check whether or not a conditional $A \to B$ is true in situation π we look at a (nother) situation, $s(A, \pi)=p$, the one that would have been the case if A had been true (which is π itself if A is true in π). And we check simply whether B is true in that situation π. Stalnaker put the following conditions on s:

1. (i) $s(A, \pi)=\pi$ if π is in A
   (ii) $s(A, \pi)$ is in A if A is not empty
   (iii)   if $s(A, \pi)$ is in B and $s(B, \pi)$ is in A then $s(A, \pi)=s(B, \pi)$

and he then characterized the conditional by the relation

   (iv) π is in $(A \to B)$ if and only if: $s(A, \pi)$ is in B, or A is empty.

(All this is Stalnaker's theory adapted to a new context, with minor variations; for example, we concentrate on propositions, identified with the sets of situations in which they are true.)

Some of this is inapplicable for us, since we are concerned only with the propositions m^* as antecedents. These are never empty, and are mutually incompatible. Hence clause (iii) and the part "or A is empty" of clause (iv) are not applicable. This means that we are in the area common to two theories of conditions, Stalnaker's C_2 and the system CE of [3]. Moreover, in contrast to those theories, we are here concerned only with "first degree conditionals", that is, we do not construct such propositions as $m^* \to (E_1^* \to E_2^*)$ or $(m_1^* \to E_1^*) \to (m_2^* \to E_2^*)$.

There will be one definite twist. Working with probability we have one advantage: we can allow into our models all sorts of violations of intuitive requirements, without harm, provided only they receive measure zero. There are limits to this of course, because we would like the logically impossible to occur in no sense at all. But we don't have to be so strict about what is logically impossible. What we shall allow here, to be specific, is situations π for which $s(M^*, \pi)$ is not defined at all – so π belongs neither to $m^* \to E^*$ nor to $m^* \to (R-E)^*$. (This may not sound so strange – for in a real situation in which m was not actually measured. no one could say what the outcome would have been if m had been measured. But that is not quite to the point: if $s(m^*, \pi)$ is not defined, that is like saying, in situation π, that if m had been measured, there would have been no outcome.)

Now let us reconsider physical situations. They can no longer be identified with the simple couples $\langle m, r \rangle$. For example two possible situations might be alike in that m is actually measured and r is the outcome; but in the first situation, if m' had been measured the outcome would have been one and in the other zero. These physical situations we shall represent – and the only criterion is that we shall have enough of them, the redundant part can be assigned measure zero – by means of sequences of members of K. These sequences must be long enough, and we shall make them as long as the set Q of observables (considered as a well-ordered set). To do this most conveniently, we just treat Q itself as an index set.

$K^+ = \{\pi : Q \to K\} = K^Q$ in product notation

$F^+ =$ the least Borel field containing $\{\pi : \pi(m_1) \in A_1, \ldots, \pi(m_n) \in A_n\}$ for sets $A_1, \ldots, A_n$ in F

$P^+ =$ the probability measure on F^+ such that $P^+(\{\pi : \pi(m_1) \in A_1, \ldots, \pi(m_n) \in A_n\}) = P^{m_1}(A_1) \ldots P^{m_n}(A_n)$.

This is the usual Kolmogorov product construction, which applies because for each m in Q, P^m is a probability measure defined on F. (In product notation, the sets described in the definition of F^+ and P^+ are abbreviated to $A_1 \times \cdots \times A_n \times K^q$ where $q = Q - \{m_1, \ldots, m_n\}$. For example, $E^* \times K^{Q - \{m\}} = \{\pi \in K^+ : \pi(m) \in E^*\}$.)

There is a simple relation between the Popper function P obtained in the preceding section and the probability measure P^+ above. (We may think of K itself as the bottom or lowest layer of an infinite pile of copies of itself.)

2. $$P(A/m^*) = P^+(A \times K^{Q\{m\}})$$

If we let m_0 be the first member of the well-ordered set Q, then the absolute part of the Popper function appears as follows:

3. $$P(A) = P(A/K) = P^{m_0}(A) = P^+(A \times K^{Q - \{m\}})$$

Hence A in K may be newly reidentified with $A \times K^{Q - \{m\}} = A^+$. Our task is now to define $m^* \to E^*$ in such a way that

4. $$P^+(m^* \to E^*) = P(E^*/m^*).$$

We now define, for each member π of K^+ and each observable in Q:

$s(m, \pi)$ = the function π' like π everywhere except that $\pi'(m_0) = \pi(m)$

$s(m^*, \pi)$ = $s(m, \pi)$ provided: $s(m, \pi)$ is in m^{*+} and, if π is in m^{*+} then $\pi = s(m, \pi)$. Otherwise $s(m^*, \pi)$ is undefined.

$m^* \to E^* = \{\pi : s(m^*, \pi) \text{ is in } (E^*)^+\}$

In view of 2 above, we must now show exactly that

5. $$P^+(m^* \to E^*) = P^+(E^* \times K^{Q-m})$$

But π is in $m^* \to E^*$ only if $s(m^*, \pi)$ is in E^{*+}, hence only if $s(m, \pi)$ is in E^{*+}, hence only if $\pi(m)$ is in E^*. Therefore

6. $$m^* \to E^* \subseteq E^* \times K^{Q - \{m\}}.$$

That establishes half of Equation 5. Under what conditions is π in

$E^* - K^{Q-\{m\}}$ but not in $m^* \to E^*$? Only if $s(m^*, \pi)$ is not defined, i.e. if π belongs to the set

$$\{p: s(m, p) \text{ is not in } m^{*+}, \text{ or}$$
$$s(m, p) \text{ is in } m^{*+} \text{ and } p \text{ is in } m^{*+} \text{ but}$$
$$s(m, p) \neq p\}$$
$$= \{p: p(m) \notin m^*\} \cup \{p: p(m) \in m^* \quad \text{and}$$
$$p(m_0) \in m^* \quad \text{and}$$
$$p(m) \neq p(m_0)\}$$
$$= Y \cup Z \text{ for short.}$$

It will suffice now to show that $P^+(Y \cup Z) = 0$. But $P^+(Y) = P^+((K - m^*) \times K^{Q-\{m\}}) = P(K - m^*/m^*) = 0$ by Equation 2.

And $P^+(Z)$ is less than or equal to $P^+(\{p: p(m_0) \text{ is in } m^*\})$ for the case $m \neq m_0$, which equals $P(m^*/m_0^*) = 0$, by Equation 2 again. Hence the two sides of Equation 6 differ only by a set of measure zero, and Equation 5 is established. (This argument shows, along the way, that $m^* \to E^*$ is in F^+, because it is a difference of two sets in F^+.)

Apart from the frustrating technical detail, this construction may still feel unsatisfactory because two functions, P and P^+ are involved. What we should like, really, is an *extension* of old function P such that

$$P(m^* \to E^*/\text{tautology}) = p(E^*/m^*)$$

which means, recalling that $P(A/K) = P(A/m_0^*)$,

$$P(m^* \to E^*/m_0^*) = P(E^*/m^*).$$

Now this can quite easily be obtained. We need only switch from K to K^+, identify each old proposition A in F with new proposition A^+ in F^+, and we can so extend P. First of all, note that P_0^m has effectively been extended into P^+, in that $P^{m_0}(A) = P^+(A^+)$ for each A in F. Secondly, note that for each m in Q, P^m has a simple extension to K^+ and F^+, namely as $P^{m^+}(\{\pi: \pi(m_1) \in A_1, ..., \pi(m_n) \in A_n\}) = p^m(A_1) ... P^m(A_n)$. The sets m^{*+} form a measurable partition of K^+ like the sets m^* did for K. So by the same construction as before we get a Popper function

$$P': P'(A/B) = P^{m^+}(A/B) \text{ for the first } m \text{ such that } P^{m^+}(B)$$
$$\neq 0, \text{ and } = 1 \text{ if there is no such } m \text{ in } Q;$$

for all sets A and B in F^+ this time. Since m_0 is the first observable, and $P^+ = P^{m_0^+}$, it follows that

$$
\begin{aligned}
P'(m^* \to E^*/K^+) &= P^+(m^* \to E^*) \\
&= P(E^*/m^*) \\
&= P^m(E^*) \\
&= P^m(E^{*+}) = P^m(E^{*+}/m^{*+}) \\
P'(E^{*+}/m^{*+})
\end{aligned}
$$

since m is the first observable such that $P^{m^+}(m^{*+}) \neq 0$, and of course $P^{m^+}(m^{*+}) = 1$.

This Popper function P' has the required agreement with the old function P to be called its extension to this new model.

VI. SITUATIONS, STATES, AND PROPOSITIONS*

It may now seem that we have gone rather off the track. In the preceding section we envisaged situations in which a certain observable m_0 was actually measured. In addition, in most such situations, it was true for all or most other observables m that we could say "if m had been measured, the outcome would have been r" for some value r. That is not the way Bohr would have it, nor does it square with our own general exposition in Section III.

Indeed, in accordance with Section III we will have to say that for each physical situation e there must be some pure state α such that

1. $M \to E$ is true in e iff $P(\alpha, m, E) = 1$

This is required by conditions (a)–(c) stated there. So the situations π in K^+ of the preceding section are wild idealizations, produced in a search for nice results about probabilities. On the other hand, the situations $\langle m, r \rangle$ of Section IV were much too meager; if we know a state α we know a good deal more than what an *actual* measurement may yield. We will have to pare down our wild idealizations, without paring away the desirable results.

---

* We here acknowledge that credit for the first suggestion of using supervaluations in the explication of the Copenhagen view of quantum mechanics goes to Karel Lambert – see his essay 'Logical Truth and Microphysics' in Lambert, K. (ed.) *The Logical Way of Doing Things*, New Haven: Yale University Press, 1969.

This is not an unfamiliar state of affairs. We can often produce a reasonable explication or modelling in two steps: first we describe extrapolations or idealizations, and then we take as true what is *common* to all the idealizations that fit the actual case. In the preceding section the physical situation $S = S(\alpha, m_0)$ – state α, observable chosen to be measured m_0 – was represented by a formal object π in K^+. In the ideal situation π, each question

What would be the outcome if m were measured?

receives an exact answer, a specific real number. But the actual physical situation S is not thus according to Bohr. Alright then, what represents S is not any particular member π of K^+, but the totality of all these, that is

2.   Physical situation $S(\alpha, m_0)$ is represented by the Popper
            probability space
            $[S] = \langle K^+, F^+, P'_\alpha \rangle$
            and a statement X is true in S if and only if its representing
            proposition $[X]$ is such that $P'_\alpha([X]/K^+) = 1$.

In order for 1 and 2 to cohere, we need only point out how statements are formally represented:

3. M is represented by $[M] = m^{*+}$
            E is represented by $[E] = E^{*+}$
            $M \to E$ is represented by $[M \to E] = m^* \to E^*$

and the results of the preceding section show that these statements receive the correct probabilities in our representation.

Now that empirical statements have received a formal representation as propositions in model structures $[S] = \langle K^+, F^+, P'_\alpha \rangle$, we may ask about the logic of empirical statements. Roughly we should have.

4.   Argument $(A_1, ..., A_n$; hence $B)$ is valid iff:
            B is true in every possible physical situation S in which
            $A_1, ..., A_n$ are true.

I said 'roughly', because it is here crucial whether we think of S as 'really' having hidden variables in it, or accept the Bohrian equivalence expressed as 2 above. This choice yields two distinct semantic relations:

5. (i) $A_1,\ldots, A_n \| \vdash B$ iff $[A_1] \cap \ldots \cap [A_n] \subseteq [B]$ in every model structure $[S]$;

   (ii) $A_1,\ldots, A_n \|\vdash B$ iff, in every model structure $[S] = \langle K^+, F^+, P' \rangle$,

               if $P'([A_1]) = \cdots = P'([A_n]) = 1$ then $P'([B]) = 1$.

(We should point out here that two model structures can differ only in their third member P', which alone depends on the choice of m_0 and α.)

It might be thought that in an explication of Bohr, the relation $\| \vdash$ can hardly be of much interest, but this is not so, because:

6.   If $A_1,\ldots, A_n \| \vdash B$ then $A_1,\ldots, A_n \|\vdash B$

follows from elementary probability considerations. Since we know that conditionals were construed in the Stalnaker way, we know a good deal about the relation $\| \vdash$, and hence about $\|\vdash$ also. For example,

$$X, Y; \text{ hence } X \to Y$$
$$X, \neg Y; \text{ hence } \neg (X \to Y)$$
$$X, X \to Y; \text{ hence } Y$$
$$X \to Y, X \to Z; \text{ hence } X \to (Y \cap Z); \text{ and conversely}$$

are all valid arguments (where $[\neg X] = K^+ - [X]$) in accordance with the remarks of Section III.

In what ways does the relation $\|\vdash$ go beyond $\| \vdash$? That is not entirely a logical question, since it depends on what states α there are; and that is determined by quantum theory. To put it another way: not just *any* Popper function P' on F^+ is such that $\langle K^+, F^+, P' \rangle$ represents a physically possible situation S. There are statistical correlations between measurement outcomes, determined by the physically possible states α. The empirical content of quantum theory lies exactly in this specification.

Indeed, the nearest purely logical question has a quick answer. How does $\|\vdash$ go beyond $\| \vdash$ if all conceivable states are physically possible? Not at all. For if π is in $[A_1] \cap \ldots \cap [A_n]$ but not in $[B]$ we can make up a Popper function P' such that $P'(\{\pi\}/K^+) = 1$, and this would refute the claim that $A_1,\ldots, A_n \|\vdash B$.

Though pure logic can say no more, quantum logic can and does. The next section will show how quantum logicians have answered questions that involve the empirical content of quantum theory.

VII. RELATION TO QUANTUM LOGIC

In the preceding section we came to a question: exactly how does the Bohrian valid argument relation $\Vdash$ go beyond the "logical hidden variable" valid argument relation? The answer, we saw, depended on quantum theory, which specifies what conceivable states are physically possible.

We shall now show that, as far as the conditionals $M \to E$ are concerned, this question is answered by quantum logic. As is well known, there are various quantum logics. But still, the answer is not ambiguous, for these differ only in the operations they study, while directing themselves to the same family of propositions.

Let us consider specifically the family G, a part of F^+, of all propositions $(m^* \to E^*)$. Because K^+ was taken so large that each statement $M \to E$ is represented by a different proposition $[M \to E] = (m^* \to E^*)$, we may think of the relations $\|\vdash$ as defined on G also. Here $\|\vdash$ is just the natural partial ordering of set inclusion. $A \|\vdash B$ iff $A \subseteq B$. But $\Vdash$ is not a partial ordering, because it is quite possible that $A \neq B$ although $A \Vdash B$ and $B \Vdash A$. Hence we begin by giving a name to the reduction that identifies $\Vdash$ equivalent propositions:

$$A^0 = \{B \in G : A \Vdash B \text{ and } B \Vdash A\}$$
$$G^0 = \{A^0 : A \in G\}$$
$$A^0 \leqslant B^0 \text{ iff } A \Vdash B$$

The relation $\leqslant$ is well-defined on G^0 because the relation $\Vdash$ is transitive. It must be understood that we now regard $\Vdash$ as defined with reference to the set of physically possible states (of a given system) specified by quantum mechanics to be a Hilbert space H, and also the probabilities $P(\alpha, m, E)$ as specified by that theory.

To find out what the relation $\Vdash$ on G is like it clearly suffices to investigate the relation $\leqslant$ on G^0. Next, therefore, we represent G^0 in terms of the set H of states. We have defined $\Vdash$ and produced G^0 in such a way that

1. $[M \to E]^0 = [M' \to E']^0$ iff for all states α,
         $P'_\alpha([M \to E]) = 1$ iff $P'_\alpha([M' \to E']) = 1$

Hence the map

2. $g([M \to E]^0) = \{\alpha \in H : P(\alpha, m, E) = 1\}$

is one-to-one. Also, from the definition of $\Vdash$ and $\leqslant$ we see that

3. $g(A^0) \subseteq g(B^0)$ iff $A^0 \leqslant B^0$

and therefore if we define

4. $(m, E) = \{\alpha \in H : P(\alpha, m, E) = 1\}$
         $HP \quad = \{(m, E) : m \in Q$ and E a Borel set$\}$

we see that the structures $\langle G^0, \leqslant \rangle$ and $\langle HP, \subseteq \rangle$ are isomorphic.

Our work is now finished for HP is in part the family of subspaces of H, and $\langle HP, \subseteq \rangle$ is the structure which is the prime object of quantum-logical research. Depending on which operations on HP we care to study, we shall say with Kochen and Specker that this structure is a *transitive* (also called *associative*) partial *Boolean algebra*, or with Gudder that it is a *compatible orthomodular poset*, or with Jauch that it is a *weakly modular lattice*. Each of these assertions answers, in a different way, what arguments are valid, when the premises and conclusion are all conditionals about measurement outcomes.

VIII. CONCLUSION

For a long time, more than 30 years, Bohr's writing on the understanding of quantum theory have been regarded as obscure even somewhat mystical, and certainly far from the hard-nosed analytical approach to the detailed understanding of modern physics. It is taken for granted in the professional community that Bohr's approach to physical theory is radically different from the various analytical approaches, in particular from the so-called quantum logical approach.

With the development of a semantical approach to understanding Bohr ([2]) it became possible to provide a much more precise formulation of Bohr's doctrines, albeit still a relatively informal one. Now that account has here been precisely formulated. We hope that it will remove forever the charge against Bohr of ineradicable obscurity.

The formulation turns out to develop in the most surprising and pleasing way into a general reconstruction of a physical descriptive language that is rich enough to contain within itself much of the quantum logical approach. This would surely have satisfied Bohr deeply, though it would have been exactly what he would have expected and he would have been impatient with the technical details. The striking way in which this development requires recent work in the theory of conditionals and conditional probabilities leads to an intimate connection between the conceptual structure of quantum mechanics and other fields of rational analysis, a point made much of by Bohr. All told, it provides a striking demonstration of the penetration and fecundity of his thought.

It would be a mistake, though, to think that we have exhausted the content of Bohr's thought, or removed any of the mystery – Bohr's ideas on the conceptual structure and evolution of human thought remain as provocative and 'deep' as ever. Our analysis only serves to reflect them in clarified form in a formal structure.

Equally, it would be a mistake to suppose that any and all of the quantum logical approaches to physical theory are nothing but special cases of Bohr's analysis. Some might be. What our study now raises in acute form is the necessity of clarifying precisely the relation between the approaches.

REFERENCES

[1] Hooker, C. A. (ed.), *Contemporary Research in the Foundations and Philosophy of Ouantum Theory*. D. Reidel Publishing Company, Dordrecht, Holland; 1973.
[2] Hooker, C. A., 'The Nature of Quantum Mechanical Reality: Einstein Versus Bohr', pp. 67–302 in R. Colodney (ed.), *Paradox and Paradigm* in *Pittsburgh Studies in the Philosophy of Science*, Pittsburgh: University of Pittsburgh Press, 1972.
[3] van Fraassen, B. C., 'Probality of Conditionals', Volume I, pp. 261–301.
[4] van Fraassen, B. C., 'Semantical Analysis of Quantum Logic', pp. 80–113 in ref. [1].

THE UNIVERSITY OF WESTERN ONTARIO
SERIES IN PHILOSOPHY OF SCIENCE

A Series of Books on Philosophy of Science, Methodology, and Epistemology
published in connection with
the University of Western Ontario Philosophy of Science Programme

Managing Editor:

J. J. LEACH

Editorial Board:

J. BUB, R. E. BUTTS, W. HARPER, J. HINTIKKA, D. J. HOCKNEY,
C. A. HOOKER, J. NICHOLAS, G. PEARCE

1. J. LEACH, R. BUTTS, and G. PEARCE (eds.), *Science, Decision and Value.* Proceedings of the Fifth University of Western Ontario Philosophy Colloquium, 1969. 1973, vii+213 pp.

2. C. A. HOOKER (ed.), *Contemporary Research in the Foundations and Philosophy of Quantum Theory.* Proceedings of a Conference held at the University of Western Ontario, London, Canada, 1973, xx+385 pp.

3. J. BUB, *The Interpretation of Quantum Mechanics.* 1974, ix+155 pp.

4. D. HOCKNEY, W. HARPER, and B. FREED (eds.), *Contemporary Research in Philosophical Logic and Linguistic Semantics.* Proceedings of a Conference held at the University of Western Ontario, London, Canada. 1975, vii+332 pp.

5. C. A. HOOKER (ed.), *The Logico-Algebraic Approach to Quantum Mechanics.* 1975, xv+607 pp.